STEAL THE KEY

WILDE CONTRACTS
BOOK 2

MAZ MADDOX

Thank you to Jess, Shen, all my betas, editors, PA and readers. I can't do this crazy dance without you. And most of all Alex, who untangles plot knots and brings me coffee. Love ya.

"THIS IS A STUPID IDEA," Zane, my unhelpful, undead jackass of a bodyguard said as I continued with my master plan.

My fingertips burned from digging in the snow, my gloves protecting them from getting wet but shit at keeping them warm. Trying to drive stakes into the frozen earth wasn't optimal, but it also wasn't impossible. And the damn plan would work regardless, it was just a pain in the ass.

I shook out my numb hands so I could get enough feeling back to flip him off.

"You're a stupid idea."

"You're assuming that they're going to take the bait when it's freezing outside. How do you know they'll even smell the blood through the snow?"

"Because they're animals." I grunted as I drove the stake down enough to keep it upright and placed the enchanted stone onto the top. "Animals will come out when they're hungry."

Zane crossed his arms, watching as I did all the work, standing there in his leather jacket acting like was cool.

"What exactly is that enchantment supposed to do?"

"Well, we're running very low on life essence and the possibility of us getting more is unlikely," I reminded him, wiping some sweat from my face. "So I got some clear quartz enchanted with a grounding spell. They'll flock to some nice, fresh blood, then I'll put down the last quartz in the circle and BAM." I tried to snap but I was wearing the gloves. "They'll get locked into the circle and we'll pick them off. Fish in a barrel kinda thing."

My stoic, unnecessary partner continued to just stare at me.

"You've done this before?"

I paused my digging to glare at him. "It'll work."

"That's what I thought."

"If you're not going to help me, can you just go be broody somewhere else?" I got back to work torturing my hands with more snow shoveling. "You're giving me heartburn."

"I'm going to go wait for this to fall apart so I can ambush a couple of them."

"I hope they bite you in the ass," I called out as his boots crunched in the snow. He popped off with something I didn't catch, so I just said, "Yeah, you too, dickhead."

"I said your phone is ringing, dumbass."

"You're a dumbass." I fished my phone from my pocket, pulling off a glove with my teeth in order to hit the button. "Wilde Contract Killing and Fish Training, can I take your order?"

Whatever freezing numbness that was settling over my body melted into simmering pools of lust when Sias's voice rumbled into my ear.

"Dinner tonight at seven sharp," he commanded, sending all kinds of dirty signals across my body. "Don't fill up on junk before you arrive."

"I wouldn't dream of it," I promised, unable to hold my grin back.

"I'll send a car at six thirty."

"I feel so spoiled," I teased, knowing it was more to keep me punctual than anything else. "Is this a private dinner or are we doing another uh…buffet situation?"

"Private. I don't feel like company tonight." There was a beat before he added a cheeky, "Unless Zane would like to tag along."

"No," I said immediately. "He's not invited."

"Dallas," he scolded, which I hated myself a bit for getting a little turned on by it. "I share my toys with you. Why can't you return the favor?"

"Oh my God. That is not what's happening here." I rubbed my eyes with my fingers. "Not a toy. He's more like a thorn in my ass, and not in the playful, sexy way."

I could feel Zane looking at me so I flipped him off.

I added for good measure, "I'm not bringing the thorn."

"Fine, fine. Have it your way. I'll just have to give you my undivided attention."

A small thrill danced up my spine and I had to chew on my lip to keep from smiling too big.

"It's a date."

Sias hummed. "Don't be late, Wilde. I don't want anything to be cold by the time you arrive."

He hung up without saying "good-bye" because he had too much big dick energy to be bothered with parting words. Goddamn he was so hot.

Attractive, dominating, suave-as-hell incubus business daddy who could make me melt with just a few touches.

He also made my heart do goofy little flutters, even when we weren't going at it like sex-crazed bunnies.

"Meeting Sias tonight?"

Zane's sudden voice broke my fun little horny spell and I threw some snow at him.

"Are you listening to my phone calls?"

"No." Zane tapped his chest. "You got all fluttery."

"Fuck you, I don't flutter," I lied, because it was none of his business and I hated that he could feel my emotions. "You're not supposed to be keyed in, remember?"

"In order for me to mute the connection so you can have your private time, I have to meditate or read. Not gonna happen when we're hunting grunt vampires at an old, freaky hospital." Zane motioned to the large, square building behind us that was all shattered windows and rot.

"I can handle myself just fine. I was doing this long before you started tagging along." I started stabbing the earth with my stake, pretending it was Zane's face.

"Uh-huh. You set up traps like this alone too, or just when you have backup?"

"Best time to experiment is when your life is tethered to an undead dipshit." I twisted the stake into the ground and put my body weight into it. "You can't let me die. So maybe I'll get lucky and you'll get some chunks taken out of you."

"They're not going to be interested in me, hunter." Zane glanced over the circle, the sunlight catching on the angles of the quartz.

"We'll see about that." I stood once the stake was pushed in, and dabbed at the sweat on my brow with my sleeve. The cold wind stung my wet skin and made howling noises through the busted windows of the old hospital. Icy teeth hung from the ledges, giving each dark entrance a sense of hunger. Deep within the belly of the empty building was an infestation, mindless husks of what used to be living people now feral with death magic and blood thirst. They had been turned by a necromancer I had yet to find; made to be attack dogs and vessels of brutality and terror.

My job, along with training exotic fish and assassinating regular folk for money, was to purge this world of all the death magic I could find.

Even if I was now part of their twisted little family, by no fault of my own, and had to haul around an unhelpful Thrall with a bad attitude and no sense of fucking privacy.

My backpack sank into the snow as I slung it off my shoulder, the zipper sticking a bit as I slashed it open. Inside the cozy confines of my now soggy canvas bag were a few bags of borrowed blood I'd acquired completely legally and not at all from shady dealings with sketchy people who work at a blood bank.

These non-existent people might also have sold me some drugs on occasion, so we had a good working relationship.

The sun was hidden behind thick winter clouds packed with unfallen snow, and the tangle of dead trees shrouding the ground near the hospital ER entrance was optimal for lesser vampires. Direct sunlight would cause them to burst into flames, but desperate, hungry monsters would take a risk on an overcast day with ample shading.

It wasn't a guarantee, but it was worth a shot. It was a hell of a lot better than going into their lair and fighting on their turf. The last thing I wanted to do was get myself trapped in a dark corridor with bitey vampires looking for an easy meal. I was fairly sure Zane would let them gnaw on me awhile before helping me.

The blood in the bags was cold, but still dented the snow as I splashed it onto the ground. It sank into the white, staining it crimson and corrupting the footprints we had left behind. Soon the center of my trap was bloody and wet, and I tossed a half-empty bag down as extra incentive before backing away to the perimeter. The smell of pennies and death stuck to the cool winter breeze, and I pretended it didn't cause dark memories to uncurl in the shadows of my mind.

I flexed my fingers to help with blood flow, resting them on the gun strapped to my hip. There were only a few bullets left that had life essence fused to them, and as long as I kept my glove on, I couldn't feel the sharp tingle of the life magic yelling at my necromancy blood.

Loading these little bastards had been as equally exhausting as it was terrifying, since I had to get Barnaby to do it for me.

Have you ever tried to get a fussy antiques dealer with a chip on his shoulder to load a firearm for you before?

No? Just a me problem?

Well, it sucked.

Fun fact: Barnaby "dislikes" weapons and thinks bullets will kill him even when they aren't inside of a gun. He's also perpetually annoyed and thinks I'm gross.

It wasn't a fun afternoon.

Since I only had a clip left and no hope of getting more, I also had to bring a sword with me to do things the old-fashioned way. While it is kinda badass to run undead monsters through with a blade, it's so much easier to just shoot them.

Like, so much easier.

And way less cleanup.

But, when life gives you lemons, you bring a sword.

The wind whistled through the glass teeth of broken windows, the building groaning as its bones froze. An eerie lack of birdsong made the sound seem to bellow, the stinging cold promised more snow in the future. The smell of freezing blood made my mind go static for a bit, eyes overfocusing and blurring at the red criss-crosses.

"So. A date, huh?"

I blinked at Zane's comment, the scene around me coming back into view.

"What?"

"You said 'it's a date.'" He had come to stand beside me, watching the hospital entrance with his hands in his pockets. While I was bundled in a down jacket and snow boots, Zane just had on the "cool guy" leather jacket he'd stolen from a bar fight, jeans and black boots. No gloves, no scarf, not even a damn knit cap.

It wasn't fair that I had to look like a rosy-cheeked five-year-old in layers of protection while he had an icy breeze caressing his hair like some model for "Undead Passion" cologne.

"Thought you weren't listening to my phone call."

Zane shrugged. "A little bit."

I rubbed my hands together to help warm them and kept my eyes on the hospital.

"He invited me over for dinner."

"Regular dinner or incubus dinner?"

"Pretty sure when Sias says 'dinner' he means sex." I formed a cave with my hands and blew into them, my breath heating the inside and giving me some temporary comfort. "It's never meant food, at least in my experience. Last time he said we were going to buffet, he meant me and some of his other favorites getting fucked by some of his friends." I grinned at the memory, my body tingling. "That was fun. He had us all line up—"

"Okay. I get the picture," Zane cut me off, sounding bored.

"Prude," I teased. "You've never been presented as a dessert to a buffet of hot incubi dudes while your business daddy pampers you?"

"I'm more of a main course with maybe one extra side type of person." He lifted a shoulder. "Buffets get messy."

"So you *do* have sex!"

"I never said I didn't. Don't fucking point at me like that."

I kept pointing, because he wasn't the boss of me.

"I've never seen you so much as flirt with someone. You just sulk around like a moody goth kid."

Zane slid his red eyes over to me, the ever-present look of bored annoyance at my existence plastered on his dead face.

"Exactly."

"Oh my God." I think I gasped, but I pretended it was a cough. "You covert slut."

"Can we focus on the vampires that will be crawling out here soon?"

"Hell no. We're talking about you slinging dick on the down low. That's way more interesting." All efforts to warm up my hands were forgotten, my heart pumping with the opportunity to tease Zane had warmed me up plenty.

"Hunter. Focus."

"So, do you go after the pretty goth girls who swoon for the moody vampire types? Fishnets is pretty hot, right?" My elbow was knocked away as I tried to jab his ribs.

"How the hell has Sias put up with you so many times a week? He doesn't strike me as a man with patience."

"He keeps my mouth full." I wiggled my eyebrows and Zane furrowed his as he rubbed at his eyes.

"You're giving me a migraine."

"C'mon, you know my dinner habits!"

"Not by choice," he argued with a huff. "I'm forced to tag along while you constantly get takeout."

"Hey, I'm a hungry boy."

"Goddess, strike me down now." Zane shut his eyes and leaned his head back. "Bring me back to the void and end my suffering."

"I bet that makes the honeys melt. So broody. So tragic. Is that why you're growing your hair out?"

He exhaled a long sigh from his nose, his body too cold to activate steam. It had been a while since he'd had any blood, likely a month or so, and I realized with a needling guilt that he was likely starving.

Since he could only have my blood, which I hated him drinking, he never dared ask unless he was gravely injured. Thralls could only heal and recover their powers from their necromancer's blood, which made the whole situation uncomfortable.

No wonder he was such a moody ass. I would be hangry too.

"You know," I supplied after a second, restarting my effort to get my hands warm again. "There is a pretty sweet goth club I haven't been to in a while. You would clean out the place easily if we wanna go one night."

"I do fine at your normal haunts, hunter."

"Mostly dudes where I go though." I moved my knees a little to wake my cold feet up. "If you want more options, I mean—"

"I'm an immortal vampire born from the void." He sliced me open with his eyes. "I don't limit my dinner options. Now, stop being a jackass. We have company."

I smelled them before I saw them, the familiar stench of dry blood and filth permeating the frigid air. Glowing red eyes floated near the entrance, their bodies slinking over each other as they tried to gauge the risk of sunlight verses the free meal in the snow. The hissing, gulping noises of them swallowing down the scent of blood made my skin crawl, no doubt my own beating heart teasing them as much as the open blood bag.

They knew I was there. I wanted them to.

It made the trap all the more irresistible.

I positioned myself just outside of the circle, my hand resting on the trap's trigger.

"C'mon, you nasty bastards," I whispered, trying to will them into action.

Zane drifted away to flank the swarm, and I kept my focus on the entrance. Two pairs of eyes turned into six, then eight, the hissing growing more agitated and desperate.

My heart kicked up into a steady dance as the first grunt vampire slinked out from the shadows. They had once been a young teen, an imp, a band shirt torn at the collar and marred with blood. Fangs flashed as they snapped their jaws, eyes smoldering embers of undead magic. Whatever life had been in that young imp was long gone—it was only piloted by corrupt necromancy driven by the need to eat and destroy.

It didn't move like a person anymore, more like an insect with too few legs trying to scurry across the ground. Once it realized that the sun was too weak behind the clouds and through the canopy of tree branches, it rushed the stained snow and started chomping at the ice. Its little friends followed, grunt vampires of all sizes and races, slithering from their den to fight over scraps.

The shredded blood bag was ripped into smaller chunks by the fighting animals, fangs gnawing at the plastic to try and sip every drop from within. It didn't take the dead oni teenager long to remember I was there, and it turned its gross, glowing eyes my way. With a hiss, it began its slow approach, testing to see if I was going to run in panic and give it a reason to chase me.

"Let's see how much of a badass I truly am." I tossed the last piece of my trap into the air and caught it. "C'mon, ugly. You gonna just eyeball me all day? Or you going to make a move?"

"They can't understand you," Zane tossed from across the circle.

"It's called showmanship, dick."

"I'm the only one watching the show and it sucks. Put the rock down so it can fail and we can kill these things."

I flipped him off as I held up the rock. "It's gonna work."

Zane checked his watch, and I made a mental note to kick him in the balls later. Why the hell fate had tied me to this jerk was an act of cruel and unusual punishment, and frankly, I was way too nice of a guy to be saddled with such aggression and rudeness.

Especially from a dead guy.

He should be *dead*. Not giving me crap from wanting a little fanfare with my vampire killing escapades.

The hissing imp kid took advantage of my flipping off my sassy vampire Thrall and lunged, springing from the ground with all the power in its legs to try and tackle me full force. As it was airborne, I slammed the last enchanted crystal into place and pulled my gun free just in case I was somehow wrong about my master plan.

A surge of power rippled out from the ring, my magic blocker humming with the warning of a spike of activity, and the imp leaping into the air to rip out my throat was suddenly face down in the dirt with a delightful thump. The swarm that had been ravishing the empty blood bag all crumpled to the ground, teeth gnashing and hissing with anger.

My mocking laughter took the form of a happy spite cloud puffing out into the air, and I aimed a few at Zane for good measure.

"Oh, look at that! What was that about it not working? Hm?" I put my hand to my ear to wait for his response. "Can't hear you over there, Zane. I think you said how great I was and how badass this trap is? Who's stupid now?"

"Are you done?"

"Hell no. I'm going to lord this over you for a week, you mopey goth boy." I chambered my gun. "Now if you'll excuse me, I'm going to pick these vampires off without even breaking a sweat."

The charm in my pocket pulsed then went still, the ripple threading itself through the crystals stumbled and went slack, one of them shattering like a busted light bulb. The vampires in the circle collectively lifted from the ground like one combined inhale, eyes and teeth aimed my way. A particularly dirty imp face snarled up at me, snow and mud stuck between its fangs.

"Crap."

"Called it," said the absolute asshole that was my bodyguard.

Taking my grounding trap personally, the imp vampire let out a screeching scream that shattered like shards across my eardrums before it sprang forward. I put a life magic infused round between its eyes, sending its body into a mist of fire and ash. The other vampires fanned out and rushed me like a pack of wolves, and I picked off two more before switching to my sword.

So much for not breaking a sweat. Switching to my sword meant that things were about to get less ashy and more bloody since the blade wasn't blessed with life magic. Gross.

"Are you going to help me?" I yelled to Zane as I sent a head flying from another's shoulders.

"No, you got it." He crossed his arms. "Doing great."

"Is this because I made fun of you growing out your hair?" I dove to the side and slid onto one knee, driving my blade up through a grunt's chin and out the top of its head. "Because you don't look *totally* douchey."

"Is that your attempt at an apology?"

"I'm not apologizing." I dodged a snapping set of teeth and cracked my knuckles across its jaw before slashing at its throat with my blade. "For being honest."

"This is why you don't have friends, hunter."

"I have friends!" I turned one of the grunts into a kebab and rushed forward, using it as a shield to fire a few shots at some faster vampires who were trying to rush me.

"Name two. Sias doesn't count."

"Barnaby is kind of a friend. We bonded a little once rent was caught up."

"Barnaby called you a drug-addled hussy less than twenty-four hours ago."

My sword came up and out of my shield, and I grabbed the vampire that had tried to sink its teeth into my neck and tossed it onto its back before shooting it twice for the offence.

"So? He calls everyone names." I panted, spitting some blood from my lips. These fuckers had a habit of splashing their nasty fluids everywhere when you sent blades through them.

"Doesn't call me names."

"That's because you make my life hard and he thinks it's funny." I stepped over a vampire I had decapitated and paused in reflection. "Okay, I might not have *close* friends, but I have some acquaintances that don't hate me."

"Yikes."

"I don't exactly see you with tons of friends, Mr. Undead Asshole." I gave my sword a shake to get rid of some of the bloody and nasty bits.

"I'm a vampire Thrall. I'm undead, immortal, and bound to do the bidding of whatever necromancer holds my tether." He shrugged one big shoulder. "What's your excuse?"

I had a really witty response to him being a jerk, but it was cut short by my phone ringing again.

"Wilde Contract Killing and Fish Training, please excuse the gunfire." I popped off a round at a grunt rushing my direction. "How can I help you?"

"Bad time?" Dex asked, the sound of a gum bubble popping following directly after.

"Dex!" I swung my gun to connect the butt to the temple of a vampire, then snapped its knee backwards. "We're friends, right?"

"Friends?" she repeated slowly, like maybe she was mispronouncing an unknown word. "Are you about to ask me something weird?"

"What? No, I mean like…we're friends. Buddies. We'd go grab

a beer together or…you know, do normal people shit." I wiped some vampire carnage from my chin.

"Are you asking me to go get a beer with you?"

I was a little insulted she sounded so disgusted, and I ignored Zane as he chuckled.

"Never mind," I grumbled, turning away from Zane so I could kick a dead vampire and pretend it was him. "You got good news about my super-secret project you've been working on?"

"No updates there, but I do have some info about a certain imp you have beef with."

"You're gonna have to be way more specific."

"The one who's boyfriend you fucked," she added with a sigh. When I didn't respond back immediately, she added a flat, "Dallas."

"I sometimes make bad choices!" I pointed at Zane before he had a chance to chime in. "Shut all the way up."

"Marthas," Dex sighed. "I'm talking about Marthas, from the Broken Horn, one of many people whose homes you've wrecked."

Marthas. How could I forget the big, angry, leader of the imp gang Marthas. Last I saw the guy, he was trying to kick my ass in his club after a tryst I could barely recall at this point. Zane had gotten stabbed, and I'd been permanently banned from my favorite hook-up location.

Oh, and then Marthas broke into my apartment and stole a lot of very rare, expensive magical shit I had lifted from Omar's place. So that was also really fun.

"Oooh, right."

"You're a dog."

"Woof, woof." I dodged a vampire trying to tackle me and tripped it before shooting. "Whatcha got?"

"According to my sources, Marthas has been looking for a buyer for some really upscale, expensive artifacts. From what I understand, Florence Pierce has tapped him as a potential buyer."

That was not what I had been expecting.

"Florence? Like the health guru lady?"

"The superstar health guru who owns ReNew, yeah," Dex clarified. "She's all about utilizing inner connections with magic. Like, this bitch has yoga for aligning your magic chakras or some shit."

A bone-deep chill went up my spine at the mention of ReNew.

Visions of Omar staring at me with crystalized spikes coming from his smoky eyes clouded my brain; the memory of his voice commanding me, my wrists bleeding.

Sias walking off into the night, stoically trying to drown himself.

The terror I had felt when I thought I had lost him, knowing it had been my fault he was there.

Feeling Zane pull me from the void just as I had seen how endless it truly was…

"Hunter!"

I turned at the sound of Zane's voice, just in time for a set of teeth to latch onto my leg. One of the grunts I had incapacitated hadn't fully died, and in one last desperate attempt to piss me off, had sprung up and bit me just above the knee.

I hated how familiar the sting was, how vicious it squeezed my heart.

The thing was already at re-death's door as it was, so it died quickly when I shoved a blade through its throat to finally push it back to the void.

"Dex, I'll call you back," I managed through my teeth, terminating the call to examine the bite.

Zane had materialized beside me. "Why the hell did you just stand there?"

"I thought it was dead! Er. Dead *again*." The cloth of my pants stuck to my skin from the blood, the wound hot in the frigid air. "Some fucking bodyguard you are, by the way."

"Who called? Whatever it was had to be pretty interesting to have you that damn distracted."

I slapped his arm away when he tried to help me walk, managing to limp along just fine.

"Dex," I spat. "You remember all those cool, rare, magical arti-facts we stole from Omar's place a while back that got lifted from the apartment? Marthas is planning on selling them to the owner of ReNew."

"Shit. When?"

"I don't know," I explained slowly, contempt boiling over. "I got bit by a vampire while getting the intel, because my body-guard *sucks*."

"You'll live," he deadpanned. "You can't get turned into a vampire as a necromancer."

"You are terrible at apologizing."

"I don't apologize for being honest."

I threw the keys for the car I had stolen at him, annoyed that he caught them when they were very clearly aimed at his head.

"Go get the car. I'm going to check inside."

"Alone?" He pinched his brows into a frown.

"I got it." I made a shooing motion with my hands. "Go get the car."

"I can go with you—"

I dramatically motioned to my bleeding leg.

"Go get the fucking car, Zane. I need medical supplies."

The vampire threw up his hands in surrender, turning to fetch the stolen sedan while I peeked inside for any lingering traces of the elusive necromancer. Whoever had created this batch of ghouls had been slipping through my fingers for weeks, leaving very little in the way of clues or motive. The last place I had found even the smallest little whiff of this jerk's trail was almost a day away from the city.

They were getting bold by creeping closer to the city. I didn't like it, and I knew I needed to find *something* soon, or I'd be chasing down fangs in the damn market district next.

My boots crunched on dead leaves and debris as I pushed through the double doors of what had once been an emergency room. Dark streaks of grime and decay clung to the high corners of the stained hallways, outlining everything in black and deep green. Busted light fixtures drooped from the ceiling, an old fire alarm switch had met a grisly fate on the dirty floor.

Sunlight had reached as far as it could from the dingy windows, shadows taking up permanent residency in the quiet hallways. A few drops of owl's eye helped sharpen my vision, piercing through the darkness so I wasn't completely blind as I continued forward. A sticky, rotten smell grew worse the deeper I went, trailing downstairs and punching me in the face as I made my way into the basement.

I had smelled all stages of decomp for years, and it still wiggled like worms in my stomach when I got too close. A smear of menthol-coated cough suppressant under my nose helped curb it, but damn if it wasn't rancid.

It was absolutely annoying how uninspired and clichéd it was that they had set up their little paradise in the damn morgue. To be fair, having a decent sized room with little hidey-holds to crawl into during the day would be mighty temping for a group of undead. I was more disappointed they gravitated to the dead body room instead of surprising me with something else.

But hey, dead husks weren't exactly brimming with imagination, so I wasn't exactly surprised.

Inside the morgue was evidence of long-term stay, with discarded corpses and gnawed bones thrown to the corners. The amount of leftover scraps told me that the vampires had been there at least a month, which settled like a cold blanket over my shoulders.

This necromancer was an expedient little fuck. I was further behind than I thought.

It meant they might already be inside the city.

I kicked a ribcage in annoyance, feeling a little better as it shattered against the wall. How the hell this necromancer was giving me the slip was beyond me, but I had to light a fire under my ass to find them. If the vamps got into the city and made a nest, it would cause absolute chaos, not to mention really screw up the whole monopoly I had on the vampire killing market. Keeping these undead shits out of the city kept the general population and government unaware of their existence. They were getting too damn close to exposing themselves.

My charm gave a pulse, a little warning sign the same moment I heard something fall to the ground a few feet from the morgue. It wasn't strong enough to be the necromancer, but I had been wrong in thinking all the vampires were outside. My sword slid free as I peered out from the morgue's door, listening to the scraping, hissing sounds slipping down the hallway.

The bite on my leg throbbed as I moved, the fresh blood no doubt exciting the vampire close by. I adjusted my grip, fingers wrapping around the hilt, my charm humming with warning as I crept toward the noise. An office door was hanging half open, the plaque beside the entrance molded over so completely that the name was forever lost to time.

I kicked the door open further and lifted my sword to swing, only to realize my readied strike wasn't necessary. Pinned to a dusty desk with a hunting knife through its jaw was a grunt vampire, still very feisty but completely unable to move. Its red eyes flashed at the sight of me, the fresh blood from my leg wound sending it into a starving frenzy. Its hands slapped the desk and clawed, sending dust flying like it was a bull stomping before a charge.

It was not what I had been expecting.

Someone had clearly been here, gone through this whole office and stripped it for information, and run into this bundle of sunshine.

So much for my fucking monopoly.

The much more disturbing part of the whole situation wasn't the trapped grunt nor the threat to my income. It was the reality that very few people had the training to handle these undead bastards, nor the knowledge of how to find them. It was a very small pool of people.

And none of them were fans of me.

I dodged the swiping, bony fingers of the starving grunt to

look at the blade, noticing a thick piece of paper pieced between the handle and the thing's jaw. The paper tore free with a gentle tug, the blade sharp enough to cut through it clean. I had to shake the sticky, clotting blood from the paper before I could unfold the calling card that was no doubt left behind for the slippery necromancer.

My heart began to thunder once the note was opened, the familiar, clean handwriting ripping me down the middle as cleanly as the blade through paper.

By the light of The Saint, you shall be found, cleansed, and brought to order.

There was a good chance this note wasn't for the necromancer.

I had been knocked so senseless by the message that I had missed the trap pinned to the goddamn vampire.

I knew better. I knew better than to get so lazy about checking for traps, but it had been years since I'd had to think about it. The enchantment was basic and punchy, a concussive ward that ignited with a simple tear of a piece of paper. The energy inside the room expanded like a bomb, sending me through the doorway I had come through and knocking the door off its hinges. I met the wall like a bug to a windshield, the liberated door following me like an unwanted guest.

My vision and hearing were momentarily gone, the volume of my existence turned up far too loud in my skull. For a few seconds, all that I knew was my heartbeat and darkness. It almost felt like dying, like touching my toes into the void before jerking back from the chill.

Then I moved, and the screaming confirmation I was alive ripped over me like a lightning strike of pain.

Debris and glass ground into my palm as I pushed myself up, an awful numbness settling over my body. I thought I yelled, but it sounded like I was underwater, my head ringing with the memory of the explosion. Slowly the shock cloud faded from my vision, and I took stock of all my body parts.

Two arms, two legs, a head and a dick.

Thank all the Gods and Goddesses twice for that.

I wanted to lie there for a while and recount all of my bad choices, but that seemed like a bad idea. Instead, I did some more underwater screaming and kicked the door off me, forced myself to my feet, fell a little bit, and spit some glass from my mouth.

While I wasn't broken or bleeding any more than I already had been, the whole exploding through a room did make me a little jumpy and kinda pukey. When Zane came rushing in to help me, I fired at him before I realized what was happening.

Then I puked.

The asshole had the audacity to yell at me, even though I had once again missed his head.

"Concussive ward," I yelled, because my hearing was still calibrated wrong. "Didn't notice until after. Stoppit." I tried to bat his hand away as he grabbed my jaw, turning my head from side to side. "You're gonna make me barf again."

"You're lucky you're not dead."

"Yeah, that's kinda my whole vibe, man."

"Anything broken?" Zane's hands ran down both arms and my torso, and I groaned a warning as he spun me in a circle. His palms were ice on my cheeks. For a few blinks, Zane had four red eyes that were peering into mine.

"No. But I wouldn't argue if you wanted to give me a piggyback ride."

"I'm not doing that." Zane looped my arm over his shoulders to steady me. "What the hell was a concussive ward doing in a vampire den?"

"Rival hunter," I grumbled. "Left a note for the necromancer that set off the ward."

"Great." Zane sounded murderous, apparently not thrilled with the idea of more vampire hunters on the loose for some reason. "You know this person?"

"No," I said immediately, then remembered he could tell when I felt uneasy. "I don't want to talk about it."

"That's deeply obvious, but I should know who we're up against."

The sedan we had borrowed had been pulled closer to the overgrown parking lot, and I hobbled into the passenger seat where my duffel was waiting. I dropped into the seat and settled into the cushion while my body hummed from the events of the last thirty minutes.

"We have other things to focus on," I told him as he climbed into the driver's seat. "Like Marthas selling shit to ReNew."

"Hunter—"

"Zane, give me a break." I looked at him, bone tired and sore. "One catastrophe at a time. My head hurts and a vampire chewed on my leg."

Zane's jaw bunched, the engine rumbling to life as the subject was dropped.

"How is Marthas able to get a sit-down with ReNew?" Zane asked as I fished my first aid supplies out, the sedan rocking us as he pulled back onto the long-abandoned road. "I didn't think Florence Pierce took meetings with mid-level thugs."

"Apparently she does when they have priceless artifacts for sale." I lifted my hips and wiggled out of my jeans, hissing as the wound pulled from the rough denim. The bite punched deep holes into my skin, blood dripping onto the tarp we had earlier placed over the seats. The sting of the antiseptic made me wince, and the frigid cold settled into my bones enough to force a shiver from me.

"Would Sias know about deals like that?" Zane asked, the bumpy road giving way to something better traveled and smooth. "He seems like he'd be given a heads-up if something expensive and possibly deadly was floating around on the market."

"I'll ask during my dinner date."

Zane grunted, pulling out his phone to check the screen. I

sealed the wound with some gauze, holding tight to help stop the bleeding.

"I still can't believe you let a damn grunt bite me. You literally have one job."

"Not my fault you got complacent, hunter. Maybe you need to do some training."

"*Me?*"

He pivoted the conversation into a hard left turn. "Sias is inviting me to dinner tonight."

That made my already pounding head throb like a war drum.

"Gods, he's relentless."

"How often am I invited without my knowledge?" Zane cocked a brow. "Maybe I want to have dinner with Sias."

"You're ruining my really clever metaphor."

"I wouldn't call it clever," the moody goth boy retorted.

"I'm not into policing who Sias enjoys his time with, but I swear to the Gods I will set you on fire if you follow me to dinner." I jabbed my finger at him after I finished wrapping my leg. "It's a private dinner. No asshole bodyguards allowed."

"What do you know about how these deals are brokered?" Zane sliced the conversation in half and moved on. "Who would be the middleman on something like this?"

"Marthas is a thug, but he's also the leader of a wide network of imps. The Broken Horns aren't small, they have their connections all over." I checked on the bite and sighed. "I have some people we can tap for answers if Dex—"

The rumbling noise of a growling stomach interrupted me so severely that it made me lose my train of thought. For a few beats of very pregnant silence, there was only the hum of the road and the dying gurgles of Zane's hunger.

The mumbled "Sorry" sounded much more genuine that time.

CHAPTER
TWO

SHOWERING AFTER MURDERING vampires was a must.

Not only did I need to wash all the nasty, undead blood splatter from my hair, but the chill and ache I carried home from the day needed to be cleared away.

It wasn't even a big bite, but it had fucked with me. I hadn't felt teeth in my skin in a long time; long enough that I had felt too confident. It had been a brutal wake-up call today to feel it again, to feel that prickling, childish fear crawling up my spine and into my stomach, exploding into a winter storm.

The warm shower helped temper that sharpness somewhat into a dull stab that was easier to mask.

The note, the handwriting and the warning was something else entirely. I'd need some drugs and sex to curb that one down.

"You, my good man," I said to my reflection, wiping the steam away to check if I'd missed a spot shaving. "Need to get out of your head."

While my face was very handsome and clean-shaven, I was keenly aware of the dark rings under my eyes. I was long overdue for a good, deep sleep, but I had run painfully dry on Dallas's Super Fun Time Sleep Drugs, after burning the bridge with Marthas. After years of dabbling in recreational drug activities, melatonin wasn't going to cut through my insomnia, and I wasn't sure if asking Sias to charm me so I could sleep was appropriate yet.

Hell, I wasn't sure what was appropriate at all for us, other than wild, fantastic sex.

I wasn't even sure if saying "us" was within the realm of appropriate. We never discussed it, even after I saved him from drowning after Omar's spooky shit. Somehow, after all that, we just fell back into the same pattern of "dinners" and avoidance of deep conversations about relationships.

And for some reason, it was starting to hurt my feelings, which I really didn't know how to manage.

I didn't get my feelings hurt. I was an assassin. A vampire hunter. A goddamn menace.

Menaces don't get their feelings hurt. We kill things or do drugs about it. The whole thing was throwing off my groove.

The brisk bite of cold air on my body helped dispel the clouds in my brain as I threw my bathroom curtain open, steam breathing out into the apartment. My skin rolled with warmth, the towel around my shoulders protecting me from too much chill at once. I closed my eyes and inhaled, getting back into character.

I had work to do, a "dinner" to attend, and fuckery to accomplish.

"Other people live here," Zane commented from the kitchen. "Can you put your dick away?"

"Never."

"Marthas is going to be at a gala tomorrow," he added as he turned his wide back to me. The sound of a can of cat food popping open set off the Twig alarm, the tiny rat-kitten dancing at his feet for the processed tuna.

"A gala?" I transferred the towel to my waist and sat on a barstool near the kitchen so my ass didn't stick to the vinyl. "What kind of gala?"

"The kind where Florence is going to be."

"How the hell do you know that?"

Zane emptied the contents of the metal can into a dish, cutting it into tiny pieces with a fork. Twig sprinted ahead of his footsteps, jumping up onto the counter beside Kevin's tank and continued to scream.

"I called Dex and asked," he explained, following after his kitten. "You owe her two hundred bucks for the intel by the way."

"Me? You're the one she gave the info to!"

"Mm-hm. You owe me a hundred for the relay." Zane placed the small bowl that was full of pungent, fishy cat food next to Kevin.

"Fuck you. Also, are you feeding your feral little goblin beside my betta's tank? The hell is wrong with you?"

"Keeps his ego in check." Zane cut his eyes to Kevin, who blew a bubble at him.

"Dick." I waited until he turned around and pushed the bowl away from the tank. Kevin flicked his fin. I agreed with the sentiment.

"Where is the gala going to be?" I asked after Kevin and I exchanged mental notes about murdering a vampire and feeding it to a cat.

"Metro Gardens. It's an exclusive, invite-only situation."

"Easy. Did she say if he was bringing the goods with him to this gala?"

Zane rinsed the dirty fork and put it away, leaning on the sink. "According to her intel, he's bringing everything he has. Florance is going to make him an offer at the location." He wiped his hands off and crossed his arms over his chest, face settling into his normal scowl. "What are you thinking?"

"If we can catch him before he gets there, we can grab the shit before it gets into the heavily guarded VIP, rich person party."

"You know where he might be stashing everything?"

"Not a clue," I admitted with a sigh. "All my contacts went quiet after the…uh…club incident."

"Where you fucked his boyfriend and caused a fight?" Zane said it like he was bored.

"Didn't know it was his boyfriend, and it wasn't that big of a deal."

Zane's scowl shifted to the more grumpy kind.

"I got stabbed, hunter."

"But you got that jacket," I pointed out. "So silver lining."

"Do you have any means in finding out the route or travel arrangements Marthas is going to take to his gala?" he asked, ignoring my positive spin on the stabbing situation.

"Yeah. I got a last-ditch effort sort of contact. What are your feelings on acquiring human meat?"

"Human meat," he repeated slowly. "If this is your weird term for sex stuff—"

"I would just say 'sex stuff.' I mean actual meat. Fresh is better. Like a newly dead person, optimally a chunk from the upper thigh or butt." I shrugged. "I'm not asking you to kill someone. The general hospital near the Swallows has a great morgue guy who'll leave you alone with a corpse for a bag of Dust."

It was always a delight to watch Zane's face twist like he just ate a bug.

"What in Goddess's name are you talking about?"

"It would really save me a trip." I slid off the stool. "I'm going to be a little busy tonight, so if you pop down there, we could get a jump on this intel."

"You're not joking," he realized out loud, possibly amused in his horror.

"Not even a little bit."

"You're honest and upfront with me about you bribing morgue workers and acquiring human meat for intel, but you're cagey as hell about injuries." Zane gave a knowing nod to my leg.

"It's fine." I adjusted my towel a bit to make sure it was covered. It stung, and it made me feel sick each time the skin pulled around it, but I'd live.

"It's not fine," he countered coolly. "It's bothering you."

"Mind your own feelings, Zane. I hate that shit."

"I can heal it for you. It just takes a little blood—"

"No. Fuck no. We're not doing blood stuff." I felt my heart ricochet around, bouncing off sharp barbs of intense disgust and excitement that I couldn't wrangle into cohesive thoughts.

"Fine."

"You're getting me stressed before my dinner date." I checked my bare wrist for a watch I didn't have, then patted my towel for pockets. "What time is it?"

"You're going to be late," the vampire said just as I heard a knock at the door.

"Damnit! Stall him!" I sprinted to my clothing, throwing my pile into smaller piles to find something clean. "Don't let him leave without me! Break his leg!"

"You're more upset about being late to your booty call than you were about defiling a corpse," Zane mused. "Each day I learn that you're more depraved than I had originally thought."

"Gotta keep the boys on their toes." I extracted a pair of pants that seemed cleanish, and tugged them on while wrestling a shirt free. "Adds some spice to life."

The knock came again, a little more demanding the second time around. It became very apparent that Zane had decided not to assist, instead opting into poking around on his phone while his kitten gobbled down processed fish. The knocking continued, agitated and quick, whatever patience this driver had was waning quickly.

I tugged my shoes on as I made my way to the door, barely getting my left foot into the damn thing before beginning the process of unlatching all of my security mechanisms. By the time I swung my front door open, I was aware that I must have looked like a sweaty mess of horny desperation.

What greeted me on the other side wasn't a pissed-off driver wearing a nice suit, getting paid handsomely to bring Sias his dinner.

Honestly, I wasn't sure what the hell I was looking at. A few seconds of confusion hung in the air as I stared dumbfounded at a stone statue positioned right in front of my face, a grinning Barnaby just outside of frame.

"Hey, Barns," I finally managed. "That's a really nice stone vagina you have there."

The *extremely detailed* carving of what I assume was a very lovely vulva was retracted, replaced instead by Barnaby's grinning face.

"Isn't it beautiful?"

"Sure," I lamented, turning to let him inside. "If you're into sex toys for rocks."

"This is an authentic fertility offering from almost two thousand years ago." Barnaby swept inside, placing the graphic totem near the whiny kitten and the unamused betta fish. "They use these to burn incense during sex in order to please the spirits. Isn't it simply *stunning*?"

"Where the hell did they put the incense?" I asked, immediately regretting my question as Barnaby extracted a stick from his pocket, putting it exactly where I knew it would go. "Women really had a crap time in history, didn't they?"

"Oh, there's a male version too," Barnaby informed us, lighting the incense unprompted. "I've yet to track that one down."

"How progressive," Zane added, waving the vagina smoke away from the cat.

"You hoping to please some spirits?" I teased.

The fussy incubi rolled his eyes, dusting the figure off with his sleeve.

"I came to see if you are going to drop off a crystal tonight. I'm getting hungry and the last three you gave me weren't great quality."

My pride was stung, Zane's snicker an extra little stab that made me a bit more defensive than I wanted.

"You try having a fulfilling self-love session when you share a one room apartment with a guy who doesn't sleep." I smoothed my cleanish shirt down, the movement fidgety instead of cool.

"Sias is back in town, so tonight's sex crystal menu is going to be much better."

In addition to being a fussy prick at the best of times, Barnaby had apparently been working on his passive aggressive stand-up because he popped off with, "Thank the Gods for that. It was like chewing gum that lost its flavor after three bites."

I wasn't a fan. Zane sure as fuck was, because he laughed like it was the funniest goddamn thing he'd ever heard.

"You know I've trained Kevin to poison people, right? They'd never find your bodies," I reminded them, but was overshadowed by an undead Thrall giggling. Even his little goblin got in on the action, meowing along too.

Barnaby pretended like he wasn't proud of the jab but failed to hide his little smirk. "I didn't mean it as a joke."

"Uh-huh. Why don't you go enjoy your weird smoking vagina statue back at your shop. I'm waiting on someone to pick me up."

"You mean the gentleman downstairs?" Barnaby tossed a lazy gesture over his shoulder. "He's been parked for about twenty minutes."

Of course he had been. Of. Fucking. Course.

"Great!" I announced, snatching my jacket. "Fuck you both very much, I hope you fall down the stairs."

"Don't forget rent is due in three days!" Barnaby called after me, and I slammed the door behind me.

As expected, the driver was pissed.

He didn't even greet me as I sprinted over to his town car, only checked his watch slowly, and walked to the driver's side door.

"Mr. Llon'nai wanted us there by seven," he growled.

"Yeah, blame the idiot with the patchouli pussy."

He gave me a look and I just shook my head.

"Never mind."

To say the ride to Sias's office building was uncomfortable was an understatement. Not the car itself—that was all premium leather with heat-controlled seats—but the driver decided that I had lost my music privileges. I had to ride in silence the entire way, listening only to the man's contempt for making him fail to meet Sias's expectations.

To be fair, I wouldn't want to disappoint Sias either. The Gods themselves didn't have a presence in the city, but he sure as hell did.

I was unceremoniously dropped off in front of Llon'nai tower, a glittering monument to the power of the all-mighty dollar placed right at the heart of St. Athesall's business district. The spiral of glass and steel captured the city lights and played with them, sliding neon signs and streetlights lazily across the surface like the world itself was its toy. Automatic doors whispered greetings when I passed through, a security guard waving for me to go ahead.

It was after hours, which made the building hum at a low boil, only a few floors still active. Sitting at the very top of his castle, Sias's suite was waiting for me, guarded by a blond dragon with a killer resting bitch face.

Claudia flicked her eyes up at me as I sauntered in, perfect eyebrows bored with my audacity.

"What the hell are you still doing here?" I demanded. "Also, hi, Claudia. How are you?"

"I don't leave until Mr. Llon'nai leaves." She made a show of checking her watch. "It's like you're not even trying anymore."

"I was ambushed by a very excited landlord bearing a new stone sex toy." I angled my head to the closed door. "I'd rather not be later by having to explain that."

Claudia hummed, lifting one finger and taking a million years to push down on the com.

"Sir, your late dinner has finally arrived."

The office door clicked, a lock sliding open. Claudia wiggled her fingers at it and cut me with a judgmental up and down.

"He'll see you now."

I still disliked Claudia.

All the windows facing the lobby were tinted too dark to see through, but the windows overlooking the city were clear and wrapped around the expanse of Sias's immaculate office. A never-ending lake of electric crystals shone up at us, blinking and buzzing with life. The inner lights of the office were dim and calm, Sias's lithe form leaning against his marble desk.

Tonight he was wearing a bespoke, gray suit with sapphire shirt, his hair a waterfall of honey blond cascading down his shoulders. The golden tips of his incubi horns caught the soft light, reflecting as sharply as the tumbler he sipped from. Tan skin under his open collar looked warm and delicious, his long fingers curled around the edge of the desk.

"You kept me waiting, Dallas."

"I had a wild landlord hold me up." I crossed the office, pausing just within arm's reach. "And I kinda got exploded earlier. Had to make sure to get all the debris out of my hair."

His eyes were a smoky swirl of lavender and magenta as he looked up from the tumbler, a galaxy of splendor I could never navigate.

"If you're trying to be intimidating, it's just making it worse," I teased. "I like it when you glare at me like you want to literally eat me."

He finished his drink with one final toss, throat moving hypnotically.

"You don't think I could punish you properly, darling boy?"

A thrill of excitement slid down my spine like it was a stripper pole. Every bit of me that liked being touched by Sias tingled, and I failed to hold back my smirk.

"I'd love to see you try."

Sias lifted from his causal lean, his eyes flashing a shade of fuchsia only reserved for when he was about to bend me over something. The long fingers that had been cooled from the glass pinched my chin, forcing it up as he stepped in close. There was only a few inches of difference between our heights, but when he was a breath away from me, he was a tower of sex peering down a perfect nose at me.

A beautiful warmth curled up from my chest and flooded my

brain, the charm magic pulsing from Sias a drug I was hopelessly addicted to. The city lights faded away, reality tunneling into only bright eyes and the rich taste of amber and tobacco.

Incubus magic was the blissful venom used to relax prey before devouring, a non-lethal poison that made their meals drooling simps that would do whatever they wanted in order to reach the height of sexual pleasure. When Sias's venom was pumping through me, when his magic had a grip on me, I wasn't just a horny jackass ready to fall to my knees at his command; it gave me a way to forget, to get lost in the fantasy that there was nothing else out there but that moment.

No necromancers. No death.

No disappointment or regrets.

No mistakes.

No loss.

No loneliness.

Only pleasure, release, and priceless distractions.

Sias was my escape, and I was in love with it.

Warm breath traced over my lips as he spoke, spiked with the sting of the drink he just finished.

"Lie on your back across my desk. I want to watch your face when I make you come."

A brutal chill shook me, my body responding immediately to not only the promise of ecstasy, but in the authoritative, boss daddy tone he used when he was ready to eat me alive. I hadn't realized his other hand had hooked into my belt loop until I was manhandled in a circle, my ass hitting the edge of his desk. As ordered, I lifted myself and sat on the cold marble, bringing us eye to eye. Fuchsia pinks shifted to rose under hooded lids, and I nearly gasped as he finally pulled me into a kiss.

Sias's tongue tasted like hundred dollar whiskey and sex magic, an impossibly delicious aphrodisiac that made me groan and wiggle around like a touch-starved deviant. My fingers grabbed his designer shirt in an effort to keep myself from floating away as well as bring him closer, my tongue dancing with his like it was going to solve all my damn problems.

Long, elegant fingers gripped the back of my hair, the tug of his magic feeding on my mounting excitement made me almost lift off the damn desk with need. I felt my jeans being unfastened with such speed and dexterity that it was almost distracting, but my dick had taken the wheel at this point.

God, had I needed his touch, his magic, his taste. My mind had been crowded with the growing vampire population, the risk of Marthas doing something stupid with those fucking artifacts, the necromancer I couldn't seem to track down.

Not to mention the goddamn note.

It had been a long time since I had seen that handwriting.

But that was future Dallas's problem, and I sure as hell wasn't going to think about that when Sias was about to have his absolute fill of me.

My body was on fire, lit within the electric pulse of incubus magic and Sias's hunger. I was making noises only Sias got to hear: the desperate whines and pants of a man drowning in an ocean of lust and happily ready to sink to the bottom.

When the spell was broken, it happened so suddenly I exhaled like someone had punched me in the gut.

Sias's palm had landed right on the vampire bite on my leg, the sting a shrapnel bomb that ripped through the fantasy. The devastation was so severe, so complete, that I was left embarrassed with my ass on a very cold desk.

Worse yet, Sias blinked like he had just woken up from a dream.

"Are you alright?" he asked, more surprised than concerned.

"Fuck." I squeezed my eyes shut, an ache of shame creeping over like a storm cloud.

"Did I hurt you somehow?" Sias lifted his hands off me. "When you said you exploded earlier, I thought it was a joke."

"It wasn't the explosion." I scrubbed at my face, hoping maybe

I could just erase myself from the situation. "I got...this fucking vampire surprised me earlier. On my leg."

"How bad?"

"Not bad. It's fine." I rolled my head from side to side to try and ease the tension knotting between my shoulders. "Just give me a second. I'll be good to start again."

"Dallas."

"Can we start back from the kiss and go from there?"

His fingers weren't icy anymore when he took my chin again, my eyes forced up from the ground to meet his. They weren't pink anymore. They had shifted to a sapphire, the fire gone.

"You should go heal and rest."

"Sias, I'm fine. I'm not about to leave you hungry."

His brow quirked a fraction. "I didn't invite you here just to eat."

The fist around my heart unclenched, and I felt a new wave of something complicated.

"Really?"

He hummed in affirmation, and gave my chin a soft squeeze before letting me go.

"It also matters to me that you're healthy and rested. I don't want you keeping injuries from me in the future."

"I don't plan on letting this happen again," I practically growled, pushing myself from the desk.

Sias extracted a billfold from his pocket, plucking a few hundred from the fold before tucking them into my pocket.

"Go heal, and get something to eat. You were too excited to notice but your stomach was growling."

"One of these days we need to go get food dinner after sex dinner." I managed to force a smirk, even though I wanted to sprint out the nearest window.

Sias leaned down to kiss my lips, a gentle, sweet thing he didn't give out often.

"It's a date."

THREE

I DIDN'T THROW myself off Llon'nai tower, but only because I didn't want Zane feeding Kevin to his stupid cat.

Otherwise, after the soul-crushing moment of losing my steam in front of the guy I had the ultra hots for, I was game to test out if I could fly. I didn't know how in the holy hell I was going to face Sias again after that, and I had realized only after I was a few blocks away that I hadn't asked him about the stupid gala Marthas was going to be attending.

Overall, probably the shittiest day I had endured in quite some time, and I was duke of Really Shitty Days (TM).

Wanting to walk around being miserable, the annoyed driver that had picked me up late didn't argue when I declined a ride home. My leg hurt from Sias's grip on my thigh, a constant reminder of my failures following me. I needed to focus, get my head back in the game, and figure out how I was going to manage everything at once.

I needed drugs and/or tons of alcohol, my leg fixed, and something to eat—not necessarily in that order, but absolutely all three.

St. Athesall during the winter months had an extra coating of grime. What had once been glittering, pure white snow falling majestically from the sky was quickly turned to brown sludge and piled high on either side of the street. Sidewalks were constantly wet and gritty with salt, and attitudes were about as bitter as the chill biting through your jacket. Between the tall buildings the wind tunneled and transformed into a bully, shoving you around just for fun.

It set the mood perfectly as I moped my way across town, leaving the commerce glitz for somewhere I felt a little more at home. While the tourist areas of St. Athesall and the shining monuments of capitalism were cold and covered in brown snow, the Swallows had that but at least threw better parties. Since there were so many different holidays and celebrations that took place in late winter and early spring, the cold often brought with it spiced food and strong drinks, often meant to share with friends and neighbors.

I couldn't remember all the block parties I had stumbled on, strangers shoving hot wine and cookies into my face. It hadn't mattered that I didn't live there, they were too drunk to care that some human dude had wandered in.

I would have given my right arm for some type of makeshift community at that moment. I needed somewhere to go and feel less like a piece of shit, but only had a pissy fish, a grumpy-ass vampire and an ancient vagina-obsessed landlord waiting for me at home.

Wee.

The Swallows wasn't throwing any parties that evening, but the cold helped keep fewer of Mathas's goons off the streets for me to run into. It was no small secret that I wasn't welcome in most of that section of town, but the only clinic I knew of that took cash and didn't ask questions was sitting right at the edge of the Broken Horn's territory.

So, I had to roll the dice.

The frigid wind followed me through the door, muddy foot-prints trailing from the tile onto the soggy carpet near the entrance. My head had begun to hurt from overthinking and replaying how bad my day was, which helped distract me from the pain in my leg. I didn't want to focus on the lingering feeling of teeth marks in my skin, nor the nausea that accompanied it.

The clinic was small, and thankfully sparse, only a few people with sniffles in the open waiting room watching a television playing a drama from twenty years ago. I had been so annoyed and sour that I didn't even give the nurse at the front a stupid name to annoy Dr. Reynolds with.

The day kept getting better and better.

Despite there only being a few people ahead of me, I sat just long enough to get lost in the plot of a movie I'd seen at least a dozen times before Reynolds finally called me back.

"Not at your best today I take it, Mr. Wilde," he teased with his wry doctor humor.

"Understatement."

"It makes this go a little faster when you're not putting "Thundercock" on my paperwork." He waved me into the exam room, barely glancing up from his clipboard. "Remove your pants and have a seat."

"If I had a dollar for every time I heard that."

Reynolds didn't react, because he had been over my shit for some time. It felt good to at least get a zinger in.

I tossed my jeans over the little swivel chair and climbed onto the stiff, paper-lined cot masquerading as a bed.

"Any stiffness?" Reynolds pulled on some rubber gloves, snapping the hem before gently prodding at the bite. "Chest pain? Difficulty breathing, like if you're battling an infection?"

He motioned for me to lean forward so he could listen to my heart. His gloved fingers jabbed at my throat and ribs for a moment. When I shook my head, he let me lie back down again. "I'm going to do an x-ray to be on the safe side."

"If you say so, doc." I shut my eyes, folding my hands over my stomach while he zapped me with radiation to look at my insides. Whatever my torso told him seemed satisfactory because he parked himself on the squatty, rolling stool and got to work on the bite.

"This doesn't seem like an animal bite." He tossed a glance at me. "Human and demon mouths are particularly riddled with bacteria."

"This was an animal. Trust me on that." I tucked my hands behind my head when I felt the first tingle of the healing magic march over my skin. The itchy feeling of tiny ants crawling over my body made me wiggle despite myself, and I set my teeth to hold still.

"Fucking hate how this feels."

"Everyone reacts differently to medical healing magic," Reynolds parroted his normal doctor speech, placating, and a little bored. "Try to relax."

While the good doctor proceeded to torture me, I let my mind wander to the far corners of wild, obsessive overthinking-ville. Despite my best effort of trying to forget about the embarrassing moments with Sias, I kept replaying the look on his face when my baggage snapped his spell. The dazed look on his face killed me, as did the fleeting look of concern that had drifted past.

The misery I had felt was icy and sharp, a frozen knife twisting between the ribs. I had felt nothing quite as miserable as disappointing—

Ah, shit.

Zane.

I had forgotten about fucking Zane.

There was no way he hadn't felt the moment I had shattered Sias's spell and fell ass first into embarrassment, because I was still feeling the effects way after the fact. I wasn't sure what was worse: the fact that it had happened or the knowledge that someone uninvolved was *painfully* aware of how badly it had gone.

I mused on how much I'd have to pay Reynolds to give me a lobotomy.

My misery was interrupted by the itchy ants taking a much

more aggressive assault against my skin. The soft, irritating pitter-patter of healing magic grew fiery and fierce, scratchy limbs growing into hot daggers.

As the pain grew sharp and sudden, my eyes flew open the same time I heard the doctor performing the healing mutter, "That's not right."

The golden glow of the healing magic glittered in a halo around my wound, the skin quivering as it started to pull apart.

"Uh," I started, hissing through a wave of pain. "Isn't it supposed to be going the other way?"

"Fascinating…"

"Yeah, super interesting and kinda…painful!" I yelped as the glow pulsed for just a moment, before everything got way too intense way too damn fast. The weird, quivering skin situation took a hard left turn, going from slightly unnerving and gross to terrifying in a heartbeat. My skin began to split and tear apart at a rapid rate, the muscle under it falling into ash like I was a mummy that stood up too fast. Blooming from the bite, the halo ballooned out over my thigh, eating away at skin and meat so all that was left was an obsidian bone.

"Saints and fucking Gods, man!" I tried kicking the halo off the table. "Make it stop!"

Reynolds sprang off his chair in a panic, hands up like I was mugging him.

It was the second time that night I had shattered a spell, and while my leg was turning into bone right before my eyes, I still thought the Sias one was worse.

Way worse.

The golden halo died away, slowing the rate in which my leg was becoming a skeletal mockery of logic exponentially.

But not stopping completely.

"I don't understand," Reynolds was repeating in a whisper. "I've never seen someone react to healing magic this way. I don't understand."

The sharp pain of the attack had faded back into the normal

itchy march of healing ants slowly eating away at my body. From just above my knee down to the middle of my tibia and fibula was inky black bone that looked charred, the skin and muscle flanking either side seared by golden magic.

What made less sense was how I was able to still move my toes and bend my knee. It was like my whole leg was powered by horror and nonsense.

Whether it was because I was in shock or morbid curiosity, I reached out and poked the patella of my newly charred leg.

It kinda tickled.

Reynolds fainted.

That was my cue to go ahead and see myself out.

I decided since he likely marred me for the rest of my life, but also knew that I apparently had a new allergy to note on my patient form, I'd only pay him half of his normal fee. I thought that was a fair compromise.

I wiggled back into my pants, tossed some bills onto the counter, and left the clinic trying to not throw up or scream. My heart was desperately trying to jump ship since there was a massive hole in the lower deck, and I couldn't stop trying to make sense of how my leg was still functioning.

If I stopped believing it would work, would it stop?

Why wasn't I bleeding?

What was going to happen when it reached my foot? Would my shoe fall off?

I curled into myself as the wind blew hard against me, the mind-numbing sensation of feeling the breeze against my skin and my bone almost made me start laughing out of hysterics.

Since I was already feeling a little crazy, I hedged my bets and ran like hell to the bus, tucking myself near the front so I could dive out the moment I was close enough to home.

It was the longest bus ride of my damn life.

Also, my knee looked ridiculous as it pressed against my jeans as I bounced it in anxious anticipation, but I couldn't stop. It was the soothing thing I needed to keep from screaming.

The bus stop was just a block or so away from my apartment but it felt like a marathon to get home. I sprang from the bus the moment its doors hissed open, and I rushed up the stairs in a flurry of bony panic.

I had been right about the shoe. It fell off as I crashed through the front door.

"I fucked up!"

Zane lifted his gaze from his book, annoyed confusion pushing his eyebrows up as Twig blinked sleepily from his lap. He pulled one earbud out and checked his watch.

"You're home early."

"Zane," I said through the panting hysteria. "I really fucked up."

Whatever meditative state the book had put him in slowly wore off, and the confusion was replaced rapidly with visible concern as he stood.

"What happened?"

"I went to Reynolds to get the bite healed—" I began unfastening my pants.

"You went to get *healed*?" he barked, shifting into anger. "What the hell is wrong with you?"

"So many things!"

I shoved my jeans down, horrified that my sock slipped right off my onyx, skeletal foot.

"Why in the love of the Goddess would you intentionally put yourself in the presence of healing magic? Did you somehow forget that healing magic is a branch of *life* magic?!"

"I got healed before!" My voice had taken a delightful edge that made me sound angry instead of terrified. "You were there! You held me down!"

Zane grabbed me by the meat of my upper arm, tossing me onto the couch with a strength I hadn't expected. My bony leg stuck out as I lost balance, crashing into the cushions like a drunk toddler.

"That was before your necromancy powers had fully manifested. You hadn't been resurrecting dead bodies or puppeting them across islands yet," the very mad vampire Thrall growled at me, grabbing a knife from my discarded jeans. "The magic is in you now, it's changed your essence."

"Is that why my skeleton looks like barbeque?" I spread my toes to watch the little pebble bones shift. It was terrifying and I wanted to throw up, but it was still kinda neat in that unhinged, numbed mind state of panic.

"Lie back."

"Why?" I peered up at him, immediately suspicious of the knife. "What are you going to do?"

"I have to heal you with necromancy magic."

"Damnit. It's blood stuff, isn't it?" The way Zane did his disappointed dad sigh made me groan. "Not the blood stuff. There's gotta be another way. What if…what if I try and use my powers? Maybe it'll trigger the…the super creepy death magic and I'll start healing myself! No awkward blood ritual needed."

I thought this sounded like a grand idea, but the big goth grump didn't agree with me.

"You know that sounds legit," I added quickly. "Has anyone ever tried that? Maybe I'm a damn savant."

"I'm glad you're enjoying yourself, but that creeping healing magic is about to reach your dick."

I swung my legs onto the couch and lay back, no longer driven to come up with more brilliant ideas.

Zane kneeled beside me, touching my blade to his wrist. His red eyes connected to mine and held them hostage, his tone serious as always.

"You have to drink my blood until I tell you to stop. It's going to be intense, but don't fight it. Whatever pull you feel, follow it. Do you understand?"

"When you say intense, do you mean like how it is when I give you my blood?" I hated that the idea made me fidgety and weird, and I was aware I was adjusting my hands a lot on my stomach.

"Yeah," he admitted with a less bitter sigh. "Probably."

"Can we just agree that this is a life and death thing and that any boners we get is just a side effect? Strictly business boners."

"Focus, hunter."

Zane slashed the blade across his wrist with one quick motion, his fingers curling into his palm to squeeze the blood from his veins. It was too dark to be human, taking on the viscosity of long-dead blood and dripping down in rusty drops. His skin was cold against my lips, the smell of metal and death almost overpowering as I forced myself to let the icy drips fall on my tongue.

It tasted like what I imagined a dead body would taste like, until suddenly I couldn't taste anything.

The world around me sank like I was being pushed under water, plunging so fast and deep that I barely had time to attempt a scream.

I wasn't falling, I was sinking. Dropping like a heavy stone in a black pool of nothingness, endless waves of shadow and nihility. Zane was gone, my apartment was gone, St. Athesall and the connecting world—gone.

I was in the void.

The panic that had squeezed the breath from me faded with my reality, leaving me hovering in a state of death and acceptance. What the hell else could I do?

I died. Or…

I couldn't see my body, which made it strange to feel something under my feet. Black tides rolled under me, rippling where my limbs should have been. The shadows coalesced into forms, my hands and feet outlines of what they should have been.

In the endless expanse of forever, I saw something.

She was faint at first, a ghost barely corporeal enough to be visible. She was the outline of a faded dream, something you'd see out of the corner of your eye that would disappear the moment you looked for it.

The Goddess of Death stood before me like I was expected to

do something impressive. Even in the void, surrounded by nothing, I could tell she was waiting on me for some untold task.

It would mark the second time tonight that I had performance issues.

The Goddess was formless and comprised of second glances and passing shadows, but when her arm moved, I could follow it somehow. A closed fist was presented to me, and I held out the idea of my hand to accept whatever it was. Dust fell from her fingers, slipping silently into my palm with the heavy weight of sand and expectations.

Her hand transferred the dust to mine, then she turned her palm upward and closed her fingers. I followed her lead, mimicking what she did in order to try and unpack what the hell was going on.

In the nothingness, something happened.

Something wiggled in my hand.

It was Kevin, jumping around in my palm like he had when I had pulled him back from the void. I had crafted him from dust or…maybe it was his soul?

I didn't know how to ask. I didn't know what it meant.

Are fish souls made of dust?

Are *all* souls made of dust?

What the fuck was with the dust?

I closed my hand again, feeling Kevin crumble like a sandcastle against my palm.

The Goddess waited. She opened her palm again.

And so did I.

She smiled, and I felt a terror like I had never felt before in my life. It pierced through my chest and turned to ice, branching out like razers that cut me into small, shriveled pieces that would never fit together again.

Kevin flopped around in my hand, and the Goddess reached out and grabbed the center of my chest.

The carved handle that had landed in my chest when I killed Esdras twisted and locked into place as she touched it.

Then she pulled all my pieces back together again.

And my sandy Kevin exploded.

I arched my back and gasped for air, the tug so vicious and sudden that I felt life snapping back into my limbs like an electric shock. The void paled and melted, receding back from my vision.

A shadow with red eyes peered down at me, icy hand on my head, and thumping heart pounding in its chest. The pounding muscle was cupped by a bony hand, the fingers flexing as the heart beat against them.

The heart was warm, a soft candlelight in a dark room, the eyes a lighthouse leading me safely to shore. I tried to reach out and touch the hand holding the heart, wanting to feel the warmth, to be back from the emptiness of the endless void. The rhythm of the heartbeat pulsed through me, a current of life bringing a delicious sensation back to my body.

Each beat ricochetted through me, shredding my senses to oblivion. I was hungry for it, desperate to feel alive, and I pulled the shadow to me like it would save me from sinking again.

The lips were cold at first, carved from ice and stone, but the more I kissed it, the more heat I felt. The heartbeat quickened, the shadow leaning over me, a hand cradling my jaw as I demanded more and more. I kissed the void shadow until I could feel my own heartbeat again, and I sobbed against its lips when my chest began to breathe again.

I didn't want it to end, I wanted to keep kissing it forever, but the thing eased away.

The shadow thing spoke, voice calm and familiar.

"You're okay," it said. "Take some breaths."

"Is Kevin okay?"

"He's fine," the shadow promised. "Kevin is safe."

"I want to go home." I swallowed, my head was starting to get fuzzy.

"You are home. You're in your apartment." The shadow smoothed my hair back, its other hand blanketing mine as it rested against the beating heart. "It's late at night. You're on your couch. Can you feel it under you?"

My fingertips touched the fabric of my couch, and my reality faded into view.

I was home. I was on my couch. There was a leak in the ceiling. My mouth tasted like hot pennies.

I was alive. I was whole and alive.

The shadow thing was gone, disappearing back into the void like a lost dream.

Zane came over to me holding a glass of water, dry blood still on his wrist. I forced myself up into a sitting position and peered down at my legs to verify they were back to normal.

"You weren't kidding about intense," I mumbled, accepting the glass of water.

"You've been out for about an hour." Zane sat on the couch by my feet. "You started mumbling about Kevin."

"Had some weird dreams." I rubbed at my temple to try and remember them, but they were jumbled and weird. I couldn't make sense of half of it, and the other half was too bizarre to recount properly. "I'm just glad I'm not ultra horny this time."

"What do you remember?"

I shook my head. "Not much. Something about dust, I think. Or fish souls."

Zane grunted. "Explains the Kevin mumbles then. Nothing else?"

He had to wait for me to finish downing the entire glass of water before I could answer, using the last swallow to wash some of the blood from my tongue.

"No," I managed after a burp. "Why? Did I do something weird?"

It was almost refreshing to hear his disappointed dad sigh again, the couch dipping as he pushed off of it.

"You always do something weird."

"I'm nothing if not consistent."

I got lost in watching my fleshy foot move, barely noting that Zane had moved to the kitchen.

"What did you learn from Sias?"

His question wasn't meant to be a sharp slap to my ego, but it landed hard just the same.

"He was busy," I lied. "We had to reschedule."

Thankfully, he didn't push, shifting topics to something strangely more pleasant.

"I got the dead body meat."

"Oh?" I leaned back to stare at the leak in my ceiling again. It was in the shape of a lumpy dragon swallowing a lightning strike. A fat droplet of water careened to its demise beside the couch. "How'd that go?"

"About as terrible as I thought it would."

A brown bag was tossed into my lap, the top crumpled into a makeshift handle. The sudden delivery made me jump, but the most concerning part was that the contents inside were *warm*.

"Oh, God." I cringed. "Did he give you parts from a body that was burned or something? This feels oven hot, man."

"That's not the body part, idiot."

It felt like a trap, so I carefully uncurled the paper bag away from my face. When nothing sprang out or hit me with a wave of nasty funk, I peered inside to see a foil-wrapped plate inside. The wonderful smell of cooked, spiced meat kicked my stomach into a growl.

"You got me dinner?" I asked, dumbfounded.

Zane ignored me, his headphones already plugged back into his ears. He scooped up his little mangey cat, his book and his scowl and parked in a chair near one of my few working lamps.

I guessed that was his way of apologizing for letting a vampire bite me earlier, or maybe he didn't want me slamming stuff around in the kitchen while he was trying to read.

I didn't ask.

Instead, I inhaled the food, took a few shots of whiskey, and crawled into my bed to wrestle with nightmares for a while.

CHAPTER
FOUR

ZANE DID NOT APPRECIATE my summer picnic-themed freezer bag.

Apparently, storing cadaver parts in a bag covered in smiling sun and fluffy clouds was somehow inappropriate. I disagreed, because what was more summertime than fresh meat and meeting an informant? Plus, it was all I had.

"Are you going to fill me in on the plan or is this a classic 'I'm winging it like an idiot' sort of day?"

"It's a classic, 'Fuck you,' sort of day." I adjusted the absolutely appropriate and functional bag on my shoulder as we hopped off the bus. "But as a treat, I'll let you know we're meeting an old friend. They work at a lot of places Marthas frequents and overhears a lot from the kitchens."

Zane strolled beside me, hands tucked into the leather jacket that didn't need to try and warm him up. I had noticed how cold his body felt beside me on the bus, almost matching the smuggled dead meat in my summer bag.

"And you pay for them with body parts?"

"Everyone has a price. This is theirs."

Zane grunted a response, tired. "This'll be interesting."

Midtown was bustling by mid-morning, the local shops open

and the family-owned restaurants leaking customers waiting in line for breakfast. The smell of coffee and frying sausage hung in the air, snippets of passing conversations ranged from family gossip to complaints about the economy. Small children not yet old enough to be shoved into a classroom followed parents trying to hustle at the outdoor market.

During the weekday mornings, Ushen worked a few different locations throughout Midtown, so it took me a few failed attempts to find them. I struck out at two diners and a cafe before finally tracking the tall, mild-mannered wendigo down at a breakfast nook next to a flower shop.

The place was small, maybe enough for ten people to sit inside comfortably, with a long counter in view of the kitchen. Ushen's antlers were capped with tiny socks to keep them from scraping paint off the ceiling, the serving window just big enough for them to stretch a bony arm through to pass along orders. Each of the barstools at the bar had asses in them, so we inched past the munching crowd to find the swinging kitchen doors.

The waitress was an imp woman with a messy bun and blunt horns, she held up two fingers to ask us how many menus. I countered with one and she passed it over someone's shoulder.

"If you two don't mind waiting, I'll get to you when I can," she said. "I think the two at the end are about to finish up."

"No problem." I snagged the menu and strolled toward the kitchen doors, pretending to look over the plastic offerings of fried eggs and buttery toast. Her attention was divided in several directions, so it was a breeze to pass the menu to Zane and dip into the kitchen.

Ushen moved in the kitchen with the grace of a spider; long limbs floating from one task to the other like they were spinning a web of breakfast foods. Pancakes were flipped as eggs were cracked in clawed hands, their body hunched over a griddle with the type of placid grin only a skeletal face could have. There was no work uniform that day, only an apron over bone and moonlight silver fur.

Their face turned to me, head lifting to sniff from the hole where a nose should be. Fiery red orbs in their eye sockets drifted from me to my cute bag, then back to me.

"Dallas," Ushen said, voice calm and haunting. "What do you have for me?"

"Prime goodness, fresh from last night." I gave the bag a pat. "Thought maybe my good friend Ushen needed a nice dinner."

"Your good friend Ushen is grateful." They scrambled some eggs with cheese, plating it next to some perfectly made toast before sliding it through the window. Ushen held out their hand, claws curled out so I could place the offering without nicking myself on the tips.

To keep things sanitary, I decided to give Ushen my whole bag instead of pulling the meat out inside of the very small kitchen. They lifted it curiously, still managing to flip hash browns before pulling the zipper aside to peek inside.

Ushen's eyes flared, and the bag was closed again.

"Choice cuts. Very fresh. I will return the bag."

"Keep it. My treat."

Ushen nodded, placing the bag into the freezer before starting on some toast dipped in a sweet egg batter.

"Speak your request, Dallas."

"I need to know where Marthas might be stashing something important and very valuable. Not just drugs or guns, but something he'd want to protect, something that would make him a lot of money."

Ushen tilted their head in thought, reaching up to adjust a sock that went crooked from the gesture.

"There's an old warehouse near the Swallows, it has a picture of a top hat faded on the side." Ushen paused to consider something, tossing the egg-soaked toast onto the griddle. "He stashes valuables there, where the machines used to be on the third floor."

"You're a lifesaver, Ushen. Always a fountain of information. I know where you're talking about, it's near—"

"Or," Ushen interrupted, and my triumphant stroll out of the kitchen was stalled.

"Or? You're not sure?"

"It's one of two places, that I know." The wendigo scratched at their cheek with the very tip of the razer claw, the sound of bone scraping terrible. Did they have an itch or was it a gesture they learned from watching fleshy friends contemplate?

They continued, "The top hat warehouse, or a club called Rubber Gloves."

"Never heard of it."

Ushen made a noise that sounded like a rock tumbling in a dryer. Their broad shoulders shook, antlers knocking a sock loose. It took me a few dazed seconds to realize the skeletal chef with a hobby of eating human flesh was *laughing.*

"That is very telling," Ushen commented after the rock settled down in his ribs.

"What does that mean?"

Ushen plucked an old ticket from the line and reached into the pocket of their apron, extracting a pen. It was fascinating to watch them manipulate an ink pen with such massive claws, their penmanship was neat and crisp. Scrawled across the wrinkled receipt was an address near the business district of the city.

"The door is around back. Ask for 'rubber gloves' when they answer the door."

"Where the hell are you sending me, Ushen?"

"Somewhere you've never been before," the cheeky monster joked, the toothy smile ever present. "Good luck, Dallas Wilde."

"I'm not loving how ominous you're being." I waved the receipt in thanks, taking the hint when Ushen shooed me out of the kitchen with their claw. I almost asked for something to go, but the waitress handling the front of the house was throwing a ton of tickets onto the line by the time I was slipping out.

Zane followed me as we started inching our way through the crowd, people hovering near seats waiting for a chance to pounce.

The outside air was crisp, morning starting to fade into early afternoon.

Zane took the receipt when I held it up, examining the address.

"This where we're going?"

"Second stop," I corrected. "Ushen wasn't sure if Marthas has the stuff stashed at that shady address they didn't want to elaborate on, or the old textiles factory near the Swallows. We'll start with the old building then try out the mystery joke Ushen wrote down."

A paper bag was placed against my chest and I caught it before it fell to the ground. The bottom was warm, the contents inside sweet and delicious.

"What's this?"

"Pancakes." Zane shrugged his shoulders up defensively when I cut him a look. "She asked me what I wanted and I just picked something."

"Are you serious?"

"You handed me the menu."

"This is the second time you got me something to eat." I folded one of the warm, flat confections and took a bite. "You keep this up and I'm going to start thinking you tolerate me."

"Those are business pancakes."

I laughed, because despite the fact it came from Zane, it was funny. I decided to let him have the victory because the business pancakes were good.

We had a decent walk ahead of us to get to the old factory, and I wasn't exactly in a rush to scope the place out in the middle of the day. It would be extremely obvious for two guys to be casually strolling through a long-abandoned area of town, one that was fenced off and covered in weeds. The only people who made it a habit to hop the failing security measures were usually peddling hard drugs or doing something equally dicey.

It doesn't get much more illegal than infiltrating a crumbling building to look for a gang leaders secret stash, so in this specific scenario, I think we were worse than the drug dealers in the realm of dicey.

"How did you meet a wendigo in this massive city?" Zane filled the silence while I finished chewing a massive bite of pancake.

"Wendigos don't sleep," I said around my bite. "So Ushen works in kitchens in the Swallows at night. Most of the places they work are the same ones these big leaders run or operate. I made friends with them when I was trying to locate a necromancer who did some dealings with the Broken Horns a while ago. When I asked them what it would take for intel, Ushen didn't hesitate to let me know."

Zane's brows lifted, almost impressed. "Bold. DHAP would arrest them for defiling corpses, wouldn't they?"

"Big time." I stuffed the trash into a bin and shoved my freezing hands into my jacket. "But at the time I was also running odd jobs for Marthas, doing some wet work stuff on the side. Ushen figured I'd know where to find some fresh meat. They weren't wrong."

"You've been moonlighting as an assassin for a while then," Zane mused out loud, like it was a piece of a puzzle.

"Few years."

"You could have used your training to be a DHAP officer. Why not go that route?"

The question didn't so much take me off guard, but the reference to my "training" sure did. I knew he felt the bouncing squirrel of anxiety climbing up my chest, digging its icy claws in deep.

"You're going to be surprised," I deadpanned. "But I don't do well with authority."

Zane's snort was the second time that day I had been surprised by a nocturnal creature laughing. His didn't sound like a rock rattling in a dryer, so much as a low tumble down a cliffside.

I focused on the sidewalk, an unsettling bundle of nerves winding up in my stomach.

"I guess you had plenty of run-ins with Saint's Army."

"I have," Zane admitted coolly. "It's been a few decades, but there's no mistaking the fighting style. Only a mercenary group hellbent on eradicating vampires wield swords like you do."

I said nothing, because I didn't want to talk about it, but he wasn't done.

"You never mentioned it before," he said.

"That's right, and I don't plan on starting now."

"It couldn't have been easy, being part of that group with your abhorrence of authority. That's about as authoritative as it gets."

Zane stopped when I did, a frown creasing his forehead when I jabbed his cold chest.

"Fuck off, Zane. Boundaries. I said we're not talking about it."

"I'm not trying to provoke you, hunter."

"Then shut up. I don't ask you about your shit, right?" I kept walking, trying to shake the knot from my stomach. "Nosy, undead butthole."

"Alright," the vampire said somewhere behind me, the bustle of the busy Midtown starting to drop away. "Then ask."

I was half paying attention, turning us down a calmer side street to avoid street construction. The old factory's retired exhaust pillar stood as a beacon in the distance, the faded lettering almost washed away completely. The height of the thing made it seem deceptively close.

"Ask what?"

"My past, my time with the necromancers. Whatever you want to know." He wasn't fazed when I gave him a dismissive snort. "You're right, if I'm asking you about your past, you should have the same luxury."

"The difference is I can't feel the barbs going into your stomach when I ask you about crap you don't want to talk about. Or keep pushing after you said to fuck off."

Bitterness and anger coiled in me like a viper, and I knew he could feel it slithering around just as strongly as I could. The quiet apartments we passed had a lady outside sweeping salt from her stoop, the rhythmic brushstrokes matching the surge of blood in my ears.

"If I could make it go the other way, I would," he said after a stretch, the understanding in his voice a needle in my heart. It was a prod into a tender spot, a jolt that sent me into a knee-jerk reaction of malice. I didn't want this vampire's sympathy. I didn't want his friendship, and I sure as hell didn't want him knowing any part of me that was vulnerable.

That wasn't fair, and I reacted in kind.

I whirled on him, temper hot and voice lethal.

"You wanna do this? Fine. What the hell happened to your necromancer? Not Edras, but the one that pulled you from the void. You were his bodyguard, his protector, so you either betrayed him for Edras or you fucking failed him like Edras. Which is it?"

The assault was brutal, unforgiving, and I had meant it to hurt. I wanted him to feel sore and tender, poked at and exposed.

Zane's face was always a slab of ice, a blank, dead thing with two stains of blood for eyes. He was starving, which made the veins in the thin skin near his tear ducts blue, his lips colorless with cheeks that had stopped growing dark stubble.

As far as dead things went, his emotional range had been a short scale of annoyed, angry, bored or apathetic. I had seen him both in writhing pain and ecstasy only once.

I'd never seen him emotionally hurt.

Until that moment.

It melted the ice, a slow drip of a memory I couldn't see or feel, but he didn't try to hide it even though I knew he could have. It would have been easy for him to keep those walls up, the door shut tight, but he kicked it open to let me know the blow had landed as viciously as I had wanted it to.

When he spoke, his voice carried the burden of a lifetime of regret.

"I failed him."

We stood together on the street, two people unfortunately bound together by circumstances neither wanted, having just flayed each other open to bleed out a few decades of unresolved trauma. I had hit a damn vein.

"You cared about him," I told him, because I knew. I could see it all over the melting ice.

"I did."

"Did you love him?"

"Deeply," Zane admitted immediately, the knife of my question twisting. "He was a dear friend, a man I respected immensely, and someone I miss every day."

"He was like…?" I almost pantomimed a sex act, but decided maybe that was a little crass in this situation. I know, I was shocked too. "A boyfriend? Husband?"

"No, not at all," he corrected. "More like a brother. Platonic admiration and affection, a man with a love for life and passion to help others."

"Bullshit," I spat out of reflex. "No one who manipulates the dead does it for altruistic reasons, Zane."

"Of course they do." He said it so easily, like he was telling me a truth as obvious as the color of the damn sky. "He wanted to keep people from dying, to extend life by controlling death itself."

"Yeah? How? By murdering people and turning them into hungry husks that rip people apart? By unleashing hordes of vampires into neighborhoods?" I tossed my hands up, frustrated with his delusions about his bestie. "What the *fuck* are you talking about, Zane?"

"Sandros didn't make vampires, Dallas. Not a single one, besides me, and I wasn't a tool for destruction. I was his friend."

"Dude needed to rip a soul from the void to have someone to talk to? Is that what you're spinning right now?" I laughed at the absurdity of it. "So what did you two do then if he wasn't toying with human lives or trying to dominate the living to his will? Movie night and fucking checkers?"

"We worked to prolong lives in the terminally ill. Sandros could push death back by weeks, sometimes months, while healers tried to knit things back together, fight off sicknesses that spawned too fast for magic to extinguish." Zane placed his hands into his pockets, eyes unfocussed as a memory swept over him. I knew that look; he was years away. "The frustration and anger he carried with him was like the cancers he fought, all-consuming and rotten. It pushed him to make the wrong connections. Trust the wrong people."

"Zane." I waited until he came back from the memory, eyes blinking toward me. "I'm not finding this easy to believe."

"Why would I lie about him?"

"To have empathy for your story? Unless you can make this guy sound really likeable, there was no way I would mourn another dead vampire factory. I think if altruistic necromancers were floating around, I would have heard about them by now," I scoffed. "I think you want me to like Sandros."

Saint, he looked exhausted from dredging up the memory of his necromancer, from the verbal assault I had slashed him with. The sigh that left him was silent, his shoulders sagging under the weight of the day. I knew better than to assume the vampire Thrall was harmless; I had seen Zane tear lesser vampires in half looking more tired than this. I was ready for the next barrage, the new maze to navigate, the new string of bullshit he was going to try and choke me with.

Instead of an attack, or what I had thought was manipulation, Zane knocked me off balance with the hurt in his blood-red eyes.

"Of course I do," he admitted, the raw honesty punching me in my cold, mean heart. "Hate me all you want, hunter, but know my maker was a good man. That's deeply important to me."

I hadn't just hurt him. I wounded him.

We both stood in silence as a wave of cold shame hit me like a wall of spikes.

The chilly guilt made me shuffle my feet like a kid who just realized right from wrong.

"I feel a little bit like a dick."

"You didn't know," he whispered after a time. "Plus, I had been asking you tough questions. I guess we're even."

"I um…" I huffed a cloud of steam into the air, envious I couldn't disappear into vapor from the situation. "I didn't leave the Saint's Army on good terms. Sort of bailed in the middle of the night after torching some bridges. I guess you could say I failed them."

Massive understatement. It was like saying a volcanic eruption was a tiny upset in the planet's tummy. The comparison was similar to what my gut was doing while still being as vague as possible.

I had made the mistake of thinking the quiet Thrall was done bleeding, but he got in one last bite to level the playing field.

"Did you love them?" he asked me, the same way I had asked about Sandros.

Ouch. Fucking *ouch*, man.

"They were all I had. I loved the idea of people caring about me." My body shivered as anxiety forced my feet to move. I felt too naked, too exposed, too much of myself open. Zane had been the first to ever ask, and the only soul to know.

"Okay, now we're even," I tossed over my shoulder. "No more deep, dark secrets today."

CHAPTER
FIVE

DEATH.

It hangs in the air like a poison, a noxious shroud that spreads out like spores and crawls up the walls. We didn't have to go far into the old factory before it landed on us like a disease, causing us to change our approach.

The fence surrounding the place had long ago lost any ability to keep people out, the barbs at the top stripped away and falling in lazy spirals. Several spots around the bottom of the failing perimeter were bent back and split, easy enough to slip though. The true defense was where the artifacts were supposedly stashed.

Ushen's intel was always reliable, but sometimes the details weren't exactly correct. In this instance, the wendigo was mistaken about there being a third floor. There were only two floors above ground, which were barren landscapes of crumbling flooring and rotting machinery.

There was, however, a dark basement that would be perfect to hold goods they didn't want found.

It was also where the death smell was coming from.

Because of course it was.

I was *less than* thrilled about going into the dark, especially when I knew dead things were down there.

Sure, I charged into vampire dens often, and was—dare I say—pretty damn good at it. Zane's previous mention of my "training" (which still bothered me) was rooted in the specifics of vampire extermination, and I had years of honing those skills to become a professional fang murderer.

The first rule of killing unnatural dead things was simple:

Prepare.

Before any of us dashed into the unholy hiding places of the damned, we had to stock up on all the fun equipment needed to not only turn the bloodsucking beasts into soup but to also keep ourselves alive.

Guess what I hadn't done before we left?

Sharp stabs of ice had begun to form at the base of my belly, crystalizing up my spine once I realized the smell was too strong for it to have been an animal. It was a body, a person, somewhere in the darkness that we had to wander into.

And my stupid ass wasn't prepared for it to be anything other than regular dead.

The awful embarrassment of my lapse in training compounded with my ever-present *unhappiness* about being in the dark made the back of my tongue acidic, along with my attitude.

Zane was blissfully quiet, and didn't remark on my heart hammering through my ribs as we made our way down. The metal stairs rattled as we descended, one of the steps falling below after we passed over it. Grit slid under my boot as we stepped onto the bottom floor, the light stopping just shy of the basement entrance.

"You have your owl's eye drops so you can see better?" Zane asked, his voice echoing up the groaning stairwell.

"Of course not," I answered like a viper strike. "I would only have enough for one eye anyway. I'm almost out." I fished my phone from my pocket and tapped the front-facing light on, handing it to Zane. "Point that over my shoulder as I lead. I need my hands free."

"Is your charm sensing anything?"

The magic detector charm was humming in the baseline aggravation of being next to me, perpetually warning me of my own death magic. There were no spikes, no pulses, nothing to indicate anything obviously magical.

"No. But that doesn't mean there aren't magic-suppressing charms or something in there." I pulled my gun free and checked the bullets, grinding my teeth that they weren't blessed. If it was a vampire den, it was going to be a rough ride. I told Zane over my shoulder, "Follow my sightline."

Zane gave a single nod, calm and cool wandering into the darkness that reeked of death.

We entered slowly, Zane following my sweep of the area with my phone's light. The basement was a long stretch of open floor with support beams, dusty crates and machine parts. Decades of spider lineage hung from the corners and draped over busted gears, rodents taking up residence in the machines and wooden crates.

The dirt under our footsteps crunched and scraped along the cement floor, dusty footprints made by modern footwear led further into the belly of the basement. Had the place not been monopolized by the foul odor of decay, we probably would have picked up the stench of old grease and animal waste.

Zane followed behind me, matching my pace, the light following wherever I aimed the barrel of my gun. Darkness and death made my heart bounce around my torso like it was a rubber ball thrown by a sadistic child. A scratching sound of a fleeing mouse caused me to whip around and aim, cussing at it, myself, and the world.

"Ahead," Zane told me once my heart was done having an attack. "There's a body lying near a beam."

I followed where he aimed the light, the cause of the death smell coming into view.

At the far end of the basement, near some busted crates and a tangle of wires, the top of a man's head was poking out from behind a cement beam. A pool of dark, sticky mess haloed out from his hair, the exit wound obvious even from a distance.

The body was too still to be anything dangerous.

Relief washed over me like an ocean wave warmed by a summer sun. There were no undead things lurking in the dark just out of view, nothing that was hungry to stab its teeth into my neck. That warmth would be short-lived as we pieced together the scene around us.

We approached careful and cautious, mice no longer terrifying me for sport, until we could get close enough to take in more of the scene. The man was an imp; two black, short horns among the messy hair on his head. Remnants of broken wards were scattered across the ground, crystal and gem fragments catching the light in earthy rainbows. A string that had once been a simple binding spell was tangled up and tossed aside.

Someone stormed through here like a tornado and destroyed everything.

They also knew how to dismantle spells, which meant this guy might be worth knowing.

In the mess of broken rocks and shattered bits of charms, drops of blood arced around the beam and led back in the direction we had come from. Seemed like one of the charms may have worked before it was torn down, probably a tripwire reaction paired with a defense ward.

The magic itself couldn't physically harm anyone, but the force of an expanding ward with some knives or a box of nails attached would fling them at you like a soundless bomb.

Deadly shit if you knew how to set it up.

Our poor imp had been shot between the eyes, probably only a day prior, the look of surprise still stuck to his face.

Beyond the crime scene were long trails of pushed dirt, evidence of something massive being wheeled around and moved.

Like crates filled with important, illegal goods that were now long gone.

"Shit," I breathed. "I think someone else had the same idea."

"I imagine Marthas has plenty of people who would want to come after his stash," Zane mused. "But does anyone in particular come to mind?"

"No one that would want to start a war." I put my gun away and kicked at the shoe of the dead guy. "That's one of his guys for sure. Someone surprised him."

"There's a lot of charms and wards here." Zane kneeled and picked up a piece of rock. "Tourmaline. It still buzzes a little bit with the protection ward that was attached. That's impressive."

"Marthas can afford the pricy witches."

"Can we get a tracking spell? Maybe whoever was here can be traced." Zane tossed the rock down and stood, knocking dust from his jeans.

"We'd need fresher blood or some hair for that. These drops are too old."

Zane stood over the body of the dead imp, giving him a passive once-over.

"I think even with the brain damage, you'd still get some useful information from him."

I knew it was coming, but I still groaned my frustration to the ceiling.

"It's the best lead we have, hunter," Zane reminded me. "Otherwise, the trail is as cold as he is."

"Yes, yes, funny vampire. I get it." My hands started to tingle with the phantom sensation of feeling them turning to bone. "I can agree with the idea and still hate it."

"It won't be as bad as the first time."

I stared at the dead guy for a long time, only a little distracted by the smell and my creeping dread.

"I don't like how the necromancy magic makes me feel," I said to the dead body and therefore Zane by proxy.

"I can ground you, and keep you from reaching too far into the void."

"How?"

"My purpose is to be the grounding rod and to protect you." Zane nodded to the body. "Put your hands on him, let the magic travel through you into the beyond. I'll be right here."

Shards of rock poked through my jeans as I kneeled, the sticky smell of death cloying and invasive. Tiny pinpricks of magic danced over my palms and the tips of my fingers as I reached for the body, hungry for the excuse to come out to play.

"Did Sandros—" I started to ask, feeling unsure if I should. I knew Zane could feel my guilt nipping at me for being such a jerk earlier with my questions.

"Go ahead."

I wiggled my fingers as I asked, "Did he ever get the weird skeleton hands?"

"No, but he also wasn't fighting the magic either."

"Fair." I adjusted in the dirt, exhaling all of my feelings out through my lips. "God, I hate this."

"Focus." Zane took a knee beside me and placed my phone down near the body. The light remained bright, casting stark shadows across the floor, cutting the body into fragmented angles. "Don't resist the magic. Let it guide you."

I shut my eyes for a few moments, willing my heart to slow down. Butterfly wings and sticky ant feet danced up my arms from the pads of my fingers, the death magic humming as I hovered my hands over the body. My charm was pissed, warning me constantly that the magic I was summoning was dangerous.

I didn't know why it made me feel worse, why that dumb little thing warning me of my own magic prodded a tender spot in my process, but each little buzz was like a kick in my side.

Zane wordlessly held his hand out, taking the thing as I ripped it from my pocket.

The dead imp's body wasn't cold; it was the same temperature as the floor under me, which somehow made it more disgusting. I had expected him to be icy, or like he'd somehow *feel* dead. He didn't feel like anything.

His sweater had been soft, but his body was void of anything else.

Magic crawled up my arms, stopping just short of my elbow in freezing, slithering tendrils. I wanted to shake my hands out like they had fallen asleep, it felt like they had bugs living just under the skin. My molars hurt from grinding my teeth, and I wanted to wiggle and fidget like I was in the doctor's chair again.

"Focus, hunter," Zane's voice came again.

"It feels awful. Why does magic feel so damn gross?"

"Because you're fighting it. Relax. It's not going to hurt you."

I scoffed, wincing as the magic tendrils tightened and summoned more ants to torture me. "We just talked about skeleton hands, Zane. Forgive me if I'm not thrilled with this whole fucking process."

Something heavy and cold settled on my right shoulder, a familiar feeling that lived far back in my memories. The temperature was wrong, far too chilly to be the warmth of a supporting hand, but it was there all the same. Zane gave my shoulder a squeeze, the connection of Thrall and Necromancer sliding into place.

The tendrils on my arms relaxed, the ants washing away into soft streams of trickling water. My palms stopped itching. My fingertips cooled like I was tracing the water's edge. I took in a full breath, the smell of death lost.

I shut my eyes to the living world, and was plunged into darkness.

I sank my hands into black waters and the center of my chest knocked once.

The hand on my shoulder kept me steady, steering me through the sensations.

The void is yours to command something whispered in my head, sounding eerily similar to the red-eyed shadow I had seen before. It was…comforting…hearing his voice again.

The tendril magic spiraling up my arm squeezed, tugging my arm through the darkness of the endless nothing. It pulled me, guiding me through the void like I was a lost child. Cold understanding rippled as my fingertips touched the top of a buzzing energy.

Fear, loss and panic called out from that simple touch, my body lurching.

There, it whispered. *There it is.*

It.

I knew what "it" was in a sickening, nauseating wave of realization. Such an overly simple yet insulting dismissal of someone's essence, their embodiment, their *soul*.

Don't fight it, the red-eyed shadow warned me as my fingers curled back, my stomach churning. *Focus. Focus —*

If there was a proper way to rip a soul from the void, I sure as hell didn't know it. My body was shaking, sick and crawling with guilt as I grabbed onto the dead man's soul and dragged it through the veil, the tendrils gripping my arm a vise of icy malice. A searing pain clawed down the center of my chest, my arm plunging into frostbite as I pulled the soul kicking and screaming into the corpse.

Dead eyes opened wide, milky and blue; a scream pierced through dry lungs.

Zane pulled me back up from where I was slumped, cold sweat raking my body.

"Breathe, hunter," he was whispering to me. "Well done."

"Why did that suck so much worse than last time?" I fought a shiver that ran down my spine. "Ugh, I might barf."

"His soul was deep. There was no death magic lingering like there had been last time." Zane squeezed my shoulder, fingers frozen. "You did this on your own."

I felt the soul vibrate in my hand, the control slipping for a moment.

Dead eyes stared up at me, groaning whispers stuck in the corpse's throat. His limbs jerked like he was struggling to get the muscles to work, confusion inching over his features.

"Am I…" the corpse managed, mouth dry and tongue thick. "Am I dead?"

"Yeah," I answered with a wince.

Its milky, pale eyes swiveled in my direction. "Like…*dead-dead?*"

"Pretty dead, I'm afraid."

Disappointment twinged with horror twisted its decaying face.

"Oh. That kinda sucks."

"I'll let you go back to the void, just answer my questions," I promised. "I need to know what you were guarding here. Was this where Marthas kept his stash?"

The corpse's eyes floated around the room, deep pops sounding from its stiff neck as it turned its head.

"Oh yeah…that old, creepy factory. Yeah, he kept stuff here…" it trailed off, stiff arms jerking as it tried to move its hands.

"What was here? What were you guarding?"

The dead man manipulated its arms up to its torso, patting itself down with clumsy, jerky movements.

"How did I die?"

"You got shot," I placated. "You gotta try and focus, man. I don't know how long I can hold this spell. What were you guarding at the old hat factory? What was here?"

"Old, ancient stuff," it said, brows lowering in thought. "That guy did shoot me…I remember the gun, the bang. I tried to tell him it was already gone but…" One hand lifted, touching the ripped skin of the bullet wound.

"Gone?" I asked. "The artifacts weren't here anymore?"

"No, they got moved. Boss moved them to the club yesterday, but that guy…he wouldn't listen to me. I tried to tell him that but…"

"Club? You mean Rubber—Oh *dude!*" I turned away in disgust

as the corpse slipped his finger right into the bullet wound in the center of his forehead.

"Gods," the corpse marveled. "Right between the eyes!"

The soul in my grip shook with my distraction, slipping between my fingers. I gripped tighter, the pressure of tendrils tensing my jaw.

Zane reached over and pulled the hand free, forcing it back down to its side with a muted crack.

"If you throw up on me, I'm leaving you down here," he warned me.

"Saint, that was nasty." I swallowed down any sickness lingering and focused back on the dead guy. "Did they take the artifacts to Rubber Gloves?" It nodded at my question, so I added, "Where in the club?"

"I don't know," it said softly. "Never had club duty." The features on the man's face lifted as much as the state of his decay would allow, devastating hope in his sad, dead eyes. "You're a necromancer, right? Can you bring me back? Undo this?"

"No, I'm sorry." I adjusted my fingers around his soul, and felt the grief trail up to punch my heart.

"This is it for me? This is everything? I wanted to travel…I have a new motorcycle I only got to ride once."

Regret and heartache rippled out from him in a radioactive beacon of sadness, scorching me with the burn of loss. The soul in my hand fought against me, seeking the void, seeking escape from this torture of realization. Zane tightened his grip on my shoulder, and I struggled to keep my control over the magic.

"Who shot you?" I demanded. "Rivals? A double cross? Who was trying to get these artifacts?"

The corpse's face crumpled like it was trying to cry, but no tears could ever fall.

"I can't believe I died for…what? *Marthas*? That guy is a dick!"

His soul slid in my grip, the tendrils on my arm tugged so hard I almost toppled over. I fought against it, my chest burned with the strain.

I struggled to keep my hold, my arm shaking like his soul was made of steel.

"Listen to me," I managed through my teeth. "Tell me who killed you, and I'll make sure to take them out for you."

Its attention moved back to me, searching for solace. "You will?"

"Yes. Tell me." I wrung my eyes shut as pain seared up to my elbow. "Who killed you?"

The dead man lifted its hand and placed it on mine, the sensation almost as horrible as the bullet wound situation.

"Human. None of our guys. He had—it…scar…"

The corpse groaned and began to flail, eyes rolling back into its head. A quake radiated up from my palm, I felt the soul begin to sink.

"Don't fight it," Zane warned me. "Let it go."

"I'm not done." I gripped the soul in my hand as hard as I could and jerked it forward, the corpse screaming in agony.

"Hunter, let the soul go." Zane pulled at my shoulder. "You're not strong enough yet to keep a soul out too long."

"Just a bit longer." I set my jaw, almost blind from the searing pain. "I know I can get more information. I just—have—to—"

The corpse screamed; fueled by anguish and magic, splitting into octaves that only existed in the realm of the dead. A force knocked me into a backwards tumble, the soul in my grasp falling away. The icy tendrils that had wrung themselves tight around my arm slid off, the rippling pulse of the void fading into shadow.

Everything fell silent and deathly still for a few moments, until I became aware I was panting hard from exhaustion. I was lying on my back, something hard and cold under me, the light of a phone casting a pale glow over a cracked ceiling.

I pulled in a breath, the exhale stuttering and shaking.

"That. Sucked."

"I told you not to fight," Zane scolded from under me, pushing me off onto the dirt as he sat up. "You're too fucking stubborn for your own good."

"I wasn't fighting it, I was controlling it," I shot back, rubbing the back of my head. "I knew he had more information to give. If I could have just held on a little longer—"

"You'd be worse off than you are now," the vampire interrupted, catching my arm. My black, bony fingers mocked me as I stared at them.

I sighed.

"Crap."

"Yeah." Zane deadpanned. "Crap."

"Can you do the Thrall magic thing you did before?" I wiggled my bony fingers at him. "Like you did after my first attempt at the museum with Mia?"

"My 'Thrall magic' is not kicking your ass when you do stupid things." Zane placed my skeletal hand in his fleshy one, his fingers curling around it gently. "You could have hurt yourself fighting against the pull of the void. You need to listen to those tugs, move with them until you get the strength to bend them."

"I don't know how I was able to find his soul so fast," I mused, watching the skin of my arm start to reform over bone, crawling like spiderwebs up my wrist. "I thought it would take longer."

"He was still fresh—the blood and bone guided you." Zane's brows twitched, a wince creased his forehead. The bruising of exhaustion around his eyes seemed to darken.

"I guess it gets harder to track as they decay then?"

The skin of my hand crawled over my knuckles, and I could feel how cold Zane's palm was.

"Extremely. The more of the physical body that rots, the deeper into the void the soul goes." He spread my fingers as the skin stretched over it, giving my hand a once-over before letting it go.

"So, like a pile of bones would be a no-go? Mummies and old shit is just off the table?" I flexed my hand and watched my fingertips grow pink from the blood rushing back into place.

"For you." Zane stood, knocking dust from his jeans. "Powerful necromancers can train to bring back whispers to the ancient dead. The Goddess's inner council was supposed to be able to animate and talk to mummies, but I've never seen it myself."

"Inner council, huh?" I grabbed my phone and dusted myself off as I got to my feet. "That sounds ominous."

"They're from hundreds of years ago, hunter. Don't get excited."

"Aw. Fighting a council of necromancers sounds badass." I aimed the light at the now still body of the imp. We stood there staring down at the poor, informative corpse for a few heartbeats. "We should move him, right? Feels weird to leave him down here to rot after we talked to him."

"Grab his feet." Zane looped his arms under the imp's and lifted after I grabbed his ankles. Balancing my phone light while piloting a dead body out of the darkness was trying, but we managed to do it without tripping over anything. We left the poor bastard just inside one of the busted doors with his arm in view, hoping that someone would spot it from the distance and make a call.

Hopefully no one was waiting for him, but if they were, at least they'd know what happened to the guy now. It was my good deed for the year.

"Are we heading to the club the imp mentioned?" Zane asked after we vacated the property. "If it's one of Marthas's places, we'll need some glamour."

"Yeah, my glamour contact was the guy we beat up after he jumped me, remember?"

Zane tilted his head in remembrance. "Oh, right."

"We'll have to do this old school and just keep a low profile. Stop fucking laughing, I can be covert when I need to be." Zane snorted a dismissive response and I continued. "We won't go totally empty-handed in the glamour area though. Dex has glamour tech that will mask us from cameras, so at least we have that."

"So, we're going into a club, having no idea the layout, relying only on some homemade glamour tech you buy off a black-market dealer that barely tolerates you based on intel you bought with human flesh from a wendigo diner cook?" Zane lifted a brow. "Did I miss anything?"

"You forgot that I fucked the club owner's boyfriend while high in his other club."

"Right." Zane sighed. "How could I forget that?"

I slapped him on the arm. "Chin up, vampire. We have more fuckery to accomplish."

CHAPTER
SIX

LIKE ALL GOOD UNDERGROUND, highly illegal magic tech operations, it was run out of the upper apartment of a twenty-four-hour convenience store.

The store itself was nothing special, it had the same layout and overpriced snacks found in literally every single little stop-and-rob across the city. The shelves were stuffed with processed garbage and cheap, cold beer waiting in glass freezers. The only thing under lock and key were the cigarettes being guarded by the clerk armed with a revolver and some basic spells. Beyond the "employee only" restroom and stacked milk crates near the exit was a set of stairs leading up to the real operation, which was run out of an oni family's living room.

Dex sat with her legs curled under a low table, metal blasting in her headphones as she wired together a tapestry of magically infused gems with metal-teethed rectangles. Two small tusks escaped her bottom lip, curled at the edges like backward fish-hooks, her blunt horns almost disappeared under the shaggy state of her mohawk.

Her father, who she got her tusks and cheery personality from, watched a movie at a high volume on the couch behind her, not bothered by his daughter's blasting music or her criminal activity.

She had been so hyper-fixated on her work that her brother had to all but wave his hand in front of her face to get her attention, which she snarled at him for. I was given almost the same amount of snarl when I waved from the front door, but she slipped her headphones off and unfolded herself from her work.

"Came to drop off my intel money?" She stuck her tongue through the elastic, pink gum in her mouth before she breathed life into the thing, expanding it out in a balloon.

"Yeah, and ask for some goodies. I need some glamour tech to keep us from being noticed on security cameras. Got anything available?"

The gum bubble popped, and she gathered it back into her mouth with a quick jerk of her tongue. It was always impressive how she did that without ever getting it caught on her prominent tusks.

"Basic," she yawned. "I always have that. I was hoping you'd give me another interesting, custom project to work on." Dex strolled over to her workstation and snagged a few things from the table, her father leaning to the side so he didn't miss anything on the television while she sorted through the bits and bobs.

"Another interesting project?" Zane asked me. "What custom thing did you request?"

"Just a little experimental thing."

"Such as?" he prodded. "Is it of the exploding variety?"

"Don't worry about it, Zane."

"Fuck, that means yes." He rubbed at his temples.

"Will you relax? You're giving me just as big of a headache."

"If we're about to try and blow something up with whatever the hell Dex rigged together, you need to tell me. This isn't a 'relaxing' scenario, hunter."

"Not a bomb," Dex clarified as she strolled back over. "But if you want one, I am working on a really badass pulse device that sends off the same lust waves as succubus enchantments have."

"Yes," I said the same time Zane barked a firm, "No."

Dex grinned, her nose ring catching the light with the movement.

"You lovebirds can hash it out later. In the meantime, it's two fifty for the boring glamour tech, and…" She dropped the glamour tech into my palm, the small thumb drive-shaped device a familiar sight. The second thing she dropped into my hand was new, a plastic circle with a rolling switch in the center and a nylon cord looped through it.

"Is this…?" I prompted, mirroring her grin as she nodded.

"Yep. It's finished."

"Is that the not-bomb?" Zane quizzed, sounding less than convinced that the little device wasn't going to murder us all.

I slipped the small device around my neck, the plastic circle landing against my chest bone, and gave Dex a glance.

"You sure this works?" I asked.

"I'll wait patiently for my praises." She picked at her nails a bit, shifting her weight onto one leg.

Zane took a cautious step backwards as I gathered the device into my hand.

Sliding my thumb to the button, I held my breath as I rolled it the other direction with a solid *click*.

For a heartbeat nothing happened, and I watched Zane's face to see if I had gotten my hopes up too high. Confusion creased his brow a moment, his eyes darting around like he was trying to listen for a sound I couldn't hear. A scowl set into his features, jaw jumping.

It had worked.

I couldn't stop myself from smiling. "You can't feel my emotions anymore, can you?"

"What did you do?" Zane demanded of Dex.

"Trade secret," she said coolly, cocky grin on her face. "What I can tell you is that the tech is set to nullify very specific frequencies. You can praise me now."

"You are a genius, Dex. A mastermind. A gorgeous, badass, oni princess and I would kiss you if I knew you wouldn't immediately punch me in the balls." I grasped my new shroud of privacy in my hand and held it to my heart, ecstatic that Zane couldn't feel how happy I was. He couldn't feel how tired and stressed I was, or that I kinda had to pee and wanted a cigarette for some reason.

All those emotions, feelings and desires were just for me. Mine. A solo experience I had missed since he came barreling into my life.

"Oh, I rarely say this, but thank you sweet, loving Saint. I needed this today."

"Hunter, I don't like this," Zane countered, frustration all over his dead face. "We don't know what kind of magic was used. We don't know what effect this might have on our bond."

"Relax." Dex brushed his concerns away with a wave of her hand. "It's enchantment manipulation and a touch of blood magic. Plus, if it starts messing with your 'bond'—cute by the way—he can just flip the switch again and it'll shut the nullification down. Everything will snap back into place."

Zane was shaking his head as she spoke, either not believing her or set on dismissing whatever was explained. Dex was forgotten, his attention back on me.

"You cutting yourself off from me is dangerous," he insisted in a low, angry grumble. "I know you don't like that I can feel your emotions—"

"'Don't like?' That's a hilarious understatement," I spat before he could continue. "Zane, you know every single thing I feel all the time. *All the time.* I have *zero* privacy. It's bad enough I know you can feel when I'm fucking Sias, but knowing you can feel the deep, personal shit? Do you have any idea what that does to my mental health?" I tapped my temple. "It fucks with me, man. I'm constantly aware someone else is in my head, feeling how I'm processing things, how I'm dealing with stuff I'd rather no one knew about. I need this. I need to be alone with my thoughts. You have to understand that on some level. You're not a fucking robot."

Zane's molars continued to grind as I spoke, his temper a razor's edge from exploding out in all directions.

"Not to break the tension or anything," Dex said, not so much breaking the tension as just adding cracks to the thinning resolve of a pissed-off vampire. "But do you guys wanna take this outside? Dad said he can't hear his show."

I turned to stare at her, not masking my annoyance. "Seriously?"

"Y'all's little spat is loud." She presented the room behind her. "And you're standing in my living room."

Zane remained deathly silent as he broke away from the group, storming outside like a mute hurricane. The door slamming shut behind him made her dad glare at me, like I had somehow given the order for Zane to be a prick.

"Sorry," I called over to him with a wave, and he growled as some of his oni magic made his teeth seem sharper. "I'll take that as my time to go."

"Yeah, think so." Dex counted the money I gave her. "You want to take a sleepy enchantment for your gloomy Gus? I think he needs a nap."

"He'll get over it," I said, though I didn't believe it for a second. "Thanks for this, Dex."

"Anytime. Your money's always good here." Dex popped another gum bubble and strolled back over to her workstation as I followed after my pissed-off Thrall.

Zane was waiting at the convenience store back exit, fuming in the cold. The wind tossed his shaggy hair, his eyes sharp against the paleness of his skin.

"You just going to be pissed off at me forever now? Is that the deal?" I asked him as I made my way over.

"You do a lot of stupid things, Dallas, but this one is record breaking."

"Saints and devils, you are a real diva sometimes, you know that?"

Zane turned his fierce gaze to me, anger lifting his shoulders like the cold was getting to him.

"Don't dismiss my concerns. What if you need me and I can't feel it? What if something happens to you and I don't find out until we're both dead?"

He was nervous. Not of me dying and subsequently him dying along with me—maybe it's better to say it wasn't *just* that, because I'm sure he didn't want to go slinking back to the void. I had been there before and it sucked.

Zane was nervous, possibly even afraid of something just as monstrous.

He didn't want to fail. Again.

A lot of things were clicking into place with Zane. He was a Thrall with pride, an undead creature with scars. Having this piece of tech blocking me from sharing my emotions with him was making those scars burn, but it was something he'd have to learn to ignore.

"Look, I know I'm going to take you by surprise here, I think that's a valid point. But Zane, you gotta trust me to not get us killed."

"Hunter," he said through his teeth. "You got blown through a wall a few days ago. You're wild, unpredictable, and constantly rushing into death. You told me it was 'your whole vibe, man.' How in the Goddess's name am I supposed to trust that?"

"Believe me when I say I've been through worse," I lamented, relieved he couldn't feel the icy fingers tugging at my ribcage, the tattooed, cloaked bite marks on my neck itchy. "Getting shot through a wall isn't shit."

"You've lost your fear of death," the vampire spoke softly, like death itself might be listening. "I haven't."

The weight of those words was heavy enough for two, but really only meant for one. In my very center, in the tiny, protective part that I kept all to myself, I let myself hope he was talking about me.

It was selfish and sad, exactly the embodiment of who I was, clinging to a hope someone would be stupid enough to care about me despite it all.

"I'll make you a promise," I told him, chest achy from private feelings and my body shivering from the biting wind. "If I feel like a situation is getting out of hand, or if I get the smallest hint that one of my plans isn't working out exactly right, I'll flip the switch and turn this off."

He said nothing, his jaw tight and eyes locked on anything but me.

"And," I added with dread. "I'll be more upfront about plans. I know I'm not great at communication. It's my one flaw."

The pressure in Zane's jaw eased as he snorted a bitter laugh.

"I'm trying here," I told him, relieved when he pulled his attention away from being mad and looked at me.

Zane studied me like I was a weird little worm that had crawled out of his apple. With the blocker in place, he had no idea if I was being sincere, no idea what I was thinking or planning. It didn't seem to trouble him so much as it worried him.

"I'm your partner, hunter," he told me, the anger starting to fade. "Not a burden. Not a curse. A partner. Treat me like one."

"Business associate," I corrected. "Tolerated co-worker."

"Partner," he insisted firmly. "I'm involved in plans. I'm not in the dark. I'm trusted, as I am trusting you."

Zane presented his hand to me, and I only hesitated a moment before shaking it. He was cold, a walking corpse, but his grip was somehow comforting.

I believed that he trusted me, and I had no reason not to trust him. Zane was a lot of things: annoying, grumpy, and a pain in the ass—but he was honest. He'd never once lied to me, played me for any reason, or tried to manipulate me into anything. For an undead guy, he wasn't horrible. Hell, he bordered on being a tolerated presence in my life.

Maybe even liked.

"Alright. Deal. But I'm not calling you 'partner.'"

Zane let my hand go, his unease still resting near the frown lines in his face, but no longer on fire with anger.

"What's the plan?" he asked as we continued along, leaving the convenience store behind. "To the club?"

"We're going to go change because we've been hanging around dead bodies today. Then yeah, we'll head to Rubber Gloves, break into wherever it is that Marthas is hiding the artifacts, and take his shit. In and out, no complications."

Zane sliced his eyes over to me, blood red with skepticism.

"That's it? That's your whole plan?"

I grinned at him. "Always leave room for some fuckery, Zane. Who knows how the night is going to go."

CHAPTER
SEVEN

SHOPPING FOR CLOTHES wasn't something I did often, so it unfortunately limited my style selection.

I preferred to spend my hard earned, and sometimes stolen, cash on fun things; like protective enchantments to keep me safe from undead creatures and murder toys for murdering. Zane on the other hand, who didn't need enchantments to protect himself from dead creatures and had vampire abilities that meant he didn't need murder toys, spent his cash on cat toys and nice jeans.

Between the two of us, I looked like a cute homeless guy and he looked like a classy corpse.

We were quite the pair.

"You know what I like about you, Kevin?" I asked my fish as I went over my shirt with a lint roller for the fortieth time. "You don't shed like a certain kitten who is squatting in the apartment."

Kevin agreed with a bubble, glaring out from his coconut shell cave. Twig was on thin ice with him as it was for taking up his counter space with her existence. That cat had no idea how often I had to remind him to play nice.

Said kitten was busy watching Zane put on his socks, very enthralled with the chance to try and pounce on his foot. The hair on her tail never grew in, leaving her with a permanent rat tail that curled at the end in curiosity. When she finally committed to flinging her tiny body onto his foot in a full kitten attack, the deadly vampire parried her attack by scratching the base of her tail.

It worked every time.

Kevin and I exchanged looks, mentally agreeing that we were way cuter. I gave him some bloodworms as a treat because he was the best pet in the apartment, probably the world.

"God, are you ready?" I agonized from the counter. "Do you need to go style your pretty locks again?"

Zane slipped his shoes on and stood, his black sweater and dark jeans made him ghostly white. He tossed something my way, a folded piece of fabric I had to shake out to understand.

"Change into that," he commanded.

"What's wrong with what I'm wearing?"

"Besides the fact it has a pancake making a sex face on it?" He gestured to the sleeve. "There's a blood stain. Wear the shirt I got you, because you're an adult going to a club."

"Some people find my punny sex shirts charming," I reminded him as I made the swap.

"I'm not one of them."

"Good thing they're not for you then." I tugged the shirt over my chest and admired the fit. Unlike the secondhand shirts I lifted from the targets of my assassination jobs or out of thrift stores, the fabric still had some shape. It fit my body in a flattering way, and I had to grunt in approval.

I looked good in it. Zane gave me a smug look, and I didn't call him an asshole because of the new partnership rule. I called him a butthole instead.

Growth.

The weather had taken a sharp turn as the sun went down, the cold almost unbearable when the wind went on the attack. Zane wore his beloved jacket, which of course went great with what he was wearing. I had to toss on a less insulated coat to not mess up the hot vibe I was giving, which caused me to have chattering teeth by the time we got onto the subway. The weekend crowd was out in droves, the subway ride packed with various walks of life determined to have a good time wearing minimal clothing despite it being freezing outside.

We surged out of the subway car like a kicked-over ant pile, the squealing brakes of a passing train mingling with the chattering buzz of voices and flittering laughter of excited youths traveling toward parties. Normally on nights like this, the real fun was in Midtown or Market, with bustling shops, endless bars and great dives tucked away in cozy corners of the city.

Tonight, we were braving the upscale crowd by meandering into the Business district. Most of this area catered to the corporate nine to five, with a cornucopia of coffee shops and tiny cafes that only served lunch. Llon'nai tower was a sharp knife stabbing into the dark skyline, all the floors still alive with activity except for the top.

Sias wasn't there tonight. I couldn't help but wonder where he was.

He hadn't called since my…incident…with performance. It was bittersweet to let that mess of mangled shame cloud my chest knowing that Zane was blind to it. Checking my phone for any missed correspondence didn't help to dispel it, since there was nothing new waiting for me.

I couldn't help but feel like I really fucked something up.

"Are you going to see Sias tonight?" Zane asked. "You were looking at his tower."

"Oh." I checked to make sure the device was still hanging from my neck. "Maybe. It would be nice to have privacy."

"It would be nice not to have to meditate," he agreed. "Even at a distance, it can be hard to block you out sometimes."

"I'm not sorry that my sexual energy is so great that it defies distance."

"Pretty sure Sias's incubi charm magic is what's amplifying it, but sure." Zane fixed his hair with his fingers as some wind knocked it out of place. "I thought you'd be over at his place more after what happened at the island. I assumed saving his life would have promoted you to his top favorite."

"Who's saying I'm not?" I defended.

"Are you?"

"Fuck off, Zane."

"I'll shut up," he offered, placing his hands in his pockets. "Or, you can talk to me about it. Partners do that."

I scoffed a puff of steam into the cold, curling my shoulders up as a blast of wind punched me in the chest.

"You don't care about my relationship with Sias."

"I don't care about the sex part, but the other stuff I don't mind talking about," he corrected without a trace of sarcasm or judgment. "But I'm not going to drag it out of you if you don't want to talk about it."

I pulled at the skin of my lips with my teeth, the dry, winter air cracking them in places.

"You ever date an incubus or succubus?"

"Not long term," he admitted. "But yes."

"You never got close with them?"

"Hard to do as a vampire. She had a harem, which is very common, but I never ranked high. She had two favorites she'd known for years, and it was hard to break into."

It had been the first time I had asked about his dating history, and while I wasn't surprised he had one, it did shock me that he was part of a proper harem at one point. Sias didn't like the "harem" label. He had favorites, a small group he enjoyed, and I always prided myself as being part of that. The dynamics of sex demon partnerships were complicated, which Sias was always upfront in trying to avoid.

He didn't do complicated. That's what had attracted me to him in the first place.

Now, I was disrupting my own status quo by yearning for something beyond "fun time fuck buddy."

"I thought we'd be closer after what happened," I admitted to

Zane, the wind biting at my nose. "I'm not expecting him to prioritize me, I know better than that, but…I dunno."

"What were you hoping for?"

"Sleepovers?" I laughed, hating how pathetic I sounded to myself. "He usually sends me home after. I would like to stay with him, maybe hang out a while afterward. Fucking cuddle? I dunno. God, that sounds so desperate. Erase that from the record, I hate everything I just said."

Zane, for his part, didn't seem to notice how badly I was floundering. Saint bless the stupid device on my neck.

He asked without a hint of pity, "Have you told him that you want to stay?"

"God, no." I shrugged my shoulders up from the wind attack. "When he invited me to his group of favorites, he was very upfront that it was casual, and that he doesn't keep people at his house overnight."

"Sounds like you don't want this to be casual anymore."

"I don't want him to propose, but…yeah. Maybe a step up at least. When I pulled him out of the water, when I thought he was going to *die*, I was devastated. He has to know I care about him beyond just wanting to have sex." I blew out a breath. "Damn, I think that's the first time I said that out loud."

Zane hummed, glancing my way. "You're worried if you tell him, the relationship will change again?"

"I *know* if I tell him that I'm catching feelings that it will change things. It's not worth it."

"Sounds like it already has changed, hunter." The vampire handed me his jacket as I desperately tried to rub warmth back into my arms. "It changed back on the island, and neither of you have addressed it."

I tossed the jacket on. It smelled like leather and Zane, which was a combination of wilted flowers and ozone. It always made me think of a grave wreath on a rainy day or a very gothic novel with water damage.

I didn't hate it.

"Yeah, well…" I trailed off, not knowing how to commit to any real response. He wasn't wrong. We hadn't talked about that night. We hadn't talked about anything. A few months ago, that sort of silence surrounding personal stuff layered with random, casual sex would have been perfect. After seeing him almost die, heaving his limp body from the water—something shifted.

I wanted Sias as more than just a friend. I wanted something else. Something more.

Maybe not a "boyfriend" per se but, maybe a partner—

Except not a "partner" because Zane ruined that damn word for me. Zane is my partner now. Damnit, he ruins everything.

Opting to move on from the conversation, and thankful Zane couldn't feel my mental misstep, I decided to segue the conversation.

"I need a drink."

"So do I," the vampire mused dryly. I didn't take the bait.

This time Ushen had not been mistaken about the location. We didn't have any weird surprises when we arrived to the address they had scribbled down for us. It wasn't missing a floor, nor was it decrepit and freaky looking. Instead, it was the opposite; the most unassuming building in the complex, a small square structure boxed between some department stores that were closed for the evening. True to their advice, we spotted a large man standing near a back door around the side wearing a dark jacket with yellow "Security" across the chest.

"Lost?" he asked as we approached, giving us a once over.

"I hope not. We're looking for 'Rubber Gloves.'" I motioned between us. "We were told to look for the back door."

The guard did the eyebrow lift of "If you say so," as he pulled open the door for us. It didn't do great things to my confidence, but I trusted Ushen enough to know they wouldn't lead us astray. Not to mention the dead guy we questioned earlier in the day had reaffirmed their intel.

Still. I wasn't excited about whatever it was that made the security guard make that face.

The entryway was dark, a simple hallway with not much else of note other than the heavy doors waiting for us at the bottom of some steep stairs. The pulsing music of a hidden, underground club wasn't noticeable until we were about halfway down. Had I known what was on the other side of those fucking doors, I wouldn't have thought the very flirtatious, cartoon rendition of a rubber glove with a ball gag in its mouth was funny.

Listen.

I'm not a prude. Obviously.

Probably the biggest understatement of a lifetime. But when I tell you that walking into a gothic kink club made my jaw drop, it has to paint a picture for you. I was quasi-dating an incubus, I had romantic trysts all the damn time, and I had my fair share of situations wherein there was more bodies in a sexual encounter present than myself.

I am not lying when I say I had never seen so many liberated goth babes in my life.

The club opened into a main dance floor with poles positioned on the upper stages, with a large bar that wrapped around the left side. Around the wooden dance arena were tables and corners shrouded in just enough darkness to feed into the scandalous vibes. A massive, gaudy chandelier hung in the center, draped in black crystals and flickering, fake candlelight. Two hallways broke away from the main area like antlers, with different music and lights filtering through.

"Holy Saint, this is…wow." I plucked at my shirt. "I'm not dressed appropriately."

"You have some latex lying around somewhere, hunter?"

"You don't know my life." I snorted. "But no. I might get some though. Damn." I followed a very well-formed ass clad in leather as someone strolled by, his long, black hair hanging just above the dimples. "*Damn.*"

Zane sighed his catch phrase. "Focus."

"Worried I'll poach all the cute goth boys for myself?"

The vampire didn't appreciate my expert eyebrow wiggles.

"We need to find where Marthas is holding the artifacts, not chase after cute goth boys—which you're not going to catch."

"Fucking pardon me?" I laughed. "You don't think I can reel in hunky goth boys who are literally walking around half naked? That guy is wearing a black string and nothing else."

"No. I don't."

My pride was not going to allow Zane of all people to throw that amount of shade my direction without a fight. We were standing in a club so dark I could hardly make out the ghostly white girls spinning around on poles with platform boots on, I was tolerating no additional shade from him.

"You wanna make this interesting?"

"No. I want to find what we're looking for so we can leave." Zane narrowed his eyes at me like me standing next to him was giving him a headache.

"I bet I can land more goth boys than you."

For the second time that night I was surprised. The strangest thing happening in that club at that moment wasn't the man getting lifted off the ground by hooks in the meaty part of his back, or the girl wearing a bodysuit of a nun with a zipper for a mouth.

It was Zane tossing his head back laughing.

This undead prick was *laughing*. The strobe of red lights that kicked on when the music shifted filtered through his fangs, his hair painted with streaks of black, red, and raven feather blue.

"Yeah, is it funny?" I snapped, realizing I was watching his grin a little too long. It pissed me off. "When I win, you gotta give me a piggy-back ride all the way back to the bus station."

"Oh, hunter," the vampire crooned in a pitying, amused voice. "You're not going to win this."

"Bet." I stuck my hand out. "And stretch your back."

Zane grabbed my hand with his icy, dead fingers, and pulled me in close to glare his crimson gaze into me.

"You're going to have to clean Twig's litter box."

"Deal," I hissed back at him. "Good luck grabbing onto people when you're that icy, corpse."

"We're in a gothic club, dumbass." He dropped my hand. "Being a corpse is why I'm going to enjoy watching you scoop up cat shit."

I might have misjudged the situation a bit, but I sure as hell wasn't going to let him think he had the upper hand. Was he tall, pale and handsome? Sure. If you're into dead guys growing out their hair, wearing nice clothing and smelling like grave flowers.

Shit.

Yeah, I fucked up.

Zane dropped my hand and turned away, melting into the throngs of bodies filtering in and out of the dance floor. I touched the device around my neck as I made my escape to the bar, refusing to acknowledge that he moved like liquid shadow when he was on the prowl. If I was going to win my bet against the vampire in a goth club—damn it, I was really fucked—I was going to need some alcohol and a big-ass heap of charm.

I parked myself at the edge of the wraparound dark wooden bar smothered in band stickers and faded water rings, and did a sweep of the offerings. The beat of the gothic music was quick and industrial, the synthesized drum beat grinding against bass. Beautiful bodies slid around each other in various stages of undress, hips swaying with the beat and hands reaching up to the ceiling to catch the lights on their fingertips.

The few times I was able to make any type of eye contact with someone was quickly shut down; a quick, bored glance skipped over my body before ignoring me completely. A particularly adorable man wearing low-cut black jeans with a scorpion tattoo on his back landed next to me for a heartbeat, and I got to admire the lovely scars resting just under his pecs.

I tried to yell a greeting, offer to buy him a drink or two, but he swept past me to reach the sweet thing wearing a leather pencil skirt and spiderweb bra.

"I think I hate this place," I mumbled to myself.

The bartender, a woman with black-out, tattooed eyes drifted from one end of the bar to the other, too busy twirling glasses to notice me trying to wave her down. By the third attempt, I leaned against the bar with my elbows and contemplated trying to steal something.

A shoulder brushed against mine, pulling me from my temporary misery. A woman with short, curled bangs streaked in green and black leaned her torso onto the bar and lifted one heavy boot into the air for balance. Fake, iridescent fairy wings were strapped to her back, flowing down like a pair of wispy capes. They matched the plastic pair hanging from her ears, and while I wasn't a patron of goth clubs, I knew a dealer of party drugs when I saw them.

This girl was the saint of Wings, Dust, Vibe and a hell of a lot more.

How she was able to move with the tight corset cinching her waist was impressive, but she caught the bartender's attention with a wink and a wave.

"Hey, gorgeous," the bartender purred, already sliding her a drink.

"Hey, Bonnie. Thank you, baby." The corset woman put her hand on my shoulder. "Can you get my friend here a drink?"

I blinked in surprise, but didn't leave the opportunity on the table.

"Whiskey sour," I told the bartender, before turning my attention to my gothic knight. "Thanks."

"I saw you struggling," she teased with a smirk. "First time here?"

"Yeah. This place is…something else." I was mildly hypnotized as another very cute boy wearing a skirt and thigh-high boots walked past.

"Sure is." She passed over my drink as it was set down. "Cheers."

"Cheers." I knocked my drink against hers. "Thanks for the assist."

"We gotta stick together." She took a mouthful of her drink, the sip making the thick collar around her throat move.

"Sure," I agreed, sipping my wonderful glass of liquid comfort. The music shifted down into a slower melody, the lights dropping into a twirling spiral across the floor. The rhythm of the dancers changed, people moving closer together as the sensual vocals gave them more of an excuse to touch. In the slow wave of bodies melting together, the sharp, cascading light slicing across the floor swept over Zane.

He was at the edge where the dance floor ended and the dark corners began, his head ducked down near someone's ear with one hand resting on the small of their back.

The guy in his grasp tilted his head back, eyes shut, leaning back as Zane slid his other hand behind their head.

I gulped down my drink in envy.

"Your Dom is cute."

My new goth girlfriend chewed on her straw while I choked on my drink, suffocating on the audacity.

"What??" I managed through my coughing.

"It's sweet he lets his sub off the leash. My Dom is a lot stricter. I can't fool around without her here." She lifted a shoulder.

"Gods." I wiped at my chin. "Not a sub. He's not my Dom."

"Boyfriend then."

"Partner," I corrected, then choked again. *"Business partner."*

She slow blinked at me. "Kay."

"What gave you that wildly incorrect notion? Do I seem like a sub to you?"

"Well, a bratty one, yeah." She shifted the straw in her mouth. "You have the vibe. And he has big Dom energy. But," she relented before I could counter with how wrong she was. "My mistake."

"Yeah, you don't sound as horrified as you should. My Dom. Saint help me." I exhaled and polished off my drink. "I know how you can make it up to me, though."

The fairy goth princess tilted her head expectantly.

"Tell me more about fairies," I told her with a wink. "I'm a big fan."

"I can tell you all about them, and their friends." She hooked her arm with mine. "Let's go to my office."

We abandoned the crowded bar, slipping through the wiggling mass of people filtering in and out of the dance floor. Zane had disappeared, his prey also vacant, which meant they were no doubt lost in the shadows somewhere probably making vampire babies. The night was still young, and I had plenty of time to reel in more bodies than him.

Still stung that he had a head start though. It had been a while since I had failed so miserably at picking up guys. My newly acquired freedom from Zane's emotional nosiness was somehow throwing me off. I had gotten so used to keeping my guard up and my emotions in check that I had forgotten what it was like to just be my normal, unhinged, awesome self. A few hours ago, he would have been able to feel my eagerness to get some fun party drugs in my system, or my annoyance that he was doing better than me in the hookup arena. Now, he couldn't feel anything.

I was alone with my feelings again.

It was kinda fucking with me.

My new best friend—

"Hey, what's your name?"

"Salem."

Salem led me through one of the branching hallways, the end of which ended in a lounge area with couches and tables, some occupied with bodies that were either tangled together or sipping cocktails. Her "office" was on an elevated platform near the back left, two plush, high-back chairs angled toward one another which were currently empty. I had a feeling her "office" moved depending on where there was space, but the back area of the club was dark, quiet, and out of view.

A perfect place for either making out, or doing a little bit of Dust.

Salem sat at the edge of one of the chairs and unlatched her corset, revealing a small pouch sewed into the lining. It was genius, and I also got to see the cool spider tattoo that curled around her ribs. The pouch was unzipped, and she tugged a few little baggies loose of items I was very familiar with. Each one was wrapped in the packaging one would know if they were a deviant of narcotics, and I was thrilled to spot something I hadn't seen before.

A small envelope no bigger than a postage stamp had a glittery rabbit sticker on it.

"What's that?"

"Rabbit Hole." She handed it over for me to inspect. "It's a melt-away. Put it under your tongue and it kicks in after a little while."

"This like a hallucinogen? I'm not into the mind-fuck stuff."

"Not at all. It's more…" She thought for a second before landing on, "Manic euphoria. You feel everything at eleven. Great for dancing and sex."

"Manic euphoria," I echoed. "Now that sounds fun. You just take one?"

"Well, normally yeah. But if you're familiar with Vibe and take it often, you can manage two. Space them out though, because otherwise it's intense." She took my money as I paid her and tucked the bills under one of her breasts. "Remember it takes a bit to kick in. Give it time."

"Got it." I unwrapped one of the little stamps and glanced at her. "You're a regular here, yeah?"

"Most nights." She latched her corset up after getting everything back in place. "Why?"

Under the plastic wrapping was a thin, opaque slice of pink. I peeled it off carefully and placed it under my tongue, adjusting so it fit flush against it.

"I'm guessing Marthas is cool with you dealing at his place? I know he has a steep fee."

"Criminal fee more like. And yeah, I know the irony of that, but Gods, he really cleans us out." She cut me a look I was very familiar with, her posture growing rigid. "You're not going to narc on me, right? For talking shit?"

"I hate that bastard," I said with a laugh. "Relax. I'm actually wondering if you can help me out with something."

"Depends on what you're about to ask me." Salem fixed one of her fairy wing earrings and narrowed her perfectly painted eyes. "I don't want to risk losing my spot here. I love this place."

"You're not. I'm a ghost, and I don't make it habit of tossing good people under the bus, especially if they get me free drinks." I leaned on the arm of the chair, closing the distance between us. "You know where Marthas typically hangs out? Or maybe stashes stuff here?"

"You're going to rob Marthas of the Broken Horns? Have you already taken drugs tonight?"

"Not rob," I corrected. "Take something back. He sort of stole a bunch of stuff from me so I'm just…reclaiming it."

It was Salem's turn to lean in, or lean as much as her corset would allow.

"What did he take?"

"Expensive museum-quality crap I stole from a rich dead guy that I did not kill." I was quick to add that last part on just in case. "Found him dead fair and square and stole his stuff. I just want it back, and if anyone asks, I seduced some cute goth boy who told me everything in the throes of passion."

Salem, who was a magical fairy goth goddess of sass said, "To make this convincing, you're going to have to actually seduce someone."

"Wooow, you bitch. I think we're best friends."

She tried to keep her stoney face, but I saw the cracks.

I pressed, "C'mon, Salem. Marthas can't keep taking big slices. He needs to get humbled."

Salem exhaled and scanned the room quietly with her eyes before pointing them back at me.

"There's a back office around the corner past the bathrooms. It's behind the curtain backdrop they use to hide the stone walls.

I've seen Marthas's people go in there sometimes. That's all I know."

"That's all I need." I gave her some extra money for the tip and for her silence. "For the drink and the company."

"You want my advice, Mr. Not Sub?" She tucked the money away and stood. "Goths are like cats. Some of us love attention and cuddles, but most need to come to you."

"I'm more of a fish guy."

"You're weird," Salem sighed. "Don't get killed."

I gave her a salute as she sauntered off, making her way back to the bar for more free drinks and customers.

THE DOOR WAS HIDDEN behind the curtain just like Salem had said.

I guessed whoever they hired to turn this place into a gothic haven thought that exposed bricks weren't black and edgy enough, so their solution was to hang thick slabs of velvet across the walls. Tugging on the curtains and fishing out the opening did break the immersion of the kinky crypt, and the plain, brown wooden door with a faded "employees only" sticker across it was a mood killer. They could have at least sprung to paint the damn door or get a bat-shaped sticker or something. A little effort goes a long way, guys.

While the ugly door wasn't worthwhile enough to paint, they did spring for a keypad lock to keep nosy people from trying to get inside. The thumping, electric bass of the music warped into a dramatic flair, killing any chance I had to try and listen for any life inside the locked room. There was no telling if Marthas had someone inside guarding his treasures or not, but knowing him, he'd be paranoid enough to keep someone close by.

I was going to need to move fast, in and out, and neutralize anyone who was in my way. How the hell I was going to casually meander out of the club carrying the stolen goods was the part of the plan I hadn't figured out yet, but I was decently sure I could muster something when the time came. The first piece of the puzzle was figuring out the combination of the lock in front of me, or hoping like hell the very expensive lock picking tools I had bought would be able to crack it open for me.

Out of base, lizard-brain instinct I gave the handle a jiggle to see if maybe luck was on my side.

Turns out, it was.

But not the good kind.

The doorknob caved immediately, the keypad never beeping or acknowledging my existence. It was unlocked. No alarm set.

Not good. Red flags. Tons of red flags.

Marthas was a paranoid bastard with the same amount of business sense as he did a mean streak, so having his back office casually unlocked was a huge fucking deal. My heart started demanding to leave through my ribcage as I eased my gun from the hidden holster, inching the door open just enough to peek inside. The room was lit by a standing lamp near the entrance, a dated, pattern carpet stretching out in awful zigzags. I ducked low and eased the door open more, keeping my body to the side of the door in case someone tried to shoot at the uninvited guest.

I waited a few beats, hopeful I wasn't going to be shot dead as I budged the door open enough to peek fully inside. A short hallway ended at another door labeled "office," neighboring a private bathroom that was dark inside. I eased in, closing the door behind me and locking it.

A lazy camera flirted above the office door with a lazy red wink, alerting me that my movements were being watched. Shadows moved under the bottom of the office door, and I kept close to the ground as I darted over to confirm the bathroom was unoccupied. There was a chance that whoever was inside knew I was there from the camera, and I was praying to whatever god wanted me that it wasn't Marthas.

That guy was huge, and like previously stated, mean as hell.

I had the fabulous displeasure of seeing what he did to guys who got on his bad side, and it usually ended with pliers, hot pokers going in no-no areas and teeth being *extracted* in less than friendly ways. Dude was cruel, and very thorough.

Plus, you know.

The whole…banging his boyfriend behind his back in his own club…thing.

Total misunderstanding, but there was no talking Marthas of the Broken Horns down when he was that level of murder.

This could be a trap. This could be a huge setup that I was merrily barging into.

But I had made it this far, and I sure as hell wasn't going to flee now. Those artifacts were mine and I had stolen them fair and square. If anyone was going to get rich off them, it would be yours truly.

I crept, low and steady, inching to the office door to try and listen in. The bass of the club rumbled the soles of my shoes, but was far enough away to allow me to get a baseline on the activity inside. Footsteps moved around the office slowly, either unbothered or unaware of my presence. One of those scenarios was great. The other, not so much. They sounded heavy, someone formidable, and I exhaled the nerves tightening around my lungs.

This was going to suck.

My fingers touched the device around my neck, checking the button was still set to "off." Zane didn't know yet, and I was alright with that. I could handle myself, but knowing I had a Thrall in my back pocket did help bolster my resolve. If shit went sideways, I could flip the switch and have him come running.

Hopefully he wasn't too deep into his activities. Though it would be kinda hilarious to make him do a mad dash to find me with his pants around his ankles. That would serve him right for being a cute goth boy magnet. Stupid walking corpse and his pretty vampire hair.

It was time to commit, to rush headfirst into something dangerous and terrifying and hope like hell I'd come out the other side. I lived for these encounters, these life-or-death moments that reminded me that

I was, in fact, still very much alive. My heart thundered, my temples pounded, and my drive to keep clinging to this strange, terrible existence punctuated with bursts of euphoria drove me to swing the office door open and aim my gun in the face of whoever was inside.

A large back was to me, hunched over a desk he was in the middle of rifling through, and I breathed out in relief that it wasn't Marthas.

"Hands up, handsome," I said to the stranger. "You move too fast and I'll drop you."

The guy froze, the muscles in his shoulders bunched under the shirt that stretched across them. The lack of horns narrowed him down to either human or jinn, and I had a cold realization wash over me that I didn't have my magical charm in my pocket. If this guy was jinn and wanted to wield some influence magic at me, I was going to be in for a ride.

"Hands," I reminded him. "I'm known for my aim, not my patience."

Reluctance rippled over him as he lifted his hands, his spine slowly uncurling from his perch. He wore a plain black shirt and jeans, but I could see the outline of his gun at his ankle and knife in his back pocket. His hair was cropped short, a deep, rusty brown color that most people had to dye to achieve. His skin was a light brown, almost golden, and I appreciated how nice it looked in the soft lighting.

If I wasn't pointing a gun at him or in the market to steal from his possible employer, I might have asked for his number.

"I mean this in the most non-sexual way: get on your knees. You move too fast and I'm going to—"

"Risk firing a gun in a crowded club? I know you're not that stupid."

His voice curdled in my stomach.

Sour, rotten, terrible nostalgia diseased my heart, stealing my breath away so completely I had to gasp to restart my lungs.

He turned, hands still raised, glaring at me with a decade of hate and betrayal; the same look I had tried to desperately drown through years of chemical ecstasy.

Nothing had changed. He was bigger now—we both were—but he looked exactly how he did the night I turned my back on the family.

Austin still hated my fucking guts.

And it still broke my heart.

"Austin." I adjusted my grip around my weapon. "You're looking tall."

"You're not." He gave me a slow once-over. "I told you those gross, cheese puff things you ate as a kid would stunt your growth."

"Hey. I'm a solid five-ten. That's average for a human," I defended a little too enthusiastically. "Plus, I like dudes being taller than me. It makes me feel cute."

"Makes you look punt-able."

"If memory serves me right, I won most of our grappling matches in practice." I glanced quickly behind him to make sure there wasn't anyone hiding behind the desk. "I'm nimble, like a cheetah."

"I was really hoping these years would have made you less chatty, Wilde," Austin sighed. "You gonna shoot me or just talk me to death?"

"I can do both things." I drew the hammer back on my weapon. "Let's start with the basics. What the hell are you doing here?"

"Testing out my new bondage gear," he said with the arid sarcasm from my childhood. "What the fuck you think I'm doing here?"

"You're here for Marthas?" I narrowed my eyes when he didn't respond. "He isn't involved in vampire shit, and sure as hell doesn't mess with necromancers. He's a thug, a gun seller, and drug runner. Nothing that the Saint's Army would care about."

Austin bristled with annoyance, his frown set so deep in his features that it aged him by ten years.

"Then your boss has done a phenomenal job keeping secrets from you, Wilde."

"*Boss?*" I barked a laugh that was more in line with a clown horn honk. "Marthas hates me."

"Smart man," he said with a tone so arctic it made me shiver. "I have strict orders that if you get in my way, I should deal with you however I see fit."

"Are we still talking about your new bondage gear?" I tried to shake him, but he deflected it with the ease of a fellow smart-ass.

"Sure. I'll let you try out the clamp that goes on your balls. The safe word is 'backstabbing asshole who I loved like a brother.'"

"Kinda wordy."

"I'm done fucking around, Wilde," he hissed, anger starting to break through. "I don't have time for your bullshit and I'm not here to reconnect with you."

I adjusted my fingers to keep them from shaking, the tips had gone wet and cold.

"You're here looking for the artifacts, aren't you?" When he didn't respond, I knew I was right. "What do you want with them? Why does Magnus want them?"

"Your fingers are shaking, Wilde."

"Can we stop with this alpha bullshit, Austin?"

The hate fueling him curled his lip into a vicious snarl. It took a cheap shot at my heart.

"No, we're not doing that," he snapped. "We're not on a chummy, first name basis, Wilde. We're not family anymore."

"I get it, you hate me. Join the club. Everyone hates me." I steeled my grip and took a step to the right, glancing at the upturned office behind his large frame. "From the looks of this place, you came up short. And I'm also guessing you were the human that took out the imp at the warehouse."

"If you tell me where Marthas has them, I'll give you a quick death," Austin promised, failing to reel in the malice in the offer. "Far better than you deserve."

"I'm not about to hand over any information to you without knowing why the Saint's Army wants some old relics stolen from a dead jinn's place. If you guys want them, that means they're not just expensive shit to sell. They're important. Why?"

"Last chance, Wilde." Austin rolled his head from side to side, three quick pops ran along his spine. "Keep being defiant, and I'll happily remind you who actually won those grapples."

I exhaled the nerves I felt inching up my chest, my stomach alive with terror worms wiggling around in harmony with my thundering heartbeat. I rolled the dice, hoping that there was some small part of him that was still the boy I knew before I fucked everything up.

I really wanted Austin to not hate me so much that he couldn't remember a time when we were brothers. I had to believe that was true.

My gun's clip slid free, the bullet in the chamber ejected, and I disarmed my weapon before tossing it aside. I mirrored how he held his palms; I showed him surrender.

"Cards on the table," I told him, my former best friend. "I wasn't lying when I said I don't work with Marthas. I'm the one who stole those artifacts in the first place. I know they're supposed to be relics of the Gods. If they're really…godly or whatever…I can help you."

Austin's jaw ticked, his hands dropping to his sides. He didn't give an inch in his hatred, his eyes burned like hazel coals.

In that moment of withering under his stare, feeling small and horrible, I could smell the wood fire smoke of my deception, follow the embers dancing in the night sky. Witnessing the hurt in my brother's eyes, I could see the plumes of smoke rising from the structure that had been my phoenix nest.

They had trusted me.

Loved me.

And I had burned it all away.

If I had any strength in me, any humanity left, I would have told him how sorry I was, how much he had meant to me, how badly I missed everyone.

"Please," I managed. "Let me help."

It was too much to ask. The bridge was so burned it was in cinders, my plea throwing the ashes in his face.

Austin moved with all the rage and hurt from that night, fermented over a decade of silence and resentment.

It wasn't until his fists were curled into my shirt did I have the unfortunate realization that the drugs had kicked in.

Salem hadn't been lying when she said you would feel everything at an eleven, because I felt every inch of the desk he threw me over. My shoulder screamed when I landed on it, paper and pens clamoring beside me in a storm of office supplies. While my brain chemicals were dumping endorphins in the wrong direction, I had the passing thought that the carpet felt plush under my palms as I tried to push myself up. It was a silver lining in the absolute ass kicking I was about to receive.

Austin rounded the desk as a totally sober, pissed-off, highly trained fighter with all the right in the world to take his frustrations out on me. But I couldn't let him kill me. Not yet. I had so much shit to do, and I couldn't trust Zane to keep Twig away from Kevin. I was not going to be responsible for a kitten's death, even if her would-be murderer was a very cute betta fish.

I was hauled to my feet by the back of my shirt and spun around to face him, his fist cocked back to knock my jaw off.

Here's the thing about Austin: he's what I would refer to as a "bruiser." He hits like a freight train and doesn't expect anyone to get back up afterward—and rightly so, because they usually don't. Getting socked in the face by this guy would be lights out, even if you're experienced in getting smacked by large guys who are often very angry at you.

If I were to throw a punch, it would tickle him.

So, I had to go with something a little spicier.

The coffee mug I scooped off the desk shattered into dust

when I cracked it across his skull, giving me just enough wiggle room to roll away with my jaw still attached. It was painfully obvious that he had kept up with his training more than I had, because he tackled me before I got halfway across the room. Normally, feeling a guy his size on top of me was fantastic, but it was less fun when he started beating on my kidneys.

His fists were like bricks, solid and unforgiving. The blast of pain from his assaults made me scream. My body was on fire with chemically-induced nerve ending overload, bypassing the lovely safety measures of going numb when the pain got a little too intense. His weight crushed me, the carpet smelled like old beer and cigarettes, and I was fairly certain in that moment that my left kidney was about to divorce me.

My world spun in a halo of desk lamps and pain as Austin forced me onto my back, his knee pinning my right elbow to the gross—but still *so soft*—carpet. My instincts were on overdrive, my left hand reaching to try and take out his eyes or at minimum knock some hesitation into him.

He was cruel to go for my throat, he knew what it would do to me, and he was right. The moment I felt his grip tighten, I panicked. I went from tactical training to raw terror, my free hand slapping and grabbing at his arm.

Austin hated me so much. So much. The anger in his eyes made me weak, left me stupid and fragile. He loomed over me, his face red from strain and bitter hatred.

It gutted me to see tears in his eyes.

It was too much. It was too damn much.

I tried to navigate around my fear, around the terrible panic that drove my movements. I tried so, so hard to tell him how sorry I was.

Austin's knife flashed its blade with a flick of his wrist, the concealing handle folding away with the mechanical dance. The tip stung as it bit through my shirt and into the meat of my chest, only a few inches more and I would be back in the void, only this time I could finally commit to settling down there. It was my one-way ticket, the end of my shitty saga of heartbreak, loneliness, loss, and hurt—with side stories of betta fish and epic sex.

The Tale of Dallas Wilde: He Was a Real Piece of Shit. Foreword by Kevin.

Austin's throat bobbed, his hand shook as he strangled me. I watched a tear slide down his nose, and I prayed like hell he'd kill me before I saw him cry.

Death didn't come for me like I had imagined. Instead, he materialized as a large, pale, snarling man with red eyes and hair he was trying to grow out.

Austin's face lifted in shock as Zane pulled him off me with such power and ferocity that he didn't have time to react. My vision swam as blood rushed back to my brain, my lungs kicking into full speed as I vacuumed air into them. Zane had tucked his arms under Austin's, pushing them up so he couldn't do anything other than flail them in defiance.

A flash of fear ripped across Austin's features as Zane gripped his hair and shoved his head to the side, neck exposed to the fangs of a raging Thrall.

Zane bared his teeth, opened his mouth, and his eyes blazed like the fires of hell.

"No!" My words ripped from my throat like sandpaper, my throat as raw as my chest.

Zane hesitated, the flames in his eyes dying. Austin didn't waste the opportunity. It was a simple yet effective move, the full body weight of the stomp on Zane's foot made him yell in pain, his grip failing enough to give Austin his opening to escape. The trained Saint's Army soldier spun and sank his knife deep in Zane's chest, the force knocking him back into the disheveled desk.

For a heartbeat I was sure he was going to rip the damn thing out and do the same to me, murder me while I lay winded and gasping on the floor. I didn't have it in me to fight.

I didn't know what to do when he ran.

I watched Austin bolt out of the office in a flash, the chaos dying without so much as a "fuck you" on the way out.

I didn't know how long I stared at the office door that hung open, the distant club music thumping away in blissful obliviousness of the madness just beyond the walls.

"This is why I said that fucking device was a bad idea," Zane was raging, pulling the knife from his chest with a pained hiss. His blood was black and thick, corpse blood instead of vibrant crimson.

It hit me like an acid wave of horror that the blade in his hand could have very easily been blessed, that it could have disintegrated him into nothing. It made me sick. It made me feel cold and nauseous.

"Are you okay?" I heard myself ask. I didn't feel present, more like a passenger in a sinking car.

"I just got a knife in the chest so, no, I'm not *okay*." The blade hit the ground with a tumbling rattle, and I felt my heart go with it. "Who the hell was that?"

It was a valid question. He had every right to ask who it was that had almost killed me, who'd pushed a few inches of metal into his chest. I would have asked the same thing, probably more forcefully and just as annoyed.

But that question was the final push for me, and I did something I had never done in front of another person before.

Especially not a vampire Thrall.

I started crying.

My world melted into liquid, my chest seized with strangling sobs. The pressure of repressed, unpracticed crying made my head start to pound, my body not used to the ejection of emotions quite like this. In a feeble attempt to hide the evidence of my misery, I covered my face with my palms and bit my lip hard enough to sting, failing hilariously to stifle the process.

Zane didn't have a follow up question, which meant the room was now silent except for my rough, raw gasps of pure despair. Eventually even my pathetic attempts to keep my noise to a minimum slipped, and I let out a few real, gut-wrenching sobs that were too strong to be contained.

I didn't know how long I lay on Marthas's office floor crying my damn eyes out. It felt like an eternity, and my body felt like I had been wrung out and thrown into a ditch by the time I got my hiccupping tears under control. My palms were slick with tears as I scrubbed my face, my lip sore from where I had bit it, and my chest stuttered like an engine that wouldn't turn over.

Zane had sat beside me at some point, his hip almost touching mine, keeping watch in case someone walked through the door. I appreciated his silence as I heaved myself upright, my brain sloshing behind swollen eyes. Had a devil appeared in that moment and offered me an ice pack in exchange for my soul, I would have taken the deal. I did my best to will the aches into submission, to try and dull the overwhelming pulse of emotions that thumped through my bloodstream, but it was like fighting gravity.

I lied to myself that the breakdown had been because of the drugs. Sure, maybe it had pushed me into being a touch sensitive about confronting my past, but there was no denying that this emotional breakdown had been a long time coming. At some point, even through years of thorough denial and mentally burying everything, your mistakes and trauma come out somehow.

Mine was in my trail of bad relationships and a breakdown in a gang leaders office in front of a vampire.

No big deal.

I inhaled some mucus back into my nose and forced my eyes open. The carpet didn't feel soft under my hands anymore.

"This day sucks," I announced.

Zane grunted in agreement, only daring to glance my way after I took a full, albeit shaky, breath.

"I know you're going to think I'm teasing you, or trying to be a jerk, but I'm not. I mean this authentically, and without any judgment. Alright?"

I nodded that I understood, keeping my words limited so I didn't fall back into the cycle of sobs again.

Zane asked simply, with no hint of malice or his regular arid, vampire attitude, "Do you want a hug?"

The very loud and confident facets of my personality voted to retaliate in various versions of "fuck off" or to punch him for even offering. How dare this undead asshole pitch something like that to me, a professional vampire hunter, a killer of the damned, slayer of necromancers and overall badass. I didn't need pity, especially not from him.

I wasn't feeling very loud and confident in that moment. In that moment, the professional vampire hunter, killer of the damned, slayer of necromancers and overall badass needed a hug.

I nodded, or more, I jerked my chin down in a weak agreement to the offer.

For a dead guy who was the constant source of migraines, Zane didn't half-ass his hugs. He pulled me close like I was someone who mattered to him, both arms around me so that one hand squeezed my shoulder. While he was cold to the touch, the embrace was warm with sincerity. Zane tucked his head against mine, making a point to angle himself so that his mouth was nowhere near my neck.

That simple gesture meant the world to me.

Since we were already crossing some boundaries, I decided to just lean into the damn moment and accept the hug for all it was worth. I couldn't remember the last time I just hugged someone like this, a true, base connection of comfort and safety. Zane was solid when I wrapped my arms around his torso and pressed my forehead into his shoulder, holding on in hopes the ache in my chest would subside.

It was too much to face in one day. Seeing Austin had been a decade of festering guilt and shame body slamming into me all at once. I was beyond relieved to feel the emotional blocker still hanging from my neck, smooshed between myself and the vampire Thrall I guess I didn't hate completely anymore.

I kinda liked that he smelled like old flowers. This close, I could make out the more subtle notes of rose and deep, cold earth; the kind of wet soil after a rainstorm. His hair was softer than I had imagined it, the tips tickled my skin.

Zane adjusted his arms around me as I clung to him, his hand drifting up to rest at the base of my skull. His fingers were icy as they slipped through my hair, encouraging me to rest my head and relax. A shiver of guilt stabbed at me knowing that it was my fault he was so corpsy lately, because I didn't like him drinking my blood. Yet even with him starving and dealing with me crying on the floor, he still cared enough to—

Cared enough.

Now that is a bitch of a thing to wrap your mind around after an emotional backhand.

Did Zane, the big, mean, beastly vampire Thrall, actually give a tiny bit of a shit about me?

Is that what was happening?

"This day is weird," I said into his shoulder, wiping my face on his shirt.

"Yeah. Hey—" He eased his hand off my head and snarled down at me. "Are you wiping snot on me?"

"Be nice to me. I'm having a bad day."

"Get off me." Zane dropped his arms from around me and examined his shirt, more bothered by my face leakage than the stab wound in his chest. "You're a damn animal, do you know that?"

"I've been told." I wiped the rest of my tears on my wrists before accepting his outstretched hand. Zane hauled himself up then pulled me to my feet, knocking some debris off his jacket that I was still wearing. I thought for a moment he was checking me for injuries, but he was actually making sure his jacket wasn't ripped.

That was fair. I did get tossed over a desk and thrown around a bit. I decided him fussing over the borrowed jacket didn't trump him offering a non-judgmental hug, so I didn't comment on it being a dick move.

The club wasn't nearly as interesting or exciting after getting my ass kicked, both in a literal sense as well as emotionally. We weaved through the masses after we made a discreet slip out of the upended office, dodging the happy, drunk people enjoying their night. The cool night air was bliss on the hot skin under my eyes, the crisp sting of the temperature drop lovely on my aching skull. I watched my breath bellow out in a steam of cautious relief, staving off the needling revelation that we had failed in snagging the artifacts, that the Saint's Army was in the city, and that I still didn't have an invite to the fucking gala Marthas was going to be at.

There was something warm threading its way through my chest, and I wasn't sure where to place it within the mix. I still needed to untangle it from the complicated weave of hatred that made up the foundation of my existence, but I didn't have the energy to yet.

"I guess it's safe to assume you didn't get them," Zane said after Rubber Gloves was far behind us.

"No." I rubbed the grit from my eyes. "Marthas had already moved the artifacts. We'll need to get into that gala if we want any chance in obtaining them."

"Not the artifacts." Zane cut me a look. "The goth boys."

I blinked at the cheeky fucker, confused for half a heartbeat before I remembered our bet.

"Fuck you, Zane."

"You were *so confident*, hunter," he teased with an annoying air of superiority. "Did you manage at least one?"

"While you were off getting black lipstick on your dick, I was focusing on the mission," I spat back.

"Right." Zane nodded. "How'd that go?"

"I don't like you," I decided. "I don't like you and I did wipe snot on you. Deal with it."

Despite my declaration that I hated him, his laughing made me grin.

I guess he wasn't all that bad.

CHAPTER
NINE

FOR SUCH A TINY THING, Twig could scream like a banshee when she wanted food.

We were immediately accosted by the feral fuzzball the moment we walked into the apartment, the wailings of a *starving* creature that hadn't had wet, fishy goop in a few hours. Kevin, of course, was a perfect angel who wanted nothing but to judge, and did so by blowing a snarky bubble when I called him handsome.

With the adrenaline fading from my system, I could feel the lingering bruises from the previous fight. My chest didn't just ache metaphorically from the emotional beating I took, it still actively bled from the stab wound Austin had inflicted before Zane's intervention. Unlike the previously stated psychological damage, this one wasn't deep, but it did hurt.

Peeling the fabric of my shirt off the wet wound stung. "I kinda liked this shirt."

"You had one adult shirt without a stupid saying on it, and it got ruined in less than two hours," Zane announced as he carried his hellspawn around in his palm. "That has to be a record for you."

"Probably." I jabbed at my wound to test how badly I was

stabbed, annoyed as a new, tiny stream trailed down my chest. "Hell. I think I need to stitch this up."

The screaming banshee was momentarily silenced by the vampire's offering of tuna-flavored nasty flakes, her little naked tail shaking from excitement. Zane left the creature to feast while he grabbed my first aid kit, setting it beside me on the couch. I noticed that he didn't look in my direction while I had blood on my chest, his jaw bunching from the proximity.

While my chest was dripping, his was horribly static. The black, old blood from his much deeper stab wound was dry on his sweater, barely a halo around the tear. Blue veins had started to show on the backs of his hands, icy rivers under a sheet of pale ice.

He looked like he could sleep for days if given the chance, and since Thrall vampires didn't sleep, I imagined it was torture to be that exhausted without any relief. Zane sat in his favorite chair, a well-worn, threadbare recliner that had come with the apartment, and stretched his long legs out in the universal slump of a man who was bone-tired.

Maybe it was the events of the night that had made me sentimental, or maybe it was the drugs, or the open wound in my chest that made me feel guilty for him being so worn down. I knew he was hungry. I knew he was struggling. I had pushed it out of my mind to keep myself comfortable, to shield myself from getting lost in the past.

The final nail in the coffin was watching him close his eyes as if to take a nap. I knew I had to stop being such an asshole to the guy.

"How often did Sandros give you blood?"

Zane opened his eyes like a groggy toddler, face scrunched in sleepy confusion.

"What?"

"You needed to feed off him, right? Isn't that...how it works?" I tried to sound casual, but I was floundering like an awkward teenager asking the hot girl for a dance at prom.

Zane rubbed at his exhaustion-bruised eyes with his finger and thumb.

"It was different with him. He and I didn't have the...same reaction...as we do."

"What was it like? I mean—" The floundering sequel was so much worse. "If, um...if it's okay to ask. Is it weird that I asked?"

"You sure as hell are making it weird."

"I don't know how to ask about the emotional mechanics of blood drinking and it not be weird! This is all weird!" I wiped some blood off my chest with my ruined shirt. "If you don't want to answer, never mind."

Zane sighed, sinking down into the chair more to rest his head against the plush cushion.

"It didn't feel intense. There was a connection, like a string being pulled, or like feeling the vibration of a guitar string being plucked." He watched the ceiling as he recounted it, lost in a memory I couldn't see. "It was nice. Warm."

"What about Esdras?" I asked, wincing when he scowled.

"Very cold. Transactional. His blood tasted bitter, but it was all I had. It was like learning to love drinking pickle juice out of a cold jar."

"Saints, that's gross." I shivered. "How do you know what pickle juice tastes like?"

"I try food sometimes." Zane shrugged, the gesture barely there. "I can't swallow it, but I want to see what the fuss is about. Pickles are fucking disgusting."

"To a vampire, yeah." I fished for some gauze absently. "How often did you get blood from them usually?"

Zane exhaled slowly, like the question was something he had been dreading.

"Every day."

If I had been floundering before, I was in a full-on frazzle at Zane's admission.

"*Every day*? Are you serious?"

"Like I said," he repeated slowly. "It was different with them."

"Saints, Zane. It's been…over a month, at least. Why didn't you say something?"

"I'm fine, hunter," he growled. "You sound like Twig before dinner."

"Hey, I am way more charming than that little gremlin," I retaliated.

"Disagree."

"How long can you go without blood?" I asked, but he ignored me, just shutting his eyes again and lacing his hands on his stomach. "Zane, I'm being serious."

"Not having blood doesn't kill me, it just limits my abilities," he answered after a few breaths. "I can't move as fast, my mist powers are harder to control. The sunlight burns a bit."

"You also look dead. Well. Deader."

"Still got more goth boys than you," he mused back.

My stomach was in slippery knots as I gathered my nerves, my heart reminding me how loud it could be when I was about to do something dangerous, exciting or stupid. My new reflex was to check that my magical Zane blocker was still on, and I touched the plastic device hanging around my neck as I committed to my dangerously exciting, stupid idea.

"Once a week. Let me get used to it."

"Hm?" Zane cracked his eyes open again. "What are you talking about?"

"Giving you blood. It's…going to be…weird, and I can't promise it's not going to freak me out, but I think I can do once a week for now. That seems fair."

"Hunter—" He sat up as I got to my feet, tossing my bloody shirt aside. When I approached him, he shook his head. "We don't need to do this tonight."

"Yeah, we do, because I might chicken out tomorrow." I tugged my knife out from my back pocket. My heart was pounding, my gut on fire, and I didn't try to hide my discomfort as I exhaled a long, silent curse.

Zane pressed, "Dallas, I'm serious. Tonight's been difficult enough."

"It's always going to be difficult," I parried. "It's always going to be uncomfortable and rough for me, but I want to do this. Let me return the favor."

In the soft light of the tableside lamp, Zane's face settled into an expression I hadn't seen on him before. The hard lines around his mouth softened, the crease in his brows melted away. The hunger tugging at the corners of his eyes strained the blue veins near his cheeks.

"You don't owe me anything," he whispered.

"Yeah, I do." I nodded for him to lean back. "We'll do like before. Try and curb the sex noises."

"Hunter," Zane warned gently. "I've never gone this long without feeding. When permission is given..."

"Yeah, and I'm sure it's going to be *intense* for both of us so..." I exhaled through my lips as I flicked my knife open. "I'll give you blood, you'll be fed, and we'll both just, you know, ride the wave until it's over. This is strictly—"

"Don't say it."

"—Business boners."

In order to try my best to keep blood from dripping onto the recliner, I braced my knee on the cushion next to Zane's thigh, leaning my outstretched arm over him. I didn't like having to cut my hand, but it was the least awkward way to get blood into his mouth while staying far from it. One clean cut to open my palm, and I could squeeze a steady stream into his mouth without our skin touching.

I had felt his lips and tongue on me before when we had to feed in front of Sias and his friend, and I wanted to try and mitigate that as much as possible.

I knew the moment blood hit his tongue, the sexual high would turn us both into horny idiots, so we didn't need touching in the mix. It was going to be awkward enough as it was.

Distance was key. As much distance as possible while still getting the job done.

Zane's pupils began to dilate, the burning red irises swallowed by a slow expansion of obsidian hunger. His vision swam over me, trailing down the stream of blood on my stomach before floating back to meet my gaze.

"You're sure?"

"No, but we're gonna do it anyway." I shook my hand out and clenched my fingers in anticipation. "You ready?"

"Yes," he said in a rush.

"No teeth."

"No teeth," he agreed quickly.

"Alright. I hate this part." I gave myself a beat to settle my heart rate. "Do you…damnit. Do you want my gift inside of you?"

"I do," he confirmed, eyes now black with all-consuming appetite.

"I really hate how that is phrased."

"Hunter, please," Zane gritted out through his teeth.

"Right. Sorry. With this gift, I give you life." I put the knife to my palm. "Tethered to me from the endless void."

"Permission," Zane breathed out, voice shaking. "Give me your permission."

"You can drink my blood. Just lean your head back more so I can—"

Zane's hands flew up to my hips before I could react, my body forced forward with icy fingers digging into the fabric of my jeans. The greedy, blood-starved vampire didn't wait for me to cut my palm and drizzle blood on him. Instead, he heaved me onto his lap like I was nothing, and licked the trail of blood from my stomach to my chest.

The first time I gave Zane blood, he was writhing on the floor after being stabbed and was in horrible pain. He was still well-fed back then, alive enough to bleed and suffer. The sensation of my blood on his tongue had been overwhelming—like my nerve endings were being seared by sizzling lust. I had never felt anything quite like that: a slow, constant burn that had risen and exploded into a very awkward night on Barnaby's kitchen floor.

This time, Zane was *starving*.

And I was not ready for what it felt like to have a starving Thrall feed after fasting as long as he had.

Whatever part of me that should have been offended by a vampire licking me died a miserable, silent death by the volcano of lust that boiled within me, my entire body reacting so strongly to his tongue that I became the sex noise problem. I didn't care that I was straddling his lap like a stripper, or that his breath was about as frigid as an open freezer door. His tongue was icy on my skin, his fingers frozen iron on my hips.

I *hated* how turned on I was. It was embarrassing, but I couldn't control how viciously the magic between us caused my body to respond.

My knife was tossed onto the ground to free up my hands, and I raked my fingers through Zane's hair and grabbed a fistful of it. His mouth was getting warm from the blood, his tongue less arctic as he licked at the stab wound. Each swipe of his tongue was a bolt through me, a churning wave of molten passion that nearly lifted me off his lap. His hair was soft in my grip, the motion of his skull erotically similar to someone giving me head, which did not help the thundering want that was raising my body temperature.

Zane's skin grew warm, his breath hot as it tumbled over me in humid waves. In one of his upward laps, his tongue grazed my nipple, and I responded by bucking my hips.

I felt a very obvious ridge rub against mine.

My chest knocked hard as Zane let out a slow moan, a shiver danced down my spine as his fingers trailed up my sides. The frantic feast on my blood paused, his bottom lip catching on my skin for just a breath. My pulse was rounding the corner of a marathon, galloping full speed into the next bend as Zane planted his hands on my ribs and drew me in closer.

My fingers gripped his hair, his soft, pretty hair, and I yanked his head back to look him in the eyes.

It was a mistake.

I made a horrible, stupid fucking mistake.

Because Saints damn me, Gods curse me, I was lost in what I saw.

The pale, deathly sallow of Zane's complexion was gone, lost in the flush of rose that now painted his features. Sickly white was warmed to a living cream, lips pink with life, eyes bright and crackling with red fire.

Zane wasn't technically alive, but in that moment he was. He was warm under my fingers, hot under my thighs, boiling in my gaze. His stubble darkened his jaw, finally growing back, and I was amazed at the sweat beading at his temples. I could smell the moisture and heat on him: grave flowers and ozone mixed with musk.

But the worst part, the part that pushed me a little too far, was how his fangs looked outlined in red.

He was…

Zane was…

Oh no.

Oh no.

The knocking in my chest turned into a hammer, heat curled through me like a lightning strike, and Zane was knocked in the forehead by a bone white stick that suddenly shot out of my sternum. We both yelled in different pitches of outrage and alarm, Zane's tinted in pain and mine in pure surprise. In the throes of the sexy, blood-drinking spell, I had forgotten that the end result was always this goddamn thing making itself known.

Thank the damn Gods for that.

Because I had almost made *another* horrible mistake. One I wouldn't have been able to walk back from.

"Shit!" I crawled backwards off Zane and hit the floor, staring down at the stick rotating in my chest. The ivory rod protruded out about eight inches, the carved inscriptions clicking and locking into place as it spun slowly counterclockwise. There was no pain when it shot out of my body, or as it twisted, only a little pressure and a whole lot of confusion. The moment I tried to touch it, tried to reach up and grab a hold of it, the mystery stick retreated back into my chest and disappeared without any trace it had ever been there.

"What the *fuck* is that thing?" I rubbed at my chest, not sore and not exactly soothed. "And why does it only show up when you feed on me?"

"I don't know." Zane rubbed at his forehead, scowl back on his face. He was alive enough that the rod had left a red circle on his forehead and the stab wound in his chest was healed and gone. It was amazing how different he looked with color back in his cheeks, how human he seemed with black stubble peppering his jaw.

I needed to leave.

I escaped to my bathroom and scrubbed the Zane spit and dried blood off my skin, disinfected the holy hell out of my wound, and stitched it closed in record time. It was truly amazing how fast I could be at routine tasks when I was sprinting away from a problem. Since my "adult shirt" had been slashed and bled on, I had to default to my normal, punny, secondhand stuff to make my exit.

"I'm going to Sias's," I announced to the apartment, grabbing my jacket on the way to the door. Zane was still stuck to the chair, rubbing at the newly grown stubble with his palm. He barely reacted, nodding that he had heard me but nothing more.

I didn't wait around for the awkwardness to balloon out further, and I locked the door behind me before flying down the stairs.

This night was fucked. My heart felt like there was a vise grip of guilt wrapped around it, but it had been placed near a cozy blanket covered in vampire stink. What the hell was I supposed to do with this? Where did I compartmentalize these very conflicting, very painful, very *powerful* feelings when I was still coming down from a drug high and desperately lonely?

I decided, stupidly, to let my heart decide.

CHAPTER
TEN

MY BRAIN HAD BEEN REPLACED with scrambled eggs, but my body knew where to go. The eggy mixture was able to decipher that it was way too late for Sias to be at his office, but not late enough that he wouldn't be up on a weekend night. It was the twilight hour, the part of the night when he was usually feasting. He'd be hungry and ready for a meal, and I needed to be on a silver platter.

I had a lot of pent-up energy I wanted to expel, and he was the best catalyst for it.

I could salvage this day yet, if I could just get my mind off of things for a little while. Incubus charm magic mixed with Sias's touch would be exactly what the doctor ordered.

It was the best time of night to travel the city, especially getting into the Lower Lovett. The buses weren't running their normal route that late, but the train was nice and quiet, giving me plenty of time to be alone with myself before being dumped a few blocks away from Sias's neighborhood. Lovett was a beautiful mix of extreme luxury and inherited wealth; big houses with too many bedrooms and an abundance of iron fences. The rich really thought crime would permeate their territory at any moment, like we'd collectively realize how much they all had and make a run for their properties.

The only thing stopping us was a lack of planning.

Sias's estate didn't need to be lavish, because his damn tower was the beacon of the city. His city home, which I'm sure he had a few of, was a modern masterpiece of understated wealth. It was an homage of turn-of-the-century industrial influence, with chic modern arches and automatic lighting. Even the security guard's booth blended well into the ivy-covered stone fence, and I was waved along as a returning guest.

It was too cold for the crickets to sing, but the night wind was whispering through the large, skeletal trees that had dropped their leaves months ago. The perfectly maintained shrubbery looked fake around the perimeter of the house, but the warm light inside was very real. I held my arms to keep the cold away, wincing from the tug on the stitches, and rang the doorbell twice.

Sias was a dream when he answered my summons.

The heavy wooden door swung open, the demon of silk and sex smiled at me like candy had just been dropped into his hand.

"Dallas," he purred, eyes swirling into cotton candy dipped in grape sprinkles. The gold at the tips of his horns glittered, his red silk robe open enough that I could see his golden skin. "What a lovely surprise."

"I was in the neighborhood," I obviously lied. "Thought I'd drop by for a midnight snack."

"My favorite." He pivoted his body to allow me inside, the door sliding shut as soon as I was past the threshold. "I'll make you a drink."

"We can skip that part." I ran my fingers down the seams of his robe and pulled him closer. "I just want to fall into something soft with you for a little while. Bed, couch, a particularly comfortable rug, I don't care."

His long fingers tipped my chin up, the flurry of colors in his eyes slinking into magenta and velvety blue.

"Long night?"

"You have no idea." I sighed at the soft kisses of charm magic that teased me. "I need a nice, big distraction for a little while."

"I have just the thing for that," Sias whispered near my lips, his breath vanilla with hints of fine brandy. His long, honey blond hair curled down his shoulders, draping over my fingers as I tried to pull him closer. I wanted to drown in amber and tobacco, to get lost in his expert touch while I drifted into the bliss of his charm magic.

This night could go to hell. No more lingering pain from past mistakes. No more weird, hot feelings for the dead guy in my apartment. No more fear that the artifacts would be lost.

"Right," I mused out loud once the reminder of the shockingly difficult to obtain artifacts came back into my brain. "Before we get into the fun stuff, I do have a favor to ask. I was…too distracted to talk about it last time we hung out."

"Does this favor involve you thrashing in ecstasy? Otherwise, I'm not terribly interested right now, darling boy."

"Two favors then." I grinned at him, lifting a brow in horny interest. "The first one is the thrashing bit. The second is I need an invitation to the gala Florence is holding tomorrow night."

Sias's hooded eyes lifted in surprise.

"Why in the hells do you want an invite to an art gala held by a wellness guru at the botanical gardens?"

"She's going to be buying the artifacts I stole from Omar's apartment, and I want to intercept that deal. Or at least get a cut of it." I moved my fingers from his robe to his waist. "Could you get me in?"

"I can," he said, voice dripping with sinful promise. "But it will cost you."

"I hope it does."

Neon pink flashed over his eyes, a wave of beautiful lust floated over me like a current, and his fingers plucked me from my inner melancholy. I loved how his touch felt on my skin, how sweet his lips tasted when he angled my chin up for a kiss. I could get lost in him so easily, escape all the obligations banging at the walls for my attention.

Tonight, it could be just us, whatever we were, and I could pretend I would be sleeping over afterward. It was pathetic how badly I wanted to melt into the blankets with him, hold him, fall asleep to the sound of his heartbeat and plummet into a dreamless sleep with the promise of a sweet tomorrow.

The melodic laugh of Vix in the dining room shattered the illusion into sharp shards, and I was standing in the nebulous unknown again.

"Oh," I managed, proud that I didn't sound disappointed. "You have other snacks over."

"Vix and Bastian are here," Sias confirmed, trailing his fingers down my cheek before releasing me. "They'll be happy to see you'll be joining us tonight."

I forced a smile, because I wasn't going to be the favorite that brought the mood down. They sure as hell didn't deserve that, even if I was having a crap night. It was an unspoken rule that baggage was checked at the door, and that only fun sexy times were to be had within the walls of Sias's domain. No complaining, no sad tales, just unbridled fun and orgasms.

Sias placed his hand at the small of my back and led me through the foyer, the dark wooden floors heated to keep the chill away. Vix and Bastian were lounging together on the leather couch near the fireplace, silks barely covering their gorgeous bodies. They were a snapshot of indulgence: Vix, a succubus sculpted from calla lilies, silver threads weaved around her ram horns and spun through long locks, and Bastian, a silver-eyed jinn with a braided beard and dark tattoos covering his earthy brown skin.

Since Vix didn't have the anatomy I'm into, we didn't spend a ton of one-on-one time together, but she was often tangled up in the mix during past rendezvous. I liked her in a fuck-buddy-adjacent sort of way, and appreciated that she seemed to adore my presence, even if we kept our hands to ourselves. Bastian had his perks. He was a slab of hairy meat with an easy laugh and talented hands, but more than once I felt like I was in his way when he wanted a little more time with Sias.

As far as Sias's favorites went, they were the ones I was the fondest of and spent the most time with. I liked them, but I never saw them outside of Sias's place. I had a sneaking feeling that our camaraderie began and ended around Sias's pleasure.

On any other night, when I wasn't emotionally bruised and wanting some quiet, sort of monogamous time with the guy I currently had squishy feelings for, I would have been happy to see them. It was hard to maintain the smile and make it feel anything less than a performance.

"Dallas!" Vix sat up when she saw me, making grabbing gestures for me to come to her. "Sias, you spoil us. I love it when Dallas comes to play."

"This was an unscheduled surprise," Sias chimed in, easing me forward into Vix's demands.

"Hey, Vix." I crawled onto the couch and hugged her, immediately wrapped in sweet perfume. "Sorry I didn't get the memo to wear a silk napkin over my nipples."

"You're ridiculous," she teased, adjusting one of the tiny strips of silk over her breasts. "I'm sure Sias has something you can change into, but we're not going to be dressed long anyway."

"Adding an extra set of hands into the mix is always a good thing," Bastian mused. "The plan tonight was going to have Vix center stage, but we can pivot."

"Didn't mean to derail the plans."

"You didn't." Sias set his wine down near the fireplace, the soft sound of the glass resting against brick almost lost in the crackle of the fire. "Even numbers make it easier for everyone to be involved."

"Oh," Vix purred, uncrossing her long legs as Sias prowled

over to the couch. "I do like the sound of that. I haven't eaten all day so I could have my fill tonight."

"Good." Sias melted into the couch beside her, moving like a stalking cat slinking onto his prey. Her chin was angled toward him, her thighs nudged apart. "I want you starving for me, darling."

There was something truly magical, in every sense of the word, when you got to be near two powerful sex demons feasting off of each other. In my demon biology and culture 101, I knew that incubi and succubi could sustain themselves on fellow sex demon energy, and had for centuries before they realized how delicious jinn, imps, humans, and even oni were.

When two sex demons love each other very much, they put themselves in a sex energy cycle and sometimes make babies.

Not really, there were like…family treaties and marriage bonds that go into sex demon procreating, and it was all very complicated and boring. There's a lot of politics and paperwork that go into baby incubi, like a crazy amount. Barnaby told me all about it once and I almost died.

But I knew from personal experience, when two godly demons were in the throes of passion, they could break the cycle right at the tipping point and turn their attention to the other bystanders in the room. It was like edging for demons who feed off ecstasy, and god*damn* was it fun. The charm magic was at its most potent when they were ready to burst, so it hits like a shot of pure lust directly into your veins. It's so powerful, so all-consuming and glorious, that it was actually illegal for them to do that without written consent because they could basically turn us into walking sex zombies.

I'm not kidding, Bastian and I had to sign contracts before we could experience it.

This is the thrilling content you don't see behind the scenes, kids.

The moment Sias's fingers touched Vix's skin, the sizzling presence of their charm magic made the hair on my arms stand up straight. It was the dancing spark of a lit fuse, the beginning pop of magic that pinched at the anxiety sitting like a brick in my belly. I hadn't wanted a hot and heavy, sex-zombie night because I was already wound up too damn tight but, I was here now, and I needed to figure out how to relax into it.

Otherwise, I wasn't going to have any fun, and they'd notice.

No bad vibes, no excuses.

Bastian's thick arm wrapped around my waist and pulled me into him, my back pressed up against his big chest.

"Easy, big guy," I teased, forcing myself to not seem prickly at his aggressive maneuver. "We should enjoy the show."

"That's the plan." His beard tickled my ear as he spoke, voice husky with the brewing excitement. "Look at them together. Two beautiful specimens enjoying themselves just for us."

Vix wasn't my type, but she was beautiful. The charm magic helped sway me into appreciating her more, the way she moaned into Sias's touch added a certain seductive ambiance to the scene. While she was a stunning woman and absolutely deserved to be worshipped, it was Sias I was praying to. I was a devout worshipper at his altar, and couldn't wait to get on my knees to show him my faithfulness. The way his hands moved over her skin, the ease in which he moved onto his knees in front of her, the smirk when she shivered from his touch.

I was ready to take over countries in the name of that damn smirk. All would know of the good word of Sias's talented, sinful lips.

The swell of charm magic that bloomed from the foreplay helped me relax into Bastian, and I reached back to bring his hand around to my jeans. I tried to give him the signal to go slow, make the night a gentler dance while we enjoyed the delicious deities tangled up together on the couch. He responded by giving me a less than gentle squeeze, chuckling as I hissed.

"Easy," I whispered.

"Since when do you like it easy?" He nipped at my ear, too

many teeth greeting the flesh. "What happened to, 'Snap me in half like a candy cane'?"

"That was then." I put my hand on his and urged him to ease the grip. "Just to get the party started."

The grip eased, palm sliding up before dipping under my waistband. His big hand felt fantastic on my skin when he wasn't wringing the life out of me. The sensation of a man's hand on my cock made me exhale some of the tension in my chest, and I shut my eyes to pretend it was Sias who was making me feel relaxed. Bastian's warm breath bled over my neck, the smell of brandy almost distracting.

"I know what you need," he growled, beard rough on my earlobe. I almost told him to stop talking so I could fall back into my daydream, but thought maybe that was rude.

Vix began to groan in mounting pleasure, body arching and sliding on the leather from Sias's undivided attention. The charm magic fell upon us like shattered starlight, crackling across our bodies in electric kisses. Bastian had pulled me into his lap, his skin white hot against me, obvious excitement pressing against the seat of my pants. My jeans had been undone to give him more room, and I was just about to shuck the damn things and get more into the festivities.

But, because this is my story, and things hadn't been going great, it was doomed to fucking fail.

I don't know what the hell got into Bastian that night. I don't know why the guy couldn't take the hint that I was maybe in a weird place and needed a gentle touch. Either way, the message wasn't received, and he hit the gas forgetting my very few limitations.

Thick fingers ran through my hair in an almost loving fashion, caressing over my scalp so sweetly that it made me smile. The sudden shift in demeanor hit all the wrong buttons as he grabbed ahold of it and yanked my head back, freezing me in mid-appreciation. That I could have forgiven, maybe course-corrected with some teasing but firm reminders that he needed to follow my lead and stop being an alpha jackass.

It was the biting that did me in.

Bastian tilted my head back and raked his teeth over my neck, and my body was immediately lost in a firestorm of soul-deep panic.

I reacted so fast, so severely, that I didn't even feel the impact of my elbow hitting his face. It was a series of movements I couldn't control, a body running off of blind fear and bone-deep training that kicked in when my brain went into dark mode. One moment I was enjoying the heat of his touch against me, the next I was backing away from the couch while a fountain of blood poured from his nose.

Bastian made a terrible noise, a groaning scream of agony as he tried to stop the bleeding. The glittering fireworks of Sias and Vix's magic withered into a cold vacuum, the warmth draining from the room in a heartbeat. Vix was at Bastian's side, urging him to tilt his head back, worry marring her features.

Sias was on his feet, somehow manifesting a towel for Bastian to bleed into.

"What the *fuck* is wrong with you, Wilde?" Bastian was wailing, whatever else he wanted to toss out there lost in a sharp inhale through his teeth.

"Gods, you need a healer." Vix's attention turned to me expectantly. "You could at least heal him enough to stop the bleeding."

"Me?" I blinked, stupefied. "I can't heal anyone."

"All humans can heal," she said so confidently that I questioned my abilities for a second.

"No, we can't," I argued. "We have to go to school to hone that shit. Plus, you don't want me using any of my magic on him."

"Don't let him touch me," Bastian snarled, glaring at me through eyes squinted in pain.

"Enough," Sias chopped our bickering short, encouraging Vix to place the towel over Bastian's bloody fountain. "I'll call a doctor. Bastian, stay still. Vix, stay with him. Dallas." He motioned for me to follow him and walked out of the living room in a quick stride.

The shock from Bastian's teeth on my neck started to wear thin, replaced by a growing boil of anger, regret and heaps of guilt. It poisoned me like a snake bite, icing my veins and knocked my heartbeat off rhythm. I usually liked seeing Sias mad, because the heat was never directed at me. He would get pissed off, ask me to kill someone for him, then we'd have fun, grumpy sex across his desk.

He'd never been mad at me before, not in any real sense.

Not like this night.

I was led back to the foyer, and Sias came to a stop only a few feet away from the front door. The chill of the snow falling outside made me shiver, even though I hadn't felt the cold just yet.

"What the hell happened?" he hissed, eyes a storming cocktail of dark blues and sharp teal.

My shoulders had tensed up too much, my bones started to ache.

"Fuck. I'm sorry. He knows not to touch my neck. They *know* I hate that! But I know—" I cut myself off before he could. "I know that's not an excuse. He didn't deserve to have his nose busted because I have a *thing*."

"I don't tolerate violence in my home, Dallas."

"I know." I rubbed at the prickling shame trailing down the back of my neck. "It was instinct. I felt teeth on me and..." I couldn't make myself continue. "I don't like people touching my neck, Sias. Especially teeth. I've been so up-front about that."

"You're jittery, under-slept and on edge." His eyes churned from icy to cobalt. "You weren't in a place for this tonight, and you didn't communicate that to me."

"Yeah, no fucking shit." I shut my eyes, hating how sharp I sounded. I scrubbed at my eyelids until I saw stars, blinking them open to stare down at the floor. "I had such a shit day, Sias. It's been so hard. I wanted a night with you."

"You cannot come here in that state of mind and put people I care about in danger, Dallas."

My heart was too fragile for that kick.

The fine cracks that had spider-webbed over my bruised, sad excuse for a functioning emotional core shuttered and faulted, the pain so brutal it knocked the wind out of me.

"Saints," I breathed out in disbelief. "That fucking hurts."

"Dallas—"

"No, I get it." I struck out verbally like a wounded animal. "Sorry your fun little fuck buddy came in and crashed the party. God forbid your favorites have a bad night."

The cobalt in his eyes sharpened into a vicious gold, jaw bunching as he gnawed at my audacity. I didn't know if he was mad because I called him on his bullshit, or if I missed something else entirely. I had a pretty good feeling I not only overstepped, but struck a little too deep when he finally spoke.

I had never heard him sound so cold to me before. It strangled me with the distance of his words.

"I surround myself with people I care about, and I choose who I spend my time with very carefully. If you can't respect that, can't see that you are part of the chosen, then maybe we need to take a break from this arrangement for a while."

I didn't know what to say, so I said nothing.

I probably should have tried, should have apologized and owned up to the fact that I was in the middle of a crisis, that I was grappling with too much crap and I sucked at communicating that. I was sore, tired, and confused. I couldn't handle anything else complicated in that moment, including trying to unpack how deeply hurt I was that he couldn't see how much I needed him.

I wanted him to magically know that I cared about him, even though I was a total fuckup who had just ruined something special, I didn't mean it.

Sias opened the door to his home and didn't look at me as he tacked on, "I'll get you your tickets into the gala, but don't come here again unless invited."

I don't remember hearing the door shut behind me, but I remember how cold I felt when I stepped out into the street.

It had been about a decade since I had felt that type of cold, the type of freezing hurt that only came when you had only yourself to blame.

My heart was in shambles, my feet didn't know where to go, so I just meandered across Lower Lovett until something made sense. The snow stuck to my boots, my hair was soggy with the bitter weather, and I mused the idea of finding a dive bar and getting blackout drunk for a bit.

It wasn't the worst idea by a mile. What else does a miserable jackass do after they get dumped by a sex demon billionaire who was also your best client?

I knew I had to fix it somehow, but I wasn't in any place to summon a decent plan. I needed time to wallow, maybe get into a fight and get some sense knocked into me.

My plans for getting assaulted and drinking were interrupted by a buzzing cell phone, the bright screen informing me that my high-strung landlord was calling me well past his grandpa bedtime.

"Barns?" I answered, befuddled. "Is the apartment on fire?"

"What the *hell* did you do to Zane?"

"What?" I blinked, checking to see if maybe the reception was bad before clarifying, "Is Zane different than normal in some capacity? Because he was whole the last time I saw him."

"Well, you broke him somehow, because he's acting insane. Truly bonkers. A maniac."

"Uh…" I faltered, the gap in my dialog a moment of opportunity for Barnaby to pounce.

"I normally don't mind him coming into the store, since we usually meet for breakfast in the mornings anyway, but this is *ridiculous*. He's rearranged several displays, and I caught him polishing my rare collection of brass codpieces."

"Sorry, did you just say that Zane meets you for breakfast?" I cut in when he took a fussy breath.

"Well you sleep late like a delinquent teenager, so we do the newspaper crosswords over coffee."

"What the fuck?"

"Get home *now*, Dallas. He's trying to alphabetize my books by author instead of subject! No! Zane, I have those exactly how I like them!"

The phone politely beeped that Barnaby hung up on me. I stood in the snow, brokenhearted and now gobsmacked, wondering what the hell I was doing with my life.

"YOU LOOK like you're about to tell me your grandkids never call you."

Barnaby didn't appreciate my observation of his sleep attire, which was stolen directly out of a cartoon about a curmudgeonly old man who foils children's antics. The long nightshirt he wore almost reached his ankles, complete with a matching floppy hat that I refused to believe he slept in. He'd told me it was to keep his horns from wearing down his pillow, but I think it was because he bought the outfit as a set from an old folks' home.

Unlike the more striking incubi who had just stomped on my heart, Barnaby's eyes didn't fade into a colorful spectrum of emotions. His remained inky black and angry, and he was the only incubus I had ever met that had frown lines.

"I'm going to be up all night fixing my books," he complained, stomping around in his shop with his slippers on. "I don't know what the hell you did to him, Dallas, but it really ruined my evening."

"Why the hell do you assume this is somehow my fault? I was out for the past hour." I didn't see a single thing out of place except for the books Barnaby was shuffling around.

"Because it usually is your fault. That's what you do. You're an agent of chaos and heartburn." Barnaby exhaled as he sorted some hardbacks and slammed one back onto the shelf. "He has my ancient linguistics mixed up with my post-classic fertility rituals of the Sarbon empire texts. This is all a mess!"

"I'd offer to help but—yeah, that was the face I was expecting to see from the offer." I glanced around at the quiet shop, the shadows of his erotic antiquities casting hilarious shapes on the walls. "Where is said maniac book organizer?"

"He insisted he was going to teach Kevin a new trick and bolted right after I called you." He took a step back and set his hands on his hips, aging from sleepy grandpa to scolding ghost who died from being disappointed. "I like Zane. He's decent, and nice, and can actually carry a conversation. I would be upset if you chase him away with whatever nonsense you've done tonight."

"I didn't realize you had such a big crush on my vampire Thrall, Barns."

"I don't like him that way, you impossible dick, but I do consider him a friend." He crossed his arms and uncrossed them, turning to glare at his books before deciding that he did want to cross his arms after all. "Probably the only friend of yours I think is good for you."

"Good for me," I echoed, exhausted. "Sure. The vampire is good for me."

"Compared to the usual ruffians you hang around with, yes." He started busying himself with shuffling books again. "The vampire is the least of your problems."

"I'll agree with you on that point." I turned to leave but rotated around when Barnaby did his "I'm not finished" sigh.

"Two DHAP officers stopped by. I think they were former clients, but they were looking for you."

"Human and jinn?" I asked and Barnaby nodded. "They say what about?"

"Only that you should call them. I didn't get their card."

Preston Cheslock and Seyyid Taleb; Demon Human Alliance

and Protection officers I had helped over a year ago. Seyyid had been bitten by a vampire and started to turn into a messenger, and his buddy turned boyfriend had dragged him to my doorstep for help. It had also been the first time I met Zane—well. The first time we tried to kill each other, anyway.

While I managed to help the two and Seyyid made a full recovery, they were quick to let me know they could only turn a blind eye to my assassin profession to an extent.

We had a complicated history, but for the most part they didn't bother me.

Still didn't love that they dropped by. It probably wasn't good, but I had other fires to deal with.

"Thanks," I told Barnaby. "Anything else?"

"Rent is due next week." He exhaled a few more years off his life. "And I thought you were visiting Sias soon? I was hoping for an intimacy crystal."

A slice of bitterness ran through me, but I managed to keep it from leaking out.

"Yeah, sorry about that. I'll get one to you as soon as I can. Night, Barns."

He mumbled some sort of departing words, but his attention had been set back to the books by the time I was leaving.

I felt heavy as I hauled myself up the stairway, my body demanding rest but my mind whirling too fast for any sleep to arrive. I had done this dance for so long that I knew the nights I wasn't getting any sleep way before my head ever hit the pillow. I had been naïve to think the emotional turmoil and earlier drugs would help knock me on my ass for some deep, dreamless sleep, but I thought I was building up a resistance to such things.

Lucky me.

While my body ached and my mind was in pieces, I had somehow managed to still set an expectation of what I was going to see when I entered my apartment. I hadn't known Zane long, but the word "manic" was not one I would ever use to describe him, even when he was in intense situations. Whatever I had imagined seeing when I came home was shoved off the tallest tower in my imagination and replaced by the scene before me.

My bed had been stripped of its sheets, blankets and pillows repurposed for an honest-to-God pillow fort, erected in the middle of my very small living space. All my swords had been taken down and rehung, my guns in perfect order beside them. All of my laundry was folded, my sink void of dishes, the smell of fresh cookies hung in the air like I was being lured into a trap.

As I stood in my doorway, taking in the lunacy, Twig sauntered past in a little vest made from a sock.

My vampire Thrall had apparently gone insane.

"Zane?" I stepped inside and shut the door. "You uh…you alright?"

Zane stood from where he was bent over Kevin's tank, face set in intense concentration.

"It took all night, but we figured it out."

I glanced between the crazed vampire and my fish, who was building a bubble nest near the top of his tank.

"Figured out the bubbles? 'Cause he does that when he wants a fishy wife so…whatever you have planned, I'm vetoing it."

"Bubbles? No." Zane drummed his fingers on the counter. "The double backflip."

"You or Kevin?"

"Kevin. The landing is still a little sloppy but he has done it twice so far."

I cautiously went over to my fish and peered into his tank. Kevin paused his aquatic architecture to glare at me. He did not like to be bothered when he was working, and from the amount of bubbles made he had been at it for some time. His little gills flared, his breathing normal, and he puffed his tail in absolute outrage that I would dare speak to him while he was constructing his future wife's palace.

"We just need to adjust the angle of the second flip," Zane went on. "Otherwise he splashes everywhere."

The counters were dry, nothing fish-floppy about the situation.

"Sure, man," I placated, steering his attention away from my poor betta fish. "You've been...busy."

"I had a lot to do. The apartment needed revamping and Barnaby had his books out of order." He tried to peel away from the counter, whatever compelling him to move won the battle, but I caught his arm and piloted him back in my direction.

"Look at me a second," I told him, amazed by how wide his pupils were. His stare was glassy and jumpy, his arm buzzing with the desire to do anything but stand still. "Saints, Zane. Are you high?"

"Do humans like cinnamon in their cookies or is that just an imp thing? Because the recipe I found was an imp one from someone's grandmother, but it seemed like everyone could benefit from them." He looked at the fresh batch sitting on the counter, then back at me.

"Everyone likes cinnamon."

"I'm going to make more."

"No more cookies. That's plenty of cookies. Zane, focus on me. What did you take?" I snapped my fingers to get him to stop staring at the cookies and repeated myself before he realized I was asking him a question.

"I didn't take anything," he insisted. "I feel great."

"How great?" I probed. "Obviously you have...an abundance of energy. What the hell is with the pillow fort, by the way?"

"I read about them in a book. Did you know kids make these and sit inside them to read?" He lifted his eyebrows like he just told me a very coveted secret I should be amazed by.

"Kay. You didn't find something in here and swallow it? Little pink pills or some powder maybe?" I quizzed. "You didn't eat any of the cookies, right?"

"Do you want more cookies?"

"No, stop it." I steered him out of the kitchen. "Hey, show me the fort. Let's go sit down."

Watching a tall, brawny vampire crawl into a pillow fort was hilarious, even if he had stripped my bed to make the damn thing.

His wide shoulders scraped the sides of the entry, and there wasn't a ton of space inside with his large body dominating the narrow space. I managed to squeeze myself in and sit, though the close quarters meant I was basically sitting in his lap.

"Did you ever make these as a kid?" Zane asked, shoulders hunched to bring his head away from the blanket ceiling.

"I didn't have that kind of childhood." I scooched forward and watched his eyes dance around. "Zane, when did you start wanting to do all this stuff? Can you remember?"

"I made the fort right after you left. But then I wanted to go see Barnaby." He drummed his fingers on his knees, wide pupils aimed at me. "I wanted to keep myself busy."

"You've done a great job at that." I reached up and snagged a piece of cookie dough from his hair, surprised when he leaned into the touch. His fingers stopped tapping, his eyes shut, and he took a long breath.

"That feels amazing," he confessed. "Relaxing. Like my whole body feels it."

It was a simple gesture, and something I hadn't thought much of, but his reaction was the missing piece I needed.

"Ah, hell." I winced. "Barns was right, this is my fault."

"Hm?" Zane opened his eyes sleepily. "What is?"

"My blood. I took some Rabbit Hole earlier and I forgot. When you um…when we did the…" I motioned to my chest, felt my cheeks burn and moved on. "The drugs were still in my blood. You got a kick from it. You, my good sir, react very strongly to this shit."

"Your blood…had drugs?" He screwed up his face like I was trying to trick him.

"Yeah. Sorry about that."

"Oh." Zane rubbed at the spot between his eyebrows. "What do I do? Will it go away?"

"Normally I'd try to get you to eat something and lie down. That's what I do to try and curb it—Zane, if you're about to get up to make cookies, I'm gonna punch you."

He paused in mid-rise. "You said you needed to eat something."

"No, *you* need to eat something, but you don't eat! Hell, you don't sleep. Are you just going to be stuck like a hyperactive vampire puppy forever? Because only one of us can be the jackass. We both can't be, it fucks up the dynamic."

Zane watched me for a moment, eyes drifting to the exit then back to me.

"So, that's 'no' for cookies? They have cinnamon."

"Oh my *GOD*. Zane, lie the hell down. Rest. Meditate. Stop moving and relax so this can pass."

"Let me just get you one—" He tried to crawl past me, which was impossible because there was no room, so it turned into him crawling on me to try and escape. The guy was strong and determined, and from the personal experience of me trying to kill him more than once, I knew there was no way I was going to out-muscle him into submission. He could toss me off him without batting an eye, and had several times in past encounters.

Instead of trying to grapple him to the ground and force him to stay still, I used his current affliction to my benefit and pacified him the easiest way I could think of. Just as he knocked me over to go fetch some fresh-baked, imp recipe, damn cinnamon cookies, I reached up and ran both of my hands through his hair.

I knew from earlier when the drugs had still been rolling through me, that everything felt extraordinary when at the peak of the high. The maneuver was risky and a little awkward, but damn if it wasn't effective. Zane's manic quest to grab sweets stalled out at the feeling of fingers on his scalp, and he deflated like a heavy balloon.

I had made one fatal error in my plan in that I hadn't moved out of the way fast enough. When Zane melted into my touch and lay down, I had become the only resting place that made sense. He settled down like a meat blanket on my chest, head over my heart, one thick arm thrown over my stomach.

It wasn't ideal. He was heavy, and a vampire. I didn't want vampires lying on me.

But he wasn't cold anymore. In fact, he was pleasantly warm, and the construction of the fort had padded floors that felt nice as I lay on them.

I had to grudgingly acknowledge that his hair was silky soft. Running my fingers through it to keep him peaceful wasn't awful. His shampoo smelled crisp, pleasant, and I decided I was going to steal it. I wanted my hair this soft. The entire situation, while weird—and I vowed not to speak of it later—was…

Nice.

Comfortable.

I didn't hate it.

My deep sigh brought his head up and then down again, and I couldn't tell from the angle if his eyes were closed or not.

"You know Barns has a big ol' crush on you?" I asked, not able to bear the tranquility any longer.

"No, he doesn't," Zane countered immediately, voice slowing into his normal cadence.

"Hm, I dunno. He was pretty mad that I might chase you away. He absolutely likes you more than me, that's for sure."

"He cares about you," he said, which took me by surprise. Before I could dismiss the accusation with something funny but likely shitty, he nullified it by adding, "He's losing his shop."

"What are you talking about?"

"He's drowning in debt and can't make enough to keep the bank off his back." Zane adjusted his head on my chest a bit.

"How bad?"

"Bad."

"Goddamnit, Barns." I kept petting the vampire but took a moment to rub at my eyes. "He never said anything to me."

"He's not going to. He's too proud." Zane started moving around a bit too much, so I put both hands in his hair again.

"I thought he was some rich guy with endless sources of

income. Who else opens a shop like that other than eccentric millionaires with trust funds?"

"I don't know about that, but I know he only has a few weeks left. I saw the bills shoved in his desk."

"Damn." I stared up at the sheets above us, worry picking at my chest. I'd have to move, find something else low profile and cheap, with a landlord that wouldn't ask a ton of questions. Kevin hated moving, it was always stressful for him.

I quietly mused how the hell I could convince Barns to move with us. I couldn't stand the thought of him being out on his ass, even if he was a major pain in one.

"I think I fucked up with Sias."

"Oh?" Zane sounded surprised, which was fitting because I was too. I wasn't sure why the hell I blurted it out, but it was out there now. "What happened?"

"I sort of...punched one of his favorites in the face? Don't fucking sigh. It wasn't on purpose. Mostly."

"How do you accidentally assault someone?"

He was starting to sound like his normal grumpy self, which was good, but I decided to keep him still with my platonic hair petting for a while longer. Just to make sure he was resting long enough to let the drugs wear all the way off.

"When they cross a line," I explained to him, the leftover venom of guilt starting to work its way into my bones. I was getting tired of constantly messing up. "I don't like people biting my neck. He got lost in the moment and...well, I reacted strongly, we'll say that. Sias..." I wasn't sure how to proceed, and almost let the sentence die on the vine. "Sias told me that I couldn't hurt people he cared about, then kicked me out."

Zane, who was growing to be a master at shooting me with perfectly aimed insightfulness, landed a well-placed bolt through my chest.

"You know he wasn't excluding you from that, hunter."

I didn't know when my hands stopped moving, but they had found a nice little nest in his hair.

"I know."

"Did you talk to him?"

"I wish I could have him borrow your emotion reading abilities for a while," I said. "So I could just feel things and he'd know."

Zane hummed thoughtfully. "You spent a small fortune obtaining a device to keep someone from knowing your feelings."

"You're not Sias."

"No, I'm not."

That was Zane's cue to finally lift off of me, his pupils retracting back to their normal size, or at least close to it. He rubbed at his eyes, which I knew from experience were dry, and blinked them at me.

"I don't have the luxury of getting pissed off at you and shoving you out the door," he explained. "Instead, I have to force you to talk to me. Which, to your credit, hunter, has been the hardest fucking fight of my life."

"Do you charge for your special vampire therapy by the hour or is it a weekly fee?" My words were as deadpan as my posture, and I glared up at the vampire from his stupid damn pillow fort. "Why the hell do you even care?"

Zane watched me, my blood in his veins giving him an almost alive, human glow to his cheeks. He needed to shave, and his locks were wild from being ruffled into submission. He wore a different, but equally black shirt and dark jeans, and looked more like a pasty model than an undead creature of the night.

He hadn't been the toughest vampire I had ever encountered until that moment.

Until he spoke, he was just a burden, a weird, hilarious fluke that had been cursed upon me from years of bleeding necromancers and vampires dry. Zane was a heavy suitcase I had to drag around behind me, who could feel all of my insecurities, and was filled with aggravation and annoyance.

But then he spoke, and everything changed.

It set us on a new path.

"I care about you, Dallas."

And that was it.

He was the first person to tell me he cared about me to my face.

No vague remark, no phrasing that could be easily tossed away as manipulative or toxic.

He just simply cared. About me.

"I don't know what to say to that," I told him, because I honestly didn't.

"You don't have to say anything," Zane affirmed. "I just wanted you to know."

"Okay." I continued to lie on the base of his pillow fort, wondering what the hell to do next. "You're not about to go make more cookies, right? I don't like that you're standing up right now."

"No. I'm going to go shower, then sit and read my book. Feel free to sleep in the fort, because I'm not remaking your bed. I'm tired."

"Gee, thanks."

As Zane disappeared, sober and not nearly as whimsical, I was left lying on the ground as a tiny kitten wearing a sock found a home against my leg. My thoughts had taken a gelatinous shape, bouncing violently each time I tried to latch onto any of them. Each time I tried to unpack my run-in with Austin, an intrusive plop of guilt squished into my mind. When I replayed the image of Sias's eyes flashing yellow in anger, Zane's admission dripped over it.

Eventually I was too exhausted from trying to fight my own messy brain to stay awake, and I fell asleep to the sound of Twig purring.

CHAPTER
TWELVE

OK, look.

I'm a big fan of men in suits. They accentuate their body shapes. They look classy as hell. You can pretend to be a spy. And we all know that when guys wear tailored vests, they are instantly, and always, fuckable.

It's like a law of nature.

That being said, I hate wearing them for more than an hour. While they are, in fact, deadly sexy, and I know I look like a rakish rogue about to cause mayhem, I hit my limit when I have to fight while wearing cufflinks on my rented tux.

We don't have time for me to scream about how asinine the concept of renting articles of clothing is right now. I'll come back to it.

Zane and I arrived at the gala fashionably late, because the train we needed to take to get there was delayed and because I wanted a burrito. But we did arrive, looking like two handsome rich dudes, and I only had a tiny stomachache from anxiety and the previously stated burrito.

I knew that Sias wouldn't have told me he would get the tickets if he didn't mean it, but there was a small part of me that wasn't sure they would be waiting for us. After resting and replaying the absolute shitshow that was the previous night, I wouldn't have blamed him for leaving me high and dry when I needed a favor.

Somehow the tickets being there made me feel worse. It was salt in the wound that I had let him down, but he hadn't.

"You think this place has an open bar?"

"Probably." Zane made a sweep of the place with his eyes, which looked strange as hell with the colored contacts in them. Since I didn't have access to glamour anymore due to past bullshit involving an ambitious imp trying to rob me, we had to go back to the basics when it came to covering up Zane's vampireness. The pale skin wasn't nearly as bad since he had fed recently, but there was no denying his red eyes were harder to explain away.

We decided that some basic brown contacts would work best for him, and for the most part they did the trick. To everyone else he looked normal, but to me, he looked weird as hell. I had finally gotten used to the gross red eyes, and now he was just...normal.

I didn't like it.

"Any sign of Marthas?" he asked me, turning the fake brown eyes my way.

"Nothing yet, but I have a feeling it's just a matter of time. Even in a sea of formal attire, eventually he's going to realize we're here."

Zane followed me as we politely skirted around elegant gowns and crisp suits, making our way deeper into the lion's den.

"What's the plan?"

"We need to figure out when the handoff is and snatch them. The security is tight, but I didn't see any guns on them. Did you?"

"You want to steal them here?" His brows creased, voice shifting to annoyed dad pitches. "That's idiotic. We trail them afterward, hit them outside the gala."

"You think Florence Pierce doesn't have muscle following her expensive purchases? C'mon, Zane."

"Hunter, going after the artifacts in the middle of a gala is going to start a damn panic."

"No shit." I snatched a flute of champagne off a tray and sipped it, hated it, and put it down on a table. "Chaos is the best cover."

"No, it isn't. Not when there's this many people. It's risky and stupid."

"Assuming we'll be able to tail them after the exchange and get away without being seen is a worse idea," I countered. "We wait until they're loading the artifacts into her car, then we knock over the help and steal them back. If we wait until they're on the road, we may as well write them off."

"If we do this plan, we go in quietly. Don't start a riot, and we should be able to do this without getting shot or arrested. Hunter." Zane scowled at me as I turned back in his direction, spitting the drink I had grabbed off the bar back into the glass.

"Ugh, Saints! This isn't alcohol! What the hell is this? Fucking kale??"

"Focus," Zane growled.

"Who the hell sells green juice at a gala? Gods, that's gross. Can you believe this? Everything on the menu is pressed juices and vegetables. Look!"

My very rude vampire bodyguard ripped the menu from my hand and slapped it down on the bar.

"This is a gala run by the queen of vitamins. What the hell did you think she'd be serving if not *her products*?"

"Fair," I lamented. "But I'm still outraged. Hey, you can do the mist trick now that you had some blood, right? Can you go do some recon?"

"Can you stay out of trouble for a few minutes?"

Between my question and his response, I decided that I actually did like the drink and grabbed another one. It tasted better the second time, and I felt my liver thanking me.

"I can guarantee a soft ten."

"Make it a solid ten and I won't kick you in the ass."

"Aye-aye."

Zane did not like my salute, and mumbled something about me being an idiot or something like that as he meandered away.

We hadn't talked about last night.

After I woke up, the pillow fort was dismantled, my bed tossed back together, and our normal bickering bullshit was back in play. Zane was back to his standard grumpy self, maybe a little worse for wear after being accidentally drugged, but all in all, the same vampire. I wasn't sure if he even remembered most of what happened.

Or what was said.

I had a lot to process between what Zane had bombed me with and how badly I'd screwed up with Sias, but it was much easier to narrow my focus on finding the artifacts. Taking on a gang leader and ripping off a supplement tycoon was much less scary than dealing with crushing guilt or confusing feelings.

Even better if it turned into a chaotic mess I could lose myself in for a while.

While Zane was off vampiring with his cool ability to turn into black mist, I got to work Dallasing by mingling through the throngs of rich jerks who spent lavish amounts on crap that didn't matter. Honestly, it was how I found some of my best clients. Every person in power had enemies they needed dead or fish that needed training.

Polite conversation hung in the air like the perfume of manu-factured flowers, the soft music of the live orchestra almost lost in the equally plastic laughter. I floated around in a bored haze for a while, scanning the tables for signs of Marthas or Florence, eventually finishing my blended juice drink. Zane had five minutes left before I got to go full chaos and attempt to break into locked backroom areas. It was a perfect excuse to go order another drink.

I parked myself at the juice bar musing between another kale thing or maybe jazzing it up with an avocado affront to my senses when the inevitable happened.

The tip of Marthas's knife was a sharp kiss against my kidney, his hand on my shoulder to keep me from whipping around at the sensation.

"You have some nerve, Wilde." Marthas spoke close to my ear, like he was leaning down to speak to an old friend. I was impressed he was able to school his ugly mug into a pleasant placid look of ease, instead of the snarling fury dripping from his words.

"Hey, Marthas. Want a blended juice thing for that chronic constipation?"

"You think you're funny. That's fine." The tip of the knife bit through more of my rented tux, and I winced more at the fact I wasn't getting the deposit back than the pain. "I'm going to enjoy carving your kidney out after all the stupid shit you've done."

"Which part? Busting up your office or figuring out your stash spots?" I slid the menu back across the bar. "You stole my pilfered goods and you're acting like I'm the bad guy here."

"Get up." Marthas squeezed my shoulder, knife refusing to budge. "You do anything stupid, I'll end you."

"I promised my bodyguard that I'd wait ten minutes before causing chaos, otherwise I'd flip you over this bar." I got to my feet carefully. "You have five minutes left, hot shot. Actually, make that four."

Marthas steered me away from the bar, the knife tip biting into skin as we weaved through the crowd. It was a strange sensation feeling cold metal jabbing into the meat of your back while also smiling at party guests who had to step out of your way. Out of everyone attending, Marthas and I were absolutely the eyesores. He was a huge imp with knuckle tattoos, and I was some random human trying to pass out assassination business cards.

Quite the pair.

Marthas piloted us down a quiet hallway where the bathrooms were, and ducked into one that had been marked off as "under repair." I was shoved into the empty room, tiles ripped from the floor and new toilets waiting to be installed, and Marthas made a show of locking the main door behind us.

"What was your plan, Wilde? Show up at the gala and try and steal back your shit before I sold it off?" He shucked his tux jacket and tossed it over the sink, rolling up the sleeves to his button down.

"Yeah. Or rob them afterward." I pulled my jacket off and checked the hole in the back. "Ugh. You could have just showed me the knife, you had to fuck up the rental? You're such an asshole."

Marthas rolled his neck until his spine popped, then flipped the knife around in his hand.

"I'm done playing with you, Wilde. When I'm done beating that pretty face into a pulp, I'm going to slit your throat and my boys will come collect your corpse. We're not doing this crap anymore."

"I know you hate me because of Danny—"

"Dancer," he said through his teeth, vein throbbing near his eye.

"Sorry. Dancer." I cleared my throat. "But listen to me for a second. Those artifacts you took? They're dangerous, and I don't know what the hell Florence Pierce has planned for them. Trust me when I say she's up to some really wicked, mad scientist shit, Marthas. She can't get her hands on them."

"I don't care."

Marthas charged like a bull, shoulders low so he could try and tackle me to the messy tiles. I danced backwards and pivoted into a stall when he got close, kicking him in the hip to throw him off balance.

"They're not just historical pieces, they might actually have some magic in them," I explained as I dodged one of his meaty fists, rolling across the ground to get around him. "If she gets them, she might use them to make magic tech."

"I don't *fucking care*, Wilde!" He grabbed one of the toilet seats and chucked it at my head, the plastic bouncing off a sink as I ducked. "I'm getting paid, and you're getting your face bashed in."

"Counteroffer—" I whizzed a tile at his face like a Frisbee and used the moment he took to dodge to grab a piece of discarded piping. Craning back, I swung the thing full force like a bat, aiming to clobber him in the temple and knock him out cold. The sound of the weapon whiffing over his head as he ducked made my stomach flip, and I was soon airborne.

My shirt choked me as he grabbed my collar with his fist, lifting me up so my feet kicked off the ground before he slammed me back down on my shoulders. All the air in my lungs left in one glorious grunt, and I got to see fun little sparkles of air deprivation around the flash of his knife.

The tile I grabbed off the ground shattered into powder as I slammed it into the side of his skull, and I used my forearm to block the downward swing of his knife. The fabric of my shirt bit into my skin as he twisted his grip, but my quick, sharp punch to his throat forced him backward in a reeling gasp.

His weapon was dislodged after I twisted his hand and forced it limp, and I took my chance to try and roll away from him. I didn't get far, his fingers grabbing the back of my waistband and dragging me back his direction so he could slam his fists down on my liver.

Whatever good that juice had done hopefully cushioned the blow, because it stung like a bastard.

My hair was wrung in his fist and my head pulled back, and I knew he was about to slam my face down on the sharp tiles that had cracked during our brawl so I grabbed his wrist and spun like a crocodile, landing two brutal kicks between his legs. Sure, I lost some hair in that exchange, but it got him to let go and sent him pitching backward.

I used my body weight to tackle him fully to the ground, snatching up the pipe I had missed with earlier and arched back to land the final blow onto his stupid face.

"Gentlemen."

I paused in mid-strike, pipe still above my head, panting from pain and exertion. Marthas tilted his head backward, still reaching for his knife that was just out of reach, and we both stared at the woman standing in the doorway.

She wore heavy fabric pants that flared toward the bottom, but were tapered tight to her ankles. The wide sash used as the belt narrowed her thick frame, broad shoulders covered with a similar fabric that gathered at her wrists. Her long, white hair was braided in a rope of elegance, her oni tusks curved inward in very slight crescents.

I recognized her instantly.

She was the same woman from the island—the same deadly oni with ruby eyes we had run into while trying to flee with Omar's animated corpse.

She regarded us, unbothered and polite.

"Miss Pierce is requesting your presence." She presented the door to us with one hand, the other remaining at rest in the small of her back.

"Can you give us a few minutes?" I tried, but she shook her head.

"She insisted on you joining her immediately."

I glared down at Marthas, who was snarling up at me, both of us still very much ready to pick up where we left off. When Marthas presented his palms begrudgingly, I climbed off him slowly.

I didn't drop the pipe until he moved away from his knife, and both of us grabbed our jackets off the sinks. The oni woman waited patiently as we tucked our shirts back in and dusted away tile fragments, nodding with approval once we no longer looked fresh from a fight.

"You're still a dead man, Wilde," Marthas growled as we followed the woman. "I'm going to hang your guts over a light pole."

"Does it help at all that I honestly didn't remember he was your boyfriend?" I whispered, feeling the spot on my head where Marthas ripped some hair out. It didn't feel too bald but I still raked some hair over it just in case. "He came onto me, dude. Maybe he's not worth it."

"You don't care about anyone but yourself. You never even apologized, Wilde. You just act and hurt people and you don't *care*."

Well.

I hadn't expected that level of introspective honesty from Marthas. Nor did I expect it to sting that much.

Marthas was a gang leader, and I could argue that the Broken Horns weren't exactly an altruistic group of charitable sweethearts, but he had never hurt me directly. He never busted up any of my relationships because of bad choices and selfish intentions.

So, yeah.

Marthas was the good guy in this scenario.

Great.

The oni woman, who was mysterious and terrifying and kinda badass, led us to a private suite overlooking the garden outside. In the false moonlight, the garden was a perfect snapshot of serene tranquility, with a meditation rock garden in the center and stone benches to reflect on.

"Please wait here." She motioned to the two seats angled across a bamboo coffee table with warm tea waiting, each of us receiving a cup we didn't ask for.

We sat in silence as she left, the tea smelling like flowers and antioxidants. The steam curled up in thick swirls before disappearing, my sigh dispelling it further.

"I'm sorry."

"Fuck you, Wilde."

"I know it doesn't change anything, and you're still going to hang my guts or whatever, but you're right. I didn't apologize and what I did was shitty. I do act and hurt people, and you never gave me a reason to do that. So. I'm sorry."

Marthas adjusted in his seat.

"Too late for that," he said, but he sounded tired.

"I know."

When the door opened again, I lifted my gaze to see Zane being escorted in by the oni woman. He lifted a brow in my direction and checked his watch.

"I made it about eight minutes," I told him. "Full disclosure though, Marthas found me, not the other way around."

Zane grunted and sat beside me in a matching chair that was brought over. Like before, the scary woman sat her new hostage, offered him tea, then left.

"Where's my jacket?" Marthas demanded from Zane.

"At home. You want it back, we can go another round." The vampire stretched his long legs out. "If you lose this time, I'm taking your watch."

"How'd they find you?" I asked, pulling Zane's attention back my way. "I thought you were gonna do the mist thing."

"I did. They caught me coming back looking for you. I have a feeling they were watching the entire time." Zane set his tea aside after smelling it. "We might be in over our heads on this one, hunter."

"Nah," I dismissed his concerns, but I knew he was right. Something about the situation sat weird with me, like I was slowly becoming aware that I was running through a maze and the cheese had been a lie. "I've gotten out of worse."

Zane didn't seem convinced. "Sure you have."

The door opened again, and this time the mysterious oni woman was following instead of leading. In front of her, almost one fourth her size, was the petite, iconic frame of Florence Pierce. She was human, dressed in the type of impossible high fashion that looked like one panel of cloth draped around her like a blanket, wearing the ugliest damn shoes that had likely cost a few grand. Pale, almost white-blond hair was slicked back into a ponytail, and she obviously spent a long time applying makeup to make it look like she was wearing absolutely nothing on her skin.

She smiled at us like a content shark, and took a seat across from me, picking up a cup of tea.

"Thank you, Hei," Florence said to the oni, who inclined her head politely. "Sorry to keep you all waiting. I had to finish my conversation downstairs before I could join you."

"I hope my…run-in…with this jackass hasn't affected our deal, Ms. Pierce." Marthas set his tea down, none of us actually drinking any of it. "I can make sure he's not a problem for you in the future."

"I'm not worried about that, Marthas." Florence sipped her tea, taking out her phone and gave it a few taps. "Hei already checked on the items you sold me and everything is in order. I just sent you payment. I prefer to do business face to face, otherwise I would have sent it earlier."

Marthas checked his phone, a grin sliding over his face. My stomach shriveled at how pleased he looked.

"Pleasure doing business with you, Ms. Pierce. You sure you don't want me to—"

"No, thank you. Please, go enjoy the gala."

Marthas stood, straightening out his suit. He cut me a very happy "go fuck yourself" sneer before making his exit. Hei shut the door behind him and stood at her post after he left.

"You're totally going to have him killed later, aren't you?" I whispered, leaning over the tea. "I have really competitive rates if you wanna talk shop."

"Dallas Wilde." Florence smiled, razor sharp and amused. "I have been waiting to meet you since you first came to the island. Did you enjoy the amenities during your stay?"

"Mud bath was pretty legit." I set my teacup aside to make sure my hands were free. "I'm going to go out on a limb and assume you had us pulled into your suite because of Omar. He's very dead now, if you were worried about him testifying against you or anything."

Something about my statement puzzled the supplement queen, her brows twitching as her smile warped into a bent angle.

"Testify against me?"

"Yeah. For the whole nightmare eye situation." I mimed spikes coming from my eye sockets. Omar had been a haunting example of Florence's influence, his jinn powers mutating into a crystalized waterfall that formed out of his eyes.

I continued, "Whatever crazy-ass supplements you had him on turned him into a terrifying experiment gone wrong. His powers were incredible though, so bonus points there."

"I see." Florence sipped her tea and set it aside. "I appreciate that you think my supplements have the capability to make a person's inherent magical abilities that of a demigod, but no, that wasn't because of ReNew. Those were the artifacts Omar kept at his home."

"The ones he had for years that just suddenly caused him to sprout spikes out of his face?" I couldn't control the snicker that bubbled out of me at her statement. "Can we pretend to still respect each other for a second here? I'm not wearing a wire, I'm not a snitch. You don't have to lie. I kill people for a living, so you don't need to dance around morality for me. Offer is still on the table to talk about taking out Marthas, by the way."

"And you hunt necromancers." She topped her tea off quietly. "That's why I wanted to chat with you."

"We can talk about that after you admit you fucked with Omar's jinn powers and turned him into a monster," I pressed. "I'm not letting that go. That crap was intense, and I want to know how you did it."

"Dallas, if I had the ability to enhance people's biological magic to that degree, don't you think I would have monetized it by now?" She lifted a brow. "I could sell that to any politician or member of royalty across the world and be the richest woman on the planet. My supplements are the best in the world, but they can't do that."

"Then why the fuck was Omar on your pretentious island hiding out in your VIP beach condo? Why were you *hiding* him?"

I watched as her smile returned, calm and tranquil like a lion. Her easy posture and relaxed tone let me know that she didn't regard me as a threat by any means, and that I was more entertaining than anything.

"Because Omar very publicly did business with me and was a loyal customer," she said. "He was a PR nightmare in his current state. When I saw how far gone he was, I hid him on my island to help try and reverse it. I was in the process of obtaining power of attorney to get his artifacts removed."

Hei materialized at my side, handing me a very official-looking envelope stuffed with papers. I flipped over the documents inside, the legal jargon made my head hurt, but it looked solid enough. Florence had pushed for seizure of Omar's assets, claiming he was mentally unwell after the disappearance of his fiancé, and that she needed to take control of his estate.

It was a black and white stack of evidence of how ruthless she was, and how powerful her money made her.

"Saints." I flipped through the documents, before passing them to Zane. "You took everything he had."

She sipped her tea.

"His death certificate says nothing about his eyes," Zane pointed out. "Nothing is mentioned about it."

"Of course not." Florence almost sounded offended. "That would raise questions. I had it removed."

"Questions about your supplements," I supplied.

"Yes," she agreed. "People would assume I could reproduce that level of magical ability, and I can't. Not yet."

"There it is," I said with a flare of triumph. "I knew you were ramping up to something evil. No one has a suite like this over a moonlit garden and doesn't have evil shit planned."

Florence took a long, quiet breath.

"I think we misunderstand each other, Dallas Wilde."

"Nah, I think I got you figured out, Florence Pierce," I countered. "You are a self-righteous billionaire who peddles bullshit that's not regulated by the government because you have enough money to cheat the system. You manufacture cheap placebos at best, and literal god juice at worst, then sling it out there to make yourself untouchably rich. Omar was a mistake that almost cost you too much, and now you want us to…what? Tie up loose ends? How close am I getting?"

The way Florence Pierce smiled at me after I spoke my mind would have been bone chilling if I knew what was about to follow.

"I am a billionaire, and you're a necromancer. I think we can work together."

"What the hell makes you think I'm a necromancer? Maybe Zane's just really pale."

Florence actually looked offended. "Did you think Hei couldn't tell that Omar was very dead when you piloted him off the island? Not to mention the fact that you radiate death magic like a beacon, Mr. Wilde, as does your vampire. Let's respect each other enough to skip past the very obvious lies."

"Alright. Fine. I might dabble in necromancy sometimes, and this guy follows me around." I shrugged, ignoring the blaring warning horns going off in my mind. "So what?"

"I want to hire you."

"Pass," I practically interrupted her. "If you wanna hire me to kill Marthas, I'm all ears. Anything else, you can choke on it."

"Allow me to change your mind," she insisted.

I gestured for her to go ahead as I leaned back in the offensively comfortable chair, crossing my arms over my chest.

"You're a ghost, you know," she said softly. "After you came to the island and handled Omar for me, I looked into who you were. I wanted to know who this person was that somehow convinced Sias Llon'nai to follow him, and had a vampire tagging along."

Zane didn't speak, just watched her with his normal glare of annoyed boredom.

She continued.

"Dallas Wilde doesn't exist. There is no record of you anywhere I could find. No birth certificate, no fingerprints." More tea was added to her cup, her ponytail swaying as she shook her head. "It's impressive, because there's always a trace. There's always something that isn't fully scrubbed when someone tries to hide, but that's not the case with you. Somehow, you are here, and no one else in the world knows who you are."

"I am pretty awesome," I agreed. "Fail to see your point though."

"You might be a ghost, but your friends aren't." Florence crossed one long leg over the other, one ugly shoe suspended. "If I hire you, I could help fund your landlord's failing business. I assume you know the bank is about to seize your apartment and his antique shop."

My heart punched itself at the mention of poor Barns, but I bit my tongue.

"You and Sias are fairly close, right?" she added once I didn't take the Barnaby bait.

"Sias doesn't do business with you," I snapped. "Especially not after the shit on the island."

"Not with me," she agreed. "But with some mutual acquaintances. I could nudge various associates of mine to increase their real estate assets, and encourage them to look to Llon'nai for various business dealings." She smiled again, seeming almost sweet. "He could have you to thank for countless new business ventures."

I wasn't naïve to think this offer wasn't a double-edge sword. She was promising riches and opportunities, but she was also threatening the reverse. Florence Pierce had influence, power, and the ability to change lives in beautiful as well as terrifying ways.

She could make Sias richer, or cripple him.

She could save Barnaby, or take everything away.

And she put that burden directly on my shoulders.

The brilliant, evil, impressive bitch.

I had to relax my jaw so I didn't bite through my tongue.

"I'm listening."

Hei appeared again, handing me a leather book that weighed enough to be used as a deadly weapon. Stuck in the middle was a collection of printed papers in a language I didn't recognize.

Embossed on the worn, leather cover was a golden title, and a toothy, grinning skull.

"I was really hoping you weren't about to ask me about necromancy shit," I sighed. "But I have a feeling a thick-ass book called 'Ancient Death Rituals and Practices' is exactly the kind of thing that precedes necromancy shit."

"I need to hire you to look into finding a very specific burial site," she explained, without acknowledging the necromancy shit accusation. "The book and the printed information is all that is known about it."

"You want me to go grave robbing? You know you can hire historians and archaeologists to do this, right? Hell, you can probably just wrangle up some jerks from the Swallows who will do it for some Dust and a hamburger. Why the fuck do you need me?"

"Because everyone else has failed," she explained calmly. "I need a necromancer for this job, because it's a necromancy item I'm after."

"She wants you to find the Tomb of the Necromantic Council," Zane spoke up for the first time, sounding the same level of irritated he usually directed my way. I was a little offended. "She's trying to find the Goddess's key."

"The what?" I cringed. "Is that a euphemism?"

Zane sliced his fake brown eyes at me, the annoyance burning behind the contacts.

"I know we're supposed to be a united front right now, hunter, but if you make a vagina joke about my Goddess, I will slap you out of your seat."

"So, it's a literal key then." I pivoted, because I believed him. "To what? And is it real?"

"It is real," Florence chimed in. "The key is the missing artifact I need."

"Artifact of a Death Goddess," I said slowly. "You want me to find you a powerful Death Goddess artifact? Are you fucking insane?"

"I want you to help me find a piece of magical history that can slow down or even stop death," Florence said, the ease of her voice hardening into a steely resolve. "The key to defeating death and unlocking immortality."

"I am not going to help you find a way to obtain the key to unlocking death, you impossibly insane jackass." I handed the book over to Zane as he reached for it. "That's so many red flags, Florence. You have to hear how crazy you sound right now. The last time a human had that kind of power, they unleashed an undead army and almost took out St. Athesall. We have a fucking museum about it!"

"I don't want to create vampires and take over a city." She laced her fingers together and placed them over her bent knee. "I can't make money off of a horde of undead. I want to harness the ability to delay death, to push back the effects of illness and to prolong life so I can market it and sell it."

"That is incredibly fucked up," I told her.

"It's brilliant."

I looked at Zane after he spoke, dumbfounded.

"You agree with her?"

"No," he corrected, flipping through the pages of the book. "It's evil to hold that kind of power behind a paywall. Absolutely soulless and horrible, but it would make her the most powerful person in the world without having to lift a finger."

"There's more to necromancy than conquering vampires and raising the dead, Dallas. The key will help unlock all of its potential." Florence rubbed some lotion onto her hands as Hei presented me with yet another envelope, this one something I was more familiar with receiving. As this was presented to me, Florence added, "To cover your expenses for the trip."

"I haven't agreed to anything."

"Of course you have." She smiled, which was starting to have a Pavlovian effect of making me want to throw something. "That will cover whatever supplies you need for the trip, and I will have transportation arranged."

"I can handle my own transportation." I snatched the envelope from Hei and stood. "For the record, Florence, don't ever threaten Barnaby or Sias in front of me again."

Florence didn't bother to stand, instead opting to sip more of her tea.

We left Florence's office without another word, both of us silent as we made a slow escape out of the grand gala. Zane kept the thick tome under his arm, jaw bunching with a rage he was failing to hide.

"We can't let her get that key, hunter," Zane bit through his teeth. "She's spitting in the face of everything Sandros stood for. She'll dangle the promise of immortality in front of the elite so she can buy another couple summer homes."

"She'll buy a few summer planets with the money she'd be pulling in," I mumbled.

Zane caught me by the arm as we got onto the street, far enough away from the party to not turn any heads.

"We *cannot* let her do this. Tell me we're not going to actually get her what she wants."

He was angry. Deeply angry. I didn't have to read his emotions to know that what she was proposing churned in his gut like molten coals of resentment. Behind the contacts I knew his red eyes were boiling hot, and he was ready to rip out her heart over all of this.

Florence Pierce had us backed into a corner with knives to our throats, and I sure as hell wasn't going to stand for it.

She was about to find out just how I reacted to sharp things near my throat.

"Oh, we're getting that key, Zane," I promised, my rage igniting a white-hot clarity. "We'll play her game, go dig up whatever the hell she wants us to. Then, when we have it in our grubby little hands, we're going to snap the damn thing in half, and I'm going to stab her with it."

CHAPTER
THIRTEEN

ONE OF THE things I loved most about living in a massive city like St. Athesall, was that no one batted an eye when you did weird things on the train. A couple years back, I saw a dance competition brought on by complete strangers vibing with each other's music. Another time I watched a mime break up with his girlfriend, who was also a mime.

This city was a constant source of wonderful fever dreams, especially on the Westside B line.

Zane sat next to me, the car swaying with the steady momentum of the tracks, flipping through a massive tome of ancient burial practices. We looked like we were on our way to a very expensive funeral, and Zane had only managed to get one of his contacts out. Each time he looked at me he looked haunted, so I busied myself with flipping through the provided intel and research that had been stuck inside the book.

"According to this," I told my heterochromatic vampire, "the cemetery has been excavated several times and they haven't found anything that links it to the council. Why do they think these jerks were buried here to begin with?"

"The Silent Steps have been historically notorious for thousands of years, hunter. It's the only place on the planet that still has a holy shrine to the Goddess on its grounds. All the other ones have been removed after the vampire outbreaks." Zane set the brick of paper in my lap and tapped a page, a black and white picture of the shrine in question staring up at me. "It's sacred to vampires and necromancers."

The Goddess's features were mostly worn away from weathering, the limestone bright against the gnarled branches of a tree that predated the damn dinosaurs. Her headdress was a crown of bones tangled in the braids of her hair, one arm outstretched to command her acolytes while the other stopped just below the elbow.

Her face was a stone shadow of what it once was, only a soft whisper of a mouth left after thousands of years of standing vigil over the sleeping dead.

"And apparently just filled with very dead bodies that don't move around." I offered him the paper I was reading, which was about as dry as the text he flopped into my lap. "They've dug up every inch of the place they were allowed to and only hit coffins and bedrock. They even checked under your Goddess's feet and found nothing."

"Not nothing." Zane flipped to a page in the book and shuffled some papers, bringing a picture of a chipped mural to the front. "This was inside one of the mausoleums from their last excavation thirty years ago."

"The guy had himself painted in front of the council inside of this grave? Yeesh."

"It shows him standing in front of the council within the cemetery." Zane pointed at something in the picture and added. "He's chanting a prayer they couldn't translate. It's a dead tongue from an old human civilization that was deeply isolated and devout to the Goddess. This is our lead."

"You speak it?" I lifted an eyebrow. "You know what he's saying?"

"No." He slipped the paper back into place and shut the book. "But we know someone who would."

"We do?" I stood as the train came to a sliding stop, the doors hissing open to allow the parade of feet to exit. "Who do we know that speaks old, creepy human dialect?"

"Barnaby." Zane said this like it was obvious, weaving through the masses who struggled to board. I followed, trotting after him to not get left behind.

"What the hell makes you think Barns knows this language? This is death magic shit, it has nothing to do with sex, fertility or weird genital stuff."

"Every culture has a fertility ritual, even the creepy human ones." The vampire tucked the book under his arm and escaped the train station, the cold wind slapping us in the face for sport. "Plus, he has a ton of books on ancient languages. I rearranged them a few nights ago."

"Yeah," I sucked in air through my teeth. "He might not help us because of that."

"I'm hoping the mystery of decoding the language will help smooth that over." He cut his mismatched eyes in my direction. "Also, that wasn't my fault."

"I'll accept half the blame there."

"Half?!"

"You know I take drugs all the time, you should have asked me," I shot back. "You've met me before."

"Unbelievable."

"I know I am." I raked my hair back, feeling very confident that I won that exchange.

Barnaby's shop was closed by the time we made it home, the lights turned off with a polite sign in the door that let prospective customers know they could return promptly at nine AM the next morning. Behind the building near the alleyway was Barnaby's apartment door, which we were given orders to use instead of barging through the front like before.

Somehow we got lucky that the fussy incubus wasn't already in his grandpa-style pajamas when he answered our summons, but he did frown at us like we were noisy kids disturbing his soap operas.

"It's late," Barnaby announced in lieu of a greeting.

"Hey, Barns. Wanna help us with some cool history shit?" I asked.

Zane presented the book to him. "We're trying to find information about a lost tomb. There's an ancient language we wanted to ask you about."

Barnaby eyed us with a confusing mixture of skepticism and intrigue, which made him seem like he was about to sneeze insults at us.

"Why?"

"Because you're the smartest incubus we know." I smiled my winning, million-dollar grin at him, and Barnaby started to shut the door. "And Zane will help reorganize the store if you help!"

The door hesitated, and Barnaby narrowed his inky black eyes.

"Even the stone sex position display?"

Zane inhaled and shut his eyes. "Sure."

With a reluctant grunt, Barnaby held the door and waved us inside.

While Barnaby's store was a dusty museum of antique dicks and elegantly curated vulvas, his home was ancient in a completely boring way. The fixtures were decades out of style but well maintained, fresh paint applied to the lumpy wooden baseboards and warped windowsills The kitchen was clean and tidy, with one mug resting upside down near a kettle that was sitting on the stove.

The small apartment was bigger than mine in that it had a dedicated space for a bedroom, and a carved-out area that served as his personal library near a window. A clock ticked loudly near the dining room table, which had one table setting and a candle holder that looked like a swan.

"I'm shocked you don't have more fertility stuff in your apartment." I peered over the spines of his books, which ranged from history texts to fantasy novels. "I don't see a single dick on anything here."

"Do you have swords on everything you own?" Barnaby quipped. "Some of us have multiple passions, you know. I love my work, but I don't want to be surrounded by it constantly. I'm allowed to adore other things."

"Like dragons apparently." I plucked a book from his shelf. "Look at you being all multidimensional."

"That's signed. If you so much as crack the spine I'll evict you." Barnaby got his kettle going, digging deep in his cabinet for another teacup. "What is it that you're looking into anyway?"

"Creepy human death stuff," I answered before Zane could, so I got a sharp look.

"Ancient text in a two-thousand-year-old crypt," Zane added a bit more context, and displayed the text and papers across Barnaby's table. "We were hoping you know the language."

Barnaby loosened the cuffs of his shirt and rolled them to his elbows, readying himself for the challenge. His short, black hair wasn't as lacquered this late into the evening, so a few strands had emancipated themselves to hang across his forehead. His ram-style horns were well maintained but not dipped in any metal accents, which gave him a reserved look compared to his more modern kin. Because of his species, Barns was a handsome guy, with sharp features and a narrow frame that somehow looked stylish in his ridiculously old-fashioned attire.

It was only because he didn't feed on sex energy each day that kept him from exuding the natural glow of a sex demon in his prime. Barnaby always looked a little tired, and always seemed a little irritated.

When he was reading over old text, or showing off a new piece to add to his collection, I would see the glow. I saw it now as he poured over the mural like the great puzzle it was.

"Zane, since you're so familiar with my book collection, could you run into the store and grab the third volume of *Classic Human Ancestry and Native Languages*, please?" Barns extracted his keys from his pocket and handed them to the vampire. Before Zane could take them, he added a stabbing, "Don't touch anything else."

"Do I need to apologize again for the books, Barnaby?" Zane lifted both eyebrows.

"I suppose not."

Neither one of us were convinced, but Zane left without another word.

After Zane was away on his errand, I attended the teapot that started to whistle.

"You know that wasn't his fault, right?"

"Oh, I'm very aware it was yours." Barnaby licked his finger and flipped a page. "I was curious if you'd own up to it or not."

"Don't be a dick, Barns."

"Who is helping whom in this situation, Dallas Wilde?" He leaned on one leg to sass me properly. "Because I can go back to my night and leave you to decipher this on your own."

"You're in a mood tonight." When Barnaby moved to shut the book I pivoted, "I know I haven't been doing a great job at getting you intimacy crystals. I know you're hungry. Sias and I had a…it's complicated. Another thing that's my fault, I guess."

Barnaby halted slamming shut the massive death ritual tome, opting to leave it open on the table.

"Oh." He scanned the text, lowering his sass levels by taking the weight off one leg. "I'm sorry to hear that."

"I'll see what I can do, okay? I'm sure I can stock up if I could just get a night to myself." I rubbed at my eyes, exhausted by the idea of trying to be charming and tumbling into bed with some stranger. Normally that prospect would be just what the doctor ordered.

For some reason, it wasn't the pill I wanted to swallow.

My heart ached.

I felt lonely.

Hell, I would have taken another hug from the vampire if it was offered, which sat in a weirdly comfortable spot in the middle of my chest. I touched the emotional blocker to make sure it was still on, quietly embarrassed.

"I can get crystals from other sources, you know." Barnaby leaned his palms on the table and hovered over the pages.

"Aren't they crazy expensive?"

"I can manage." He tossed a glance my way. "Do you want to talk about it?"

"You do not want to talk about my sex life," I said around a laugh.

"Not your sex life," he snapped, softening his tone as he continued. "I'm an incubus. Maybe I can help navigate whatever it was that…caused the 'complication.'"

My chest went from feeling like a pit of loneliness to a fragile little nest of comfort: gentle and finite, but more than I'd had in a very long time.

"It's not an incubus thing," I said after the lump in my throat dissolved. "But thanks, Barns."

Barnaby's lips thinned as he pursed them, giving a silent nod that the topic would be dropped per my request.

Zane reemerged from his fetch quest with the book requested, placing it on the table for Barnaby to reference with his shop key on top.

"I locked up," he said before Barns could ask.

"I'm relatively sure this language is a specific dialect of an isolated human culture that was absorbed by the takeover of the jinn empire a thousand years ago," Barnaby told us as he got busy thumbing through the newly arrived book. "The roots of which run very deep within the death magic cult. Actually, it's very interesting. The jinn empire was almost overturned by the power of the uprising necromancers but it ultimately lost due to in-fighting and corruption."

"Sounds like us," I supplied.

"If humans could just stop fighting each other, your species would be a force to be reckoned with, you know." Barnaby sighed. "A shame, really. You have truly eclectic fertility rituals. Some of my favorites, actually."

"That's not going to happen. We're too good at it."

"You think this person was involved in the Death Goddess worship?" Zane pulled us back to the matter at hand. "I know this language is tied to the old text. My past master owned some original copies."

"I have no doubt this is a passage meant to guide fellow Death Goddess worshipers to her council." Barnaby tossed the new book open to a section detailing the language and its roots, smoothing out a page. "They have very similar guides for the life deity, before the split when the Saint divided the religion. Those who follow the original life deity's text, like this group, believed that they could offer life essence to bless a womb before conception."

"Life essence?" I asked, worried about the answer. "You're going to say something gross, aren't you?"

"Blood, Dallas." Barnaby cut me a stern look. "Blood is the cornerstone of this civilization's rituals. Bloodletting was used in fertility ceremonies, death passages, the changing of seasons…it was the holy essence that brought life and death."

"Yep. Gross."

"I strongly disagree," said the vampire.

"This mural is talking about bringing the essence to the gate, or door, which is also sometimes meant to be the body. Similar to the fertility ritual." Barnaby's eyes bounced between the tomes, a crease etched between his brows. "There's something specific I can't translate though. This word here, it's giving the blood offering a property. It's a qualifier of some sort."

"How do you know?" Zane leaned over the text to see what Barnaby was talking about. "What makes you think it's meant to signify the blood type?"

Barnaby went to his bookshelf and pulled a volume from his personal collection, which was surprisingly not about dragons. He flipped through the pages and placed it down near the black book of death. In the pages of the new addition to the table was another picture of an old mural, strikingly similar to the one painted on the inside of the mausoleum.

Instead of a figure walking toward a realm of shadows and skulls, it was a person with a child in their belly, offering their palm to the holy beacon of life while it dripped crimson tears.

"This person is asking for a healthy birth, and is offering birthing blood. See this symbol? This makes the blood specifically 'birthing.' Usually given by whoever would carry the child," Barnaby explained. "They have this all over their fertility rituals. But the symbol in the cemetery isn't something I've seen before."

"Could it be death'?" I offered. "Maybe he's offering his corpse blood for a chance to talk to the Goddess?"

"The Goddess doesn't bargain with the dead," Zane spoke on behalf of his deity. "If he was already gone, he'd be in the void. This would need to be before his passing, while he was still alive."

"Something about his blood was special," Barnaby confirmed. "He offered it to the Goddess and it opened a passageway to a room with five skulls."

"The council." Zane nodded to the painting. "The five necromantic voices of the Goddess, one for each stage of a body's journey of returning to its primal elements while the soul slips further into the void."

"Ambitious goal," Barnaby mused. "Why would someone want to speak with the council?"

Zane explained, "They speak for the Goddess. A regular person would be able to ask about death and commune with lost souls. A necromancer could ask for blessings, guidance and power."

While Barnaby and Zane chatted about the council, I flipped through the pages of the tome that discussed the Silent Steps. From the few dated, grainy pictures of the graves, I noticed the mixture of sizes, shapes and wealth that went into some of the resting sites. A few understated headstones leaned with the weight of time, next door to mansions of carved elegance topped with mourning skulls. This cemetery was a smattering of diverse classes and stations, all human, all devoted to knowing where they were going beyond the grave.

It was beautiful in its macabre majesty, a statement to what humans were capable of before we took things too far. Had it just been a religion of preparing for death, it would be a peaceful art gallery of death rites and gravestones. Instead, it was a reminder that at one point, we made dying our sole personality trait and had tried to impose it on the rest of the world with black magic and void goddesses.

While the Silent Steps were still around, countless other human resting places had to be torn down in fear that the cult would try to use their corpses as tools of destruction. This was the last stand of the Death Goddess's garden, and all the thorns had been trimmed back centuries ago. Now it was just a maze of stone no one could navigate, its secrets lost or buried deep.

And that got me thinking.

"When was this mausoleum built?"

"According to the book, about four hundred years ago." Zane flipped the page back and pointed at the date.

"Well past when the cult was erased and the Goddess's shrines started getting torn down?" I lifted my gaze to see Zane nod. "Did they find a body in there?"

"They did."

"Barns, you said the language for 'gate' or 'door' is often also used as 'body,' right?"

"Yes?" Barnaby's eyebrow crease deepened. "And?"

I saw the moment Zane landed on the same conclusion as I had, his face melting from deep thought to dawning understanding.

"If the body is well preserved," he said. "It could work."

"What could work?" Barnaby was still catching up.

"The archeologists that excavated this place weren't thinking like necromancers, Barns. They were looking for a literal door to the council, but like all treasures, you need a guide." I tapped on the picture of the mausoleum. "We gotta talk to him."

"Talk to…oh. *Oh.*" His eyes widened like surprised inkwells. "You mean…reanimate his corpse?"

"Just for a few questions."

"That is horribly sacrilegious and offensive to modern sensibilities but deeply fascinating." Barnaby rubbed at his chin like the fellow detective he was.

"It's the best lead we have, so we're going with it." I pulled out my phone and tapped in the address of the cemetery, watching as the GPS app muddled over the best route for us to take. "It'll take two days to get there if we leave tomorrow morning."

"This place is locked down. They don't let visitors in." Zane shut the book gently. "We'll need to go at night to keep our profile low."

"Hey, if we're going to go break into a cemetery to talk to a dead guy, why not go full cliché?" I turned to Barnaby. "Thanks, Barns. We wouldn't have figured this out without you."

He hummed a non-committal response, replacing the book from his shelf before scooping up the other one from his collection. Placing the shop key on top, he presented it to Zane, who cocked a brow.

"Are you asking me to take this *back* to the store now?"

"I'm not asking," Barnaby corrected. "I trust you know the *correct* place it goes, yes?"

Zane did not appreciate being bossed around by an annoyed incubus, but he really didn't like me grinning at him like the whipped servant boy he was. Somehow, I was the one who got punched in the arm and not Barnaby, even though I hadn't been the one commanding him to do things.

I waited until Zane left before rubbing my arm. Damn vampire had sharp knuckles.

"Leave this book tonight, I'll go over it for any more clues to your theory," Barnaby told me, drumming his fingers over the black book.

"It's past your bedtime as it is," I teased him. "It's almost ten PM!"

"Some of us prefer to get a full night's rest, Wilde. I don't run off of idiocy and unhealthy habits like you do. The store is closed tomorrow so I have time to stay up tonight anyway."

My stomach tightened at the mention of his store being closed, though I knew he didn't mean permanently. Not yet, anyway.

"Yeah, speaking of that." I extracted the envelope Florence had given me, which was thick with bills intended to fund our trip. Barnaby eyed it as I tossed it down onto the table.

"What this?"

"Rent, plus a little extra for pain and suffering."

The envelope was picked over, the bills inside counted by running his thumb over them. Whatever appreciation or relief I had been expecting to see on his face was painfully absent, a mounting rage boiling in the way his jaw ground.

"Zane told you."

"He mentioned it in his intoxicated ramblings." I felt the urge to shift my weight on my feet, nerves crawling up the lining of my stomach. "Why didn't you say something to me about it?"

"Because it's none of your business."

"Barns—"

"Don't you *dare* pity me, Dallas Wilde. Not you." Barnaby wheeled on me with fire and pain, glass coating his stony glare. "I don't want it, and I don't need it."

"I don't pity you," I tried to explain, but it just added fuel to the fire.

"When have you ever given someone money out of the goodness of your heart?" he challenged.

"Probably once before, I don't know." I shrugged. "I can do nice shit sometimes!"

Barnaby plucked a few bills from the envelope and tossed the rest back onto the table like the thing was made of fire.

"I'll take rent, but the rest can be thrown out of the window for all I care." Barnaby shoved the money into his pocket and inhaled sharply through his nose. "It's not your job to try and come in like a white knight, Dallas. It's an insult to both of us."

I showed my palms in surrender, taking the envelope so the money didn't get thrown out of any windows.

"We're leaving early tomorrow after I get us a car. Let me know if you find anything else helpful in the book."

"Fine," he tossed over his shoulder as he worked on cleaning out the two used teacups. "You can see yourself out."

I left feeling terrible and with no idea how to fix it. A part of me thought about slipping the money under the door or finding a way to smuggle it into his pocket, but I knew it would end up back at my place once he found it. I had underestimated his pride, and how sensitive he was to feeling helpless.

That was something I could empathize with, even if I would have personally taken the cash.

I knew what it was like to feel helpless and see the pity in someone's eyes. I wouldn't wish that on anyone, especially not Barns.

Zane was on his way back to drop the key off, and I intercepted with a shake of my head.

"Drop it off in the morning."

"Alright." Zane pocketed the key, sliding a glance my way as we made our way around to the other side of the building where my apartment stairs were. "Something happen?"

"I tried to give him money for his store."

He inhaled through his teeth. "Bad move, hunter."

"No shit. You think he'd take the money from you?"

"Not a chance."

"I figured." I climbed the stairs with a sense of dread, worried that soon it would be the last time.

Twig was howling for attention when we made our way inside, only muting when she was scooped up by her undead servant and promised treats. Kevin, who was a much quieter diva, judged me by my lack of providing bloodworms for him.

Even after I obeyed and gave the little shit what he wanted, I got a side-eye in return. I loved him so much.

I tugged my tux shirt loose around the collar and tossed the ruined jacket onto my bed, battling with myself on whether or not I wanted to commit to a shower. My mind was torn in too many directions, each impending-doom situation lacing hooks into my concentration.

What the hell was I going to do about Florence?

How was I going to find the key?

What was going to happen with Barnaby's store?

How was I going to mend the rift between me and Sias?

Was I going to see Austin again?

Why was there a note in the vampire den? Did Austin do that?

I really wasn't up for a family reunion. The thought of that tied my intestines in knots. What the hell would they think of me now, after all this time?

"Dallas."

Zane's voice cut through the noise, sounding a bit firmer than usual. I blinked at him and had to do it twice, because I was distracted by his appearance.

Yet another thing to rip at my mind and destroy my already fragile concentration.

Zane.

Zane had gotten a little more complicated lately, and I desperately wanted something to stay simple. He stood watching me with his muddled look of annoyance and concern, both contacts finally out of his eyes. Blood red and probing, his gaze was starting to be a grounding rod to all the bullshit surrounding me.

What wasn't helping my overloaded brain, or my internal battle of conflicting morals, wants and ambitions, was this fucking vampire and how he wore his suit.

Listen, I know. I *know*. He's a vampire, he's technically undead, and he's a creature of black magic manifested by death worshipers to do their bidding—which often meant destroying the lives of mortals and torturing others. I had some personal past with Thralls in particular, so this made the situation very confusing for me.

But Zane wearing a tuxedo, shirt unbuttoned and untucked, hair a little messy from the wind with a scowl on his face, really sent me on a ride.

Listen.

It was kinda hot.

Which really, truly, fucked with my world view.

"What?" I felt my neck start to burn and I touched the emotional blocker around my neck in a panicked state, only breathing when I felt it was still "on."

He did not need to know my moment of insanity, and I begged the Saint that he didn't notice I was eyeing his chest a little too long.

Don't judge me. His chest hair was growing back after getting some blood, which made me remember the blood thing and—yeah.

Yeah.

"I asked you if you're going to take a shower," he said. "You were staring off like you didn't hear me."

"Yeah. I mean…no." I rubbed at the fuzziness in my eyes. "If you want to shower, go for it. I have a lot on my mind."

"You want to talk about it?" he offered.

It was tempting, because if anyone was going to help me unpack at least some of the things on my list, it would be the guy who'd been present through the bulk of it.

But then he had to rake his fingers through his hair and rub at his neck, which made his chest move, and his shirt slide aside so I could see the trail of hair under his navel and I had to shut it all down.

"Nope." I sat on my bed and rubbed my temples to massage away my very bad, dirty and gross thoughts of a vampire and his pubic hair. "I want to somehow get to sleep and forget about this shitty day."

"Don't take anything strong. I want an early start tomorrow," he scolded before stepping into the bathroom.

"Yeah, yeah." I only opened my eyes after I heard the curtain to the bathroom get pulled and the shower turn on. With Zane safely out of view, I tore my nice, but no longer returnable, tux outfit off and tossed it over a chair. My boxers weren't exactly hiding the fact that my body was more awake than I wanted, so I crawled under the blankets before Kevin or the vampire could judge me.

I needed to get my head on straight. I needed to focus on the extremely terrifying situations at hand, and I knew for a fact if I tried to "handle" anything in that moment my mind was going to wander into territories I did not want. So instead of wrangling the beast, I tried to distract myself by searching the best routes to the Silent Steps for our trip tomorrow.

My phone pinged, a message waiting for me to help destroy any heat that had been building in my body.

An arrow through my heart. A precision cut that left me quietly bleeding.

Sias simply messaged, *"We should talk."*

I didn't think my heart could take anymore, but it kept surprising me.

Instead of calling him, messaging back or handling it with any grace, I just shoved my head under my pillow and wrapped it around my skull.

I didn't want Kevin to see me cry.

"THIS IS SURPRISINGLY PRACTICAL."

Zane descended the steps of the apartment with his duffel, apparently surprised I was able to get a car for the trip. The sedan wasn't anything remarkable, but it was reliable, low profile and had plates on it that made the whole thing seem on the up and up.

Since I wasn't exactly someone with a government presence in any sort of positive way, it made renting a car legally impossible. Instead, I went to Criminals R' Us and bought a reasonably priced, stolen but seemingly legal, vehicle for our needs. This particular model was a ten-year-old four-door with working heat, working wheels and no visible reason for any officer to pull us over.

It was perfect.

"I can be a practical man when the need arises," I tossed back at the vampire. "We have a two-day drive ahead and we have to pass through some rural areas. I don't need bored cops chasing us down for a cracked windshield."

"I half expected a sports car with more muscle than trunk space." Zane tossed his duffel into the open trunk.

"That's not what we need for a trip like this."

"Uh-huh. They just didn't have any, did they?" I flipped him off as an answer, so he added, "That's what I thought."

"Keep it up, and you're riding in the trunk."

"I doubt he'd have room," Barnaby announced as he strolled over, dressed for the day in an honest-to-God sweater vest and tie, looking like he was about to teach middle grade English. The man's sense of fashion, somehow being both outdated and posh, wasn't the most out of place thing about him. That was the off-white and beige suitcase he was carrying.

"Uh," I managed just as he tossed his suitcase into the trunk. "What do you think you're doing?"

"That's as light as I can pack."

"That's great." I rounded the car and pulled the suitcase back out. "But you're not going with us."

"Of course I am."

"No, you're not." I held the suitcase out to him. "I asked you to check the book, not tag along."

"You need me, Dallas. I can translate the mural. I stayed up last night figuring it out."

"You're not going with us to a necromancer cemetery, Barnaby." I set the suitcase on the ground when he refused to take it. "There's guaranteed bad shit there. We're going to go poke around in a tomb with depictions of a necromantic council on it. That's literally a huge warning sign!"

"Good thing you know your way around necromancers then." Barnaby lifted his expression like he was explaining something very obvious to me and picked his suitcase back up. "Unless of course you've been *exaggerating* your skills all this time."

"Go to hell, Zane," I told the vampire as he snickered. "Barns, the answer is no."

"I disagree."

"I don't give a shit." I blocked him from putting his suitcase back into the trunk. "You're a liability."

"I'm an asset, Dallas Wilde," he countered with all the confidence only he could muster in this situation. "You need someone who speaks the language, who knows the culture and can guide you to the location of where this mausoleum is." Barnaby moved his suitcase behind him when I tried to grab for it. "If you want the information, you have to bring me along."

"Barns, I don't want to have to pin you down, but I will."

"If you try, I will blow my rape whistle. I swear to the Gods."

As I weighed my options of how I was going to wrangle the book from Barnaby without him blasting an alert that I was trying to assault him—all the while, mind you, my fucking vampire bodyguard was just laughing and *not helping*—an additional pain in the ass appeared out of nowhere.

"Wilde." My voice resounded with the boisterous authority of an officer.

"Goddamnit," I sighed as I turned to try and appease whoever it was that I had now upset, sighing with almost relief to see the only two Demon Human Alliance and Protection officers that weren't actively trying to arrest me for something. Preston Cheslock, human brick with a permanent scowl, and his nicer, jinn boyfriend / officer partner, Seyyid Ahmed, were sauntering over with an air of seriousness I didn't care for.

I glanced to Zane, who they hadn't officially met yet beyond him trying to super murder us a few months back, and motioned for him to get lost. Thankfully Zane didn't feel the urge to argue or complicate things, so he vanished back up the stairs before they could piece together who he was.

"Bad timing, guys," I told the pair. "I'm on my way out of town. Can this wait?"

"This is serious, Wilde," Preston pressed. "There's some weird shit going on and we need to talk to you about it."

"You getting weird vampire urges again?" I asked Seyyid. "Because I don't give refunds."

"No," Seyyid said, sounding a bit offended. "We found some vampires in the city recently. That's why we asked you to contact us."

"When?"

"Two weeks ago." Preston stepped back into the conversation. "Another DHAP officer came across them."

"He get bit?" I asked, to which both of them shook their heads. "They get away?" More head shakes. "Then what's the problem? Sounds like the DHAP force did their job, protected the human and demon population of St. Athesall and saved the day. Where do I fit into this?"

"It's not just that vampires were spotted in the city, Dallas. It's how the officer described one of them." Seyyid's expression grew concerned, his silver eyes bright under his dark brows. "He said one was a jinn that had green eyes and spoke to him, which we know is a messenger vampire, but that's not what freaked us out. He said it *compelled* him, like it could still harness its jinn abilities after turning."

"When someone is turned into a vampire, any of their natural magic is gone," I explained. "Necromancers can't puppet a messenger vampire to use any magic that is biologically tied to the body. That part of them dies when they're a vampire."

Seyyid's face didn't relax, his posture still stiff with concern. "He said the vampire was able to nudge him with jinn powers, made him hesitate before he could fire his shot."

"He was scared," I said. "You guys don't face vampires, and a lot of people think they're extinct."

"Dallas—"

"What you're describing is impossible, Seyyid," I added before he could continue. "Trust me. There is no way a vampire of any level can use demon abilities. Even the top-tier, super badass necromancers of yore couldn't turn vampires into anything other than mindless sets of teeth. Otherwise, I would know about it." I looked between the two officers, who exchanged looks of unsatisfied reluctance. "You sure your guy didn't get bit? All the vampires were taken out?"

"He's fine," Preston said. "He was able to throw the two into the sunlight after putting some rounds into them. Seyyid and I inspected him for bites ourselves."

"He's a seasoned officer, Dallas. He's not easily shaken," Seyyid added softly. "If he said he felt compelled or persuaded, I believe him."

"I promise you both, vampires cannot use magic. Full stop. I've been doing this for a long time, gone toe-to-toe with some gnarly vampires and necromancers. Zero demon magic involved, hand to the Saint." I put my hand over my heart.

"I told you he'd be useless," Preston grumbled, walking off like I was somehow being the asshole in this situation.

"What the hell is his deal?" I asked the more sensible of the two.

"He's worried," Seyyid explained. "We both are. Dallas, I believe you know what you're talking about. You're the expert. But this…doesn't sit right with me. I can feel it. Something is wrong about all of this."

"I don't know what to tell you, Seyyid."

The jinn took a long breath, watching his partner who was brooding near the street before aiming his silver eyes at me again.

"If we call again, please answer. I hope we don't need to."

"Life's been a little hectic lately." And because I was a softy and a sucker I lamented, "I will. Go cheer up your bulldog."

Seyyid gave me a friendly clap on the arm and went to go console his boyfriend, leaving me with an extra burden and a goddamn Barnaby strapped in my car. The prickly priss sat in the back seat with the seat belt fastened, a look of accomplished arrogance smeared over his pinched features.

I leaned down to glare at him through the open window. "You're proud of yourself, aren't you?"

"I'm not taking 'no' for an answer, Dallas Wilde."

"If you get eaten by some random, scary dead thing that we will inevitably run into, don't come crying to me afterward. Got it?" I waited until he looked at me before adding, "I'm only half joking, you know."

"I have no doubt that whatever paranormal business that occurs at that graveyard will be promptly handled by you and

Zane. I won't get in the way." He folded his hands into his lap. "Zane won't let me get eaten, at least."

"Yeah, well. He let me get bit by a vampire recently so I'd stay sharp."

Barnaby narrowed his eyes at me, trying to feel out if I was joking, but I hopped up the stairs to my apartment before he could quiz me.

"Coast is clear, I chased away the cops." I meandered over to my duffel, which was still tossed open from when I was packing. "I still can't believe you bought that cat an automatic food dispenser. You could just pour a huge pile and she'd be fine."

"She's not a fish, hunter. She needs her food measured." Zane recalibrated the other electronic device, which was in charge of cleaning her litter box. That one I didn't mind as much because that kitten had some powerful poops. Said poop machine was following Zane around mewing pathetically, her naked tail shaking with excitement.

"Because fish have more self-control. Right, Kevin?" I placed my cute betta fish's weekend pellet into his tank. Kevin peeked at me from his coconut shell with all the hatred I adored him for. "You're so perfect."

"Make sure you actually pack clothing and not just snacks and weapons," Zane scolded from where he was lavishing treats onto his gremlin. "I'm going to be pissed if you make us stop at a store for socks again."

"Hey, we pack for vampire killing differently. I prioritize undead killing machinery and you pack socks." I gave Kevin some bloodworms for being so cute and got back to my duffel. "Barns locked himself in the car, by the way. So I guess he's coming too."

"He'll be useful to have around." Zane paused to give Twig a few kisses on her head, and I refused to acknowledge that it was precious. Refused. "Do we know if he can handle any weapons just in case?"

"I've seen him haul a giant wooden dick twice his size across a shop so, I'm guessing he's at least competent with something long and blunt." I threw some clothing into my duffel after shoving it to the brim with knives, ammo, my gun, some rose and blackthorn bombs for emergencies and my stash of chocolate-covered pretzels. If I couldn't shoot them in time, I could at least throw a vampire repellent to make them scatter and then eat some snacks for a job well done.

As I shouldered my bag of goodies and some socks, I passed by Kevin's tank to remind him *not* to murder the kitten, and to keep the apartment safe. I was decently sure the kitten would be fine, but the rest wasn't promising.

Barnaby was still sitting like a defiant brat in the back seat as we dumped my bag into the trunk, only acknowledging our presence when I climbed into the driver's seat.

"Wait. You're driving?"

"Why do you assume my driving is something to be concerned about?" I adjusted the rearview to glare at him. "You've never been in a car with me."

"I just have a feeling," he said with about as much enthusiasm as a dead rock.

"You won't die," Zane promised, matching his energy. "Just develop some ulcers."

"Fuck you both. I drive fine." I rumbled the engine to life and bullied my phone into divulging the route to the cemetery. "Ungrateful jerks. This trip is two days long, and I'm being *nice* by doing the first leg of the trip."

"It'll be nice if we survive that long," Barns mumbled, tightening his seat belt.

Despite the fact that both of the goons I was forced to ride with had zero faith in me, we made it out of the city unscathed. Was there a little road rage? Sure. Did I hop a curb at one point to avoid a traffic jam? That's for a judge to decide.

But we made it out and onto the highway fine, our course set for the Silent Steps.

Being the wayward vampire hunter I was, this wasn't the only time I had traveled outside of the city to track down some super-natural nastiness in order to vanquish some evil. St. Athesall was my home base because it was the jewel of modern civilization, and located as close to the center of the country as one could get. Everything worth seeing was only a few days away, including the ruins of the kingdoms that had once tried to rule over this sprawling landscape.

Demons constantly fought over this space for the resources and to further their empires, humans came in and spread religion all over the place, imps tried to mind their business and live their lives, and finally we all had a sit-down and figured it out. By sit-down, of course, I mean a big-ass war that crippled everyone involved, almost collapsed the economy and forced demons and humans to come to an understanding.

That understanding as that we could all come together in a capitalistic oligarchy pathetically veiled as democracy and stop waring so hard.

Yay politics!

St. Athesall was one of many big cities across the countryside, with lots of beautiful nothingness punctuated with pockets of suburbs and ruins. Relics of our turmoil were scattered all over, most now museums and fun tourist shops, since the last war fought was over a hundred years ago. Now the sites of death, murder and political intrigue had punny t-shirts and photo-ops set up for traveling guests making their way to an amusement park. The jinn palaces that once held a tight grip over the popula-tion stood in regal majesty, the sex demon metropolises had been restored as historical sites. Imps and onis didn't bother to build shit here because this place was such a dumpster fire of fighting for so long, so all their cool shit was across the connecting conti-nent with their own history.

The human stuff was mostly graveyards and churches, because we're kinda bummers.

Then a few hours south of the city was a drag of farmland and rolling acres of nothing. The most exciting thing we passed was a tunnel that was carved through a cliff, but that was only fun for about ten minutes. The rest of the excitement came from arguing over what we could fill the silence with, which lead to us putting on a random radio station since we couldn't agree on anything. Zane actually pitched talk radio, and I wanted to somehow divorce him as my bodyguard. At least Barns was suggesting music, even if his ideas were crap.

I flicked off the classic rock station once we pulled into the gas station, my body aching to move around and be fed. Zane stretched tall arms high, giving another cheeky peek at his stomach. Barnaby did some deep lunges like a maniac, and I argued with the gas pump for a few minutes.

"I'm going to get some food. Barns, you want anything?" I asked as I hung the gas pump back into its resting place.

"I brought snacks from home." He fished out a plastic bag of makeshift trail mix that looked like it was crafted in the Neolithic era. "I have some caramel candies too if you want some."

"How are you already a hundred years old?"

"Gas station food is terrible for you, Dallas," he scolded. "And overpriced."

"You are such an old man. Fine, keep your weird horse feed, I'm getting snacks." I did a double take as Zane followed me into the simple roadside store. "You want to gander at all the food you can't eat?"

"I'm running interference."

"The hell does that mean?" I demanded, trying to make his head dent in with my mind when he ignored me. How I ended up with such annoying traveling companions, I had no idea. Maybe I crossed someone in a past life, or got cursed as a baby. Either way, I didn't feel like the punishment matched the crime.

While Zane haunted the gas station convenience store, I got busy curating my snacks. It's important to balance the sweet and salty when one is traveling long distances, so loading up on chips, jerky, nuts as well as a smattering of gummy and chocolate candy is an absolute must. Since I hadn't eaten any real food since before we got on the road, I also decided to snag a coveted, delicious, well-balanced lunch of a hot dog drowning in chili.

Apparently, that was the line crossed for Zane.

The tongs for my dog extraction were torn from my grasp and placed back in the plastic holder, and I stood there with an empty bun in my hand and offense on my face.

"The fuck, Zane?"

"You're not doing that." He offered me a replacement food item, which was—I shit you not—a salad wrap.

Who in the Saint's name tries to substitute the artery clogging, salt-soaked mystery meat tube with lettuce masquerading as something it wasn't?

"Are you trying to get me to fight you right now?" I asked. "Is that what's happening?"

"That's going to destroy your stomach."

"My stomach is made of iron. You've seen me eat way worse than a gas station hot dog, and I have never once chased you out of a room."

"Mm-hm," Zane hummed sarcastically. "Not while you're awake."

I wheeled on him, trying to summon some deep-rooted powers to shoot a hole through his head with my glare.

"*What?*"

"You fart in your sleep."

"I do NOT—"

"You do." He interrupted me, forcing the salad wrap back into my hand. "For the sake of us having to sleep in a hotel room later, skip the hot dog."

I heard the cashier near the front fail at hiding a snicker behind a cough.

"I'm going to kill you," I promised him. "Full murder, Zane. You're a double dead man."

"That's fine. Just no hot dogs." He reached over and closed the plastic lid protecting the rotating meat tubes on their grill. He then left me standing there with a salad wrap in my hand and all my well-curated self-image turned into a fart cloud.

Silver lining, it did help me forget how I had been staring at his stomach only a few minutes earlier, because all I wanted to do at that point was punch him in the face.

I didn't get the hot dog.

WE CONTINUED DRIVING through the scenic nothingness of the country until the sun had finished planting itself under the horizon. The flickering, neon lights of a motel beckoned us, promising clean beds and free cable for a reasonable price. It was the sort of small dive that was too far away from anything for it to be too dangerous, but just isolated enough that if someone did decide to murder you, they'd never be found again. We made sure to take the bag filled with weapons into the room.

For some reason, probably Zane's fault, Barnaby did not want to share a room with us, even though it was promised he'd have a bed to himself. Since Zane didn't sleep, his plan was to sit and read a book all night like usual, or go do whatever vampire shit he normally did while I slept. Barns decided that he wanted nothing to do with either of us and grabbed his own room.

I had my suspicions that my midnight gas activities had been discussed behind my back.

The weariness of the drive as well as the past few days had settled into the marrow of my bones the moment I sat on the somewhat comfortable motel mattress. Spiraling floral patterns covered the dark, brick-colored blanket, the smell of industrial laundry detergent puffed up when I flopped my weight onto it. My phone buzzed at me for attention, but I didn't want to be tempted to open Sias's text message again.

We should talk.

I knew what that meant. I knew what the future held, and I couldn't bring myself to make it reality just yet. I didn't want to face a world that didn't hold the promise of Sias's hands on my skin again, his voice in my ear, or the way his hair felt between my fingers. I missed him; missed his touch, the smell of amber and tobacco when he pulled me into his warm, intoxicating charm magic. I was starving for him, for someone to hold me, want me.

And I just couldn't deal with that loss while also battling the terror of what might be waiting for us at this creepy-as-hell cemetery. Earlier that morning I had forgotten about the fight and I had almost called him to let him know what we were up to. I wanted to hear his take on all of it, what he would think of us trying to break into a grave to look at an old painting to find a hidden Death Goddess key.

I had no doubt he'd have some opinions.

I wanted to hear his voice again.

The knot in my chest twisted at a faded memory of his voice rumbling, the way his lips looked when he smirked at me.

Gods, I was miserable.

Miserable and deeply confused about some things. One of which being the goddamn vampire who had outed me as a farting disaster in front of a gas station attendant.

"You're still mad about the hot dog."

I checked my blocker tech around my neck and turned to call him a bastard but lost my steam.

You know what was really annoying? More annoying than the fact that he was an asshole, constantly grumpy, and sometimes let wild vampires bite me?

He had those dimples right above his ass. You know the ones. The little pockets of sex that live just above the juicy bits of a round ass. Zane had those. I knew this, because he was standing with his back to me, changing shirts for some arbitrary reason. His jeans sat low, his back muscles moving as he dug through his duffel, hair falling into place after he raked his fingers through it to get it out of his face—

And there it was.

The spark.

The tiny, almost non-existent little pop of electricity right at the base of my chest where all my lusty feelings lived before torpe-doing downstairs.

Zane looked good.

Zane.

The vampire.

Looked *good*.

I had officially crossed a line with myself, cartwheeled into a realm I didn't think possible and landed right on a landmine of existential crisis.

I didn't handle it well.

"I'm taking a shower," I yelled to the room, slapping my thighs with my hands to announce the finality of the situation. "Then I'm going to bed, and I will not be answering any questions."

"Why would I ask you questions?" Zane asked as he tugged a shirt on.

"I said no questions!"

"You're losing it, hunter." Zane's voice was lost as I shut the motel bathroom door with a little too much force. My reflection stared back at me with a look of manic anger that was settling over my body. How very *dare* my hormones send me down such a dark path. Yes, I was lonely. Yes, my heart was in a state of cracking in half, but that did not give my dick permission to go rogue.

I had gone through too much too quickly, so I was clearly going insane.

Zane was undead, a corpse born of the void, and a manifestation of evil and darkness. I was not crushing on him, because that was gross and fucked up.

The only pieces of hope I could cling to was that it wasn't the first time I had made…questionable…hookup choices while I was in a stressed state. Right off the top of my head, I could think of at least three, one of which was *the boyfriend of a gang leader*.

So, yeah. I'm a horny disaster when I'm stressed out.

But getting the lusty sparks for Zane was still not okay.

The only cure for the stress sex cravings was to get it out of my system, which I fully planned on handling myself, thankyouverymuch.

It wasn't until I was already stripped down and hard as a rock that my mind allowed a non-sexual thought to weasel its way to the front of the line: I had promised Barnaby that I'd get him some sex energy soon. Had I not already promised and knew that he was getting hunger pains about my lack of a sex life, I would have said "to hell with it" and gone about my shame-shower solo sex.

But because I was such a nice guy and felt like a bastard for the whole money thing, I had to make the very awkward walk out of the bathroom to retrieve the sex energy-absorbing crystal in my goddamn duffel bag.

The large, hotel-provided towel was not the softest thing on the planet, especially when sensitive parts were being *extra* sensitive, but it kept me covered enough not to give anything scandalous away. Zane was lounging on his bed when I emerged, and even though I refused to look at him when I waltzed over to my bag like nothing soul shattering was happening in my mind, I could feel his bloody red eyes on me.

It made things worse.

Why, you ask? I don't fucking know. I didn't want him to know what was happening under that overly bleached towel, but feeling his eyes on me was like a call to action for my dick. I had to adjust the towel a bit to make sure nothing was peeking through the curtain, if you get my drift.

Horny. Disaster. When. Stressed.

With the crystal in hand, I made my escape back to the bathroom and practically dived into the safety of the shower.

Steam quickly filled the room as the shower blasted water onto the tiles, the frail fabric protecting the floor from the ricochet billowing from the heat. The water pressure wasn't fantastic, but it was strong enough to be pleasant as I climbed in, dipping my head under the stream to try and cool off. My body was demanding attention, mind fogged over with primal signals that needed tending to.

I thanked the Saint and whatever Gods wanted to take credit for Dex being a tech wizard. My waterproofed emotional blocker helped me not feel as guilty as I let my mind take some concepts and run wild.

For my own sanity and self-preservation, I focused on how it felt when I gave Zane my blood, and not so much on Zane himself. Just bringing forward the memories of how my body buzzed with electricity when my blood hit Zane's tongue helped get the engine running, but my mind wasn't in the mood to stay in its lane. Each time I held on to the physical feelings associated with letting Zane drink my blood, my mind was quick to remind me of the other parts of the ritual I had repressed.

Like Zane's hooded eyes looking up at me, my fingers gripped in his hair that was so damn soft. The weight of his hands on my hips was a particular hit with my imagination, and I cussed at how absolutely fucked it was that I was into it.

I shouldn't be that turned on by a vampire touching me—a damn *vampire Thrall* of all fucking things—but Gods help me it was hitting all the buttons. The cascading water over my body was delicious, my muscles tensing as I worked on releasing the tension coiling through me.

It wasn't the first time I've had both hands busy in the shower, one holding a sex energy-absorbing crystal for my landlord while the other was busy summoning the energy from my cock. But it was the first time I had felt such an intense pull of lust that I had to bite my knuckle to stay quiet. My body was on fire, liberated by the permission to sexually fantasize about the most taboo thing imaginable.

Sex with a vampire.

I had to let myself indulge, to shake away the guilt and just let it ride. It was just me, all to myself, and no one would ever know about my moment of weakness.

It was just once. Just one time.

I was going to make the most of it, so I let the shackles of shame get tossed away and gave my disaster horniness a free pass to get weird.

And boy, did it not disappoint.

My body was a quaking mess of mounting desire as I sank into the fantasy: warm hands on my hips, the feeling of long hair in my grip, how thick that ridge was under me when I was sitting in his lap, the buzzing high of untethered blood magic shared between us.

I thought the memory of his lower back dimples would be the thing that finally pushed me past the finish line.

That would have almost been respectable, understandable, something I wasn't remotely bothered by. Everyone enjoys good dimples, especially ones that accentuate a very well-sculpted ass.

While fantasizing about Zane's body was all well and good, and was working out very well for me, I let my guard down a little too much. My mind was traveling into the darker, less acknowledged folds of my brain, and it tapped into something I wasn't ready for. As I rocked my hips to the rhythm of my stroking, biting back the groans I so desperately wanted to let loose, something resurfaced in a flash of pure, deviant desire.

Bloodstained teeth.

Zane's bloodstained teeth.

I remembered how I felt when I saw my blood on his fangs, his lips parted as I yanked his head back to look at me. I hadn't wanted to accept what that had felt like. It was scary and horrible, a deep fear that lived in the tender parts of myself I kept locked away. It scared the shit out of me to think about another vampire hurting me, sinking their teeth into my skin, pushing me to the point of death.

But not Zane.

Seeing my blood on his teeth had done something to me, rearranged my wiring and tangled them into knots of confusion.

In a flash of something I couldn't quite unpack, I imagined Zane fucking me.

And *biting me.*

I felt a wave of heat so paralyzing I lost my breath, my body locking with pleasure so profound I would have screamed for the Saint if I'd the ability to speak. My heart knocked, my toes curled; everything debauched and wicked that had been swirling in my mind faded into a haze of fireworks, and I happily drifted away in a void of orgasmic ecstasy.

I don't know how long I stood under the stream of water while my body continued to pulse, but I was eventually able to pull in enough air to whimper as I rode out the last bit of the wave. The tiles were cool against my brow as I leaned my head on them, my legs sending dancing waves of lightning between my toes and my hips.

There was a lot to unpack with that shower jerk-off. A lot of things to sort through. Like a whole damn repressed cache of internalized trauma that had somehow leaked into sex fantasies.

I'd jerked off to the idea of a vampire biting me. That's not terrifying at all.

Not only a vampire, but *the* vampire, the only one I knew. I guess technically *my* vampire, if we wanted to get into it. Which didn't help, I'll have you know. That made my stomach feel weird. And my dick jump a little, which was a feat in itself because he was very tired.

With the bliss fading and reality creeping in with the cooling shower water, I eased my grip on the crystal in my hand to make sure it had caught the essence of my little sexcapade.

It blinked with waves of pastel fire with drops of smoke mixed in. That was definitely new.

So was the two inches of bony handle that was sticking out of my goddamn chest.

Great. So now the weird rod that burst out of my chest when I did blood stuff with Zane also came out for a cheeky peek when I was masturbating. That was so great. Loved that for me.

With the shower cooling and my mind starting to fire on all cylinders again, I did a quick scrub down while I gave my chest time to reabsorb the stick. I was fortunate enough that the steam from the previous hot water kept the bathroom warm while I toweled off, because the damn water was ice when I was finally done.

I was able to dress and hide the sex crystal in my pocket—for some reason the idea of Zane seeing the color of my fantasy trapped in the crystal freaked me out—but I wasn't able to get the really disturbing thing under control.

The stick didn't recede like before. It didn't budge.

It stayed poking out just an inch and a half or so, but had decided without my consent to just…remain peeking out of my skin where my sternum lived. For the life of me, I couldn't figure out what the hell it wanted from me.

It was just…stuck like that.

A small testament to my very, very filthy mind.

"Of course," I muttered to myself, tossing a shirt on to cover my shame. The guy staring back through the fog in the mirror didn't look as exhausted anymore. My handsome reflection was rosy-cheeked and satisfied, if only a little concerned. I did feel pretty great after releasing the tension, though it had cost me some chest real estate. And probably some weird dreams in my future.

I crept out of the bathroom pretending like everything was fine, strolling over to my bed like I wasn't deeply questioning everything about myself. To my surprise, the room was empty. Where Zane had been lounging was abandoned, only his book remaining. A wave of relief settled over me for a heartbeat, followed by a curiosity I couldn't control.

Had he…felt anything?

No, right?

I touched my emotional blocker and glanced down to make sure the little light was on and the switch was in place. Everything was fine.

So why was the vampire missing?

I tossed my shoes back on and leaned out of the room, sweeping up and down the walkway to see if I could spot him. Zane was MIA, but Barnaby was walking in my direction with a pamphlet in hand, browsing over the selection of takeout food that was nearby.

"Have you seen Zane?" I asked when he got into earshot.

"He went for a walk. Said his head was hurting him."

"I didn't think vampires actually got headaches," I mused.

"Well, if anyone could give him one, it's you." Barnaby paused near his neighboring door and blinked at me. "Did you fill the intimacy crystal?"

"What? Oh. Yeah." I tugged it out of my pocket. "How did you know?"

"I could sense it." He held out his hand for it, the pamphlet of physical food forgotten. The crystal was passed along, the colors swirling like a tornado. "Gods, Dallas. What did you do? Actually —" he shook his head quickly. "Don't answer that. I have no passion to know any details."

"Is it…different somehow?" I couldn't help but ask, stomach clenching as Barnaby huffed a laugh.

"Have you ever seen one with these colors before? It looks like liquid sunsets, and it feels…*strong*." Barnaby inhaled slowly like he was about to dive underwater, his palm neon with the colors as he began to pull the energy from it.

The storm of pastels took over his black irises, his gaze alive with the evidence of my secret passion for a few seconds before fading back to normal.

He blinked a few times to let the magic settle, burping a little from the indulgence.

Then Barnaby aimed his gaze on me, the weight of all of his opinions harnessed in one simple word.

"Oh."

Heat trailed up my neck and attacked my cheeks, my chest tightening like a vise.

"What?"

"It's none of my business," he said quickly.

"That 'Oh' was loaded. You said a thousand words with *Oh*."

"Who you sleep with is none of my business! I'm just… surprised is all. I thought you hated vampires."

"I didn't—" I began with a yell, my outrage bursting out of my throat before I remembered to whisper. "I didn't sleep with anyone. That was a solo endeavor energy charge."

The surprise on Barnaby's face could have been seen from space.

"Dallas, this crystal is filled with a supercharge of sexual energy with a kiss of black magic. It's the best-tasting thing I've ever had, and you're telling me you did this with your *mind*?" He had stepped close to me, like we were discussing nuclear launch codes outside of a roadside motel.

"You need to relax."

Barnaby's volume was starting to grow in his excitement. "I will not. You know how rare vampire energy is in the first place? If you could do this with just fantasizing about Zane—"

"*Shut up*, Barns," I hissed through my teeth, scanning everywhere for Zane. "I'm going to tie you up and leave you here if you don't chill out."

"Fine. I'm chilled. An iceberg." He smoothed his hair back with one hand and exhaled in a rush of satisfied relief. "I haven't felt this healthy in a while. I could go for a jog."

"Great. Jog away from me then. I'm starting to think you're the thing giving everyone headaches."

A bubbly laugh lifted from Barnaby that was too haute to be from joy.

"I don't think it was *me* that gave him the headache. Not with the energy you were producing." He turned tail and ran into his room when I wheeled back around to him. I wasn't going to hit him, but I was really considering pushing him down out of principle.

ZANE DIDN'T GET BACK to the hotel until after I was asleep, and I woke up with the stick still peeking out of my chest.

My phone alarm roused me early, the sun just starting to creep over the horizon. Zane was already dressed and ready since he didn't need to sleep, and had started a new book between late last night and the morning. I appreciated that the vampire knew me well enough at this point not to speak to me until I had a few cups of coffee, but Barnaby had disregarded that rule.

The spry, newly energized incubus had clearly been up for an hour or two before me, and had the car packed and ready to go while I was still struggling to put on pants.

"The quicker we get on the road, the better timing we'll make," he was saying, buzzing around the car, loading up our duffels. "I also have some route suggestions to help speed us along, and have picked out a few rest stops we can visit along the way. Oh, and as far as food is concerned—"

"Make him stop," I pleaded to Zane, sleep still sticking to my bones. "Or I will kill him."

"I'll drive this morning." Zane shut the trunk and motioned for us to get into the car. "You can sleep a little longer."

"He's not going to let me sleep. He's a monster." I rubbed my eyes as Barnaby leaned over the center console and started insisting on choosing what to listen to.

"I've never seen him this excited about anything. Did he get some espresso this morning?" Zane eyed Barns through the window.

"No, I gave him a crystal yesterday and it was really strong—" I hit the brakes a little too late on the sentence, my mind too groggy to be sharp.

"Ah."

"Yeah."

There was a stretch of silence that nearly killed me, both of us watching Barnaby poking at the rental car stereo like he was about to launch the damn thing into space.

Zane spun the keys on his finger and caught them with his palm. "So this is your fault."

"Hey. You wanted to bring him, not me."

"Who was the one that let him get into the car to begin with?" he fired back.

"That was Preston and Seyyid's fault, not mine. They distracted me." I rounded the car when he did, glaring at him from over the silver top. "You could have pulled him out and made him stay. He would have listened to you."

"Maybe. But I'm also the one not pumping him full of sex energy."

"Phrasing." I climbed into the car and put my palm over Barnaby's forehead and forced him backwards into the back seat. "I need way more coffee for this trip."

"I took the liberty of updating the route on the GPS. Now we'll get there faster and there's scheduled stops." Barnaby produced a foldout, comically large map he must have grabbed from the motel lobby, and opened the thing up like it was the main sail to a ship.

"He updated the route," I told Zane in mocked excitement. "Isn't this fun? Are you having fun?"

"Goddess," he breathed, regret dripping off him as he started the car.

We decided to follow Barnaby's new route, mainly because he was very insistent and annoying about it. To his credit, the rest stops he picked did have some good food for those of us who needed sustenance, and Zane was able to pick up a new paperback along the way. It absolutely did *not* save us time, even if Barnaby claimed it shaved off an hour, and we arrived at the Silent Steps historical cemetery at dusk.

Maybe using the word "historical" is painting the wrong picture, that of a well-kept, museum-quality landmark with a groundskeeper who gives tours with maybe a fun gift shop where kids could find tombstone keychains with their names on it.

There was no gift shop, no kitschy keychains, no lovable old groundskeeper with oodles of ghost stories to tell while they dragged you around the old, but well-maintained, graves.

The Silent Steps had been abandoned for a very long time. Left to rot. Forgotten.

Creeping vines had wrapped themselves so tightly across the double iron doors that the metal was warped and bent. Any locks that had been in place were rusted and long gone, the vines providing more security than the locks ever had. It took us a while to hack through the thick brush enough to swing the gates open, shadows coming to play by the time we eased our car inside.

The cemetery was a yawning mouth of crooked, stone teeth set on elevated rows, weeds bleeding from the gums. Proud mausoleums sank into the earth like rotten molars, some now only piles of rubble being consumed by the wild. We parked not too far from the main entrance, simply because there was no way the sedan was going to make it any further.

"Any idea where the mausoleum we need is in this dump?" I grabbed my duffel in the trunk and started unpacking my supplies, which consisted of my gun, ammo, and knives coated in some vampire repellent, just in case. It was kinda funny seeing Zane wrinkle his nose when I dumped the cocktail onto it.

"Northwestern quadrant," Barnaby answered, shining his flashlight onto the giant black book he had stashed in his backpack. He aimed the beam of light into the dark cemetery. "That way."

"Your charm picking up anything?" Zane asked as we locked up the car. "Any sign of lingering magic?"

"Nothing so far." I gave the little magic detector a pat in my pocket. "I think we should have brought some machetes to slice through this bush. I wasn't expecting it to be this overgrown."

"How could anyone let any site get to this state?" our historian incubus lamented. "Sure, it's a resting place for necromancers and death cult fanatics, but it's still a piece of history. Truly tragic."

"I think some things are best lost to time," I told him as we embarked into the dark. "This place could be swallowed by nature and be better for it."

"Just to have someone a thousand years later come dig something up they shouldn't," Barnaby retorted. "Better to educate than to abandon."

"He's got a point," Zane defended Barnaby, because of course he did. "Pretty sure this is the kind of crap that starts curses."

"We're not starting any curses this trip." I crunched down on some dead branches as we walked. "Just some light grave robbing."

"I'm going to let you two defile graves, I'm just here to translate." Barnaby swung his light around, looking for any hidden dangers. "How confident are you that you can reanimate this very old corpse? Are you sure you can get us any answers?"

"Bodies that have been dead a long time are tricky," Zane explained before I could give my own estimation of my skills. "As the physical form deteriorates, the soul sinks deeper into the void. Necromancers train for decades to master such a skill."

"What happens if we open the coffin and it's just bones and dust?" Barnaby aimed the light at Zane. "Would that mean we came out here for nothing?"

"Have some faith, Barns." I shielded my eyes after the beam

was redirected to me. "I've successfully resurrected two whole bodies now."

"If the body is bones, we're out of luck. There's no way he could reach that far into the void. My hope is that this person was wealthy enough at the time to have been buried with decent embalming." The vampire sighed up at the moon, his breath foggy against the cold. "Then we might have a chance."

"This body is hundreds of years old, Zane," Barnaby argued. "If anything is left, it'll be a brittle mummy by now."

"You're thinking bodies preserved by regular means," Zane countered. "Not a necromancer's magic."

"I guess they'd want their gatekeeper to be able to talk." I ducked under a low-hanging branch, dusting some spider webs off my hair. "Makes sense they'd keep him pickled."

Barnaby shivered. "Ghastly."

"You don't want to leave behind a pretty corpse, Barns?" I grinned as he visibly cringed.

"Gods, no. Back to the earth with me. Cycle of life and all that cheery nonsense."

"No cremation? Get scattered at one of your favorite historical sites with all the naked statues?"

"The thought of my body being nothing but ash is awful." Barnaby remembered who he was walking with and winced at Zane. "Sorry. I forgot."

"It's alright," the vampire dismissed the discomfort. "All vampires are destined to be dust. Our bodies become erased, souls plunged into the depths of the void to rejoin the Goddess's embrace, never to return."

I knew all too well what happened to a vampire after they're destroyed. Even Thralls, the most powerful vampires, were just embers and ash after a well-placed blade or bullet shattered their tether to the living world. Hell, my favorite sword was crafted with the ashes of a notorious undead foe folded into the blade.

It felt a little different now that I knew a Thrall I didn't hate.

I almost felt bad.

I had no plans on turning Zane into melty soup that burned into dust. I was starting to kinda like him being around.

He kept Barnaby company. And he was useful sometimes.

Plus, you know. He had his moments of being bearable with comfort, and between us, he did look fine as hell in a suit.

Naturally, those thoughts were left in my brain as we walked, the full moon above casting enough light to keep the cemetery from plunging into total darkness. The silver light made the crumbling tombstones shine in a haunting beauty as the wind whispered through the gnarled limbs of the old trees. The steps were silent as we weaved through them, the dead peaceful as two and a half living creatures stomped through their resting grounds.

Atop one of the steps deep in the graveyard, our mausoleum stood waiting. Thick vines with spade-shaped leaves grew like veins over the side of the pale stone building, the pointed roof framed by four pillars painted with moss. Stone walkways leading up to each step had been overtaken by weeds, but still had enough structure to allow us to use them.

All of the other graves throughout the cemetery had neighbors, the dense population nearly overlapping each other in proximity.

But not this one.

This mausoleum stood alone on the top step, solitary in its eerie majesty.

"If that doesn't scream 'creepy necromancer grave,' I don't know what does."

"I'm starting to get second thoughts about this," Barnaby whined. "My gut is telling me this is a terrible idea, and it's usually right."

"We're in it now, Barns." I noticed him hesitate as we climbed the weed coated pathway. "We'll keep you safe. Between myself and Zane, nothing is going to touch you."

"I'm not too proud to say that I'm very scared of this place," Barnaby admitted, like maybe we didn't notice this entire time.

"The pull of historic adventure is very alluring until you're staring down a grave."

"Here." I unfastened one of the sheathed daggers from my belt and passed it to him. "I don't see any signs of vampire activity out here, but if it makes you feel better, you can carry my dagger. It's coated with a vampire repellent, so if you take it out of the sheath, it'll make grunts back off."

"What will you do if a swarm shows up?" He took it carefully, clipping it to his belt.

"Kill them like I always do." I tossed him a wink. "Don't worry about me. Stick close to Zane if something goes sideways."

"You make it sound so easy." Barnaby's sardonic tone was present, but it was drowned out by the bubbling concern coating his words.

I led the way up the steps, the cool night breeze teasing the sensitive skin at the tips of my ears and nose. The winter had killed most of the plants other than the most resilient ones; the scent of frozen dirt and dead branches just a whisper on the wind. A cloud passed over the moon as we made our ascension to the crypt, shadows sliding over the ivory monument as a last warning of what was to come.

The door to the ancient tomb had been set back in place by the excavators, but it hadn't been fully resealed. Iron bars had been set in front of the stone seal, but they had fallen aside from the overwhelming presence of the vines and harsh weathering. The thick stone slab had a crack through the center from when it had been pried open, nearly crumbling in half.

Zane and I hefted the stone door aside, pushing away the fallen gate so we could each squeeze through the narrow passageway. Barnaby swept over the walls with his flashlight, the inside of the mausoleum roomy enough for us to stand comfortably. Dirt and dry leaves coated the floor, scattering around the massive marble structure that protected its coffin from the elements. The mural we had been studying was sprawled across one side, an ancient poem on the other, with a statue of the Goddess standing watch over her dead acolyte.

In the darkness of the crypt, it almost felt like she was smiling at us.

Welcoming us home with a cheeky little grin.

Her arm wasn't outstretched like it usually was, commanding her undead to march on her behalf. Instead, her right hand touched her chest where the blade of her holy scythe lay across it, her left arm that was missing beyond the elbow, open almost like an embrace.

Barnaby shivered, his light vibrating with him.

"I've never seen her look so…motherly."

"The dead are her children." Zane moved to the statue and touched the bottom of her robe gently, keeping his fingers there for just a heartbeat. "This is a sacred place."

"How does one pay respects to the Goddess of Death?" Barnaby, ever the polite historian, asked from a distance. "Maybe we can get on her good side before desecrating one of her children's graves."

"She's not that sort of deity." Zane moved away from his Goddess. "Death is unbiased and unbothered by mortal things."

"That's good news." I rubbed my hands together. "Then she won't mind if we take a quick peek at this dead dude and see if we can grab some answers. Zane, grab this marble lid with me. Let's see if we can shove it aside."

Barnaby stood aside while we did the heavy lifting, putting our backs into displacing the thick slab of decorated rock from the tomb. The grinding sound of marble scraping against itself was rough, the solid thump of the lid cracking from its impact with the floor made everyone in the room flinch.

Dust rose up from the belly of the grave, the black casket inside grayed with dirt and debris. Any smell of rot or death was long gone, only the powdery hint of old bones and decaying fabric remained. The wood used to make the ritual resting place was a native tree that had been farmed into extinction, and it held its obsidian color beautifully.

"What if it's just bones in there?" Barnaby whispered from beside me. "What will we do?"

"It won't be," I said with a confidence I had no business wielding. "This has to be the gatekeeper. Nothing else makes sense."

"Or it could be a trap." I felt Barnaby position himself behind me, deciding I'd be useful as a human shield. "Something to smite the people dabbling with forces beyond their understanding."

"None of the archeologists got smote, remember?"

"None of them were necromancers," Barnaby quipped, still hiding.

"I'm not about to turn around and go back now." I looked at Zane. "You ready?"

The Thrall gave me a nod. "Open it."

"Here goes nothing." I flexed my hands and gave myself a little mental pep talk before reaching into the tomb and lifting the lid of the old casket. The box opened without a fight: the nails that had once sealed it shut simply slipped free from being previously ripped loose.

Staring up at us from death was the messenger of the Goddess's key, frozen in eternal slumber with his hands resting across his chest. The clothes he had been buried in dented in across his torso and shoulders, dark from age, relics of centuries past. Leathery skin stretched across bony hands that were still in decent shape, the fingernails long and pale. He hadn't decayed nearly as badly as most corpses would have after centuries, which proved we had been right about some necromancy magic being used here.

There was only one small problem.

The head was missing.

In its place was an empty, black satin pillow coated in dust, leaving behind nothing but a mocking sting of bitter disappointment.

"Fuck." I scowled at the mocking, headless thing. "That's inconvenient."

"It doesn't make sense," Zane mused out loud.

"Why in the blazes would they take the head?" Barnaby demanded.

"They weren't going to make it easy." I leaned on the stone tomb, glaring at the corpse to give me the answer to the puzzle. "Something as important as the Goddess's key probably doesn't go to just anyone."

"So they make it impossible?" Barnaby exhaled, rubbing at his temple. "That seems extremely pointless. Why even tell us about it then?"

"It also would have been handy if it was mentioned in the book before we hiked all the way out here." I rubbed at my eyes, my frustration drying them out. "You think the fucker knows sign language?"

"We must have missed something." Barnaby was flipping through pages, resting the book on the edge of the tomb so he could aim his flashlight at the text. Zane paced slowly through the small crypt, checking the walls for anything hidden we may have missed.

I continued to glare at the body, knowing in my bones that the key was this mystery, headless man. The faded, withered clothing draped over the frail body were simple yet elegant, lace collar and sleeves curled at the edges from the battle with time. A dark vest wrapped the torso within, corroded buttons dotting up the sides. A black stone sat in a brooch pinned to the lapel of a velvet coat, clutched between bony fingers made of tarnished silver.

I had never popped open a centuries-old grave before, so I had no idea what to expect when it came to what was normally buried with people back in the ye old times. These days, most humans and demons alike just got tossed into giant ovens to be converted to ash, unless they followed strict doctrine that demanded other methods. The old practice of pickling people and tossing them in lead boxes had been phased out years ago, because it took up too much real estate and bodies were constantly being dug up and robbed.

Peering at the treasure pinned to this headless jerk's lapel, I understood why.

Since the corpse wasn't proving helpful, and he was very dead and no longer needing an expensive antique brooch, I decided that was going to be the tax for being useless.

It was the first and last time I was going to take something from a headless corpse.

The moment my fingers came within an inch of the smooth, onyx stone, a bolt of magic arced from the surface and bit the tip of my finger. It was as brief and fleeting as seeing a static shock pop free after rubbing your socks on the carpet, but a hell of a lot louder. A thin string of green had lept up like a snake bite, electrifying the stone into a dazzling display of colors.

Iridescent flecks of emerald, violet and crimson danced across its surface like a storm of fire and magic.

My magic detector came to life in a flurry, a pattern similar to the warning of death magic, but nothing like I had felt before.

"What did you do?" Barnaby peered over, eyes wide. "It's… glowing."

"I don't know." I rubbed my fingertips together, the tingle of the shock still present. "I reached down to touch it, and it threw off a spark."

"It responded to you," Zane said, moving to my side. "To your magic."

The dance of colors tossed out light from within, churning with a power I didn't understand.

"Do you think this has something to do with why the head is missing?" Barnaby asked. "Or something to do with a mural, maybe?"

"I think there's only one way to find out." I shook out my hands and shoved my apprehension aside. "If I blow up or something, tell Kevin I love him."

Barnaby closed the book and moved to the entrance of the

mausoleum, ready to escape if I did, in fact, start to sizzle like a bomb. Zane stayed at my side, ready to face whatever the outcome was, explosive or otherwise.

I gathered my breath and reached out again, much slower this time, to see how the black opal took my second attempt to touch it. The air around the brooch was icy, like I was trailing the tips of my fingers over the surface of a thawing lake. Flares of greens pulsed before melting into swirls of deep purples, fire dancing between them as I moved in closer.

I felt the dancing ants trail up my fingers, cold tendrils of death magic slithering up my arm. The moment I saw the corpse's fingers twitch, Zane's hand slipped onto my shoulder.

I felt his grip hesitate before he whispered, "You feel different."

"There's magic pulsing from the brooch," I told him, my focus on the body twitching in the casket. "I imagine I feel very weird right now."

"It's not the brooch." Zane's eyes bored into mine when I looked his way. "Something's changed."

"What are you talking about?"

"I don't know, hunter. But you feel…" he trailed off, and I'll be damned if he didn't look mesmerized or baffled in those few seconds. I confused Zane daily by just being myself, but I had never seen him look like this.

It almost felt like he was afraid of me.

Feeling the magic arc from the brooch again tore me away from trying to unpack Zane's expression, the stone's colors churning like the eye of a storm. Dancing green bolts of necromantic magic popped and flickered, connecting to my fingers in thick lines of power. The tendrils of death magic gripped my arm like a vise, and I set my jaw as the pressure began to build. I curled the magic around my fingers, feeling the lightning like strings being threaded through me. Zane's grip tightened on my shoulder, and I gave the black magic strings a hard tug.

The opal shattered into thick pieces, a viscous ichor oozing from the center. The tendrils of magic around my arm remained as the dark liquid trailed down the corpse's neck, dripping over the stump where the head used to be.

And it started to bubble.

"What's happening?" Barnaby called from halfway out the crypt.

"Stay back, Barns," I called over my shoulder. "Some freaky necromancy shit is happening."

"The magic feels ancient, hunter," Zane warned, his tone as grave as the one we were standing in. "Ancient and dangerous."

"Yeah, black mystery ooze from inside of a rock sure as fuck would be both of those things, especially on a *headless corpse in a necromancy tomb*." I held my position, focused on keeping the black magic tendrils around my arm calm.

The bubbling mass of danger goop began to coagulate around the neck, coating itself over where the vertebrae stuck out from the old flesh. The fingers of the body twitched and curled, shoulders jerking each time more of its neck was covered. The icy tendrils squeezed for power as a shape began to form, the ooze from inside the black crystal working its magic.

Before our very eyes, we watched an old, leathery head take form out of the black sap, connecting it to the body like it had been there all along. Bone sprouted from the neck like a flower, growing a jaw and eye sockets before dry muscle formed over it like over salted jerky. Skin stretched over its features and clung too tight around the cheekbones, the mouth a set of thin, curled lips over long teeth. White hair that behaved like brittle straw grew out the top of the head in thin wisps, and the puckered eyes of the corpse opened to show glowing orbs of haunting amethyst.

It looked at me, a knobby tongue moving just behind its newly formed mouth, and it spoke. The voice was a death rattle backwards, a language I didn't know that bounced off my chest like a hammer strike.

I felt Zane's hand on my shoulder squeeze, pulling me backward just a hair.

"W-what did he say?" I asked, my eyes locked on the horror before me.

"Uh." Barnaby had to take a shaky breath, his voice somewhere behind me. "I'm not sure on the exact question, but it has something to do with your relation to the Goddess, I think."

I swallowed the fear that threatened, and I curled my fingers into a fist. The tendrils tightened, crawling further up my arm as the dead creature's eyes flared.

"Tell it that I seek the key," I told Barnaby, my grip around the magic slippery. "Ask it to lead us to wherever it is."

"I'm not sure how to..." Barnaby trailed off as the corpse started to move, one of its bony hands lifting from its resting place.

It didn't move like the other reanimated bodies I had tugged back to life before, its motions fluid and terrifyingly similar to that of a living being. The dead thing moved like it had just woken up from a nap, not like it had been rotting for a few centuries.

The magic between myself and the creature stirred, the tendrils dancing, the glow of its eyes bright in the darkness of its tomb. Cold, leathery fingers encircled my wrist with a calm gentleness that I imagined a grandparent would have for a child. It was not angry, nor was it vicious in any way.

It was happy to see me.

I felt its relief like a warm blanket around my shoulders. We were family, this corpse and I, connected by something I couldn't possibly understand. I think Zane felt it too, because he sighed like all of his stress melted away, his hand leaving my shoulder.

That's when the bottom of the casket fell out from under the body, swallowed up by an impossible darkness that seemed to stretch forever.

And it took me with it.

CHAPTER
SEVENTEEN

THE DARKNESS that consumed me was not endless like I had thought, because I landed like a sack of bricks down a stone slope.

The crash banged my shoulder and elbow, but the corpse creature took the brunt of the impact and scattered into pieces. I slid down something that felt like a slide made of smooth stone, the adjoining walls just as slick and featureless as I tried to grab onto something. When I finally reached the bottom, I landed hip-first on more solid, cold stone, surrounded by darkness.

The only light in the endless void was the glowing eyes of a newly formed, but still rather fragile skull. The soft purple light of its eyes was fading like a dying candle, the glow only strong enough to show the grit of dirt across the ground.

I tried to look up at where I had fallen from for any signs of how far I had dropped, hoping to see a casket-shaped hole with Zane and Barnaby staring down, but there was nothing. The only thing staring back at me was more darkness, not even the faint outline of a seam.

"Zane!" I called up, panic starting to boil hot in my chest at the lack of echo. The space was small, narrow, like a grave or a cage. I stood up and reached out on either side of me, my fingers touching stone with my elbows still bent. I had maybe a foot on either side of me, and a ceiling that was only a few inches from my head.

Very narrow.

Very small.

My heartbeat was a war drum through my chest, my panting breath hung in the confined nothingness before me. Prickling fear crawled over my hairline and turned into acid in my belly, memories of fangs biting into my neck caused me to rub at my skin to force the ache away.

I fished into my pockets for my phone, ripping it free to try and summon any sort of light. The screen refused to light up, the plastic casing dented from where I'd landed on it.

Busted. Dead.

Nothing but a shattered piece of expensive garbage now.

I took a few steps to the only light source there, the fading, re-dying eyes of the mummified head.

I picked the thing up and hated how badly my hands shook, the light jumping in my grip.

"Where are we?" I demanded. "Tell me how to get out of here."

It said nothing, not understanding me.

"Where *are* we, you bastard!" I felt my heart freeze as the light dimmed more. "No. No! Don't you fucking dare die now! Tell me how to get out! Out!"

It looked at me with its haunting, deathly eyes, the pupils milky white centers in glowing jewels.

And it chuckled at a joke I couldn't hear before the magic faded, and the skull turned to dust in my hands.

I tried not to let the final plunge into darkness make me scream, but I had to vent the frustration somehow. Old fears came out to play, nightmares breathing threats into my ears as I forced myself forward. My knees wobbled for a few steps, my breath just as unsteady, and the need to cover my neck almost paralyzing.

I felt around the stone, desperate to find anything. My fingers touched a groove in the stone, a carved-out indention that ran horizontal to the ground at shoulder level. It was my guide forward, something to hold on to while I kept my other hand clamped on the side of my neck.

There was nothing ahead of me, the total lack of light made my eyes strobe with white sparks in my peripherals as it tried to make sense of the vacuum. The smell of dry dirt clung to the back of my throat, my footsteps cannon fire in the silence. I could hear how panicked I was, my breath shaking so violently it made my eyes start to sting.

I never wanted to feel this way again. I had vowed to myself years ago I'd *never* feel this again, that I would die before I became that scared little kid curled up in the darkness.

I knew something would come for me. Something would get me down there, alone, in the dark, where no one could help me. Something would come crawling like it had before, something would hurt me. I cursed at myself for shaking, I hated that my cheeks were wet with tears as I marched on unsteady feet.

The fear I felt, the certainty I had that at any moment, any second, I'd feel hands grab me, teeth puncture me, made my mind race to sounds that weren't there. I heard footsteps, panting, whispers; I smelled blood mixed with filth and carnage just out of arm's length.

More darkness. More nothingness. And my chest started to wring itself out in crippling panic. I had nothing to hold on to, nothing to keep me grounded and alert. My head started to swim, and I suffocated on my inability to take a breath.

I was going to die down there.

I was going to die.

Again.

Again.

Darkness beyond the darkness cloaked me, the dancing white lights of my eyes trying to focus dropped away. I felt the void coming for me as my brain starved for breath, my chest gripped by icy claws that refused to let me inhale. The phantom sounds of scurrying vampires in the shadows turned into encroaching footsteps, and I heard death calling to me.

Not death.

Something else.

Something shadowy and familiar, a noise I had heard before while I lay dying.

In the void, I saw the shadow I had met before, standing like a beacon. I remembered then, as my heartbeat started to slow, my mind fogged with the complacent chill of dying, that I had met that shadow after seeing the Goddess. It had stroked my brow and brought me back, it had kissed me while my soul swam through the endless abyss.

It was speaking to me now, eyes glowing, coming for me.

I had never felt more relieved.

I ran toward the shadow with the glowing eyes, grabbing it with both hands as it scooped me up into its embrace. I held it tight, the shadow that had pulled me from the void, kept me safe, kept me from plunging too far into the darkness, my lungs finally unfreezing so I could gulp down air.

The fog around me eased, my heart thundered, and I inhaled a full breath with arms thrown around me.

I felt its heartbeat, strong and fast, and I thought how strange it was that a shadow from the void had a heartbeat. I thought it was charming.

When I breathed in grave flowers and earthy rainwater, I thought I was going insane.

"Zane?" I looked up at the red embers in the dark that watched me. I saw his brows lower, gaze searching mine.

"Who did you think it was?"

I blinked at him, my head starting to hurt. I felt his hands smooth over my scalp, searching for injuries.

"Did you hit your head? Are you hurt?"

"It was you," I whispered, mesmerized by how familiar it felt to feel his fingers brush over my forehead. "You were the shadow that guided me through the void."

"That's my purpose, hunter." Zane gave my shoulders and arms a quick pat-down for any bones sticking out. "Though I didn't know I was a shadow when you're in the void."

"I'm so confused right now." I dared to shut my eyes for a second to rub at them, but kept one hand gripping his jacket to make sure he didn't vanish. "I'm terrified you're not real."

"I'm real. You're okay."

"How did you find me?" I asked, trying to scrub the tears away from my vision. When he pulled me into another hug, I didn't fight it. My ego was left back at the crypt, staying behind once I fell into the darkness.

Zane held me close, hand resting at the base of my skull while I clung to him.

"I can always find you," he promised me. "Always."

I nodded into his shoulder. Somehow, he knew I was thanking him. I could feel it.

"I want out of here," I whispered. "Please get me the fuck out of here."

"I will. There's a doorway up ahead, we'll head that way and navigate our way through."

"You can see?"

"Yes." His brows lifted, like it was a weird question to ask. "Vampires can see in the dark, hunter."

"Oh. Right." I rubbed at my forehead. "I knew that."

Zane chuckled, which made me follow him more out of relief than any actual humor-related reason. I was still trying to climb out of the pit of fear that I had been in just moments previously, fresh from a panic attack and still a little shaky. My poor brain was fumbling with reconnecting wiring that was fried from terror, childhood trauma and unpacking that Zane had been my shadowy guide—

"Wait a fucking second." I pulled back from his hug and stared up at him. "Did we make out?"

A flashlight beam shone right in my face as Barnaby raced

down the hallway, panting from sprinting full force through the underground tunnel.

"Gods and Saints, Dallas Wilde, you scared the living soul from my body!" Barnaby managed around his gasping, light still annoyingly in my face. "Didn't you hear us calling for you?!"

"Hey, Barns." I winced, blocking my vision from his flashlight. "You mind lowering your interrogation light, please?"

"I thought you were dead! Or at least lost. Gods." He put his hand to his chest and lowered his beam. "I see you're in one piece, which is fortunate. That gives me permission to kick you in the ass the moment we're out of here. You did not mention we'd be crawling through an underground maze for this key."

"Didn't know that was part of the plan." I eased away from Zane and pointed back the way Barnaby came. "How the hell did you get down here? I thought it sealed up behind me after I dropped."

"Oh, it did." Barnaby aimed the light at Zane's chest. "This one ripped the damn trap door off its hinges and ran after you, leaving me behind. I had to traverse this alone."

I looked at Zane, who pushed Barnaby's flashlight down so it stopped shining in his face.

"Ah." I ignored the little warm butterflies in my chest at knowing Zane destroyed a Goddess's altar for me. "Can we get back out that way?"

"No, it's too slick to climb back through. It's a steep slope from the mausoleum to the bottom." Barnaby scanned the walls with his light. "We have to keep pressing ahead."

"Great."

"There's a doorway down the hallway," Zane told Barnaby. "Can you lead the way with your flashlight?"

"Hold on a second." Barnaby traced the groove in the wall with his light, swinging the beam across to examine a matching groove on the other side. "I think this is something."

"Barns, I don't want to be an asshole, but I really want to get out of here," I told him as gently as I could. "I don't like being in dark, narrow places."

"I think this might fix one of those problems." The light in his hand switched places as he patted himself down on either side, finally extracting a tiny compact with a floral print of penises across the top. Barnaby popped it open to reveal a small, round mirror on the inside.

"What are you doing?" Zane asked.

"Why do you have a pocket penis mirror?" I asked.

"I'm testing a theory, and because I like it." Barnaby positioned his flashlight at an angle, moving his mirror to reflect the light off its surface. "When I was reading about the Silent Steps, the researchers discussed that while they were building the now decommissioned temple of the Goddess, the building was lit using a very old form of magic. They didn't want to use fire, you see, because it would throw off too much heat and they worried it would ruin the tapestries."

I watched the fussy incubus aim the reflected flashlight beam across the wall, running it along the carved-out groove.

"What sort of magic?"

"Very old, fae magic," he said as a line of silver fire trailed down the groove like liquid, illuminating one side all the way down to the archway ahead of us. The light traveled like mercury, sliding ahead before defying gravity by looping up and over the stone archway, following the groove to the other side. It raced past us, lighting the way we had come.

In a blink, the darkness was gone, and a heatless, ancient fire burned with the splendor of fiery glass on either side of us.

"A trick of the light," Barnaby said with a smile.

Zane was smirking, clearly impressed, and he gave Barnaby a brotherly clap on the shoulder for a job well done.

It was my turn to praise him by admitting, "Alright, Barns. That was kinda badass."

"You can thank the ancient fae and historians for that trick." Barnaby clicked off his flashlight and tucked it into his bag, then pocketed his little penis mirror. "I'm just very good at following directions."

"How long will it burn?" I asked.

"According to the book, we have a few hours, then it'll go dark."

"Let's keep moving," Zane urged us forward. "I'd rather not test the time limit on fae fire."

We followed the lit pathway through the archway, the connecting room shrouded in darkness. Barnaby repeated the trick of the light on some braziers next to the door, which caused a chain reaction across the room similar to the hallway. Instead of just trailing down a thin stream of silver light, it crawled up to bring several torches to life three stories up.

As more light came into being, we realized quickly that we weren't in a small cavern underground, but a massive, stacked crypt with centuries of skeletons tucked into alcoves. We stood in the middle of a pillar-shaped grave, rounded walls lined with the upright bodies of what I could only assume were necromancers. Tattered robes and worn-away clothing hung from their forms, jaws kept in place by a black ribbon that circled their heads. By each of their feet, a ceramic vase sat in obedient silence, painted with thick, horizontal stripes with inverted triangles drawn through the bottom.

There had to have been two hundred skeletons staring down, watching us with eyeless stares of judgment.

That was enough to make the hairs stand up on the back of my neck, but the finishing touch to the creepiness was what was waiting at the farthest wall.

I had seen that statue of the Goddess before, the resemblance from Omar's museum back in St. Athesall almost a one for one of the real thing. In the center of the crypt was the black statue of the mother of death, her features stunning instead of worn away and faded with weathering. I could see the fine lines of her eyelashes, each strand of her hair around the bony crown, the sharpness of her scythe blade against her chest.

She watched us with unseeing eyes, arm outstretched to command her army, which looked to be all around us. Even the matching, painted vases containing all of her Thralls' ashes were placed just right, waiting to be summoned back to life.

At the base of her impressive altar was something that wasn't part of Omar's reconstruction. No doubt he didn't know about its existence, or thought it was just a legend. An ornate stone base sat at her feet with small platforms raised along the top. Five skulls sat facing forward, a tapestry draped over the stone where their heads rested.

Each skull had its own banner and a circlet made from carved ivory latticed with prayers.

"I am not a fan of this place," I told my little adventuring party. "This is a lot of necromancers just waiting to pop back to life."

"Can they do that?" Barnaby scanned each floor of standing corpses. "Can they just…wake back up on their own?"

"I fucking hope not." I put my hand on my knife and wished like hell I'd figured out how to get more life magic before falling down there. "That would suck."

"This is the necromancy council," Zane told us, his voice soft with awe. "There hasn't been a Thrall born in the past century who has seen this place."

"Consider this your birthday present then." I tilted my chin up at the standing audience all around us. "Those little containers next to their feet. Are those…?"

"Their Thralls, yes. Either their favorite, or the one with them when they died."

"And the bigger ones?" Barnaby dared to try and peek into one, touching the covering over the top.

"Barns, don't touch it!" My voice echoed up the tall chamber, a little more dramatic than I intended. "That's the Goddess's Thralls. I don't *think* anything can come back to life, but let's not fuck with our luck today."

"She had a lot of Thralls, it seems." Barnaby forced his hands into his pockets to keep from touching anything else.

"Perks of being a goddess. You can make more playthings whenever you want." I kept my knife in hand as I approached the skulls near the base of the altar. Their toothy grins seemed almost mocking. "These are the five council heads, aren't they?"

"They are," Zane confirmed, following beside me. "Each one spoke for the Goddess in their time. They would pass judgment and set laws, guide necromancers to follow the tenants of the Goddess."

"Fancy." I eyed the fabric under each skull, recognizing that they listed out a word I couldn't read. "Hey, Barns? You know what these say?"

"Their names," Zane answered instead. "I don't know which is which, but if I remember correctly their names are Nex, Mors, Leti, Pereo and…ah. Damn. I can't remember the last one."

In the chilly stillness of the crypt, standing before the heads of the necromancy council, under the vacant eyes of the Goddess, surrounded by the loyal acolytes of their cult, snickering started echoing up the walls. One voice, then two, goading little chuckles trailed up and swirled in the air around us.

I stepped back, gripping my knife, Zane curling his fists beside me. Barnaby held his bag strap tight with both hands and stuck behind us, trying to find the source of the noise.

The laughter was joined by another giggle, before a long, annoyed sigh undercut the mocking sounds of merriment.

"It's Funus," a voice announced, irritation dripping from each word. "My name is Funus."

It didn't take us long to figure out where the voice had been coming from after Funus made his name known, because the other skulls on the altar began laughing their non-existent asses off. Three out of five skulls had their jaws bouncing from laughter, only the two at the farthest left side remained stoney. One of which was Funus, who rolled glowing, yellow orbs that sat in his eye sockets.

"It's not *that* funny, you simpletons," Funus growled.

"Oh, it's been so long since I've been able to laugh," a woman's voice came from one of the skulls on the right, her eyes glowing icy blue. "It's even better that it gets to be at Funus's expense."

"Hundreds of years waiting for a new disciple and this is how it kicks off? What a state we're in," Funus complained.

"Oh relax, old friend," said another male voice, eyes orange. "You'd be laughing too if it was one of us he forgot."

Funus grumbled in defense that he absolutely would not have, but it didn't sound very sincere.

"Alright, everyone, that's enough," a fatherly voice soothed, pink eyes swiveling to his neighboring skulls. "Let's get back into character."

"Don't be shy, young lad, step up." The only other skull that hadn't laughed with the group watched us with green eyes, her voice matronly and commanding. "You're in the presence of the council of the Goddess. Speak your name."

"I'm Dallas Wilde," I told the council, sheathing my knife and placing it back into my pocket. "I'm going to assume you're not going to try and kill us while we're here?"

"Not much we can do in this state, my boy," the pink-eyed skull said with a warm chuckle. "Unless you stick your fingers in Leti's mouth."

Leti chattered his jaw, orange eyes amused.

"Step up, child, step up. When did these new disciples get so timid?" the green-eyed woman chided.

I glanced at Zane, who shrugged, and we approached the altar with Barnaby inching along with us.

"He's not timid, Mors. He's cautious." The other female voice with the blue eyes gave us each a long once-over. "A warrior from the looks of it. How devastatingly interesting."

"Oh, Pereo, for the love of the Goddess," Mors scolded. "I don't see how you can flirt without a damn pelvis."

"Sweet Mors, there are more things I can do without the hindrances of a pelvis. Some of us have imagination."

"I can see the red-eyed creature beside you is your Thrall, disciple Dallas Wilde, but who else do you bring with you?" Leti asked, causing everyone's gaze to land on Barnaby.

"This is Barnaby. He's a friend."

A long beat of quiet stretched, their eyes moving from Barnaby to me, then to each other in confused judgment.

"A historian, translator, and collector of fine artifacts," Barnaby added with a small bow.

"And those things," I tacked on. "He's the one that solved the mural in the tomb above us."

"A historian!" Funus swung his yellow gaze to Barnaby. "Goddess, I have so many questions about how things ended up. I haven't been able to read any news since well…dying, which is rather inconvenient. And that was a good two hundred years ago."

"It's more like four now, I'm afraid," Barnaby corrected. "You've been dead for some time now."

"Four! Well, that is disappointing. What ever happened with that uppity little prince that tried to claim the territory to the east?"

Barnaby's eyes lit up at the question, but before he could verbally pounce, his thunder was stolen.

"They've clearly come here with a mission in mind, Funus. They don't have time for you to prattle on about the politics of the mortal world." Mors rolled her green eyes. "Nex, could you please get us back to the matter at hand?"

"You'll have to excuse Funus," the pink-eyed skull, Nex, said apologetically. "He doesn't get a chance to hear about current affairs these days. Speak, child. What brings you to the council of the Goddess?"

"I've come seeking the Goddess's key," I told the undead council. "We know it's somewhere here within the crypt."

"Key?" Nex mused. "What an interesting request."

"Do you know anything about a key, Leti?" Pereo moved her eyes to her neighbor.

"Can't say I do."

"Are you sure it's a 'key,' young man?" Mors quizzed. "We've no key here at the council."

"Everything we've read and researched says that the Goddess's key is down here. It's an artifact that houses some of the Goddess's power." I watched the skulls glance at each other, impossible to tell if they were being shady since they had no facial expressions to read.

"I think something must have gotten tangled up linguistically," Funus said. "It isn't a "key" in the literal sense."

"Ssh, Funus," Leti hushed. "They're supposed to figure it out on their own."

"They've figured out how to get down here and seek the council, the first group to do so in a few hundred years, Leti," Funus shot back. "They're so close, it's driving me mad."

"And what would you need this artifact for exactly?" Nex asked, the eyes of the council upon us.

"Do not lie to us, child," Mors warned. "We are the eyes of the Goddess."

The line of question was most definitely a trap, or a test, to make sure I was worthy of grabbing the key—whatever it may be. All my years battling and defeating necromancers had taught me that the majority of them were self-centered, ego-inflated maniacs with the deeply rooted drive to destroy life. They turned innocent people into vampires, wreaked havoc on towns, and tore apart lives.

All of them were evil bastards, each and every single one.

I knew that the council must be more of the same, only much more powerful and ancient. They wouldn't be reasoned with or understand mercy, which meant I would need to trick them somehow, or start hurling skulls to get my point across.

"Hunter," Zane spoke, pulling my attention away from the judgment of the glaring skulls. "Remember what I told you about Sandros?"

"Yeah?"

Zane nodded to the council. "He followed their teachings devoutly."

That was a nice curve ball to throw at me in the middle of trying to navigate a high-pressure test from a gathering of powerful heads. It left me staring at him like a confused badger ready to bite someone, and I felt like going feral while my mind raced.

"Your Thrall is trying to guide you, young disciple," Nex said. "He speaks true."

"I thought his name was Dallas'?" Pereo whispered loudly to Leti.

"Tell them the truth," Zane told me, red eyes bright in the mirror light all around us. "They'll understand."

I wasn't so sure the council of the Goddess was going to be keen on the idea that I wanted their holy artifact in order to destroy it. It kinda seemed like their entire existence revolved around not only guiding newbie necromancers and being creepy in a hidden tomb, but also protecting a very sacred piece of their deity.

It seemed like a shit idea to lay all that out in the hopes that the necromancy council of the Death Goddess were the type to see reason.

Zane hadn't let me down yet, not about anything important. Sure, he let a vampire bite me a few days ago, and he thought it was hilarious when his stupid cat threw up in my shoes. But he had raced through the dark for me. He had saved me more than once.

He was a good bodyguard, a better friend.

I trusted him.

I pulled a strong breath in to make me feel bigger than I was.

"I want to destroy it," I told them. "I came here to find the artifact and make sure no one else can find it and wield it. There are forces at play here, people who are after it that have no plans of doing anything remotely good with it. No one should have the ultimate power over death."

Five sets of eyes moved back and forth between themselves, the silence deafening as we awaited their answer.

"Bold of you to come here just to ask for destruction," Mors finally spoke. "You stand before the council, promising to defile the blessing of our Goddess."

"Not defile," I confirmed. "Just make sure it doesn't end up in the wrong hands."

"And it's safe in your hands?" Nex offered.

"God, no," I said with a laugh. "I don't want it. I don't even want to be a necromancer. This shit was an accident. I hunt vampires for a living and offed this guy's necromancer." I jerked a thumb to Zane. "I ended up with his powers and this bozo."

"Oh, my Goddess," Zane mumbled, shutting his eyes like I was giving him a migraine.

"What?? You said to be honest!"

"About the artifact, you jackass."

"You didn't fucking specify!"

"Hold on a moment," Nex chimed in, his father voice on full display. "You…hunt vampires and kill necromancers?"

"Yeah, well. Kinda." I rubbed at the prickling feeling that I messed up that trailed down the back of my neck. "Just the asshole ones that torment people. I mainly freelance as a regular assassin and fish trainer now."

"A what?" Funus asked, eyes floating to Barnaby.

"He claims he can train fish to do tricks. I haven't seen it personally," Barnaby whispered, like an unhelpful twit.

"Is this some sort of…joke? Or test?" Pereo asked, desperately unsure of the situation.

"I think we got off on the wrong foot here." I rubbed at my eyes, the sinking feeling I had overshared made me feel exhausted. "May I approach the bench?"

"What bench?" Mors whispered, everyone now fully confused. I stepped over to the council's altar, all sets of eyes glued to me.

I continued, "I was telling the truth about what I am and why I'm here, because I don't have any reason to hide that from you. I hunt down those who use the Goddess and her teachings to hurt people. I don't know what it was like when you were mortal, what the religion was for you back then, but now it's vicious. They…hurt people. They steal kids and feed them to mindless vampires they raise from the dead. They destroy lives and corrupt corpses. It has to stop. I need to stop it."

Mors's eyes filled with sorrow. "I see the darkness in your soul. I see the hurt in your eyes."

"How awful," Leti whispered. "Have we really become such monsters?"

"Hurting children? Raising vampires from the dead?" Pereo sounded like she wanted to weep, but didn't have the means to do so.

"The state of things," Funus mourned.

"Dallas Wilde," Nex summoned, pink eyes searching me. "Come close to me. Place your hand upon my skull."

"What are you after, Nex?" Mors's eyes rotated his way.

"Answers." Nex gazed up at me as I approached.

"If I touch you, are you going to curse me or turn me into a ghoul or something?" I asked. "Because I have so much shit to do, Nex."

"I do not trick, mortal. I only guide."

My palm came to rest at the top of his skull, the bone cold against my skin. He had been dead so long that there was nothing left of his mortal form, no hair or leathery skin to show any signs of what he must have looked like. All that remained was bone and magic.

Nex's pink vision vanished into a darkness I knew as windows to the void, endless nothingness that lasted forever through his sockets. I felt it ripple, felt my chest knock like the stick rotated clockwise before getting stuck again.

I heard a whisper I wasn't sure was real, and I gasped a breath as Nex's eyes flared back into a pink with an intensity that bordered on neon.

"Child," he said, watching me with awe. "You have quite the journey ahead of you."

"What did you see, Nex?" Mors asked quickly, bordering on frantic. "What did she say?"

It was my turn to sound a little frantic. "She?"

"Yes." Nex's eyes softened. "The Goddess has been watching you, Dallas Wilde."

"I don't know how I feel about that."

"Council." Nex moved his eyes left to right, making sure his fellow members were paying attention. "We are to guide her blade through the path."

"Are you *certain*, Nex?" Mors prodded. "Without a doubt?"

"I am certain."

"The blade," Pereo breathed. "I always hoped I'd see it. That's the reason I joined the council, you know."

"And they said being dead in a crypt for hundreds of years would be boring!" Leti gave a hoot of laughter.

"I would kill to be able to write again," Funus complained. "This needs to be documented for history and I so miss the smell of ink."

"Can someone fill me in on what's going on?" I interrupted the excitement. "Does the blade have something to do with the key we're looking for?"

"Very much so, disciple." Nex watched me carefully. "We'll make sure you get what it is you seek."

Relief filled my chest for the first time in I didn't know how long. Finally, something was working out as planned. We had been bossed around by a terrifying health guru, sent on a mission that made us trek through a creepy cemetery, gone through a black hole of hell, and ended up face to face with the undead council. And for once, it wasn't a trap, a dead end or something that caused one of us to walk away with holes punched through us.

I'd call that I win. One we damn well deserved.

"That is, of course," Mors spoke up, popping my feel-good bubble. "If you can pass the trial."

CHAPTER
EIGHTEEN

I'D BEEN FEELING SO good about everything until that damn head spoke up.

I knew I sounded like a tired brat when I let out a dry, "Of course," to the council to the Death Goddess, but damn, was I ready to get the hell out of that tomb. There's only so much cryptic dead people nonsense I could stomach in one day, and I'd already had more than enough to last me a lifetime. I was usually elbow-deep in vampire guts by this point in an exchange with a necromancer, and I hadn't had the chance to kill anything for a few days.

It was a total rip-off.

"What do you need me to do?"

"You there. The incubus scholar," Mors called. "Barny."

"Barnaby," Funus corrected tersely. "Goddess's sake, Mors, it's not a hard name."

"Thank you, Funus," Barnaby said primly. "A person's name is meant to be respected."

"Here, here," the fussy skull added.

I rolled my eyes so hard I saw my brain. "Saint, you two are soulmates."

It was a joke, a jab really since they were getting on my nerves, but they even sputtered the same. It was kinda sweet.

"Barnaby," Mors corrected through her teeth. "See that small clay pot near Leti? Yes? Bring it before the disciple."

For a second, I thought Barns would snap at the council skull that he wasn't to be ordered around. He had the look of a man about to spit, his mouth twisted up in offense before he begrudgingly did what was asked. The small vessel Mors had told him to grab was no bigger than an apple, painted with similar stripes as the bigger Thrall urns all around the crypts, minus the cutout triangles.

"Within this vase is your trial," Nex explained once Barnaby handed it to me. "You are to pour the ashes onto the ground at your feet, not letting a single piece scatter."

With a sigh, I kneeled down to the stone floor and opened the lid gently. The ash inside was powdery and light gray, dust floating up a bit as I gently poured it into a neat little mound. It made a perfect mountain, maybe half an inch tall, and I looked to the skulls for more instruction.

"This ash is your test, child." Nex's pink eyes twinkled. "You are to bring it back to its form."

"You want me to…resurrect this?" I huffed a laugh, not getting the joke. "I thought that was impossible."

"Not impossible. Just very, very difficult," Mors said. "If you are to obtain this 'key' you speak of, you must prove yourself worthy."

"Council," Zane spoke respectfully, not nearly as annoyed as I was. "My necromancer has only had his power for a short amount of time. He's barely managed to bring a fresh body back so far."

"Hey, I did okay," I argued. "I made him talk for a good five minutes."

Zane cut me a sideways look before focusing back on the heads. "He needs time to hone his skills before he can do this."

"Your necromancer must show us this skill now," Mors bit back. "Or we will not aid him further."

"It is what the Goddess commands, child of the void," Nex clarified. "Have faith."

Zane sighed with the weight of their words and kneeled beside me, glaring down at the pile of ash.

"Thanks for the vote of confidence," I muttered to my vampire.

"Even Sandros at his best couldn't do this, hunter," Zane whispered. "Only the Goddess can bring back ash."

"So, what then? They're fucking with me?" I looked at him, and he shook his head.

"No. They seem to think you can."

"But I can't," I told him. "Because I'm not a kick-ass death lady."

"We're going to have to try."

"Maybe we can just start going through these tombs one by one." I swept my eyes up and around the standing audience of skeletons. "What are the odds there's a key in one of them? We can play corpse piñata."

"We can hear you," Pereo sang. "In case you're meant to be whispering."

Zane huffed a noise very close to a laugh at my piñata idea, a smile almost curling his lips.

"Let's try this first. Then we'll do the corpse piñata."

"Promise?" I asked, hopeful for bone smashing.

This time he did smile, and I matched it.

"Promise."

I flexed my hands and shook them out, readying myself for the impossible task.

"You gonna do the anchor thing?" I asked him. "I'm going to need a boost to even attempt this."

Zane had come to sit beside me on my right side, and instead of placing his hand on my shoulder like he had done previously, he held it out with his palm up.

I glanced at it and he lifted his eyebrow.

"In case you fall again," he said, teasing. "I'll catch you this time."

"If the floor opens up on this trial, I'm starting corpse piñata with the heads." I took Zane's hand. His skin was still warm, but he was starting to cool. Knowing that I would need to give him blood again soon sent a thrill through me, and my chest bone knocked and shifted. It made me cough and rub at the knobby bit of mystery stick that still hadn't reabsorbed.

"Alright." I put my left hand over the ash. "Here goes nothing."

In the stillness of the ancient tomb, surrounded by the eyeless gaze of hundreds of dead necromancers, I listened to the crackle of the mirror fire. The scent of dust stuck to the insides of my nose, my legs cold against the unforgiving stone. The pile of ash before me was just that—a lifeless powder with nothing to spark magic from. I couldn't feel anything.

I tried to focus on how the magic felt when it was pulsing through me, hoping that bringing it forward would help me somehow find a way to dip my hand into the void and go searching. The faintest, tickling hints of death magic slithered over my arm, cold little ants dancing at the tips of my fingers, but it faded just as quickly as it had started.

"I can't keep it activated," I grumbled. "It's like my magic can't sense there's something here. Usually, I have to put my hand on the body to help…you know. Get the juices going."

Zane hummed in thought. "Let's try something. Hold out your hand."

I rotated my free hand and watched Zane scoop the ash into his hand before sifting it into mine.

"Is that allowed?" Barnaby asked, having gone to stand next to his new bestie.

"I believe so," Funus mused. "Each necromancer has their own methods." He cut his eyes back to us as Mors hushed him.

"Focus," Zane told me, closing my fingers around the ash.

"This vessel is yours to command. Pierce through the veil and find its soul."

"This vessel is just dirt. Even if I could find its soul, what can it come back to?" The ash settled into the creases of my palm, gritty and dry. "Seems cruel to bring something back as a clump of ash."

"You won't have to hold it long, then you can release it back into the void." Zane gave my hand a squeeze. "Shut your eyes. Focus."

I exhaled and did as he suggested, plunging myself into darkness as I held the vampire's hand and a fistful of ash.

"The magic searches," Zane continued, his voice a grounding rod in the storm. "The void calls. Slip into its depths, it welcomes you there."

"I don't like the dark," I told him, feeling weirdly vulnerable. "I sure as shit don't like the void."

"You don't fear death," he reminded me, and my chest tightened at hearing him sound…

Proud.

Maybe in awe.

A shiver traced up my spine as Zane cupped his free hand over my fist, and my grip tightened.

The tendrils of my magic curled down my arms, icy and powerful, and I felt the ripple of the void just beyond my reach. The crackling mirror fire faded, silence falling around me like a blanket. I could feel the magic reaching out from my body, searching, and it felt marvelous that it wasn't gripping me while I fought for control.

It felt like an extension of myself, maybe for the first time ever.

"Good." Zane's voice sounded like an echo, a whisper. A shadow. "Don't fight it. You don't fear this place. You are the master of it."

The smell of dust and old bones was gone. The cold of the stone faded from my legs. All around me was darkness, and the mortal part of myself, the human part of myself, threatened to revolt. The icy tendrils twitched, my chest grew cold, and for a breath I thought I was going to scream.

"Dallas."

I swallowed the panic in my throat and turned to the voice, my eyes opening into the endless darkness of the void. We sat in nothingness, floating in forever as it rippled out like midnight waters.

It was nothing.

And me.

And Zane.

Zane had become my shadow guide again, a dark figure of smoke with two red beacons for eyes. In the void, I could see his teeth, obsidian and sharp, his fingers clawed, his eyes steady.

My tendrils calmed, my chest relaxed, and I squeezed the misty claws of my vampire.

I was in the void, and I wasn't afraid.

I had stepped through the veil without dying, without drinking vampire blood, without shedding my mortal body. My magic danced over me like moths worshiping a black flame, and in that moment, I felt powerful.

The dust in my grip was just a collection of atoms and elements, clay to be reforged. Through the ripples, I reached out, my magic unfurling like a flower. The smallest thing, a twinkle reflecting on a cresting wave, swam over with the ease of a mote of dust drifting on the breeze. It traveled on the summons I had called, traveling on the tip of my outstretched magic.

I felt it slip between my fingers, I felt the ash in my hand begin to move.

Light around me bloomed as the crypt came back into vision, the crackle of the mirror fire surrounding me. Zane's fingers uncurled with mine, as the dust breathed in for the first time in centuries.

It barely had its form. It was barely anything, the mere outline of a creature rested in my palm. Made of ash and magic, it had been forced back together with a soul that had been long lost in the void.

It panted for air, tail thrashing, and my heart gave a little pang of guilt.

"It's a fish," I whispered. "I brought back a fish."

The gravity of what it was, how I made it happen, what that truly meant, went sailing through the air along with my body as the tiny collection of reforged dust exploded into a fist of energy.

The air in my lungs was ripped out as I tumbled backwards, ass over head, and slid to a stop on my shoulders. Zane was beside me, making the same pained groans I was after being tossed around like a pair of rag dolls.

"What the fuck?" I rubbed at my shoulder as I sat up, staring at the dust still clinging to my palm. "Was that supposed to happen?"

"I don't…think so." Zane sat up and winced, testing the back of his head for blood. "It felt unstable the moment you opened your eyes."

"Alright, well." I climbed to my feet, complaining a bit more from the aches traveling up my hip, and smeared the remaining fish ash onto my jeans. "On to plan B then. Corpse piñata it is."

The skulls didn't seem impressed with my fish trick, but then again, they didn't have skin to show any emotion to begin with. It wasn't until I noticed Barnaby with both hands over his mouth like he just witnessed the Saint's rebirth that I had a suspicion I may have done something worthwhile.

"Uh." I finished getting fish dust off me then bowed. "Taadaa?"

"Goddess be praised," Nex breathed. "You actually did it."

"I guess?" I winced as Zane smacked my shoulder, but smirked when I saw the grin on his face. "Yeah, I guess we did, huh?"

"Not bad, hunter."

"Not bad? I pulled a fish soul into a pile of dirt and made it wiggle. I'm fucking amazing."

"And just like that, his modesty is gone," Barnaby tried to tease, but he was smiling too big for it to land. "I have to admit, that was something to see."

"It has been centuries since we've seen a true display of the Goddess's will," Mors added, all bitchiness gone. "You have passed the trial."

"You are truly a child of the Goddess," Nex praised. "We will guide you on your path, show you the way to achieve what you seek."

"You'll show me how to get the key?"

"Yes, disciple," Nex told me. "We'll help you extract the key you seek."

"You owe me three gold, Leti," Pereo sang. "You didn't think he could do it."

"I love getting proved wrong! Keeps death exciting." Leti laughed.

"I still wish I had a way to write this all down," Funus complained.

"I could write it down for you, Funus," Barnaby offered cheerfully. "I have the most fantastic quill back home…"

"What we will need to do is make sure—" Nex began, when a familiar burst of violence ripped through the tomb like a crack of thunder. The gunshot rang up the tall walls, deafening us for a moment as my body flew into autopilot.

I grabbed Barnaby and forced him behind me, my own gun ripped from its holster to aim at the entryway to the tomb. Zane had placed himself to my right, slightly in front, teeth bared and ready to attack.

The council went mute.

Nex was now a pile of smoldering dust, the life magic infused bullet destroying him completely.

The golden crest of the Saint's Army pinned to their vests reflected back the mirror light as they approached, guns trained on us, eyes hard with hate. They poured into the room like oil, flanking each side, slowly surrounding us.

Each gun was loaded with life magic.

Each bullet was a very permanent death sentence for the undead creatures haunting this tomb, and the necromancer standing with them.

"Zane, get behind me," I told him, thankful my voice wasn't shaking. He didn't move, his fists balled and body coiled to attack.

I carefully reached up and flicked the switch to my emotion blocker tech around my neck.

His fists relaxed as he felt my fear, my real, scorching fear, and he stepped behind me as I tossed my gun to the ground.

"The Saint protects and shields life." I showed my palms, my heart trying to hammer through my chest. "Casting light onto the shadow."

Faces I knew glared at me from behind barrels, people I had once seen smile. I remembered all of their laughter, all of their voices, and knew their favorite movies and songs.

We had cried together once.

Trained together. Bled together.

Standing in the tomb that night, I was a cornered rat facing down the teeth of my former family.

When one of them finally spoke, his voice felt like a dagger through my heart.

"Who figured out the trick of the light?"

I tilted my head to indicate behind me.

"My friend. I was always shit with fae history."

Magnus still moved like an old soldier, slight limp on the left side. He had sworn up and down that the shrapnel buried in his hip wasn't worth the effort to extract, and stubbornly learned to exist with the constant discomfort.

He was grayer than I remembered. His mustache was all salt with no pepper left. Age had creased the skin around his eyes, deepened the lines near his mouth, but had otherwise done little to the muscle mass he had cultivated over time.

To add insult to injury, or because he was the one that had led them there, Austin stood beside him with one hand resting on his holstered weapon, the other ready to engage if needed.

"Magnus." I didn't dare drop my hands just yet. "You're looking old as dirt."

"Old, but not dead." His eyes landed on each player one by one, sizing up the threats standing before him. "See you're keeping interesting company these days, boy. Got yourself a sex demon boyfriend and a throat ripper."

"Landlord, actually," Barnaby added, peeking out from behind Zane. "Somewhat friend, mostly landlord and historian. Barely friends, really. We're not friends. I don't even know him!"

"To what do I owe the pleasure of being stalked?" I asked, keeping my focus on Magnus as he slowly approached.

"Austin here says he ran into you a few days back." Magnus stepped up to the altar, pinching the dust of what was once Nex to rub between his gloved fingers. "Told me you were poking around looking for information about some lost artifacts."

"I was, yeah. Those got sold to Florence Pierce." It took all of my will not to inch away from him as he stepped closer to Leti's skull.

"Heard about that." Magnus was still speaking to me, but he was watching the remaining council members. "How much did that bank you?"

"Zero. Someone stole the artifacts from me and sold them before I could get them back."

"Shame." He pulled his knife free from his hip, the glow of life magic bright against the enchanted metal. The death magic in my body recoiled, and I shifted my weight to put myself more in line with being a shield for Zane and Barns.

Magnus gave Leti's skull a tap with his knuckle.

"Gonna introduce me to your friends, boy?"

"We are the necromancy council, soldier of the Saint," Leti told him, voice scathing. "You attack on sacred ground, decimate a mind ancient and wise. You've stolen knowledge from this realm."

"When it comes to some knowledge, especially that of dark magic and evil, I'm very fine with wiping it out of existence." Magnus scooped up Leti's skull and examined it like it was an interesting find at a garage sale. "The Saint shines light into the darkness, after all."

"Foolish child," Mors snapped. "The Goddess and the Saint are two sides to the same coin. We are not enemies."

"Gonna have to disagree with you there, skull. Only one deity brings back the dead and creates monsters. I don't believe the Saint ever steals children and tosses them into pits to be eaten by vampires, or pilots dead bodies around to murder folk." He sat Leti back down harder than he needed to, making one old molar fall loose. "Ask Dallas about that. He knows all about being tossed into a pit with vampires, don't you, boy?"

I ignored the cold prickling of old memories churning in my gut, and tried to shift topics.

"What do you want, Magnus?"

"What you came here for," he said. "The missing artifact."

"Well, you shot the skull that was telling me about it so…" I shrugged. "Gonna be a little hard-pressed to find the key now."

"Oh, I'm sure we can think of something." Magnus turned his head to give a command, glancing over his shoulder. "Start searching the crypts. Two per floor."

"There is nothing in those graves but the old bones of our disciples," Pereo insisted. "Leave them be."

"What you seek is not in their resting places," Leti added. "You do nothing but desecrate the dead."

"No more than you lot do." Magnus flipped his knife around, catching it by the blade so he could knock the hilt against Mors's brow bone. "Why don't you pick up where your friend left off. Make this process go a little faster."

"You fool, buffoon," Mors hissed. "You strike against us without merit, defile our tomb, and you expect me to tell you anything? Ha!"

The strike against Pereo was fast and brutal, Magnus's knife cracking her skull with the blade before she fell away into a fine powder of ash.

I bit my tongue hard, the pain keeping me grounded so I wouldn't focus his wrath on us.

"You were saying?" Magnus asked Mors, too calm for having just murdered her fellow council member.

"You fiend," Mors snapped her jaw, green eyes flaring. "You think we fear returning to the void? Our Goddess awaits us with open arms. We return to nothingness, free of grief, pain and suffering. I do not fear you. I do not fear—"

Magnus cracked her skull with his blade and twisted, eyes cold. Mors fell into nothing.

"Magnus. They're the only leads we have," I reminded him. "If you kill them off, we're back to square one."

"Last chance," Magnus told Leti. "I'll let you keep being a rotting skull in a cold crypt if you help us find the blade."

"Sir," Austin's voice didn't make Magnus turn, but he kept speaking anyway. "Maybe we should try and keep at least one talking head for information."

Magnus placed the tip of his knife close to Leti, ignoring Austin.

Leti's eyes danced, a laugh starting to bubble through him like a boiling cauldron. Somehow, the fleshless skull sighed with relief, and even though he couldn't physically smile, his voice held a joy I didn't understand.

"The blade will find you, child of the Saint," Leti promised. "And her wrath will be magnificent."

"Magnus! Goddamnit!" I yelled as he drove his blade into Leti's eye, the skull joining the others in scattered ashes of lost knowledge. I saw Austin wince, a gesture he tried to cover by turning his head away.

"Relax, Dallas." His knife was cleaned on his sleeve. "You're being emotional."

"I'm being pissed off that you just murdered the only sources of knowledge to the whereabouts to the fucking key, you jackass!"

"What did they tell you?" he asked coolly, not putting his knife away.

"Weird, cryptic bullshit, but I was making headway. They were just starting to make sense when you showed up." I set my jaw as he stepped closer to me, eyes floating from the dust to give me a look once-over.

"Make sense how?"

"Well, the first skull you destroyed said he'd show me where the key is." I jerked my head to the ashes on the altar. "But that ship fucking sailed."

"What did they give you?"

"They didn't give me anything." I motioned to my pockets but didn't move further. "Check for yourself."

Magnus had always been a stony wall of grit, especially when he was on a mission. I had only seen the man show emotion a handful of times in my life, brief little windows of compassion or joy, but those seemed impossible when he stared me down in the silver light of the tomb. There was a decade between us now, a mountain of hard feelings we'd never be able to chip away.

Magnus's eyes pinned themselves to Zane for a long time before slicing back my way.

"How did you get afflicted?"

"I killed Edras Roe," I explained. "His...affliction passed to me."

Magnus huffed a noise too bitter to be a laugh.

"You threw away your Saint's crest, didn't you?" He shook his head when I didn't answer. "I always told you the Saint would protect you from the darkness if you kept him with you."

"I didn't know you meant literally," I snapped. "It was never mentioned that the crest repelled necromantic transferal. It all just sounded like church."

"You never paid attention during church, boy, that's why you're cursed." Magnus gave Zane a disgusted glance. "I guess you gave up killing Thralls for good, then?"

"That's not fair," I hissed before I thought better of it, a bone-deep chill shaking me as he ground his back teeth.

"Not fair," he repeated, the words bile at the back of his throat. "Not fair is having my son cut a goddamn Thrall loose on our camp because he was weak. Not fair is watching him run away like a damn coward after the monster he let loose killed two soldiers and set fire to our home."

"It was an accident," I tried to say over him, hating that my eyes started to sting. His words were landing with brutal accuracy, each one hitting me like a speeding truck.

It hurt. It hurt so bad to finally hear his voice again, and to have my shame thrown back into my face with full force.

"You ran away, Dallas. You broke our trust, our home, and *ran away*. Now you stand here in a necromancer tomb, swearing yourself to the whore Goddess of Death, palling around with another goddamn vampire—"

"Enough!" Zane's voice sounded like a hurricane; powerful and deadly, with the force to sweep away everything in its path. "You've made your damn point. Now you're just being a cruel old man grinding salt in the wound."

"It speaks," Magnus mocked, lip curled. "Did he tell you how he betrayed his family? Left us there to pick up the pieces after he defected?"

"If you really are his family then you wouldn't be standing here berating him. You called him 'son.' Act like a father."

Anger flashed in Magnus's gaze, a crack in his stoney expression. As the fault grew, a similar breakdown was happening with my composure, fear traveling up my spine. I had been trying so hard to keep my poker face, but I showed my hand when Magnus moved.

He took a step toward Zane, and I blocked him.

It was a simple sidestep to put myself in front of him, my body shifting a few inches.

But it gave me away. It showed something I should have kept hidden.

I cared about the vampire.

It was a grave mistake.

The fury in Magnus's gaze metastasized, forming a wall I couldn't see through, and he took a lazy step backwards.

"Magnus, we both want the same thing," I pleaded. "You want the artifact gone, so do I. There's no reason we can't work together on this."

"I think we'll work together just fine." Magnus flipped his knife in his hand and caught it, the momentary distraction buying the soldiers just enough time to make their move.

I heard the rattle of the rock rolling under just before the grounding charm kicked in, gravity ramping up so quickly it brought all three of us to the ground. Barnaby landed with a pained grunt, clutching his bag to his chest as he curled onto his side. Zane fell into a kneel before losing the battle, falling to all fours with his fangs bared.

I ended up in a similar pose, yelling through my teeth to fight against the overwhelming tug trying to make me kiss the ground. I glared at Magnus's boots as he walked along the perimeter of the ward, the ring on the ground dancing with amber sparks.

"You're...such a dick," I ground out, managing to pull myself up to my knees. It hurt to do anything other than sit still, my joints screaming as I held myself upright. Zane's muscles bunched as he heaved himself upright, sitting back on his heels. Barns stayed down, groaning in discomfort.

"Tell me what the necromancers were talking to you about, Dallas," Magnus demanded. "Tell me everything you know about the artifact."

"I told you everything already. We came here looking for the key. The council was telling us about it when you killed them off."

Magnus flipped his knife again, catching it by the blade with an expert familiarity before handing it to Austin.

"What do you know about the key?" Magnus kept up his line of questioning as Austin strolled over to Zane, pocketing a counter charm to keep himself immune to the grounding spell.

"Just that it's been lost for centuries and was supposed to be down here." I forced myself to turn my head, tracking Austin's movements. "What the hell are you doing?"

Austin didn't answer, the life magic infused blade dangerously close to Zane.

"Where is the blade, Dallas?" Magnus continued his verbal barrage.

"What blade?" I snapped. "I don't know what you're talking about."

Austin grabbed a fistful of Zane's hair and yanked his head back, the force combined with the grounding spell made Zane grunt in pain. A vein pulsed in his neck from the effort of keeping his head from falling back too far.

"Knock it off, Austin!"

"Answer his questions, Wilde, and we don't have to do this," Austin shot back. "No one else needs to die if you just stop fucking around."

"Where is the blade?" Magnus repeated, colder this time. "The skull mentioned it before it died. It said the blade would find me. Where *is* it?"

"I don't fucking know, Magnus!"

Austin brought the blade up close to Zane's face, the glow of the life magic mottled sunlight on his pale skin. The red in Zane's eyes flared, his breathing gaining speed at the proximity of the vampire-killing magic.

"Where is it, Dallas?" Magnus again, unbothered by the clear torment he was putting us through.

"I don't know. I don't *know*, I swear it. I swear to the fucking Saint."

That gained me a nice swift backhand, my carefully balanced posture crumbling to the ground. I had forgotten how prickly they were about spitting the Saint's name out without swearing allegiance first. I also forgot how badly Magnus's backhand stung. Metallic warmth coated the lining of my mouth and I spit some aside.

"H-hey! Leave him alone!" Barnaby yelled, somehow able to gather a rock into his hand. He tried to throw it but it just rolled across the floor a few inches for his effort. "He's telling the truth, you pickled prick!"

"I don't have reason to hurt you, but I will, sex demon," Magnus drawled. "Don't speak again or I'll break your fingers."

"I lied before," Barnaby added viciously. "Dallas is my friend. My best friend, actually, even if he is somewhat of a selfish jerk who's late on his rent. And you, good sir, are a bastard. A bastard! A rude, awful, twat bastard!"

"Twat bastard?" I tried to look his way but it was too hard.

"I'm stressed!" Barnaby tried to throw another rock, but this time it didn't leave his fingers. "I stand by what I said. Every word. Even the terrible insults."

"Thanks, Barns. You're my best friend too. After Kevin."

"Don't make me regret this moment of heroism, Dallas," Barnaby complained. "It's likely going to cost me my fingers, and I'm second to a fish."

Magnus took a step, and I spoke up fast.

"One of the skulls said they were going to guide the blade," I told Magnus before he could act on breaking Barnaby's fingers. "That was all he said. I don't know what it meant."

"Guide the blade where?"

"I don't know." I was exhausted, my head pounding. "If I did, I'd tell you. Does it have something to do with a key, maybe? Florence sent us here for a key specifically."

"Did you find a key?" he asked, sounding bored.

I tried to shake my head and huffed from the effort.

"No. Just…dust. Ash. Nothing else."

My neck was starting to ache from the effort of holding myself up, my shoulders screaming from the strain. In the throbbing pain of stiff muscles and mounting fear, a surprise moment of relief came from someone I least expected.

"I don't think he knows anything, sir," Austin said. "He's a scumbag, but he is a shitty liar. He's being honest."

Magnus cut him a look so fierce I felt it land on Austin like a slap.

"I don't believe him, and that's all that matters."

"Sir—" Austin tried again but Magnus set his jaw. "Yes, sir."

"Do I need to worry about you defecting, Austin? You enjoying your time a little too much in his crypt?"

Austin's voice fell back into his well-practiced, robotic, military cadence.

"No, sir."

"Good. Then follow your orders." Magnus gave a nod. "Let's help jog Wilde's memory."

I heard the sizzle before I heard Zane's scream, and I didn't know which one froze my blood more. Austin had the tip of his dagger pressed into Zane's cheek, his skin frying under the pinprick of life magic that cut into his flesh. The agony and fear ripping through him crashed into me, my chest twisting like a torrent of blades, bone and anguish.

I felt something inside of me click into place, a bone handle aligning, dark magic igniting with a fury I couldn't wrangle. The anger that burst from me was as vast and endless as the void.

Cold tendrils slid down my arms and expanded across the room like stretching veins, crawling up the walls and into the tiny cracks in the stones.

I saw the ripple of darkness.

I saw blood red and endless nothing, Zane's screams echoing as they melted into my own.

I stood, the charm no longer binding me, the magic failing after being swallowed by the void. Austin was staring in horror, fear so pure it turned his skin the color of ash.

The skeletons standing in their crypts gave an ovation of clattering jaws, the lids of the Thrall jars warbled as their bases shook.

"Let go," I spoke with a voice dipped in death. "Of my fucking vampire."

Austin let go of my fucking vampire.

He also pissed his pants, which I felt a little bad for.

Magnus was gripping his gun so tight his arm shook, his fear buried deep under shock and anger.

My chest twisted again, more clicking and sliding, the magic pouring from me began to ease as Zane put his hand on my shoulder.

"Easy," he whispered, his cheek still red from the burn of the life magic. It blistered and bled, angry and painful. "Ease back, hunter. Let it go."

I hadn't noticed how badly I was shaking until the ripples started to fade, the skeletons around us falling back into their deathly silence. Cold magic receded back up my arms, knocking me off balance and back into reality. Zane caught me before I fell, holding me steady until I could get my feet back under me.

"Saints be blessed," Magnus heaved, breathing like he ran a marathon. "What the hell are you?"

"I am a goddamn fish trainer, you overwhelming asshole," I spat. "And sometimes I'm a very vindictive necromancer who will fuck you up if you pull that shit again."

"Here, here!" Barnaby added triumphantly, dirt smeared across his cheek. He moved to grab a rock to try his hand at hurling it properly this time, but thankfully Zane caught his arm and shook his head.

"My previous offer is off the table. Consider it an asshole tax," I told my former father, holding on to Zane's arm to keep from falling down. It made the moment a little less badass, because of the shaking and creeping horror that I might puke, but I managed to still sound pretty authoritative. "We're going to find this thing on our own, and you're going to stay out of our way."

"You have the darkness in you now, boy. There's no telling what temptations of power that artifact will have for you." To my surprise Magnus lowered his gun but didn't put it away. "If you find it, you might not be able to destroy it."

"I'm still a necromancer killer. I still hunt and destroy evil. You know I am, because you left that cheeky little note in the vampire den outside of St. Athesall knowing I'd find it." I swallowed down another surge of rage. "You knew where I was, and you never even tried to find me."

Magnus didn't acknowledge the last part, instead pivoted around it.

"Counteroffer: we stay out of each other's way. The more eyes looking for this thing, the better. I can't pull back the effort now."

"Stay *far* out of my way," I clarified.

"I'll pray the Saint finds you again, boy. This path you're on now will only lead to more darkness and suffering." Magnus slid his gun into its place and gave a sharp, whistled command. His soldiers, my former family, retreated from the tomb in the direction they had come from.

Only Austin looked back, fear almost clouding over the sorrow in his eyes.

It almost hurt to see, but my anger was still too raw to allow me to grieve.

I tried to think of something devastatingly clever to say to Magnus about keeping his bullshit praying to himself, or that I didn't need him anymore, or that he looked like a withered testicle with a mustache, but I was so damn tired I just flipped him off.

The tomb fell back into silence as the Saint's Army fled, their silhouettes fading through the hallway. Whatever they had used to rappel down was pulled back up, I heard the echoed commands Magnus gave to not leave anything behind. Once they were gone, I let myself exhale.

"Are you alright?" Zane asked, his fingers cold as he rotated me around to face him. His cheek looked terrible, and his skin was pale from me pulling too much strength from him during my outburst.

In the silver light of the Goddess's tomb, even with a big, ugly blister on his face, Zane was remarkable. He had let me borrow so much of his strength in so many ways, from forcing a dust fish back to life to telling off my asshole father when I couldn't.

I'd never had someone in my life care about me like this vampire did.

My heart did such a terrifying shuffle as I felt the knob in my chest rattle, mesmerized by the silver reflecting in his blood-red eyes.

I heard myself whisper, "Oh, shit."

And everything went black.

I REGAINED CONSCIOUSNESS UPSIDE DOWN.

It took me a few blinks to understand what I was seeing, but thankfully the moonlight helped illuminate the ground. I watched Zane's leg moving, the shadows of the tall trees around us casting long stretches of darkness across the ground.

One of Zane's arms was hooked behind my knee, my stomach across his shoulders and my right arm held in one hand. I could smell the cool breeze tossing dead leaves around, and I tried to lift my head to see the sky.

"Are we outside?" I asked stupidly, then wrung my eyes shut to blink some sense back.

"Yes," Zane answered, continuing to walk. "We're heading back to the car."

"Can you put me down?"

"You passed out, hunter. I don't think you should try walking." He grunted. "Stop wiggling."

"Your shoulder is pointy."

"Deal with it." He adjusted me a bit over his shoulders, the jabbing in my ribs worsening.

"How are you so damn bony?"

"Because I have bones," the oh-so-hilarious Thrall quipped.

"Hunter, I'm going to run you into a fucking tree if you don't stop moving."

"Then let go of me, you giant, bony ass." I used my free arm to poke his side, which caused the best reaction possible. He jerked hard and huffed a noise of annoyance, and I practically squealed with the result. "Are you ticklish?!"

Before I could try to test my theory, Zane put me down.

And by "put me down" I mean he dropped me like a sack of bricks.

I landed on my shoulder and it hurt, but it was so, so worth it.

Barnaby added aid by shining his flashlight in my face.

"I see you're back to yourself again," Barnaby said. "You were out cold for a little while."

"How did we get outside?" I pulled myself to my feet and whined a bit from the aches in my body. "I thought it was too steep to climb back up?"

"Barnaby found a secret exit behind the altar." Zane nodded his direction. "It led us through without any issues, but we're a little further from the entrance to the crypt."

"I remembered it from my research," Barnaby explained without prompting, seeming a little more sweaty than he should. He was busy swinging his flashlight around instead of focusing on anything in particular.

"Huh. Lucky," I mused. "Funny that the archeologists didn't mess with it but felt the need to add it into the book."

Barnaby coughed and adjusted his bag.

"Who knows why. We should probably keep going, right? It's getting late and we have a long drive ahead."

"Barns," I tried, but Zane distracted me by picking some dirt out of my hair. I swatted at his hand, only then remembering the horrible cut on his face. The swelling had gone down just a fraction, but the wound itself was still angry and raw. "Saint, Zane. Your face. Does it still hurt?"

"It's not pleasant."

"Will you heal if you drink blood? That's not...permanent,

right?" I took my knife out and he shook his head, motioning for me to put it away.

"Yes, it will heal, but I'm fine for the time being. We need to focus on getting to the car."

"It'll take two seconds. Here." I tried to put the blade to my palm but he stopped me, his hand touching mine.

"Hunter, you can barely stand. I can handle a little discomfort while you get your strength back."

"Zane, that's not 'a little discomfort.' You have a hole in your cheek." My heart thumped poison through my chest at how horrible the injury looked, the sound of his screams still haunting me.

He was hurt. Wounded. His cheek punctured with a slice of life magic that *my family* caused. Austin had tortured him because I hadn't answered the way Magnus wanted, and I hadn't stopped it fast enough.

Zane was hurt because of me, because I had a fucked-up family dynamic and couldn't handle my own bullshit.

"Dallas," he started softly, but I surged ahead.

"Let me do this," I told him, chest aching. "Let me help."

"This isn't your fault."

"How the fuck do you figure that?" I snapped, guilt festering into cruel anger. "All of this shit is my fault, Zane. We could have died, do you understand that? The Saint's Army kills people like us—" I heard myself say it, admit it finally, and I felt something slide apart and break.

People like us.

I wasn't human anymore, not in the same way I had been.

I had become a monster, a necromancer. A part of the Death Goddess's harem.

It terrified me that I wasn't repulsed by the idea anymore.

Barnaby cleared his throat, his discomfort thunderous.

"I'm going to…go on ahead and find the car," he told us, backing away. "This seems important and shouldn't involve me."

I heard Barnaby retreat, slowly at first but then picking up speed to let Zane and I hash out whatever the hell I was currently unpacking.

"People like us," Zane said. "Don't owe each other apologies."

"I'm sorry anyway," I countered. "Even if you don't need to hear it, I need to say it." I rolled my knife around in my grip. "This whole trip has been a nightmare. Saint, the whole damn week has been a nightmare, who am I kidding?"

"It had its highlights." He smirked when I looked at him like he was an insane idiot. "We got to crash a gala and wear nice suits."

"I got my ass kicked during the gala," I reminded him.

"Bonus." He casually dodged my attempt to hit him.

"We went through hell—or more specifically, a dark, terrifying crypt—conversed with the council, who is now ultra dead, dealt with my shitty family, and we still have nothing to show for it." I gestured around at the bleak cemetery we were still standing in. "I fail to see the highlights in this."

"We're not dead," Zane answered with a shrug. "Therefore, we have the opportunity to continue to figure this out. This isn't the hardest we've been knocked down. Wallowing doesn't look good on you."

"I fucking hate your optimism, you know that? It's annoying." I exhaled a full breath, the tension easing in my chest. "And I wallow like a champ, fuck you very much."

"Noted."

I flipped my knife open and flexed my free hand, mentally preparing myself for the slice of pain across my palm and the promise of what was to follow. It felt different that time.

I felt different that time.

"Thank you." I swallowed. "For what you said back there. For standing up for me."

Zane gave a nod, his red eyes focused on me. The weight of them was hard to bear, so I watched my skin as I rested my blade across it.

"I give you this gift…" I began, pausing when Zane started to laugh. "What the hell are you giggling about?"

"I don't giggle." He continued to giggle. "You don't need to say that."

"What are you talking about?"

"The whole, 'I give you this gift,' thing. You don't need to say it." His giggling turned into a real chuckle, the kind of laugh he wielded when I was annoyed or angry about something. "It's all bullshit."

Somehow, through his stupid Thrall magic, his laughter jumped off him and landed on me. My annoyance was smothered with the infectious laugh, murdering any hopes I had of staying angry.

"Barnaby read it out of that stupid book!"

"Yeah, I don't know what that was about. I had never heard of it before that point."

"You're telling me," I aimed my knife at him, the threat not even registering to the giggling, tall, undead jerk. "I've been saying all that stupid nonsense this whole time for no reason? Why the hell would you make me say all of that crap?"

"Because it's really funny," he explained, fully proud of himself.

"I don't like you."

"Yes, you do."

The hand that had been offered up as a sacrifice was taken in his, his skin bordering on cold from being drained. A thumb traced over the pathway the blade usually took, caressing a soft line across my palm.

"We almost killed each other the first time we met." Zane lifted his eyes from my palm to look into mine. "You tackled me over the railing of an abandoned hotel and we fell two stories."

"I remember." My smirk wasn't strong enough to stick. "I stabbed you three times; you dislocated my shoulder. It still clicks if I sleep on it wrong."

"Four times," he corrected. "I'd never been tackled like that. I had never faced a hunter that charged headfirst into a Thrall, ready to embrace the void with no fear. I saw it in your eyes that day. You were something I wasn't ready for."

Something in my chest moved. It clicked and rotated and my heart started to fight against the tug it caused. Zane's eyes were boiling blood under the filtered silver of the moon, skin ash and lips the color of a dying rose petal.

He whispered to me in the cemetery, surrounded by death and shadow, and I didn't stand a chance.

Not a damn chance.

"I knew that day I was going to be your vampire."

For the first time in my life, I didn't know what to say. I couldn't speak. I couldn't do anything other than take him by his stupid, handsome face and kiss him.

I kissed Zane. I was kissing a vampire.

No.

I was kissing *my* vampire.

If there had been any lingering part of myself that recoiled at the idea of touching a vampire in any other way than violently, it had been evaporated the moment I felt his lips on mine. He was cold but wonderful, lips catching mine as his icy palm cupped my cheek. My world fell into grave flowers and wet earth with every breath, my fingers tangled in the silky mane behind his head.

The breeze around us cooled me as my blood started to heat, my tongue teasing his lips for an invitation. I wanted to know what he tasted like, what this undead man's mouth felt like in mine. It was thrilling and shattering all at once, my sensibilities dying a slow death under the wave of molten curiosity of the unknown.

I didn't know when we moved, or when I had started walking backwards as Zane guided me, but my back pressed against the smooth surface of a mausoleum. My weight leaned back against the marble, freeing my legs to move without the burden of holding me up.

Zane caught me under my thighs as I jumped and wrapped

my legs around his waist, his hips pushing against me just how I wanted. I felt him smile at my happy exhale, his tongue finally coming out to play.

I had never tasted vampire tongue before.

It was a new, surprising experience.

While his skin was cold, his mouth was deliciously warm, tongue demanding and tasting like rain. I gripped him with my legs like I was worried he was going to escape, and Gods help me I wanted to hold on to his hair forever. I loved his longer hair, loved how soft it was, loved how it felt in my fingers. The urge to touch him was making me crazy, and I was embarrassed that I was intimidated to grab at him like I usually did with my more… carnally inspired meetups.

It was kind of delightful that Zane made me feel a little bit like a teenager again. He was new, unfamiliar—a road I had never traveled before. I felt the same type of magical ants I normally felt when wielding power march around in my belly with the idea of exploring more of him. It kept me from slipping my hand under his shirt like I wanted, desperate to touch his chest hair.

Zane pressed his hips into mine, a shudder dancing up my spine at feeling his ridge against mine. My breath hiccupped, lips parting to sigh, and I dove into his mouth to get lost in the invitation he was giving me. I wanted more; more of him, more of his touch, more of his wonderful mouth—

"Ow, fuck." I jerked back out of reflex from the pain, the sharp stab of his fang slicing through my tongue like a razer. My head bumped the marble behind me and I winced.

"Mind the fangs," the vampire said around his heavy breathing. "They're still sharp."

"No shit." I dabbed my tongue with my knuckle, a red smear painted across it. "Damn, you got me good."

I heard the shift in his breath before I realized what I had been doing. The red in his eyes flared before being eclipsed by his expanding pupils, gaze locked on my lips. His fingers dug into the meat of my thighs as he leaned harder into me, the evidence of how excited he was made me squirm a little.

"You can't kiss me without permission, can you?" I grinned at how he growled. "Oh-ho. This is great."

"Hunter." Zane bared his teeth, wild and feral with blood desire. "This is not going to end well for you if you play this game."

"Yeah? What will happen?" I bit my lip as I squeezed my legs around his hips. He shivered, and I almost melted into a puddle from watching it.

"You think you're being cute, but I warn you, I'm a bastard if you test me." He moved his hands up from my thighs to my ass and squeezed. "I can give you anything you want. I'm yours to command. But if you keep your tongue from me, your warm, blood-flavored tongue, I will leave you in this cemetery unsatisfied and whining."

"Mine to command? That's a tall order, vampire."

"Then challenge it, hunter," he snarled. "Test my abilities, but not my patience."

With *anything* on the table, my sexual curiosity won out over my almost overwhelming desire to fuck with Zane. It was a close race, I'm not going to lie, but I didn't want to be left in the cemetery unsatisfied with only myself to blame.

I gave the grumpy vampire what he wanted and kissed him, sliding my cut tongue into his mouth to taste.

Apparently having a cut on my tongue and having him licking at it counted as a feeding for him, because the jolt of ecstasy that pulsed out from our kiss was bone melting.

If I had felt like a teenager before with all my gooey feelings of hesitation, it was nothing compared to the unhinged, hormonal explosion that happened now during our blood kiss. I went from teasing him and getting tingly about imagining touching his chest hair, to basically fucking him with my pants on. Only teenage levels of horniness would excuse the noises I was panting into his mouth, or how shameless I was in bucking my hips into his.

It would have been fatally embarrassing if I gave even an atom's worth of a fuck, but in the moment, I didn't care if the entire planet saw us.

I had never wanted anything more than Zane in that moment, and I made it evident by running my tongue over his fang again.

The taste of rainwater was gone, the swirl of metal and blood was everywhere. Pain danced along the edges of the sea of pleasure my body was floating in, like sharp rays of sun biting through the waves. Zane's cheek healed, his skin brightened and came back to life, and I ran my fingers over the rich stubble that coated where the wound had been.

I felt my body tense, the curl of passion tightening with each new swipe of his tongue. His teeth nipped at my bottom lip, a fang gliding along without piercing it, making me jerk with the promise. His lips moved off mine, landing across my jaw until they came to a tense pause under my ear.

Just as the pain had danced along the edges of pleasure, fear teased the line of excitement. My heart began to storm, the twisting in my chest churning so definitively that it took my breath away. My fingers clung to Zane's jacket as he breathed against my skin, hot and hungry, one hand moving up to curl at the nape of my neck.

He took his time, lips gliding down onto my neck, his grip easing my head to the side.

"Zane," I managed to plead, my breath catching as my heart swung like an ax. I was shaking, from lust or fear I couldn't tell, because the two had combined into a sensation I couldn't fully process. All I knew in that moment, that defining, heart-pounding moment, was that I knew I wasn't going to be the same again.

When the vampire touched my neck, his lips planted the softest, most sincere, wonderful kiss right across my rose tattoo.

Right across the scars I had hidden underneath.

No teeth. No pain.

A promise—a vow.

The rotating in my chest stopped, all the pieces coming

together in a perfect line, and I felt a fuse lighting within me. The pressure across my sternum almost hurt with the sudden intensity, and I felt the warning knock come just a few seconds after.

Zane dropped my legs as I pushed back, the ache stealing my ability to explain what I was feeling. When I felt the cannon fire building behind my ribcage, I shoved Zane aside just in time for a magical burst to rip itself free from my skeleton.

The stick that had been playing peek-a-boo in my chest for the past twenty-four hours shot out of me like a spear, destroying my shirt in the process. It spiraled out in a cartwheel, arching into a sideways spin before landing with a deep slice into the thick trunk of a gnarled tree.

Not only had it taken flight from my body, but it had also changed its shape, bending into a soft curve on one end while the other changed entirely. It wasn't the sudden, mildly painful but dramatic discharge that left Zane and I staring at it in dumbfounded horror.

It was the sharp, crimson scythe blade that formed out the top that had buried itself deep in the tree trunk.

We stood in silence a long time before creeping over to it, the silver moonlight gliding over the blade's curved edge. The stick—which was now the handle of a scythe—was the ivory color of bone, etched with runes that spiraled up from the bottom. The blade was the color of crystalized blood, comprised of glassy ossified feldspars of concentrated necromancy magic. The dark magic within the blade bent the light into its own hues of black that didn't exist for the living, whispers of the void within its creation.

"You see that too, right?" I asked Zane, worried that maybe I had finally snapped or died.

"Yes."

"Is that—"

"Yes."

"Did…did we do that?"

He shook his head slowly out of my peripheral. "I have no idea. Careful," he added as I reached for it. "Careful, hunter."

I wasn't sure why I wasn't more afraid of the damn thing, but I pressed ahead all the same. The bone handle was cool when I reached out and tapped it with my fingers, slapping the thing like I was testing to see if it was hot. My hand came away intact, and the world around us didn't explode, so I reached out again for a more confident attempt.

The curve of the handle felt smooth under my fingertips as I ran them over the length, tracing the gentle wave of the scythe up to the blade. The runes were carved deep in the bone, magic beyond my understanding radiating out from it like an unwavering flame. When I dared to tap against the blade, it felt as if my body heat was absorbed into it. Where it had buried itself into the tree was cut so clean, so perfect, that it almost seemed like the tree had grown with a massive gouge down the side, instead of it being shanked by a flying, magical scythe.

I was expecting more of a fight when I gently wrapped my hands around the handle and tugged, but the thing came away silky smooth.

The weight of bone and death magic solidified felt heavy yet somehow familiar, like I had always had this weapon stashed away. I twisted my grip to rotate the blade, the reflection splintering into jagged, geometric lines. Traces of the void traveled like smoke around the crystalized edges, and I knew without reason that this blade was mine.

It was made from me; my magic solidified, the necromancy crystals from my bones, reshaped and repurposed into the divine blade of the Goddess.

"Dallas." Zane brought me back from staring at the weapon honed from my chest, his eyes locked onto the deep carving in the tree trunk. Something was wrong with it.

Or moreover, something was dead about it.

I peered into the scar, sucking in a breath through my teeth. The endless darkness that stared back at us was infinite nothing, a cold window into the endless.

We had accidentally opened up a sliver into the void.

"That's not good," I mumbled.

"We can't leave it like that." Zane took a step toward it. "If we opened it, we can close it."

"Maybe?" I followed him, not feeling particularly qualified to be making any decisions. "This is where it would be useful to still have a council member around to ask."

"I worry about it spreading or opening up wider." Zane paused by the tree and nodded to the scythe. "Try running the blade over it again."

"The blade is what made it open, so I don't think that will help." I held the scythe out to him. "Hold this."

Zane recoiled from it like it was a snake at first, then did the quick tap test to make sure he was allowed to touch it. We didn't know the rules of the damn thing, so I didn't blame him for being terrified of it. It was scary, powerful enough to rip a hole through the fabric of reality, and a tool of his Goddess.

He was correct to be a scaredy cat.

When it didn't seem like the scythe was going to bite him for touching it, Zane took it from my hands and held it with the reverence and awe of a vampire holding his Goddess's weapon. He turned the blade in his grip, tracing the runes with his fingers, and whispered a prayer I didn't catch.

While he fawned over our new toy, I went to inspect the void gash in the tree. The darkness peering back at me from the trunk was haunting, even if I was intimately familiar with the other side at this point. There was a stark difference between dying, or almost dying, and dancing on the line between life and death, and having death staring at you from the living world. Peering into the void while I was fully alive made my blood run cold, my insides shriveling up in a creeping dread that I was looking at something my mortal mind shouldn't be able to fathom.

I flexed my hand and reached for it, and the tear began to knit itself back together. The tree's bark crackled and shifted, the carved wood reforming where the tear had been. The void turned into natural shadow, dropping away like it had all been a dream.

To be sure it was gone, and for my own sanity, I touched the cold bark where the void had been, meeting with the dry, damaged wood of an old tree.

"If I hadn't seen into the void before, I would be convinced that wasn't real," I whispered. "It melted away so fast."

"I don't think we're supposed to have this, hunter." Zane turned the blade again, the awe turning into understandable concern. "This is beyond us."

"We can agree on that." I took the blade back and gave it a slow inspection. "No one should have this, especially since it can cut a fucking tear into the void. This is…Saint, Zane. This is a world-ending weapon. We *have* to find a way to destroy it."

"We'll find a way," he agreed, solemnly. "I hate to defy the Goddess, but this is not meant for mortals."

"Let's get the hell out of this place. Maybe we can figure out how to stash it back in my chest to keep it hidden until we figure out how to destroy it." I started back on the path to the car, Zane at my side. The bony handle didn't respond as I pressed it to my chest, and the rune carvings didn't seem to want to shift or rotate along the handle anymore.

The trek back to the car didn't feel as monumental as the voyage out, and we arrived back at the front of the Silence Steps with the moon still hanging in the sky. Barnaby was waiting for us in the back seat, not even budging after Zane leaned in to pull the trunk release.

It felt a little like sacrilege to drop the Goddess's death scythe into the trunk of a car, but I didn't want to throw it into the back seat with Barns. If he panicked and dropped the thing, I was worried it would rip a hole into the bottom and we'd all plummet into the void or something equally terrifying.

The trunk would have to do.

"I'm ready to get out of here," Barnaby said as we climbed into the front seats, Zane taking the first shift as driver. "I want to be back home in my bed, away from all things death themed."

"Amen," I agreed, leaning my head back. "We can all agree this trip has been a touch more stressful than planned."

Zane brought the engine to life, a smirk playing at his lips. "Maybe not all of it."

I coughed to cover the smile threatening, butterflies dancing up my chest. The deadly tingles that fired off at the memory of our little *moment* in the cemetery made me shift in my seat, and I reached up to confirm that my emotional blocker was still set.

I got a new wave of cold horror when I remembered it wasn't.

And hadn't been.

For quite some time.

Enough time for me to go through all the stages of grief for my very well-maintained stone wall I had placed between us that had been shattered to smoldering rubble.

That bastard had felt everything.

Everything.

"Fuck," I whispered, and Zane chuckled in a way only a very satisfied vampire could.

THE SUN CAME UP JUST as I had started to drift to sleep.

We cruised down the empty two-lane road surrounded by just enough wilderness to give the morning sunshine something to play with. The amber glow lit my eyelids, pulling me from the uneasy sleep that had been teasing me. Barnaby snored softly in the back seat, somehow angling his body so he could lie across the seats without twisting himself into a pretzel.

Zane was the only one of us that looked alert, skin still warm from getting fresh blood, his eyes bright and free from any sort of weariness. He had his fingers draped over the wheel, posture relaxed, a human in every sense except for his blood eyes.

"We'll stop halfway like before," Zane said before I could ask. "You two can sleep better in beds."

"I would murder someone for a bed right now." I pressed my palms into my eyes and rubbed them, the grit of exhaustion grinding under the pressure. "How long have we been driving?"

"Only about two hours." He punched the buttons on the console to summon some heat, and I melted back against the cushion in tired annoyance. "You should try and rest."

"I'm not going to get any sleep." I watched the distant forest, my mind floating back to the cemetery. None of it seemed real; it felt like I'd had a long, weird fever dream that involved confronting my old family, talking to skeletal heads and making out with a vampire. The urge to demand an explanation from the universe was almost overwhelming.

"Do you think we'll hear from them back in the city?" Zane asked, reminding me that my emotional blocker had yet to be turned back on. I touched the device, still at odds with whether or not I wanted to commit to shutting him out again.

"I don't know. I have a sneaking suspicion that they've been tailing me longer than I realized. I thought I had lost them when I ran but…I guess I'm not as clever as I thought."

Zane's fingers tapped on the wheel, his eyes fixed on the road.

"You never told me that your falling out with your family was over a Thrall."

The pressure bouncing around in my chest almost made me hit the switch, but I forced myself not to.

"Yeah, well." I adjusted in my seat, suddenly feeling confined. "Not something I toss out to people. Especially another Thrall."

"I'd like to know." Zane spared a second to toss me a glance before planting his vision back onto the road.

I listened to Barnaby snore for a few minutes, infinitely jealous that he could sleep so soundly after everything that had happened. If I had the ability to shut down and pass out to avoid talking about everything I would have, but I didn't have the luxury of sudden narcolepsy.

I also knew that I owed Zane answers.

That was the part that finally made me snap the emotion blocker back on.

I saw him shift, saw him furrow his brow and curl his fingers around the leather of the wheel. It made me feel like an asshole, but I couldn't tear myself open that much, not when I was still reeling from everything.

"You know how you know in your heart that Sandros was a

good guy?" I asked the pensive Thrall beside me. "There's no doubt in your mind that your maker was a good man, someone you loved and adored?"

Zane popped an eyebrow up as he gave a nod.

"Yes?"

"That's how I felt about Magnus. One of my earliest memories was him finding me." I pivoted my focus back to the woods and crossed my arms to keep my heart safe. "There's nothing before that—no parents, no birthdays, no awkward first days of school. Nothing good. I was eight when Magnus pulled me from a vampire den."

Zane said nothing, listening to me while staring down the road ahead, so I continued.

"He took me in as his own, trained me up, gave me a purpose and a family for a decade. I went from a half-dead blood bag for a bunch of vampires to a loved member of the Saint's Army. I got to stomp vampires and go home to people I loved. It was a sweet gig. It was the best years of my life."

"What changed?" Zane's fingers remained around the wheel, grip tightening.

"I saw that he wasn't perfect. That he had a dark side I had been ignoring." I hugged my chest to keep my heart from spilling out. "I found a Thrall he had been torturing and I...made a choice."

I knew Zane looked my way, but I kept my gaze out the window. My eyes stung and I couldn't bear the idea of him seeing me vulnerable. I was too tired to let my pride slip away, because it was the only thing keeping me upright.

"I tried to cut him loose to end his suffering, and I made a mistake. That mistake cost us two lives and our compound." I coughed to give myself an excuse to sniff back some tears. "I ran away after that and never saw them again until yesterday."

"I'm sorry, Dallas."

"I don't want that, Zane. I sure as hell don't deserve it. I got two people killed because I couldn't handle myself." I rubbed at my face to wipe away the waterworks.

"Thank you for telling me." Zane spared a moment to look my way, and I caught his gaze for just a second. "Even with that blocker on, I know it was hard to talk about."

I shrugged, easing my arms from around my ribs to give my lungs a break.

"I felt like I owed you that much."

"You don't owe me anything, hunter. You never do."

I felt like being nice, felt like thanking him for listening and caring, and hell—I almost reached out to take the hand still gripping the wheel. There was a mini battle in my bruised, misshapen heart over wanting to keep the status quo between us and giving in to the urge of just being a sappy idiot around the vampire. I didn't get to be gooey around people, and had only ever experienced the sensation to try once before.

I wanted to go full romance novel and hold his hand, do the thing where we lace our fingers together and sit in silent comfort. Maybe he could kiss my knuckles and tell me everything was going to be alright.

I would have gladly handed over my soul for that moment. And somehow, within all of that sappy bullshit, I wanted Sias to call me and tell me he wasn't mad at me, and that everything was fine between us. He would tell me that I hadn't ruined our relationship.

A boy could dream.

I was lost in my stupid imagination and let the moment pass as Barnaby sat up with a snort. He grumbled and tugged his phone from his pocket, glaring at it with the groggy grumpiness that only he could manifest.

"I don't understand how we can be so far away from anything remotely civilized, yet random phone numbers can still find me."

"Ah, hell." I pulled my busted phone out and examined it, trying to turn it on. The fractured screen displayed stripes of purple and blue, marred further with massive areas that had gone totally dark. I tried to apply some pressure into places to get the screen to respond, knocking it against my palm in an effort to bully it back to life.

"It's a lost cause." Zane adjusted his hands on the wheel. "We'll get you another one back in the city."

"They're so damn expensive to get a good model phone these days. Dex charges me extra, I swear she does." I exhaled and tossed the busted phone onto the floorboard. "I'm going to come out of this trip in the red."

"Well, at least you'll get relief from telemarketers," Barnaby grumbled, tapping his phone.

"What are we going to tell Florence when she asks about what we found at the Silence Steps?" Zane asked. "I'm sure she knows we left."

"We tell her the truth." I shrugged. "We didn't find anything."

"So, we're not going to tell her about the council, or who we ran into?" Barnaby leaned forward between our seats. "Shouldn't we at least let her know that the Saint's Army is aware of her little passion project?"

"Fuck no." I tried to find another comfortable way to lounge in the seat, but gave up and just sat like normal. "Best-case scenario, they fight each other and blow themselves up or something."

"What's the next move, then?" Barnaby looked between us. "Where do we look next for the key or blade or whatever?"

"Yeah, um…about that." I cleared my throat and looked to the vampire, who seemed to be battling indigestion from the subject. "I think we figured it out."

Barnaby blinked rapidly. "What? When?"

"Earlier in the cemetery when we were walking back."

Barnaby looked like he was about to explode and flapped his hands around as he demanded, "Well then *tell* me, you dimwit! You dragged me out here to help you solve it! Don't hold it hostage now."

"It sort of uh…" I tried to rummage through my vocabulary to piece the words together, unsure of how exactly to explain what happened without it sounding impossible or insane.

Zane did not have to rummage, and instead opted to just go full blunt transparency.

"It flew out of Dallas's chest and turned into a scythe."

"What??"

Zane and I heard it at the same time, and we looked to each other with the same level of confusion.

The outburst from the back seat sounded like it was in stereo, and Barnaby's cheeks started growing red hot.

"What was that?" I asked first, rotating in my seat.

"What was what?" Barnaby shrugged a little too defensively. "I didn't hear anything."

"I heard another voice."

"No, you didn't," he snapped. "You're tired. It's just me back here. Obviously. Who else would be back here?"

"I don't know, Barnaby. Who else *would* be back there?" I inspected his phone, which he was not making an effort to hide. The screen lit up again with an inbound call and he punched the hang up button. It hadn't been a phone call, and there was no mistaking the additional voice.

"Obviously no one." Barnaby presented the back seat and idle phone. "I think you're hearing things."

"Yeah, okay." I rotated back around in my seat. "I guess it was nothing."

Barnaby fidgeted for a bit before attempting to get back on track.

"So? What did you do with the scythe?"

"We left it in the cemetery," I said. "Seemed dangerous."

"Dallas tossed it into a grave and kicked some dirt over it," Zane confirmed. "We couldn't risk it."

The choking noises radiating from the back seat were not coming from Barnaby, and his sudden interest in his bag is what finally snapped me into action.

"Barnaby, what the hell did you do?"

"Nothing! I didn't! Ah, you maniac!" Barnaby tried to lift his bag out of reach as I began to climb into the back seat. The back of my jeans was gripped and I was yanked back into my seat by Zane.

"You're going to make us crash." Zane snapped his eyes up at the rearview to glare at the panicked incubus in the back seat. "Barnaby. What did you *do?*"

"I think the jig is up," the muffled voice admitted. "No use in hiding now."

"I had it under control," Barnaby hissed at his bag. "I told you to just stay quiet."

I was about to make another attempt at grabbing the bag when Barnaby exhaled like he was about to confess to murder and reached into it.

The moment Funus was tugged gently from the confines of Barnaby's shoulder bag, I felt my soul leave my body.

"Barns! What the fuck!"

"You saw what was happening! I couldn't just leave him there," Barnaby pleaded. "He was going to get turned into ash unless I did something."

Zane turned traitor and sounded impressed. "How did you manage that?"

"I grabbed him while Magnus was arguing with Dallas."

"Are you insane?" I pulled the conversation back to the matter at hand, which was that Barnaby was in fact, insane. "We can't take Funus back to St. Athesall. What the hell were you thinking?"

"Why can't we? What's the harm?" Barnaby shrugged like he wasn't holding the decayed head of a necromancer in his lap.

"Did you forget that Funus is one of the most powerful necromancers that has ever existed?" I quizzed the frazzled idiot. "Even if he is a head, he's dangerous."

"If I could defend myself a bit," Funus chimed in. "I appreciate the recognition of my status but I actually can't do much in this state. And with all of my fellow council members dead, I was going to be stuck in there alone with no one to talk to. Can you imagine!"

"He's also a paragon of necromancy information, Dallas, which is very useful considering you just mentioned a scythe fell out of your chest," Barnaby quipped. "So, as a matter of fact, you're welcome."

"Don't smile, you dick," I yelled at Zane so I could vent some frustration. "Whose side are you on right now?"

"He's got a point, hunter."

"God, you are the worst bodyguard. How is this not a major threat? He's part of the council, deadly as hell, and we're just chauffeuring him back to the city like he's a lost puppy we found."

"Relax." Zane tapped the strap across his chest. "And put your seat belt back on."

"Your priorities are fucked."

"Please tell me you didn't leave the scythe back at the cemetery," the head fussed. "I don't know if you fully understand the importance of what you've described."

"We didn't leave it behind." I snapped my seat belt back on as Zane grunted at me. "It's in the trunk."

"Did it actually fall out of your chest, or are you being hyperbolic?" Barnaby probed. "You have a tendency of doing that."

"It fired out of me like a gunshot and ripped a hole into a tree." I rotated to glare at him. "How's that for hyperbolic?"

"Is he joking?" Funus rotated his eyes up to look at Barnaby, who shrugged helplessly.

"When I killed a necromancer named Edras Roe, a long stick got stuck into my chest," I explained to the wary head. "It sticks out sometimes when I have to give Zane blood. Today it exploded out of me and turned into a scythe, and ripped a hole into the void. It sealed back up, thank fuck, but we left promptly after that."

Funus's yellow eyes flared.

"Goddess. Quite literally *Goddess*," he floundered. "My good man, you have been touched by the divine hand of the mother of death herself."

"I was worried you were going to say that," I grumbled. "We have some nasty people looking for this thing. Us discovering that it's been hiding out in my sternum is not ideal."

"That's why it hides within the chosen," he agreed. "To keep it safe until its needed."

"Here's the part you're not going to like, bone man. Remember when I said in the tomb that I wanted to destroy it? I meant it. That thing cannot get into the wrong hands, and there are a lot of those."

I had expected the head of the Goddess's council to object or gasp in horror, maybe even call me some choice words for even pitching the idea in his presence. Imagine my surprise when the animated skull managed to look sheepish without any eyebrows.

"The Goddess's scythe can no more be destroyed than death itself can be destroyed. It's eternal, I'm afraid, as much a part of reality as life and death."

"Fan-fucking-tastic." I slumped in my seat. "This is why I want to go full time into fish training. I hate magic crap."

"Can we hide it?" Zane asked. "Get it back into Dallas's chest somehow?"

"Why don't we put it in *your* chest?" I countered. "I don't want that thing back in my body."

"Yes, I believe so," Funus said.

I swiveled to watch the skull. "That doesn't sound confident, Funus."

"Well, I've never seen it myself though I assume it can be done." His eyes rotated as Barnaby exhaled another frustrated breath. "I've been alive a long time but I haven't seen everything, you know."

"Not you. It's this person who keeps calling me." Barnaby was frowning so hard he was sprouting gray hairs from the effort. In a moment of defiant anger, Barnaby adjusted Funus on his lap and smashed his thumb into the screen in the most aggressive way to answer a phone call imaginable. "Who is this? Why in all the Gods' names are you calling me?!"

An entire performance played across Barnaby's face in a matter of seconds. Anger melted into confusion, lifted into shock then softened into concern, before his eyes swung over to me with a look of gentle embarrassment.

I stared at him as he held the phone out and said, "It's um... it's for you."

"Me?" I plucked the phone from his grasp and turned back to sit front facing in my seat. Zane offered a brief look of curiosity as I tapped the speakerphone button. "Uh, hello?"

"Dallas."

I hadn't heard Sias's voice since that night, and it caused a ripple of old familiar tingles mixed with a sharp stab of unease.

"Sias?"

"Gods, where the hell have you been? Why aren't you answering your phone?"

"I kinda smashed it." I rubbed at the prickling crawl of nerves dancing down the back of my neck. "How did you get Barnaby's phone number?"

"Where are you? I've been going to your apartment for two days. Are you somewhere in the city?"

My stomach started to sour at the seriousness of his tone, the edge to his words a sharpness I hadn't heard before.

He was angry, but not in the way I had thought he'd be. It wasn't the type of sharpness honed from betrayal or frustration, but something much more primal.

He was scared.

Something had made the untouchable Sias Llon'nai afraid.

"No, we're about two days out." I sat up straight. "What's wrong? What happened? Are you hurt?"

"Is Zane with you?"

"I'm here," Zane answered. "Sias, what's going on?"

"Someone is using some powerful magic tech in the city," Sias said, tone grave. "They're using it on vampires."

"What the hell are you talking about?" I asked, mind fraying at the edges. "What kind of magic tech?"

"I don't know what kind, but it's something new. The vampires are somehow able to retain their natural abilities after being turned, and this reeks of magic manipulation via tech."

"How do you know it's tech?" I asked.

"How do you know it's vampires?" Zane added.

Sias was silent for a while, his breath exhaling in a long stream that I knew meant he was smoking.

He was stressed. Very stressed.

"Sias?"

"Bastian is dead." Another long exhale. "He showed up at my house unannounced, which he was not welcome to do. When I answered the door to tell him to leave, I noticed he seemed off. He had been turned, and almost got the upper hand by using his jinn abilities on me."

My heart sank into a pool of ice water, my stomach curling in on itself in panic.

"Sias, did he bite you?"

"No."

"Are you *sure*? This isn't the time to be brave or shield me from something. Tell me right fucking now if he even grazed you. Time is a factor."

"He didn't bite me. I'm alright," he assured me with the calm firmness he always had. "I would have led with that, I promise. I'm fine."

"Are you sure Bastian is dead?" Zane asked.

Sias sounded wounded when he answered, "Yes. I'm sure. I handled it myself."

"Were his eyes red or green? Did he say anything to you?" I jumped back in, my body on fire with anxiety.

"Red, and not much. I told him he wasn't welcome back since I didn't trust his disregard for people's boundaries. He had been keeping his distance until that night, so I was surprised to see him. As soon as I answered the door, he surged inside and tried to compel me to not fight back. His magic was weak, but present. It almost worked." He paused to take a drag and finished with, "I found a piece of metal tech in the back of his skull."

"Do you recognize anything about the tech? The style, the components?" I tried for anything that made sense, anything I could think of as a tangible lead.

"No, hence my concern. This is new, deeply complex, and violates about ten different Demon Human ethical magic usage mandates. Whoever crafted this has a terrifying amount of resources as well as a bottomless pit of nothing for ethics," Sias growled on the other end of the phone, his snarl carrying over the sound waves. "I want whoever is responsible found, Dallas. And I want them gone."

"Do you know of any rival necromancers who could access tech like this?" Barnaby leaned into the conversation. "It has to be a necromancer if vampires are involved, right?"

"No one that comes to mind, but you're right. A necromancer is involved if there's vampires, but they don't normally turn people in the city. It's too risky, and they sure as hell don't go after people who would be noticed if they were gone, like Bastian. Nothing about this adds up."

"Who else do we know that has access to magical tech?" Zane chimed in. "Do you think Dex would be able to analyze what Sias found if we brought it to her?"

"Worth a shot," I mused. "She might be able to help us understand what it is, or how it works."

"Can she be trusted?" Sias jumped back in, sounding understandably hesitant.

"For the right price."

"I'm serious, Dallas."

"So am I," I said. "Dex is the best type of loyal, one that can be quantified with a number. She won't double-cross a good paycheck. If you get me that tech, she can help us track down who did this to Bastian."

"My concern isn't that she'll fail. My concern is that you and

Zane are now targets," Sias explained, anger boiling with each word. "If someone is playing God with tech and death magic, then a rogue necromancer and vampire Thrall roaming the city is going to be very alluring to the psychopath doing this. I want Bastian avenged, but I want you two safe more than that. I will not allow anyone to jeopardize that."

The dread in my stomach eased just a fraction. I felt like an asshole for being happy that Sias was worried about me.

And about Zane.

"We can take care of ourselves, Sias. We know how to handle necromancers."

"When you're back in the city, call me, do you understand?" His tone gave me goose bumps and I rubbed at my arm to try and hide them. I was fairly sure Zane saw them.

"We'll be there in two days. We're going to stop to rest—"

"Zane," Sias cut me off. "You don't need to sleep. Drive straight through, don't stop. I want you both back in my city so I can get eyes on you."

"I'll get us back," Zane confirmed.

"Thank you, love. And Dallas? You will call me when you reach the city. Tell me you understand."

I had to shift in my seat a bit to remain in character.

"Yeah, I understand, Sias."

"Good boy."

The call ended with a few beeps and I glared at the side of Zane's head.

"You're taking orders from him now?"

"He's scared, hunter." Zane tossed me a look. "This is serious."

"Nothing about this adds up." I tossed Barnaby's phone into the back seat. "Who the hell has the capability to do this?"

"I don't know." Zane set his jaw. "But we'll find out."

"So…" Barnaby snuck back into the conversation. "Does that mean we'll be sleeping in the car for the next day and a half?"

"We'll stop for gas and bathroom breaks, but that's it." Zane flicked his gaze up to the rearview. "Get comfortable."

"Whoever this is needs to get stabbed extra for this," Barnaby complained, very distraught with his situation. He placed the talking skull in his lap on the seat next to him. "I'm prone to back problems and this is not going to be good for me."

"I don't know. I think this vehicle is rather comfortable," Funus said, moving his jaw to test the bounciness of the cushion. "Beats sitting on a slab of stone for a few centuries."

"Oh good," I announced. "At least the skull is happy."

I NEVER WANTED to be in a car ever again.

By the time we made it back to the city, my body felt like a tense bundle of misery. True to his word, Zane drove for two solid days, only stopping to let us stretch, eat and run to the bathroom. I didn't get a chance to sleep properly, nor get any escape from Funus and Barnaby arguing about art theory and antiques for hours on end.

It had been hell. Uncomfortable, cramped, boring hell.

Beyond wanting to rest and work out the knots in my calves, I had hoped to get some privacy with Zane. We had some *things* to figure out, which we needed closed doors to achieve. On the second day, early in the morning when we stopped for gas and Barnaby was still asleep, I had asked if Zane wanted to follow me to the bathroom to discuss some things. When I was told "no," I explained that the things I wanted to discuss involved fooling around a little, maybe making out and grinding against the sink, just in case he wasn't picking up the vibes.

I got a sideways look and a "We're on a time crunch. Focus, hunter."

Rude.

Like he's too good to get frisky in a gas station bathroom. I hadn't realized I was traveling with royalty.

St. Athesall was cloudy and soggy when we got home, and I kept my promise of alerting Sias when we were back in the city limits. Barnaby sprang out of the car like the thing was on fire, which was the only silver lining. I doubted I'd ever have to deal with him trying to go with us on a future out-of-city adventure.

"May I see it now that we're back?" Funus was asking from Barnaby's arms, eyes bouncing from me to the trunk.

I scanned the street briefly, the car parked in the alleyway between buildings near Barnaby's apartment door. There were people bustling around across the street, but the rain kept anyone from sticking around too long.

I wasn't sure seeing a death scythe from the Goddess herself would mean much to people trying to get to work anyway. People had places to be, and I'd seen people fall over dead without anyone stepping out of the line for lattes before. Gotta love big-city apathy.

The trunk swung open, and Funus's eyes flared in amazement. The Goddess's scythe sat under our duffels, the red blade warping the trunk lights into shadowy ghosts. Zane grabbed the bags out of the way so I could pick the weapon up, the bone handle chilly in my grip.

"It's even more beautiful than I imagined," Funus whispered. "Gods, I'd give anything to have hands right now."

"It's scary," Barnaby weighed in. "Like most things made of bone and blood crystals. Just looking at it makes me afraid somehow."

"It's a weapon crafted from a death goddess," I reminded him. "I think that's the point."

"Is it...you know. Safe?" Barnaby eyed the thing like he was worried it would bite him. "Should I not be around it?"

"I don't think it can hurt you." I aimed the blade away from him and held it out, bringing it close for Funus to inspect. "Maybe don't touch the blade though. It did tear a hole into the void so, you know, be cautious."

"I can feel the presence of her in this blade," Funus marveled. "Like a whisper in the darkness. The magic dances over it like shadows within shadows."

"The runes across the handle are very interesting." Barnaby dared to lean in a bit more, studying the writing. "I'd love to translate them. What is the language exactly? Maybe I can—"

Barnaby reached out a tentative hand, his fingers gliding over the handle to feel the carvings of the ancient runes etched into the surface of the bone. The moment his skin made contact, a dark spiderweb splintered up his fingers, evaporating the flesh from his bones in the blink of an eye. He screamed and jerked backwards, nearly dropping Funus to the wet pavement and shook his hand to try and get the magic dispelled.

As quickly as it had happened, the dark magic faded, his skin regrowing over black bone like nothing happened.

"Shit! Barns, are you okay?!" I threw the thing back into the trunk and caught his arm, inspecting it for damage.

"You said it was safe!" he shrieked at me, ripping his arm away from me to test his fingers' mobility. "What the hell was that?"

"I said to be cautious. This is my first Death Goddess weapon, you know. I don't know the fucking rules. Zane touched it without going skeletal."

"It seems that only beings touched with death magic can wield the blade," Funus surmised. "It must repel the living."

"Great," I groaned. "That doesn't complicate things, at all. Love that for us. Barns, you sure you're okay?"

"I'm fine." He wiggled his fingers and scowled at the scythe. "I think. Ugh. I'm going to have nightmares about that thing. It shouldn't be out, Dallas. Can't you make it…you know. Go back in?"

I opened my mouth and Zane slapped the back of my head.

"Don't."

"I wasn't gonna," I lied. "This isn't the time for 'That's what he said' jokes, Zane. Saints, be professional."

"Do you know how to get the blade back into its resting state, Funus?" Zane asked the head as I rubbed the back of mine.

"Perhaps we need to just retrace the events leading up to when it left its 'resting state' as it were." Funus eyed the blade then swung his gaze up to me. "What was happening when the scythe left your body?"

"I was giving Zane blood," I answered, straight-faced and calm. "To heal the wound on his cheek."

"Was something different from the last time you gave him blood?" Funus interrogated. "Different emotional state, maybe? It had been quite stressful."

"Uh yeah. That must have been it." I coughed. "Super stressed out. You know. With the whole…deal."

Barnaby narrowed his eyes at me like the suspicious jerk he was and Zane exhaled.

"Shut up," I told the Thrall before he could rat us out. "Shut all the way up."

"I've never seen you bashful before," Sias's voice washed over me like a wave, nearly sweeping me off my feet. Approaching from the other end of the alley, Sias's silhouette was lithe, his movements water trailing through smoke. He wasn't in his normal business attire but something closer to expensive casual: black turtleneck sweater and a long coat, jeans fitted to his hips like they were made custom. His long, golden waves were pinned back around his horns, with a few strands loose to rest across his broad shoulders.

Chromatic eyes watched me, swirling purple and blue, matching the bruise across his cheek.

"You're hiding something, Dallas Wilde. It's very rare to see you flounder."

"I'm not floundering," I argued, but my steam had run dry at seeing the wounds on his face. His brow had a split that was taped closed, exhaustion tugged at the corners of his eyes. I left my post near the trunk to meet him on the other side of the car, taking in his injuries.

"They're superficial," he answered what my face was projecting. "You don't need to be so concerned."

"Why didn't you get healed?" I reached up but caught myself. "Why stay hurt?"

Purple melted to a heartbreaking pale blue, rimmed with black remorse. He ground his teeth against the hurt, his head giving a subtle shake.

"I don't want to. Not yet."

While I wasn't sure where we stood in any official status, I knew that the pain on his face wasn't something I ever wanted to see again. My heart quaked at seeing the wounds mar his features and his eyes. I moved in and hugged him, breathing deep as I felt his arms wrap around me.

"I'm sorry about Bastian," I whispered into his shoulder.

He didn't answer, but I heard him swallow. I felt his fingers trail down my scalp before he released me.

"You sure you're not bit? You're okay?" I asked again as I stepped back from the embrace.

"I'm fine." His eyes lifted from mine, the color shifting back into a purple hue as he watched the group behind me. "Is that a skull?"

"Ah, yeah." I cleared my throat and introduced Sias to our new, dead companion. "Sias, this is Funus. He's the last er, 'survivor' of the necromancy council."

"Hello there," Funus greeted him. "Glad to meet you."

"Oh." Sias's eyes went lilac. "Hello. I wasn't expecting you to talk."

"He does that a lot," Zane added dryly. "Novelty wore off about two days ago."

Sias hummed knowingly, then gave a casual sweep over Zane.

"Zane. You're looking very fed. Flushed."

I rolled my eyes but they got stuck when Zane cracked the

tiniest little smirk, like the man had the ability to look coy about something.

The vampire said, too secretly sultry for my brain to handle, "I am."

It was Sias's turn to crack a grin and I inhaled to demand to know *what the hell that exchange was* when I was cut off.

"We were just discussing what to do with *that*," Barnaby snarled, pointing at the scythe in the trunk. "The other thing we hauled back from the Silent Steps with us, besides Funus who talks a normal amount if you're not incredibly rude."

Sias trailed over to peer into the trunk, his golden brows lifting.

"Explain."

"I'm not sure where to begin," I confessed. "There's a lot of pieces here."

"Dallas has had the Death Goddess's scythe in his chest the whole time, and we just discovered it after it shot out of his chest at the Silent Steps," Zane stepped in. "Now we're trying to figure out how to put it back into his chest so Florence Pierce can't get her hands on it."

"Florence Pierce?" Sias wheeled on me, eyes going into a tangerine flare. "Dallas, you didn't. That woman is mad."

"Oh, I'm fucking aware."

"We're trying to figure out what caused the scythe to come free in the first place," Funus brought the topic back up, and I gestured for him to shut his mouth. "It had been hiding in his chest for quite some time until two days ago."

"I see." Sias scanned over the blade, tangerine fading into violet as he turned his eyes to me. "Tell me, does this blade have something to do with when Zane feeds on you?"

"It's complicated," I hedged, stomach alive with butterflies. "But kinda. It kinda…wiggles around in my chest when Zane needs to drink. It finally decided to make itself known in the cemetery."

Sias lifted his violet eyes from me and brandished them to the vampire. The color swirled blue, then went into the pinkish hues I knew very well.

My Thrall and my incubus flame exchanged a look I couldn't decipher, but Sias's color went into a new shade of orchid I'd never seen on him. It wasn't the bright pink I normally saw before I got to be thrown into a night of passion, but something softer and bright. I wasn't sure what the hell was going on behind the swirl, but it made my chest thump.

Sias inhaled slowly, and whispered, "I see."

"Don't try and touch it," I warned him as he approached. "It turned Barnaby's hand into bones for a second. Maybe our best bet is to try and hide it in the apartment for…the time…" I slowed down as Sias came to stand in front of me, his hands reaching up to cup my cheeks.

"Relax." He stroked his thumb over my cheekbone, a soft cascade of charm magic draping over me like a blanket fresh from the dryer. "This isn't the first time I've had to calm you after that blade made a fuss, is it?"

"No." I got lost in watching how his eyes danced like a rainbow storm. My muscles eased, my heart skipped around as I breathed in amber and tobacco.

"The night I brought you both to the club and Zane fed on you, I remember you commanding me to charm you in the middle of it." He inhaled like he was smelling a newly cut bouquet of flowers. "You tasted like absinth and dissolved sugar. That's how you taste now, deadly allure and sweet poison."

A shiver radiated up from my spine to my jaw, the world falling away as Sias pulled me deeper into his charm. I wasn't in the alley anymore, standing over a trunk with an ancient, dangerous Goddess scythe. I was in a euphoric bliss with his touch. I felt safe. Hidden.

I moved without question when he steered me in a half-circle, breaking eye contact so he could hold my shoulders from behind.

"Relax," his voice rumbled in my ear, breath kissing the lobe.

His fingers lifted my chin, my eyes falling shut. "Breathe, sweet boy. You're fighting too much."

I leaned back against him, exhaling a deep breath I hadn't felt myself take. Gods, it felt amazing to not feel the knots in my shoulders, or the dread of everything pressing me into the dirt. I could breathe, I could relax.

And I had missed him so goddamn much.

I felt the thump before I could process what it was, and opened my eyes just as the last bit of the scythe's handle was absorbed back into my chest.

I blinked as the charm spell started to fade, the empty trunk massive without the burden of the Goddess's weapon inside.

"What just happened?" I touched my chest where the handle had been, only skin and my tattered shirt present.

"Wow." Barnaby's eyes were bright for a second, teal fading into his normal black. "It worked."

"How did you do that?" I turned to look at Sias, who's eyes were no longer pink. "Better question, how the hell did you know that was going to work?"

"I didn't." Sias removed himself from me carefully. "But if my charm magic helped you contain it before, I assumed it was worth testing the consistency of it."

"That's one problem solved." Zane shut the trunk. "Now we can at least keep it out of view of Florence. We just need to make sure it doesn't leap out again."

I wasn't sure what that exactly meant, considering what had made it "leap out" was something I wanted to continue to explore, but I bit my tongue and nodded.

"We'll discuss what was promised to Florence." Sias didn't keep the disdain out of his voice. "Because she is not someone who will respond to you showing up empty-handed well. This is a bigger shit show than you realize, Dallas."

"I'm fully aware of the scale of the shit show, Sias. If you had any idea of the intense fuckery we just experienced, you'd know we're ready to take on the damn world at this point."

Sias hummed, not sounding convinced, but pulled a small plastic bag from his coat pocket. Inside of the bag was a small, plastic device with smears of blood across it. He dropped it into my hand, happy to be rid of it.

"Bastian's tech?" I asked, and he nodded. The tiny piece looked like a bent square with sharp, golden teeth. The thick casing had been cracked, a few of the prongs bent the wrong way.

I pocketed the device and asked, "Do you know anyone he worked with that would have access to anything close to this? Or do you know if he was in too deep with someone dangerous?"

"Bastian works," Sias paused to correct himself. "Worked with a lot of powerful people, but no one I'm aware of that has any ties to magic tech. It's still illegal. Even tech as trivial as manipulating cameras with glamour is a felony. This would be considered a war crime."

"Did he dabble in Death Goddess stuff like Omar did?" Zane took the chip to examine it. "Did they have mutual friends?"

"I'm their mutual friend." Sias placed his hands in his coat pockets. "They barely knew each other. I've tried to think of any angle where this makes sense, or who could be remotely tied to something like this, but I haven't a clue. Why him? Why would he come for me?"

"Sometimes when grunts are first turned, they run off instinct," Zane told him gently. "They go after friends and family first, because it's fresh in their brain. I don't think it was personal."

Sias's eyes went blue for a second, jaw tight.

"I'm not sure if that makes me feel better."

"We'll go talk to Dex, try and get some answers," I told him. "Do you want me to come by the tower afterward?"

"I'm coming with you," Sias told me, with zero room for negotiation. "I'm not sitting on the side for this, Dallas. Bastain was my friend. I cared about him, and I'm going to see this through."

"I'm not going to try and stop you, but I want you to understand that if this trail leads us to vampires, I'm not putting you in front of them," I told him with the same limited threshold for negotiation. "I'm not putting you in danger, Sias."

"Of course not." Sias pushed his coat aside to take out his holstered gun, ejecting the clip to show me his new golden bullets, glowing with life magic. He slid the clip back home and pulled a bullet into the chamber, then placed it back into the holster like he was some deadly cowboy from another era. "I'm putting myself there, darling. I don't let anyone put me anywhere I don't want to be."

"You brought me some of those, right?"

"If you're a good boy."

"Gods, that's my cue," Barnaby complained, sounding nauseated. "Let's go, Funus. We'll let them handle the rest of this without us."

"Dallas," Funus called before Barnaby could carry him away. "I don't understand nearly enough of the terminology you're discussing with that small object in the bag, but if it is controlling death magic and corrupting vampires, you must destroy it. The deities put rules in place for a reason. Chaos and death magic have no place together."

I wanted to laugh, but instead gave the head a nod. "We'll get it sorted. Don't worry."

I didn't know the logistics of how a possessed skull had the ability to sigh, but Funus exhaled like a worried parent as Barnaby carried him inside the apartment.

"Does he realize that 'chaos and death magic' basically describes you?" Zane asked.

"I almost wasn't able to answer with a straight face."

"Darling, there is nothing straight about you." Sias tilted his head in the direction he came from. "I brought my car. We'll use it to get to your tech contact."

"I know Dex can shine some light on this. She's expensive, but she knows her shit." I followed him out of the alley, his beautiful, luxury car parked next to the curb. "Or she will at least point us in the right direction."

The moment my body was in daylight, the warmth of the sun daring to peek out from behind the gloom of the clouds, I should have known my luck was about to turn. Too many positive things happened in a row for me not to have had my guard up.

One second, I was thinking to myself, "Man, maybe today won't be a bucket of balls," and the next I heard a very angry cop voice.

I turned at the sound of my name being called just in time to get a haymaker to the jaw, staggering me sideways.

Preston Cheslock was baring his teeth like a rabid dog, wearing his civilian costume with enough stubble to warn me he wasn't in a good place. I rubbed my jaw as I got the world to stop spinning, blinking at the disgruntled DHAP officer.

"Friend of yours?" Sias asked casually, standing near his car.

"Uh, no." I tested my jaw then cut Zane a look. "You are the fucking worst bodyguard."

"You're not dead," he pointed out, unhelpfully. "What did you do now?"

"The fuck makes you think I did something? I've been with your stupid ass!" I yelled.

"Wilde, you fucking asshole," Preston roared. "I told you to answer your goddamn phone!"

"It got smashed, you damn psycho. What's your problem?"

"The vampires are my problem!" His chest heaved, pain rippling over his face. "Seyyid's in the hospital. We told you to answer your phone."

"It got—it doesn't matter. What happened? Is he alright?"

"No, thanks to you," he snapped. "We kept trying to get you here because we found a lead. We tracked some vamps to the south side near the old railway. One of them was an oni who was able to use fear magic to scare us. When we couldn't get ahold of you, we went in solo."

"Why the hell did you do that?" It was my turn to get angry, jaw punch aside. "You didn't take any cops? DHAP officers?"

"They didn't believe us," Preston ground out. He verbally

stabbed me, his temper flaring with his sorrow. "They dismissed it. We didn't have any help."

"You don't get to put this on me, Preston. I was dealing with my own shit," I countered. "What the hell happened to Seyyid?"

"We cornered the oni vampire near the old station, got some nets ready to trap it and bring it in. The second we got the net over it, there was an explosion." Preston shook from anger, eyes glassy with rage. "There was an implant in the thing's head, Wilde. It blew up. Seyyid got knocked back into a beam and passed out. He hasn't woken up. That was three days ago."

"Fuck." I shut my eyes to digest what he was saying and to have a break from the hurt dripping off the guy.

This was getting worse by the minute.

"DHAP officers still don't believe you? Was there any evidence left over?" I opened my eyes to see him dash some tears away, still seething.

"Of course they don't believe me. I got put on leave. I can't even go after these monsters after what they did to Seyyid."

"Did you happen to find anything in the remains?" Zane asked. "Any fragments or pieces of the tech?"

Preston hadn't been paying any attention to Sias or Zane up until that point, his anger and focus being exclusively pinned to me. His posture was about as loose as a plank of wood, but the moment he drank in the sight of Zane, his body turned to pure stone.

I saw the moment he realized who was standing there, saw the spark of rage that ignited next to the bolt of fear that sent his body into action. Preston was a trained officer who had just recently gone through a nightmare scenario with his boyfriend, so the last thing he needed was another vampire to face.

His hand flew for his firearm, but he wasn't as fast as the incubus who already had his weapon trained.

"Rethink your move, officer." Sias cocked his gun. "I don't want to put you down."

"You're working with them," Preston hissed through his teeth, raising his hands. "You're a fucking traitor."

"Dude. No. Way off."

"We're investigating the same thing you are," Zane clarified as he disarmed Preston, tossing the gun under Sias's car. "We're going to our tech contact to try and get an idea of what it is we're dealing with."

"You're the same Thrall bastard we fought when Seyyid was bit," Preston growled, glaring daggers through Zane. "Why should I trust a damn word you say?"

"Because if I wanted to kill you, I would have," Zane clarified. "Easily."

"Preston," I got him to look at me after he tried to stab Zane again with his glare. "Do you think it's worth investigating the old tracks? Was there anything there?"

I imagined that the war going on behind Preston's eyes was one hell of a battle. He cycled from looking so angry he might explode, to cooling into a remorse so profound it made tears fall from his cheeks. I didn't know what he was thinking, but I could guess it was something along the lines of "the enemy of my enemy" while still managing to call me a bastard.

"You want us to get the assholes who hurt your guy?" I probed. "Then tell us what you know. I'll bring you back a piece of them."

"There's something at the tracks," he finally confessed, heartbroken and tired. "I don't know for sure, but it seemed like the vampires were being summoned back there. Seyyid thought there might be something in the old underground medical station they decommissioned."

"You know where that is?" I asked Sias, who nodded, then turned my attention back to the disheveled officer. "Go be with Seyyid. We've got this handled."

Preston almost argued, I saw it play across his face. Wet streaks were left behind after he scrubbed his face with one hand, a long sniff held back anything else from falling.

"You said you'd bring me a piece," he reminded me. "You make them pay for hurting him."

"Hey, vampire punishment is my specialty," I reminded him as I slipped into Sias's car. "Don't follow us or Zane's gonna throw you off a bridge."

Zane rolled his eyes and got into the car as Sias brought the engine to life, and we left the DHAP officer glaring at us in the rearview mirror.

CHAPTER
TWENTY-TWO

DEX PUSHED her goggles up into her hairline, popping a gum bubble across her tusks.

"Yep." She gathered the gum back into her mouth. "That's some sophisticated shit."

"And?" I encouraged, standing out of the way of the TV so her dad didn't yell at me again. "Do you know who made it?"

"Nope." She plucked the dented piece of plastic from where it had been clamped under a magnifying glass and tossed it back to me. "What I can tell you is that whoever did make this has a setup I want to see. It takes some high-powered tools to wire together charms, enchantments and bio magic like this."

"Can you recreate it?" Sias asked, flanking her other side. "Craft something that keeps the effects of this tech from reaching us?"

"Nothing that complicated, not with the limited tools I have here. I can get you three some strong blockers, but I don't know if it'll work against this."

"Dex. They're using this shit on vampires." I pinched the tech between my fingers, feeling the bite of the prongs against my skin. "I don't know how fast this is going to spread or what their plans are."

"Hey, I believe you, Wilde. I'm just being honest. I don't have an industrial setup to match that level of technology." Dex swiveled in her chair. "The center of that chip has an ossified feldspar to boost the necromancy magic, crystalized jinn tears, enhancement charms, and a boon to keep it self-contained while also creating a frequency feedback loop. It's insane, and I don't know how they did it. That level of energy should be impossible, especially while traveling through a body."

"Undead bodies don't behave the same as living ones," Zane offered. "Maybe they can be managed since the energy powering them is sourced from the void."

"Gods." Sias's disgust was turning into horror at breakneck speed. "We might be in over our heads on this."

"If we don't stop it now, we absolutely will be." I gave the chip back to Dex. "Keep this. Take it apart, figure out what you can."

"You sure?" She caught it as I tossed it back. "You could probably sell this to a tech company and make millions."

"Did you not hear us just discussing how this is being used on vampires? I don't give a shit about millions, because we're all going to be vamp dinner if we don't destroy this."

"I'm just sayin'." Dex shrugged. "Before I go ripping it to pieces, I wanted you to know your options."

"Noted," I said slowly. "Do I need to worry about you selling it off? Be honest with me, Dex. You're the best there is, but I need someone we can trust."

"I'll make you a deal, Wilde. You finance my research, I'll keep your scary vamp tech a trade secret. I wanna know how this shit works so I can be a weird billionaire who makes flying cars and shit." She tilted her head in thought. "Otherwise, I can't guarantee I won't be tempted by future offers."

Dex's eyes lit up as Sias sighed, setting a roll of bound bills onto the desk beside her.

"Before you sell it off, or if anyone makes you an offer, come to me first. I'll outbid them." Sias kept his hand on the money before she had a chance to reach for it. "I'm a good friend to have, but I can be a real bastard when pushed."

"I can always use more friends." Dex popped another bubble. "I hear you loud and clear."

"Great." Sias lifted his hand so she could pocket the cash. "You mentioned you could make us some magic blockers? We need three. The strongest you have."

"Aye-aye." She spun in her chair, pulling out her supplies.

"What is the plan?" Zane crossed his thick arms over his chest. "We march into this place and start taking people out?"

"We approach it like we do any vampire den," I said. "We scout, look for entries, and either lure them out or infiltrate."

"What about if we find living people there?" Sias came to stand with us, joining the planning process. "Or a necromancer?"

"If it's a necromancer, leave them to me. That's my bread and butter. Any living people there we'll pull out and see if they're willing participants in whatever this shit is, or if they're hostages."

"I think we should treat this as recon and wait," Sias pitched. "Going in half-cocked sounds risky, especially with this level of tech."

"Going in half-cocked is my MO." I glared at Zane as he said my words at the same time I did. He also said, "Fuck you, Zane" at the same time, so I punched his chest.

"This would be adorable if we weren't possibly putting my life in danger." Sias watched us like we were very amusing puppies chewing on his shoes. "Let's reel in the foreplay."

"Normally, I'd agree on the recon," I told Sias. "But I want to at least cause some chaos to disrupt the operation while we figure out what's going on. I don't want to give them room to breathe."

"If you can get me into the building, I can work on intel," Sias offered.

"I'll cover you," Zane said to Sias. "Dallas can handle the chaos part."

"I have no doubt," Sias agreed.

"Gentlemen," Dex interrupted. "A strand of hair each, if you please. I need to calibrate the blocker not to interact with your natural magic."

"If you use this to track or hex me, I'll sue you into oblivion," Sias warned, plucking a string of gold from his scalp. "Or I'll have Dallas kill you."

"You say such sweet things," Dex drawled, taking each of our hairs without any care to the threats. She tied each strand of hair to the top of a round charm she was threading through a keychain, reinforcing it with a thick piece of nylon. The charms had been pre-enchanted by a witch, her skills coming from construction and tech rather than the magic composition herself.

Whoever she was using as a magical source was a mystery even to me, but I was constantly impressed with the strength of it.

Our charms were calibrated inside what used to be a small keychain-sized game with a digital pet to take care of. The guts of the game had been stripped so only the shell remained, complete with a fake screen that displayed a happy, sleeping egg to shield the truth from nosy inspectors.

Each of us was tossed a fake NanoBuddy, ready to keep the bad magic away while not tripping up our own.

"If you find any more of that interesting tech while you're dismantling the evil vampire empire, do bring it to your favorite oni?" Dex batted her eyes at us.

"That's the plan." I spun my NanoBuddy around and slipped it into my pocket. "Thanks, Dex."

She motioned for us to shoo, rotating back to her infatuation with the small device I had brought her, so we took our cue and left.

Armed with our blockers, a vague plan and some life essence bullets (that Sias loaded into my gun for me, so I didn't get turned into crispy necromancer bacon), we made our way to the old railway Preston had told us about.

The southern most point of St. Athesall was past Lower Lovett, through the posh neighborhoods that fattened the city with a growing population of suburbs. The area had been similar to the Swallows decades ago, with structured housing and old buildings abandoned after the economy took a punch during a post-war decline. Somewhere along the way, some wealthy real estate types decided to do some rebranding, scooping up properties and flipping them into high-end establishments for the wealthier city folk to flock to.

It chased out the generations that had been planted there, shoved them further into the Swallows and sprinkled them throughout Midtown, walling off the uglier bones of what had been the industrial area. The old railway was one of those leftover relics, tossed aside and left to rot after it was no longer needed. Within the bowels of this old train station was the medical area that had been used for soldiers shipped back to the city after fighting.

It sounded like it would be super haunted and was not on my "must visit" list.

But here we were, rolling up to it like it was the place to be.

The metal skeleton of what used to be the train station stood in all its decaying majesty, filled with jagged bits of stained glass and birds' nests. A lazy fence had been erected around the entrance; some wood had fallen away where it had been nailed over windows. Puddles of rainwater reflected the scenery in black and white, mirroring the gray sky.

A chill bit through my coat, and I shivered.

This place had a cold to it that wasn't tied to the weather.

"Lots of places to enter from." I eyed the crumbling building, stepping around large puddles. "Perfect nest if they've gotten inside."

"I can do a quick look." Zane scanned the area quickly. "Look for any electronic activity and take down cameras."

"Go for it. Sias and I will hang back for now."

I'd seen Zane do his cool vampire mist thing just a few times, and it was still kinda badass to witness. He fell away into a shadow, lifting up into the breeze like he was made of black vapor before whipping through the air in a swarm. The cloud of Zane traveled to the building in a silent breath, disappearing into the cracks.

"That is a neat trick," Sias mused. "Can he take other forms?"

"Not that I know of." I checked my gun out of reflex, then made sure my knives were secure. "I wish I made some explosives before we left. That would really get the party started."

"I have no doubt you can do plenty of damage with what you have."

"Yeah, but it's always more fun with dynamite." I breathed out some steam into the air, the cold catching on my lips. "This place gives me the creeps in a big way."

Sias hummed in an agreeable tone, coming to stand beside me so we glared at the foreboding building together.

"I'm glad you figured it out, by the way," he said.

"Where the building is?" I glanced at him, surprised to see him smirking.

"No, darling. Zane."

My planning brain rattled as heat trailed up my neck. I got a little fidgety, which was never attractive.

"It's ah…complicated," I stumbled out.

"Is it?"

"He's a vampire. I kill those," I mentioned, like maybe he had forgotten my other job. "So, it's been a little messy to navigate. I kinda have some hang-ups about…" I shoved my hands into my pockets to stop picking at my knife sheath. "About whatever this is between us."

There was a beat of silence, my words hanging in the cold like our soft clouds of breath. I swiveled to pin the still-smiling incubus with a sharp look.

"The fuck you mean 'figured it out'?"

"You sweet, summer child."

"Don't give me that. This—" I gestured between myself and the building. "Wasn't a 'figure it out' thing. This was a spur-of-the-moment, standing in a cemetery after confronting trauma thing. Plus, blood magic makes us horny. You know. You've been there."

"I have," he purred, eyes dancing from lilac to a rose pink. "So I know what I tasted."

My little emotional blocker must have been working overtime with how wild my heart was racing, how much of a tailspin my mind was in. It was annoying how badly my feet wanted to move, how antsy my body became under his gaze.

"I wasn't sure if…" I huffed, almost bailing on what was on my mind, leaving it to die without giving it a fighting chance. "… if it would further fuck things up. With us."

The rose pink in his eyes changed to a burned orange, then slid dark blue.

"I'm sorry I hit Bastian," I said, since I had already gotten that far. "That night sucked and I handled it like shit. I'm especially sorry now because I never got the chance to make it right. But, Sias, I really needed you that night."

"Bastian deserved to get punched for violating your boundaries, Dallas," Sias cut in immediately. "I would have done it myself. That wasn't what pissed me off."

"Seriously?" I shrugged, helpless and more confused than ever. "Then what?"

The emotions painting Sias's gaze took a deep amber hue, black-rimmed and freezing blue in the center. I had never seen something so beautiful and heartbreaking. His face remained impassive, stony and calm, all while his soul churned in a rainbow of agony.

"You called yourself my 'little fuck toy,'" he whispered. "You reduced what we were into something small and disposable. I take the relationships I have with my favorites very seriously. It hurt. I refuse to be hurt, Dallas Wilde."

I didn't think my heart could crack the way it did.

It didn't split down the middle so much as crumble, fragmenting into tiny pieces to spill like gravel down into my stomach.

I didn't think Sias could be hurt. Hell, I thought the man was made of steel and resolve, an unflappable machine of will and sex appeal. With one bad night, one moment of anger and hurt, I had wounded him with a few poison words.

I tried to speak, but the resolve I had was now dust in my stomach, a pitiful pile next to my heart. Sias said nothing, only acknowledging another presence when Zane arrived back.

The mist settled into an outline of his body, taking form as a shadow before materializing back into his flesh-and-bone self.

"I found footprints in two points, and it looks like they lead down into the medical area. No cameras. We can go in together and split down below if needed."

"Great," I croaked, swallowing down a lump of dry anguish. "Did you see any signs of grunts? Hear any noises?"

"None." Zane studied me for a second before moving on. "They must be down below. My charm picked up repellent magic, but nothing else."

"We'll go in together, start sweeping the place." I nodded. "Lead the way, mist man."

To say the silence hanging between Sias and me was awkward was like saying the ocean is wet. My chest felt like an elephant had made a nice cushion out of my ribcage, but I quietly ignored the ache as we made our way into the new nightmare lair.

Zane had been underselling the intensity of the repelling magic surrounding the entryway, the blocker NanoBuddy in my pocket heating up from the effort of dispelling the hex. It was strong—an aura that would have made us so uncomfortable it could have caused us to burst out crying or throw up. As it was, the hex made me feel uneasy and nervous, but I was able to push past it like it was merely a loud invasive thought.

Zane led the way down the dark stairwell leading into the basement level, a generator hummed beyond the stone walls keeping dim lighting trailing through the hallways. An old sign directing people to the infirmary was rusted off the screws, and there was grit tucked into the tiniest of crevasses throughout.

I didn't know what the hell was up with vampires and old, abandoned hospitals, but this was the second one in less than a month. I was over how creepy it was.

"If we end up in another morgue, I'm going to be pissed," I muttered.

"Is this a pattern with you?" Sias asked. "Should I be concerned?"

"It's not me," I countered. "It's vampires. They have no imagination, present company included."

"Focus," Zane grumbled. "What is your magic detector telling you, hunter?"

"Nothing we don't already know." I put my hand over my pocket, my tiny charm buzzing with warnings of the hex we passed through along with the hum of death magic.

Echoes trailed up the belly of the building, scraping noises and rushed footsteps skittering around like cockroaches with fangs. My charm gave a little buzz of warning, and I pulled my gun loose. Sias fell into step behind me, Zane taking rear, and we traveled forward with careful steps as we listened to the pitter-patter of dead things.

Faded and torn propaganda posters were still clinging to the walls for dear life, a frozen time capsule of when the world was ready to tear itself apart. There was a bitter irony in seeing a scrap of the "Vampire Scourge" flyers they had littered the city with during the last necromancy uprising crumpled next to some discarded plastic.

While I was thankful I could see, my warning bells were ringing that the lights were still present as we continued. Necromancers kept their little paradises dark for their pets to keep their aggression down, and this place was practically glowing throughout. There wasn't a trace of the smell of death or bones tossed around from feeding.

Something was wrong.

This place was wrong somehow.

If only I had known just how right I was.

I saw a flash of a grunt rush past the bend of a hallway, growling and gnashing its teeth. The hissing scuffle of his little pack wasn't far, and had there been a smell of blood, I would be sure they were feeding on something. The thing had run like it was zeroing in on something delicious, so they'd likely been distracted. Bonus. I heard Sias pull a bullet into his gun and ready it, his footsteps right behind me.

Over my shoulder, I made sure a set of rainbow and red eyes met mine, and they each gave me a nod before I led the way to the fight. I kept us quiet and fast, knees bent and weapon primed. Pressing my shoulder to the wall, I peered around the corner to get a better idea of just how many grunts we might be up against.

It was rare that a pack of vampires could surprise me.

I had been killing them so long, so consistently, that I knew exactly how the thoughtless, primal monsters behaved. They were easy to understand and track once you'd seen them: move fast, kill faster, feed until they couldn't anymore, then sleep until the next dinnertime. They traveled together for optimal slaughter, took orders from their messenger proxies usually, and killed anything they could see.

I had never seen them standing docile before in my life.

Especially not in their attempt at a parade rest.

Six grunts stood facing each other, framing the double doors leading into an area of the hospital that was likely used for surgery. It was nearly impossible for the mindless drones to stand still, their bodies twitching and jerking like the effort was driving them more insane. One was chewing on its own tongue to give it something to focus on, red eyes stuck forward.

That, my friend, is what I call a big-ass red flag.

It wasn't just waving, it was bellowing in the breeze from a massive air horn to *get the fuck out.*

"Nope. Nope." I signaled for us to go backward. "We're getting the fuck out of here."

"What's going on?" Sias whispered, taking a few steps back as I started retreating.

Zane furrowed his brow. "Hunter, what—"

"Fuck this place. Fuck all of whatever this is. We're out. Zane, take lead, let's go. Now." I was practically shoving Sias as I rotated around.

Of course, of fucking *course*, there was another surprise waiting for us at the other end.

The green-eyed messenger vampire smiled at us from the body of an incubus. His throat had been ripped, dry blood coating the front of his university sweater, but he spoke clear and with a false sense of friendliness.

"Dallas Wilde." The voice was splintered and wrong, magic tugging on dead vocal cords and warping the voice of the necromancer controlling it.

"No, thank you," I answered back. "Whatever this is, I'm out. Not interested."

"I think I can change your mind," the creature said. "And you'll want to see what's behind that door."

"Doubt it." I took aim of my gun and fired, putting a blessed bullet through its head. The messenger jerked and fell into a melting tangle of bone and muscle, sizzling before burning into a gray ash.

"Go, go, go," I urged my two teammates, herding them back the way we came. Another messenger was coming down the hallway, and it got one word out before I shot it. Then another.

And another.

And wouldn't you know it, a fucking fourth one.

That wasn't the part that put a thorn in my side and made me angry. I could take out waves of vampires all day. It was the fact that the way we came in had been blocked off by a steel gate and padlocked shut, forcing us to travel through an area we hadn't been before.

It didn't take a genius to know we were being funneled into a trap, but we weren't left with much of an option.

We only had so many bullets and if they decided to shut the

lights off and send the grunts after us, we were a few shades of fucked.

"Zane." I pressed my back against a wall and peered down a hallway, checking it for another damn messenger before looking at him. "If this goes sideways, you need to keep Sias safe."

"I'm not a damsel in this scenario, Dallas," Sias scoffed. "I can handle myself."

"Not against waves of grunts. Not in the dark." I looked to my Thrall. "Keep him safe."

Zane gave me a nod, his hand drifting to Sias's back.

"You don't have to sacrifice your men," another voice called from the neighboring hallway. "If you'd just listen."

A pulse of fear magic hit my stomach like a gut punch, almost doubling me over from the rush of adrenaline. Sias exhaled like he'd been struck, Zane snarled against the attack and pulled Sias closer out of reflex. The little NanoBuddy in my pocket tossed out an electric sting from being overloaded, and I hissed at the pop of pain.

"What the hell do you *want*?" I yelled, adjusting my hand on my gun. "I know you have magic tech that can manipulate vampires. You don't have to show off."

"We can keep chasing you until you run out of bullets, until we send all the grunts after you. Or, you could come talk. Door is open," the voice called, an older man from the sounds of it.

"If I come talk, will you let them go?" I countered. "You're annoying me with this cat and mouse bullshit."

"Of course. After we talk."

I moved my hand in a talking clam shell and rolled my eyes. "Fine."

The sound of a door opening made me peer around the corner, scowling at the messenger vampire occupying an older oni man's body. The fear magic had calmed but didn't evaporate, which made him seem much bigger and foreboding than he actually was.

"Go into mist and get out of here," I whispered to Zane. "Find a way to get the front open and clear a path."

Zane shook his head. "Not leaving you."

"I got this," I hissed. "I need you to get us out of here."

"We stick together, Dallas," Sias joined team Zane, like a beautiful jerk. "We're not leaving you now."

"You both suck." I rubbed my face with my free hand, exhaled the tingle of dread mixed with the soft gooey feelings of them being so stupidly loyal, and turned the corner to meet my fate.

I kept my gun in my hand as we approached the messenger, the door he was standing next to was open. The creature stood like a polite butler, arms folded behind its back as he waited patiently for us to meander inside. I didn't rush into the room without peering into it first, underwhelmed by the old examination equipment shoved inside.

A bed was wheeled to the back, a table with a flip-top, glass jars with cotton balls and tongue depressors sat ignored on a dusty desk.

"You wanna bend me over and tell me to cough?"

The messenger didn't respond, only waited as we piled into the room.

"What the hell is this?" Sias scowled at some dust that got on his coat, brushing it away. "This seems overly dramatic."

"Someone has gone out of their way to get my attention. I'm flattered, but really not that hard to get ahold of."

"Something is off, hunter." Zane flexed his hands like he was gearing up for a fight. "This was too calculated."

The messenger turned so its body framed the door, fear magic still pouring off in small waves.

"Discard your weapons and slide them to me," he commanded with easy authority.

I laughed. "Hell no, man."

"I'm going to have to insist."

"I mean, I can just shoot another messenger to make it clear I'm not giving up my weapons."

"And I can make another," the necromancer behind the messenger threatened. "You have a fixed amount of bullets; I have plenty of bodies."

The magic inside the vampire played tricks on us, warping the creature's face into a monstrous nightmare of teeth and malice. I saw Sias turn away to gag, whatever he was seeing was starting to twist him up. Zane looked pale, his scowl still in place, but I didn't miss how he barely schooled the fear tugging at his eyes.

"Saints, I'm really going to kick your ass when I meet you." I set my gun on the ground and slid it over, motioning for Sias to do the same. He did so reluctantly, and breathed a sigh of relief when the fear magic eased.

The messenger scooped our guns up and stepped aside as two familiar faces darkened the doorway.

"Reynolds?" I blinked at my shady doctor from the Swallows, who stood next to the tall, foreboding figure of Florence Pierce's assistant, Hei. "What the hell are you doing here?"

Reynolds wasn't wearing his white doctor's coat, which made him seem smaller and somehow naked. The glowering stare he had on his face was even more out of place, because I had only ever seen the guy in various states of apathy. It was clear as day this guy hated my damn guts, and I couldn't recall what I did to piss him off.

Which, to be fair, wasn't out of the ordinary, but it did make the puzzle a little harder to crack.

"Dallas Wilde." Hei gave a polite bow, her ruby eyes sharp. "I appreciate your compliance."

"Lovely place you got here, Hei. Really gross and creepy." I rotated my hand in a slow circle away from my body. "Can we speed this up? Why did you want me here and why do you have my doctor with you?"

"I'm not your doctor," Reynolds barked. "I know what you are now. I don't treat monsters."

That stung more than it should. It wasn't like we were friends, but I had been going to him for a couple years now. Hell, I think I must have personally financed the guy's second house from the amount of money I threw at him for my various injuries.

"Rude," I told him. "You could have just referred me to someone else. Didn't need to call me 'monster.'"

"What else do you call necromancers?" Reynolds set his frown so solidly on his face I thought it was going to split in half.

"Dude." I pointed at the messenger vampire hanging out by the door. "Who the fuck do you think is doing that? You're still working with a necromancer. The difference between me and that dick is that I don't make vampires out of murder victims."

"Greater good." He snarled. "Something you wouldn't understand."

"Ah. Sorry, I didn't realize you were crazy. I'm done with you." I dismissed him with a wave of my hand, turning to the big oni woman staring me down. "What is this, Hei? Is this Florence flexing her power or did you go rogue?"

"I'm here for the Goddess's blade," she answered calmly. "I need you to hand it over."

"Shit out of luck there, I'm afraid. We found the tomb, but no blade."

Hei watched me, impassive and stony.

"He's telling the truth," Zane added. "You can check the apartment. We ran into the Saint's Army down there but we didn't find any blade. Maybe they took it."

"If they have it, they'll be trying to destroy it. That's going to be a better lead than us," I tacked on. "I want to get paid, remember?"

"I want to know why in the hell you went after Bastian," Sias stepped up, anger storming his yellow eyes. "He had nothing to do with this, and you turned him into a vampire. You stabbed some tech into his brain. You tell me *why*."

"The blade, Wilde," Hei insisted again, still annoyingly calm. "I know you have it. Give it to me, and this can end much easier."

"I don't have your stupid blade. By the way, you two jackasses called it a 'key' which made things confusing. It took me getting into a scuffle with the Saint's Army to know what the fuck was going on." I scoffed at her. "This tough act is just wasting time. I don't have your shit, and you owe Sias some answers."

Hei held out her hand to my former doctor, who extracted a small vial from his pocket.

"Is it ready?" she asked him and he nodded.

"We haven't had a chance to do a lot of trials, but the results have been amazing so far."

"Good." Hei reached behind her waist, which was bound with a thick sash like always. A small gun was removed, the vial slipping into the body of the weapon with a soft, priming hiss.

"Why Bastian?" Sias yelled, his step forward aggressive enough for me to stop him. "You killed him. You explain yourself or I'm going to rip you apart!"

Hei flicked her eyes to him for just a moment.

"He volunteered."

"Bullshit," Sias hissed. "No one volunteers to get turned into a vampire."

"They do," Hei corrected, her words poison and landing with devastating accuracy. "When they have nothing else to live for."

"Easy." I held Sias back as he tried to surge forward, eyes as vicious and sharp as yellow blades. "Not here. Relax."

"I'm going to kill you," Sias promised her. "There's nowhere safe on this planet from me."

"This is your last chance, Wilde," Hei continued, back to ignoring Sias. "The blade."

"I don't have it," I growled through my teeth. "I don't know what the fuck you're doing here with the necro magic, but this shit is going to stop. This is too far. You have to see how insane this is, Hei."

Hei watched me with the bored, patient expression of an old teacher explaining something to a child.

"When a necromancer develops their power, they develop

naturally forming crystals against their ribcage, as I'm sure you're aware." She tilted her head to Reynolds. "Those can be seen on x-rays. As can an abundance of them developing into the shape of a blade."

"You're full of shit," I snapped, my heart starting to hammer. "I think I would be able to feel if there was a blade manifesting in my damn chest."

"It took me a while to figure out what I was looking at," Reynolds admitted. "But once I knew it was necromancy feldspars, I went to Hei. I couldn't stand knowing someone like you held that kind of power inside. You have to be stopped."

"I'm honestly the lesser of two evils here, man. I even paid you on time! You know how rare that is for me?" I made sure Sias wasn't going to attack before I turned to Hei again. "I don't know what the hell you want from me. Killing us isn't going to help the damn situation, nor is fucking with people we care about."

"Florence has to be stopped," Zane agreed. "This is too much. You're manipulating things you don't understand."

"I follow my master's will," Hei told Zane. "That's our purpose."

Zane studied her like she was an alien for a second, confusion shifting into horror. I didn't have time to ask him what it was he saw, what her words meant in terms of what was in store for us.

An arctic dread clouded over me, my limbs locking into place like I was a cornered mouse staring down the maw of a starving cat. My neck began to burn, my scars itching, my breath freezing in my lungs.

I was petrified, my feet stuck to the ground as my mind tried to reason with myself. The fear magic wasn't like anything I had ever felt before—it was supercharged, a nuclear blast of terror I couldn't escape from.

Hei's tusks had curled out like ram horns, eyes fire, voice of the devil come to life.

"I was instructed that I was not allowed to threaten Sias or

Barnaby, per your request," Hei told me, as she lifted her hand and fired the dart gun into Zane's leg. She moved so unnaturally fast that it seemed like a blink, the sound happening well after the needle was already in his leg.

Zane ripped it from himself, sweating and pale from the fear magic she had blasted us with.

"What the hell did you give me?" he demanded. "What was that?"

"A new type of tech," Reynolds added, glaring at Zane like he was made of spiders. "Nanotech for healing internal organs."

Whatever fear had been lancing through Zane was nothing compared to what Reynolds said, and he went ghostly white as he grabbed his leg.

"They're bluffing," Sias snapped. "That type of thing isn't real. That's science fiction."

"No, it's not." Reynolds laughed, and I knew then and there that I was going to have to murder this guy. "And it works great on vampires."

"Stop," I forced myself to speak. "Turn it off."

"The blade," Hei repeated. "Now, Wilde. You don't have much time."

The fear magic eased back to let me move, my heart hammering as I rushed to Zane. For a few hopeful naïve seconds, I believed that Sias had been right about them bluffing. Nanotechnology wasn't exactly prevalent out of sci-fi movies, and that would be one hell of a scary lie.

Zane fell as part of his leg disintegrated, hitting the ground and scrambling backwards. Sias fell to his knees beside him, whipping his belt off to try and make a tourniquet around Zane's thigh.

"Ease your breathing, slow your blood pressure," Sias was telling him, pulling the belt as tight as he could. Zane screamed from the pain of the belt and growing panic, his foot turning to ash inside of his boot.

"Turn it off!" I wheeled on Hei and the doctor. "Turn it off or I swear to the Gods—"

"You have five minutes before he's gone, Wilde. Give me the blade."

Icy tendrils curled around my arms, my fingers shaking with rage. My death magic coiled and started to flow, my chest knocking and grinding.

"I'm going to rip you apart. I'm going to kill—"

I shuddered at the punch of fear magic that gripped me, my temples pounding as I tried to fight it back. Hei stared into me with ruby spears, her magic so strong it forced me to my knees. My chest felt like the bone was splintering as I kept ahold of my death magic, the tendrils slippery and wild.

"Dallas!" Sias called out, his calm resolve slipping. I turned to see the tourniquet fall away as the magic tech in Zane's blood melted his leg away, part of his hip caving in.

"Gods, no. Please," I set my jaw. "Turn it off, Hei! Please!"

"The blade." She held out her hand. "Now."

"Don't," Zane pleaded, his breathing shallow. "Don't, hunter."

"We can get it back," Sias said quickly, meeting my gaze. His eyes were pale gray, almost white with mounting terror. "Hurry."

I squeezed my eyes shut, putting my hand to my chest where the grind of the scythe's handle made my body ache. My heart was stuck between my ribs in a rapid panic, my lungs shaking as I drew in my best attempt at a calming breath. I didn't know if I could get the blade out without Zane, but I sure as hell wasn't going to sit there and watch him die.

I couldn't. I wouldn't make it without him.

Trying to focus on anything other than my terror was almost impossible, but I held my breath and forced myself to remember back to the cemetery.

I remembered his lips, the color of his eyes under the silver moon, a silent smirk playing across his fangs after he came clean about the ritual mantra.

I held in my mind how he tasted, and how sweet it was to hear him confess:

I knew I was going to be your vampire.

My chest eased, the grind popping through my chest like it had been waiting for the door to open. I grabbed the hilt with one hand and tugged, forcing it through from my body. Once I had enough through, I used both hands to pull it free with a shout.

The blade stared back at me, crimson and dancing with void magic, the handle twisting itself into alignment.

Reynolds had gone white, Hei's ruby eyes pulsed with eagerness.

"You want it so badly?" I snarled, exhausted and shaking. "Catch."

I tossed the blade to the oni woman, grinning at knowing the moment she touched it, her arm would be turned to bone like Barnaby's had. She wasn't undead, wasn't a creature of death, so that scythe was going to eat her up until there was nothing left.

I was wrong.

Hei caught the blade and looked it over, the death magic within it doing nothing to terrorize her body. Seeing the blade for the first time in her grasp, Hei finally smiled.

And I saw her fangs.

The oni woman was a Thrall. An impossible, reality-bending vampire Thrall.

"Impossible," I breathed from the devastation of seeing her fangs. "Only humans can be Thralls. What the fuck are you?"

"Something else," she whispered. "Beyond you, little necromancer."

"Dallas!" Sias screamed, turning my blood to ice.

I whipped around to see Zane gasp, his stomach caving into the ground. One of his arms was gone, his hips and everything below now dust.

"I gave you what you wanted," I told Hei, begging. "Turn off the tech. Don't kill him, please."

Hei was done noticing me, done giving a remote shit about

what was happening beyond the blade in her hand. I watched the oni vampire turn her back on me and leave with my scythe, motioning for the messenger to shut the door behind her. Reynolds followed like a puppy, and the door was slammed in my face as I charged for them.

I pounded on the door with my fists, slamming my shoulder into it until I felt something sting, my voice raw from screaming for them to come back.

"Dallas!" Sias's wailing finally cut through, snapping me from my rage to face what was waiting for me.

I gathered Zane into my arms after I rushed to his side, the healing magic sizzling away most of his chest as he stared up at me, red eyes wide and dancing.

"Hunter," he wheezed, his one remaining hand reaching up to touch my cheek.

"We can fix this," I was saying, my mouth repeating it as I ripped my knife from my pocket and sliced into my palm. "Drink, quick. Maybe we can counter the healing, make it stop—"

"No." Zane swallowed, pressing his palm into my cheek. "Listen to me. Dallas, look at me."

"Zane, drink. Drink, goddamnit." I tried to put my palm to his mouth but he shook his head, slipping his hand behind my head to pull me closer.

"You're going to be okay," he whispered, voice growing weak. "It'll be okay."

"I can't do this," I confessed, starting to shake so badly I couldn't breathe. "Zane, please. Please."

I was pulled down so our brows touched, and I would never forget how warm he felt. How soft his hair was when I pushed my fingers into it.

Grave flowers and rain.

Stupid long hair and scowling.

Too many books tossed around my apartment, and a tiny kitten screaming from his lap.

I couldn't fathom a world without all of it.

I couldn't live in that world.
Zane whispered, a smile on his lips.
"I can always find you. Always."
Then it was dust.
And nothing.
And Zane was gone.

CHAPTER
TWENTY-THREE

MY WORLD WAS dust and devastation.

Flecks of what used to be my vampire slipped through my fingers and onto the ground, smothering his jacket in fine, gray powder. Everything sounded like rushing water, my palms didn't feel the grit of the ash as I scooped up fistfuls and squeezed.

I wrung my eyes shut, blocking out reality as I tried to focus on my magic. I reached for the tendrils, focused with everything I had on getting the tug of ice back into my arms. I *knew* I could bring him back, knew I could pull him into the ash like I had done at the tomb.

I had to.

I *had* to bring him back. It was the only shot I had to undo what had been done.

My temples were pounding, lungs stuck in a half-breath.

I couldn't feel my magic anymore.

No annoying ants, no cold tendrils.

There was nothing. It was gone.

It had left with the scythe, now in the hands of some evil bitch who had taken one of the most important people in my life with her.

The crushing weight of my magic abandoning me sent me into

a spiral, and I had been moments away from gasping my way into unconsciousness until I felt the warm numbness of powerful charm magic.

The rushing blood in my ears faded, my breathing eased, and I took a full breath to beg for Sias to let me pass out. I didn't want to be conscious anymore.

His eyes were stuck in a frozen block of ice with a golden center, sadness surrounded by an anger so sharp it bled to the surface.

"You need to breathe." His hands flanked my face, his voice a steely anchor keeping me from sinking under. His charm magic shielded me from hysteria, allowing me to wade over to the shallow end of despair. I still hurt, still bled from the hole that used to be my heart, but I could focus, I could rationalize in a weird, numb way.

"My magic is gone," I told him, my eyes still pouring tears even though I wasn't sobbing anymore. "I could bring him back if I had my magic, but it's gone."

"I know. I know." He held me still so I couldn't look back at Zane's ashes. "Listen to me, Dallas. We cannot do anything more for Zane right now."

"I can bring him back—" I insisted. Sias shook his head slowly.

"No, love. Not here, not now. Right now, we have to get out of here. It's not safe."

"I can't leave him," I cut in. "I'm not leaving him here. Not like this."

Sias slipped his fingers through my hair and wiped my cheeks, then glanced around the room.

"Stay here," he told me, springing up from where he had kneeled beside Zane and me, his magic still over me like a blanket.

When Sias returned, he was tossing out the cotton balls from one of the flip-top glass jars resting on the desk. The glass was set between us, and Sias gently removed Zane's clothing from where the ashes had collected. His shirt, jeans, jacket and boots were shaken out and folded with careful movement, Sias treating everything that had touched Zane like it was sacred.

We took our time scooping up Zane's ashes and placing them in the jar, one handful at a time.

It was the hardest yet the most serene thing I had ever done. Each handful took more of me with it, and by the time we were sweeping the finest pieces up with pinches, I felt like a ghost.

Sias closed the lid and locked it, setting it on top of the folded clothing before passing it to me.

"I need you to stand up now," Sias told me, his hands on my upper arms. I could feel the pressure of his grip, but my body had gone cold. My mind was a blaring wind of white noise, and I could barely follow what he was saying. His charm magic rippled and pulled me a little more from the paralysis, soothing my pain enough to get me to my feet.

I watched distantly as Sias took my knife and kneeled by the door, busting the lock open with a few twists and a good kick to the seam. I was led out with one hand on my back, Sias holding my knife in his other.

The messenger that had been guarding the door was gone, my magic detector had gone blissfully still, the only sound the pulsing hum of Sias's charm magic.

I kept waiting for the attack, waiting for the inevitable wave of grunts sent to finish us off. Surely at any moment, Hei would show back up to finish what she started. She'd storm down the hallway and slice us through using my stolen scythe, cut us up into pieces next to the shattered jar of Zane's ashes.

But she never came.

The grunts never came.

The building was abandoned, silent minus the hum of the generator left running. The gate that had been tossed over the exit had been pushed up, fresh footprints in the mud near the entrance.

They had left us behind to rot down there, without even the courtesy of viewing us as a threat.

Either they hadn't expected us to figure out how to get the door open, or they didn't care. They had stolen what made me powerful, killed my vampire, and locked me in a room with a disarmed incubus to wither away and die.

Honestly, not a bad plan.

I had been pretty successfully stomped into the ground from all of that.

But Sias hadn't.

He escorted me from the old medical facility, and kept me walking when I wanted to curl up and lie on the floor. His charm magic never wavered, never let me dip back into the ache that was waiting just below the surface.

He kept me from wanting to give in to how fully I had been destroyed.

Even in my grief, I saw how angry he was that there wasn't a fight waiting for us on the other side. I saw how he held the knife in his grip, knuckles white and shaking. The muscles bunched over his jaw as he held the silence, how his eyes never flickered to any other colors, holding on to the cold hurt with the boiling rage center.

I had never seen them stay in one palette before.

Moving to the car and getting into it was a blur, so mundane and unimportant that my mind erased it the moment it happened. I held everything Zane was to my chest, wondering absently if I was ever going to wake up from this terrible dream.

"We'll go get you a bag packed, gather Kevin and Zane's cat, then get you back to my place," Sias was telling me. "You can rest there and be safe. I don't want you alone right now."

"Twig," I told him.

"What?"

"The cat." I watched some tears fall onto the lid of Zane's jar. "Her name is Twig."

"Sorry. Twig," he whispered. "We'll get Twig."

The sway of the car rocked me, the bland landscape of cold city and dark clouds whizzed past as Sias drove. I listened to the rhythmic dusting of the drizzle, the hum of the windshield wipers as they tossed away the droplets. A sound of plastic knocking against glass pulled me from the deep tunnel I was in.

My emotional blocker hung between me and Zane's jar, bouncing against it as we rolled along.

It was still set to "on."

I felt a piece of myself die at seeing that, knowing he didn't feel how much it mattered to me that he was dying in my arms.

Sias glanced over as I rolled the window down, the string snapping as I ripped it off my neck and threw it out into the rain.

"I never told him how much I cared about him," I confessed. "I never said a goddamn word."

"He knew," Sias told me. "Without a doubt."

"I'm a coward," I confessed. "I was so fucking scared he'd figure it out. What the hell is wrong with me?"

"There's nothing wrong with you, Dallas. There is no wrong way to love someone."

Somehow, my heart managed to break a little more, the charm magic slipping enough to let a sob sneak through.

I had loved him.

So, so much.

I hugged his jar to my chest and cried, whispering hopes that he could somehow forgive me.

I wasn't sure how the void worked when you didn't have necromancy powers anymore, but I clung to the belief that somehow, in some way, he could hear how sorry I was.

By the time we arrived back at my apartment, my eyes were swollen and red, my head was throbbing, and Sias was working overtime to keep his charm magic in place. I had calmed, able to stop crying enough to catch my breath.

The charm helped keep me in a state of numb stasis, even as we rolled up to find all of my shit sitting in the rain.

Moving trucks were parked around the building, and people were pulling things out of Barnaby's store wrapped in plastic.

"Gods and Saints," Sias hissed, climbing out of the car the

moment he threw it into park. I followed in a haze, leaving Zane's clothing behind but still holding the jar.

My couch was soaked through, my swords thrown onto the cushions. My awesome chest of vampire-killing stuff was thrown onto its side beside my bed, which was soggy and beyond saving.

Most of my stuff was ruined, and I was apparently homeless.

It would have been really fucked up if I wasn't already at rock bottom. Instead, it was kinda funny, because I had slipped into such a state of dark humor it was basically a branch of the void.

"Did you guys wanna piss on it before you go?" I asked one of the guys throwing stuff outside. "Think it would add a nice metaphor to the day."

I thought it was at least chuckle worthy, but Sias sure as hell didn't. He flew into boss daddy mode and started snapping orders, demanding information and threatening in a way only he could manage. Within just a few short minutes, the seizure of property was halted, the workers retreated to wait for instruction, but the damage was already done.

Barnaby's shop was closed. Most of his stuff was gone. All my things were ruined anyway, and I didn't fully care.

Barnaby materialized out of what seemed like thin air as I watched my couch drip, his face crumbling with worry.

"I can't find them!" he was telling me. "Dallas, I'm sorry. I-I've been looking for over an hour."

"Can't find who?" I blinked, my brain having a hard time processing more than one thing at a time.

"Twig and Kevin!" He ran his hands over his hair to push the wet strands out of his face. "I think Twig ran off when they showed up. I opened some wet food, but she won't come when I call her."

I rubbed at the pain behind my eye.

"Wait. Kevin?" I asked. "He's missing?"

"His tank is empty. His water is still there but he's not in it!"

The stinging eased as I took a breath.

"He's okay. He's in his safe house."

"Safe house? Dallas, I don't think you understand what I'm saying to you right now," Barnaby said, flustered and panicked. "Kevin is *missing*. Your fish is not in his tank."

"He's fine, Barns. It's fine." Some wind knocked over one of my mugs sitting on a table, and I watched as it rolled off and shattered, the shards landing in a puddle next to some old magazines that had turned into soggy mulch. A prickling wave of agony bit at the lining of my stomach as a cold realization hit.

"Zane's books," I breathed. "Where are his books?"

"I put them in a suitcase." Barnaby gestured somewhere I didn't really catch. "I grabbed them before they could get too wet. Some got a little soggy but..." he let out a long breath, eyes welling. "Dallas, I'm so sorry I let this happen. I'll replace everything that got ruined."

"It doesn't matter," I said. "None of it matters."

It was about that time that he noticed the jar, and his sorrow turned into something else.

"Where's Zane?"

I didn't need to answer. He noticed how I hugged the glass to my chest.

I had never been hugged like Barnaby held me in the rain that day. He held me with the same heartbreaking strength I had felt sinking my heart since the moment Zane died.

I held on to him like the life raft he was, and we cried for everything we had lost that afternoon.

I wasn't alone. Not anymore. I had another brother to cry with, and that was more than I'd had in years.

"We're going to be alright," he promised me, leaning back to rub my arms with his hands. "We're going to get through this, you and I. Somehow we're stuck together, despite your best efforts."

"Yeah," I agreed, huffing my best attempt at a laugh. It fell a bit short, but I got a watery smile from him regardless. "I guess we are."

"Barnaby." Sias came over, a bag in his hand weighed down

with something heavy. "Pack up a bag for a few days. I'll help you navigate this tomorrow."

Barnaby accepted the bag and peered into it, wiping his eyes as Funus peered up at him.

"There, there now," Funus consoled. "Chin up, my friend. Nothing some tea and a good night's sleep won't cure."

"Gods, I'd love some tea." Barnaby inhaled life back into his soul through some tears. "I need to find a suitable hotel to stay in until I find someplace to go."

"You'll be staying at my estate," Sias corrected. "I'll have a room set up for you. Skip the formalities of refusing and go pack."

"I'm almost too tired to be polite." Barnaby slipped Funus's bag onto his shoulder. "Dallas, we still need to find Twig and Kevin."

I meandered around the building and into a neighboring alleyway, the plumes of heat from the coin laundry dryers filtering out into the street above. It smelled like fresh towels and fabric softener, and gave a pocket of warmth if you walked through at the right time of day.

I kneeled near some old crates that had been stacked near a recycle dumpster, moving them aside to reach the little alcove crafted from insulated boxes and repurposed pieces of a doghouse.

Inside our small bugout bunker was Kevin in his reserve fishbowl, sitting inside a tiki house waiting for me to arrive. His heating light was on, but it was angled to help keep Twig warm as she napped in a little circle beside his bowl.

"Good boy, Kevin."

"Now, how in the hell—" Barnaby asked from behind me, standing next to an equally confused Sias. I hadn't noticed they followed me over there, which meant we were going to have to move the bugout bunker in the future.

Kevin blew an angry bubble at me.

"Sorry," I said, giving him some bloodworms. "It's been a long day. I let my guard down."

Twig blinked up at us sleepily, standing to stretch her butt out and mew for attention. I scooped her up and passed her to Sias, who tucked her into his nice thousand-dollar jacket to keep her warm. Kevin eyed me as I picked up his bowl but didn't give me too much shit. I think he knew I was going through something.

Barnaby packed a modest suitcase of clothing and some belongings, and Zane's books were placed in the trunk beside it.

I didn't bother to grab anything besides my weapons and chest. Everything else was junk, things I didn't care to try and save. None of that shit mattered anymore. Not really.

None of us spoke as Sias drove us away from our home.

I knew I should have felt bad for Barns, should have done more to try and comfort him after losing everything he had but I was too deep into my own despair to focus on anything other than the raw ache that constantly ripped down my chest. I self-ishly didn't attempt to do anything more than exist.

In another life, only a week or so in the past, I would have been over the moon that I was staying in Sias's home. I had been trying to summon the courage to ask him to let me stay, to be closer to him. This wasn't exactly what I'd had in mind during those daydreams. They definitely involved less death and zero total, soul-crushing heartbreak.

It kind of put a sour taste to the experience.

I placed Kevin on the dresser in my room, plugged in his heater and promised to get him a better tank as soon as I could. The room was big and beautiful, with a private bathroom and a bed made of feathers probably harvested from an endangered species of silk bird. Everything was rich and wooden, perfect and pristine.

I would have really loved it if I could muster a fuck to give.

Instead, I sat on the silk bird bed and set Zane's jar beside me, wondering idly what he would have thought about the place. I knew for sure he'd want to see Sias's library, set up a little reading nook near the window so Twig could climb into his lap while he read. Said little beastie climbed the expensive comforter and marched around, sniffing everything with each step.

She nudged Zane with her face, rubbing both sides across it.

Even in death, he was hers.

"Yeah, yeah. I get it." I scratched at the base of her tail, her namesake sticking straight up. "I guess I'll be taking care of you from now on. We gotta talk about the poop box, you little runt."

Sias came in, approaching carefully to set Zane's folded clothing on the foot of the bed. Twig trotted over and climbed onto his jacket to claim the spot for herself.

It made my heart ache.

Sias's magic had eased enough to let me feel the gentle needling of grief, but still kept the tidal wave from crushing me. I had to blink more tears from my eyes as he came to sit beside me, close enough to comfort without overwhelming me with contact.

"I'm not going to assume I know how badly you're hurting, love. And I'm not arrogant enough to believe there's anything I can offer you in this moment that could help ease that pain," he whispered, the gentlest I had ever heard him sound. "Tell me what you need, and it's yours."

Twig was napping on Zane's jacket, his ashes only a few inches away. My heart was so heavy, I thought it was going to fall out of my chest and sink to the core of the planet, combust and turn into a black hole.

Beyond grief, beyond sadness and pain, the easiest emotion to grab onto was scorching and vindicating. White-hot hate blistered through and it burned me from the inside out, tempering my mind into a honed weapon.

"What I need." I paced myself, worried flames might erupt from my mouth if I spoke too quickly. "Is a powerful, rich, vicious bastard with access to resources, who can help me burn everything Florence Pierce is to the ground."

I met Sias's gaze, his eyes flaring yellow in the center while the edges stayed ice blue.

"That's what I need," I told him. "I need the worst side of you, the darkest part of you."

"You have it," he promised in a whisper.

When he offered his hand, I took it and squeezed.

Florence Pierce was done. Her legacy was done. Everything she was, everything she could have been, everything she dreamed of was going to be ash and death and destroyed.

And I was going to be the vengeful asshole who lit the match.

Out of the corner of my eyes, I saw Kevin swimming. I barely registered what he was doing until he was in midair, the display of acrobatics flipped my heart.

The double backflip.

Zane had really taught him the double fucking backflip.

The sound of Kevin landing back into his water with a little *ploop* brought a splash of clarity. Revenge was still on the table, but there was another plan in place. Something crazy, deadly and probably impossible.

But so was love, right?

"I know what I need to do," I whispered. "I need to get my scythe back."

"Whatever you need, darling," Sias agreed. "I'll help you get your revenge. There's nothing that can stop us."

"We're not going to just destroy them, Sias." I smiled, feeling hope punch through the rage, the sadness and the darkness pulling me down into dust. I felt it bloom like a flower over my heart.

"I'm going to rip the void open and get my vampire back."

To Be Continued

NEXT IN THE SERIES

Desperate to know what happens next?

Save the Vampire (Wilde Contracts, book 3)

ABOUT THE AUTHOR

Maz Maddox has always wanted to be an author.

Well, almost always.

At first she wanted to be a dinosaur, but that turned out to be extremely difficult. Giving up on her dreams to be a towering Allosaurus, she discovered her love for amazing stories and started writing her own.

Maybe one day she'll try the dinosaur thing again.

Follow Maz:

www.mazmaddox.com
Newsletter signup: subscribepage.com / subtomaz
Reader group: facebook.com / groups / maddoxsaloon
mazmaddox@gmail.com

facebook.com / AuthorMazMaddox
x.com / mazmaddox
instagram.com / mazmaddox

ALSO BY MAZ MADDOX

STALLION RIDGE SERIES

Heartache & Hoofbeats

Claw Marks & Card Games

Suspects & Scales

Rocks & Railways

Mimics & Mayhem

Runes, Ruin & Redemption

Fate & Fortune

RELIC SERIES

Smash & Grab

Sink or Swim

King & Queen

WILDE CONTRACTS

Find the Jinn

Steal the Key

Save the Vampire

STANDALONE

Ethan & Jag Destroy the World